FIRST AGAINST THE WALL

Manna Francis

This is a work of fiction. All the characters and events portrayed in this book are either fictitious or are used fictitiously.

For information, address Casperian Books, PO Box 161026, Sacramento, CA 95816-1026.

www.casperianbooks.com

Cover illustration by Orit "Shin" Heifets

ISBN-10: 1-934081-13-2
ISBN-13: 978-1-934081-13-6

This is my personal favorite out of the Administration stories, and so I would like to dedicate it to my very favorite people—my parents. It would take a book as long as this to describe everything you've done for me, and all the love and encouragement you've given me over the years. So I just want you both to know that there's no one else in world I love, respect, and admire more than you. Thank you.

Chapter One

❖

Toreth shifted against the wall, trying to get comfortable. Between bruises and handcuffs, he didn't have much success.

The situation, he had to admit, wasn't promising. On the first day, in the first cell, the lights had been on, the water dispenser working, and the prisoner feeding schedule still running. Then the lights went out, and things had gone steadily downhill from there. Now, he sat in darkness so absolute that he couldn't see a hand in front of his face, if he'd been in a position to check.

He turned his head, pressing his bruised cheek to the wall, and blinked. The gray, impervious surface was right there, but he might as well be blind.

The last time he'd been taken out of the cell it had been light in the corridors, which was something. If the power to the building failed totally, they would suffocate down here. At the moment, the air cycling was still functional, feeding chill air into the cell—like the lights, the heating systems had been switched off or had broken down. He couldn't accurately estimate when he'd last eaten. Two days or so, probably, but he was starting to feel the effects. The water system worried him most. It worked only intermittently and the water had an unpleasant, overly chemical flavor.

The systems were failing. Something had gone badly wrong, and had continued to go wrong for so long that he'd been forced unwillingly to conclude that it had to have hit more than I&I.

He shifted again, wishing they'd put his arms in front of him or, better yet, not bothered to cuff him at all. What the hell did they think he was going to do, locked up in one of the most secure facilities in the Administration? The answer was that they didn't think like that. Locking him in here was an end in itself. The resisters had control of I&I—and probably a great deal more—and now they were taking their turn. Interrogating the interrogators.

He would have talked, if they'd had any useful questions, but they hadn't. They'd asked a few things, and he'd answered them promptly, because if anyone knows how futile it is to hold out, it's a trained interrogator. Mostly they'd been doing it for fun—taking people out of the cells, beating them up for a while and then putting them back. Or not putting them back, if they'd got carried away.

They were kicking corpses, dead or temporarily still alive, and as far as he could tell their plan extended no further.

Useless bloody amateurs. Still, they'd kill him in the end—the only surprise was that they hadn't done it yet. It was easy to underestimate how much damage could be done with fists and feet. He had some cracked ribs, at least. Nothing that felt like internal bleeding, but it was only a matter of time before they overdid it. Punctured lung, that would be his bet. Not the nicest way to go.

He'd thought it would be the end, the last time they'd had him out—blindfolded, to add to the fun. Resisters with personal grudges to settle were looking for the people who'd interrogated them in the past, which was probably not a survivable experience. He'd stood for what felt like hours, listening to the noise around him, occasionally recognizing one of the voices raised in pain or fear, squinting around the edge of the blindfold as footsteps approached him, paused, and passed on. Every time, he'd expected to hear a voice say, "Him." But no one picked him out, and he'd had nothing worse than a few casual blows before they'd put him back, into a different cell.

After he'd worked the blindfold off, he could see no more than with it on. However, he'd recognized the two other voices in the new cell at once—the first people from his section he'd run into since it started. They'd talked for a while, but Chevril knew no more than he did and Sedanioni was too badly hurt to say much. Neither of them had seen Sara. In the end the conversation had faded away into the blackness.

The resisters had left them alone for a surprisingly long time, now. Maybe they were getting bored. If so, they'd no doubt soon get around to shooting the survivors. If they bothered. If they didn't simply leave the three of them here, in the dark, to die in their own time. Not a thought he really wanted to spend much time with.

There was no point trying to stand up—in the pitch dark with his wrists cuffed and his ankles chained, he'd only trip over and hurt himself. More. So he knelt and shuffled along the floor, keeping his side to the wall. It was the least painful method of movement he'd come up with. Not much of a recommendation, because it still made his ribs hurt fiercely.

When he thought he could hear breathing, he sat down again and felt out cautiously with his feet. Contact, and someone moaned. Which of them was it? "Chevril?"

"Uh?"

He kicked again, harder. "Chev. Wake up."

"I am awake. How the hell do you think I'm going to sleep, like this?"

"Where's Sed?"

He heard Chevril moving in the darkness, grunting with pain. Metal clinked dully on the hard plastic coating of the floor.

"Can't find her," Chevril said. "She was right by me. I *told* her to stay there."

"Hold your breath."

They waited in silence, for as long as they could manage, listening for even the faintest whisper of breathing. Toreth heard nothing but the low, steady hum of the air cycling.

"Stay still," he said. "I'll look."

Toreth knew how small the cell was, because all the holding cells were the same size, but in the blackness it seemed limitless, except for the always unexpected, painful contacts with the walls. Eventually he found her, in the corner, curled up tight. She was cold to his touch, already stiff, and he could smell blood and urine, much stronger here than the general stench of the cell. Suddenly the darkness didn't seem like such a bad thing.

Sedanioni. Or, at least, he didn't think there'd been anyone else in the cell. Awkwardly, he ran his fingers through her hair, judging the length, matching it with his memory. Her, as far as he could tell.

"Did you find her?" Chevril's voice, startlingly close.

"Yes. She's dead."

"Oh, bloody hell. Bloody, bloody hell."

"Keep talking. I'm coming back."

"I thought she would be, to be honest. She was shivering when they brought her in, not because she was cold. Shock. I told her she was going to be fine, which was a waste of bloody time because she knew I was lying. She kept asking for water, you know—really thirsty. She knew what that meant. Ouch!" Even with the guidance of Chevril's voice, it was still a shock to find him, bumping his knee against him.

"Be careful, for Christ's sake."

"Sorry." Toreth sat next to him, grateful to stop moving and frighteningly exhausted by the exertion. Every too-deep breath shot pain through his side. When he managed to steady his breathing, he asked, "How are you?"

"Awful."

You could always rely on Chevril for a complaint, even if for once it was justified. He waited for the rest, but there was nothing. "That's it? Awful?"

"What's the point? If you're that keen to know, I think yesterday they managed to break my ankle and crack a few ribs. I got my shoulder dislocated in the takeover, but the first place they kept us was with some of the medics and one of them put it back in. Still hurts like hell, mind. I feel sick, and my kidneys feel like some bastard has been kicking them, which is a funny coincidence because that's exactly what did happen. And my head is pounding—I keep hoping I'm concussed, but I don't seem to be. Passing out would be an improvement, all things considered. Feel better, now?"

Actually, he did. Relatively better, anyway.

There was a silence, then Chevril said, "Toreth?"

"Who the hell else are you expecting?"

"Could you... that is—I'm cold. Really, bloody cold."

Toreth thought about it for a moment, then decided, what the hell. He lay down on his better side, and wriggled carefully forwards until he found what turned out to be Chevril's back. He was shivering—not surprising, because what shirt he had left was in shreds.

He fitted himself against the other man, as close as he could. What good it would do in terms of body heat he wasn't sure, but after a while the shivering subsided a little.

"Thanks," Chevril said.

"No problem."

Chevril must have been feeling better, because he added, "I'm just cold, you know."

"I know."

"Just so long as you do. Because I don't, you know..."

"Really? Then you should watch where you're putting your hands."

Chevril jerked away from him. "They're fucking well cuffed behind me! I can't put them anywhere else!"

"I know, I know. It was a joke."

"Ha bloody ha."

He thought about getting up, but lying there with Chevril was better than sitting on his own. Marginally warmer, anyway. "A bad joke. I'm sorry."

Chevril moved back, obviously still cold enough to forgive him. But he seemed to have his fists clenched.

"Chev, don't worry. Even if I wasn't almost totally immobilized, I wouldn't fuck you if you were the last man on earth."

"Oh really?" Chevril sounded skeptical. "What about that New Year's party, then?"

God, how many years ago had that been? "Doesn't count—that was for money. Someone bet me I couldn't get you into bed. Or even on your knees in the toilets. And they were dead right."

"How much?"

"Er... a hundred and fifty euros, I think."

"Bloody hell! A hundred—" Chevril coughed painfully. "Oh, Christ. A hundred and fifty? Did you pay up?"

"I had to. There were plenty of witnesses. You ruined my reputation as well. I've won bets on men who would've sworn on their mothers' graves that they were totally straight. Although to be fair, they're the easiest ones, sometimes."

"You can't begin to imagine how much I don't want to hear about it."

"You're telling me you've *never* wanted to fuck a man? Not even felt curious? Not even found a bloke slightly attractive when you were absolutely hammered?"

"Never. Not once."

Toreth tried to imagine it, and failed miserably. Individual people, that was easy—there were plenty of people he'd never want to fuck, although Chevril wasn't one of them. But writing off a whole fifty percent of the planet because of one chromosome? "Strange."

"Not really. I don't think I'm the odd one out, here."

"I suppose not." An idea struck him, funny because of who it was. "Would you do it for money?"

"No!" A short silence, then Chevril said, "Well... it would depend on what, and how much. And who with."

"Does it matter who?"

"Yes. I mean, the whole idea's totally revolting, but there are different degrees of totally. Tillotson would need the code to the Central Bank before I'd even think about it."

"Okay, say it's me."

"Hypothetically?"

"Absolutely."

"Hypothetically, that leaves 'what,' and 'how much.' 'What' I'm not even going to think about, and 'how much' is 'a lot.' Why the hell are you interested, anyway?"

"I'm not. But it's passing the time, isn't it?" And it was. For a couple of minutes he'd almost forgotten the ache in his ribs. "Got anything better to talk about?"

"Nothing I can think of, no. And believe me, I'm trying."

He grinned in the dark. "Let me know if you do. Until then, I'll say what, and you can tell me how much."

"Oh, for God's sake." Then Chevril shrugged, and hissed through his teeth. "Hellfire, that hurts. All right, go on."

"Blowjob."

"Bloody hell! Couldn't you give me some warning before you say something like that in my ear?"

"I did. Blowjob. I get to come in your mouth. How much?"

"You don't have enough to persuade me to put it *in* my mouth, never mind anything else."

"Chev, it's hypothetical. I've got however much it takes. You don't have to swallow."

"Urgh, that's just... no. I couldn't. Really. I'd be sick."

Toreth let the silence stretch out. Chevril and money made a reliable combination.

"Ten thousand," Chevril said eventually.

"Eight?"

"Ten. I said ten, and I meant ten. And I'd still puke."

"Okay. That was giving, how about taking?"

"Um... God, that's almost worse."

"Close your eyes, you wouldn't know it wasn't Elena. Except that I'm probably better at it."

A chilly silence—literally and metaphorically—then Chevril said, "Leave Elena out of this."

"Sorry." He wondered briefly if it was outside her repertoire, before deciding that asking would be a good way to end the conversation. "But it's not that different, honestly."

"Five, then."

"Five *thousand*? Fucking hell."

"When I said 'revolting,' I meant it. Whatever it felt like, I'd still know it was you."

"Fair enough. How about fucking, then? Proper fucking."

"Meaning what, exactly?"

"I fuck you in the arse, I come inside you, and you come, too."

"I wouldn't."

"You would. It's just reflexes. Obviously enthusiasm helps, but you'd come in the end. How much to let me fuck you?" And he had to admit he was getting more interested in the idea. What would Chevril be like as a fuck? "I'd be quick."

"There isn't enough money in the Administration," Chevril said firmly.

"Sure? *Any* amount?"

Silence again, then, "Yes."

"How about you fucking me?"

He felt Chevril move, turning his head to look over his shoulder—pointlessly, because it was still blacker than midnight.

"You do that?"

"Of course I do. Why wouldn't I?"

"*I* don't know. It just seems... not you. I mean, it's a well-understood fact in the section that you'll do anything, with anyone. But... I suppose I can't imagine someone so bloody competitive wanting to be on the bottom for anything."

Toreth started to laugh, but pain quickly cut it short. "It's not like that," he said when he'd got his breath back. "It's something to do, that's all—a question of taste. Some men prefer one or the other, some of the time. I suppose I fuck more than I am fucked, but I enjoy it both ways."

"If you say so." Chevril still sounded vaguely put out by the idea—spoiling his preconceptions, perhaps. "What's-his-name does it to you? Your rich corporate?"

For a moment, he was tempted to tell Chevril to leave Warrick out of it, but that would just have been tit for tat—talking about fucking Warrick was a topic he always enjoyed.

"Yeah, sometimes."

"I heard—" And he stopped abruptly.

"Heard what?"

"Oh, just rumors. Coffee room stuff. That he was into all sorts of kinky shit, whips and chains, and that's why he was with you in the first place. Interrogator junkie."

Except when it was phrased like that. "Yes to the kinky shit, no to the interrogator junkie. I don't need to do that to get a fuck. He hates me working here."

"Hates it? So why's he still hanging around?"

"Because I'm the best fuck in the solar system."

Chevril laughed, and then groaned. "Oh, Jesus, don't make me do that. Toreth, you can't build a relationship on sex and nothing else. It wouldn't work."

Or I bet that's what Elena says, right before she tells you she's got a headache. "Suit yourself. I must be imagining fucking him and nothing else for the last however many years it is. Anyway, you never answered the question: how much to fuck me? Tell you what, I'll do myself, so you won't even have to touch my cock."

"Oh, hell, I don't know. If you could get me out of here, I'd do it for free."

He sounded pissed off and exhausted, so Toreth dropped it. Again, he thought about moving, but he simply didn't have the energy.

No sound in the cell now but breathing and the cycling air. The quiet brought with it a new awareness of the blackness, pressing close around them. He wished that he hadn't taken off the blindfold. "Have you got any idea how long it's been since it started?" Toreth asked.

"No bloody idea at all." Chevril shifted against him. "Days. I'm more worried about how much longer it'll be before someone opens the door and . . . " Silence for a moment, then Chevril said, "Do you think they'll execute us?"

"Probably. Maybe. Fuck, I don't know. What do you think?"

Chevril said nothing, but Toreth felt him nod. After a minute he heard a hitch in Chevril's breathing. A few seconds later he felt a second suppressed sob. However, that, to his great relief, was it—Chevril's breathing steadied, although he still shook slightly.

Cold, that's all. Cold could kill, though. Would kill, in the end, as surely as bullets or bleeding. Through the fog of hunger and exhaustion Toreth tried to recall the course he'd taken years ago on temperature management in detention and interrogation. All he could dredge up was that shivering was a good sign, or at least a better one than stopping shivering.

How many hours had they been locked in here? How much longer would it be before they ended up like Sed? He almost didn't care—he'd never felt so thoroughly miserable in his whole life. He curled up closer to the other man, the difference in their heights meaning that he could rest his chin on top of Chevril's head. He expected a protest, but none materialized.

Toreth closed his eyes, shutting out the darkness. He'd been trying not to think about Warrick, but now, drifting closer to sleep despite the pain, he couldn't help it.

They'd argued when he'd last seen Warrick, about something stupid and trivial and entirely Toreth's fault. As usual he'd been late showing up, but this time after he'd promised to be punctual. He should've made it up then and there. (Or he shouldn't have been late in the first place, but that was getting ridiculous.) He hadn't bothered to make up, that was the thing. It hadn't mattered, or so he'd thought—if he left Warrick alone for a day or two, he'd cool down by himself.

All it would've taken was Toreth not walking out. Then they could've rowed properly and fucked afterwards, still hot and angry, and it would've been as great as it always was. He'd still be lying cuffed on the floor of this filthy, freezing, stinking cell, bruised and thirsty and starving, with a corpse and the straightest man on God's green earth for company, but at least he would've had one more fantastic fuck in his life.

God, he missed Warrick—wanted him. Just sleeping next to him would be enough right now. To have Warrick's warm body beside him, to be able to smell him, kiss him, touch him, skin rubbing against skin . . . well, maybe not *just* sleeping, then. Why waste a beautiful bed? Imagining the unimaginably comfortable mattress and fresh sheets, clean-smelling and soft. Holding Warrick close, whispering to him, fucking him slowly, making it last for both of them, hearing him moan with every—

"I can feel that, you know," Chevril said.

He was back in the cell, cold and aching. "It has nothing to do with you—I was thinking about someone else. Move away, if you don't like it."

"I'm too bloody cold. Just don't *do* anything with it."

Sometimes you have to laugh. Even when it hurts.

"Oh, Christ, look at that!"

Disgusted voices woke him, and he rolled half away from Chevril before pain stabbed through him, pinning him into stillness and leaving him gasping for breath. His ribs, his pounding head, his hip where it had been pressed again the hard floor—these were islands standing out from a wide sea of pain. Beside him, Chevril tried to sit up, and fell back, groaning.

"Not you, him. Get up."

Toreth blinked at the light from the open door. As far as he could see, the guard was pointing to him. If he wasn't, he'd soon find out. He seemed to have guessed right, because when he finally made it to his feet, one of the guards took hold of him and dragged him out. Toreth struggled to keep himself upright, hampered by the restraints around his ankles and the agonizing stiffness in his muscles. The sharper pain in his side snatched at his breathing and he fought the urge to cough.

"Come on," the guard said.

Too stupefied to think straight, Toreth muttered, "I'm coming as fast as I fucking can."

He vaguely expected to get hit for it, but he wasn't. That should have caught his attention, made him wonder where they were taking him, but he was too thoroughly worn out to care about where, only how far.

In the end, it was a mercifully short distance. The guards pushed him through an open doorway, sending him stumbling again, and stayed outside.

An interrogation room, white and stark, and one person waiting for him. Sara.

Surprise snapped him awake. He hadn't dared hope that he'd see her again. And he'd never imagined it would feel this good, and this awful: overwhelming relief that she was alive followed at once by the fear of what might happen next. She wasn't visibly bruised, but she looked pale and terrified, her hair messy and her face smudged with dirt. When she saw him she nearly screamed, swallowing the sound before it escaped. "Toreth? Oh, God."

He wanted to put his arms around her, but he couldn't. Instead, with a glance at the guards, he went over and kissed her.

He checked her over quickly, looking for obvious injuries. No blood, no visible bruises. Her fingers were bare, her collection of rings gone; his mind processed the detail automatically. She'd obviously been crying, tear tracks showing in the grime on her face, and she was starting to cry again now.

"Shh." He lowered his voice. "Don't make a fuss. Don't attract attention."

She nodded, sniffling. Her hands were cuffed, too, so he offered his filthy sleeve for her to wipe her face. "I thought you were dead," she whispered.

He forced a smile. "You don't get rid of me that easily. Do you know what's going on?"

"I've been locked up since it happened." She darted a frightened glance at the doorway. "They separated out the admins and took us away, by sections. They put us in one of the coffee rooms. No one knew anything much."

"How long has it been?"

"Four days." She frowned at him. "Didn't you...?"

He shrugged, then wished he hadn't. "I lost my watch. Besides which, it's tricky to look at one when you're cuffed. In the dark."

"In the dark? Jesus! All this time?"

"More or less. And those were the better parts, really. Did you see anything on the way down here?"

"Christ, yes." She shuddered. "Toreth, there's...such a mess. You should see the upper interrogation levels. You can't imagine. It looks like they killed...they killed everyone. Not just the interrogators—the admins, too, even the medics. *Everyone.* There's blood everywhere. So *much* blood. And God, the smell—" She stopped, coughing, nearly retching. "They were still clearing the bodies away when they brought me through, down here. That's when I was sure...that you'd be dead, too."

"They got me coming out of the level two entrance. I finished the interrogation early so I was on my way to the gym. Lucky fucking break. What about the other paras? And the investigators?"

"I don't know." Her gaze dropped. "There were a few with us, but they were... taken away. On the second day—early Saturday morning." She looked up, her eyes pleading for good news. "I hoped you might've seen some of them."

"'Fraid I didn't see much at all. The bastards were in a hurry to get into the main building—" And massacre the Interrogation level staff. "So they threw me in with a load of specialists from Corporate Fraud. Liz Carey was there, and Chean—he kept telling anyone who'd stand still for five seconds that they were all nothing more than number crunchers. The resisters weren't treating them too badly, at least then." Toreth nodded down at the place where his senior para badge had been ripped from his jacket shoulder. "I didn't think to ditch my jacket, but a few hours later they picked out the interrogators and paras whether they were in uniform or not. After that everything got a lot less fun."

"But you didn't see anyone at all from our section?"

"Chevril. He's alive, but he's not good. Sedanioni was in the cell with us—she died last night. Nothing we could do for her. That's everyone I know about. I left Starr in interrogation with my prisoner, so he would've been down there when—" He stopped. That wasn't what she'd want to hear. "Nagra was over at Justice with B-C when it started. They'll be okay." If Justice hadn't been hit, too.

She still looked stricken, so he tried to think of something more optimistic for her. "There's a chance for all the others, too. If the resisters concentrated on the Interrogation levels."

It was the best he could do, but he shouldn't have said it. She went pale again—or rather, paler, and Toreth remembered his own thoughts earlier. Tidying up loose ends, eradicating the survivors. He was an interrogator, or at least he'd trained as one, and that was in his file. Now he was a para, and as far as any resisters were likely to be concerned, paras were as much torturers as anything else. Sara was his admin. How far was it going to go?

Why had they been picked out, the two of them? It couldn't be a coincidence.

Warrick. The only good reason he could think of was Warrick. If whatever fuckup that had happened at I&I hadn't engulfed the corporations, too, maybe he'd managed to do something. He would, if it was at all possible. Toreth hadn't doubted that at any time over what Sara said was the last four days. If Warrick could do anything, he would. *If* he could. Hope was dangerous, and he wasn't going to let it drive him into anything stupid.

Toreth spotted movement by the door, and he and Sara both turned to face it. He knew at once that it wasn't Warrick, but it took a moment for his exhausted brain to recognize the tall, blond figure, then a moment longer before he could believe what he was seeing.

Carnac, as large as life and about a hundred times as smug. He smiled at them calmly, as if there was nothing in the least unusual about the meeting. Toreth simply stared.

"Hello, Toreth. Sara."

Neurons finally fired and produced a response. "What the fuck are *you* doing here?"

"I am organizing. Planning." Carnac gestured expansively. "Directing. Creating strategy. In other words, I am doing my job. Freelance, as you might have guessed."

"Okay, what the fuck are you doing *here*?"

"Looking for you, naturally. And naturally, I have found you."

Yeah, naturally. Stupid to think things couldn't get any worse. "You're with the resisters?"

"For purposes of tact, you might consider calling them revolutionaries." Carnac closed the door to the room. "Us revolutionaries, indeed, for the duration of my contract."

"I thought you were Administration."

"Not anymore. Or rather, not that Administration."

So that's how it was. "I'm surprised the rabble we had in here stopped long enough to find out you were on their side."

"Ah, yes. The rabble." He crossed over to them. "When one is engaged in a difficult enterprise such as this, one must use whatever tools are available. Even if those tools are dangerous and hard to direct with precision. Useful, but best used as little as possible. As we speak, the rabble are being, ah, encouraged to return home, to enjoy the freedoms they have won. More reliable forces are replacing them."

Toreth hunted for a suitable reply, and gave up—he was too exhausted to play Carnac's kind of games. "I don't suppose you could just tell us what the hell you want?"

"I want you." Carnac paused, as if expecting some kind of response. "As part of my organizational duties, I have been placed in charge of dealing with this establishment. I&I is a part of the old Administration." He gestured around the room, taking in the smashed interrogation equipment. "It is also a barbaric, grotesque anachronism that symbolizes that oppressive and brutal regime. A natural focus, as you have discovered, for the hatred of the populace."

His delivery was as controlled as ever, but the hint of anger behind it—real anger—caught Toreth's interest at once. It was the first time he'd ever heard the man sound as if he cared about something other than himself. "So . . . what? You're here to finish off what your pet mob started and you thought you'd begin with personal grudges?"

Carnac shook his head. "Nothing so Neanderthal. The new Administration will be . . . well, I doubt the details of our ultimate aspirations would interest you, or mean anything to you. Suffice it to say that, regrettably, your inquisitorial skills will still be required, at least for the initial period of reorganization and readjustment."

"You're going to keep Interrogation?" What the fuck was the point of the whole bloody mess, then?

"Records will be examined by a tribunal to determine those with interrogation expertise most suitable to be—" Carnac frowned slightly. "—re-employed by the new Administration. Not a plan I designed, although I concede the practical imperative. Any, ah, excess personnel will be dealt with as appropriate."

Sara said, "As appropriate?"

Carnac turned to her. "My understanding is that, after their files are assessed and they are interviewed by the tribunal, those rejected will be executed as 'political criminals.' An ironic and somewhat amusing redefinition of the term."

My understanding, my arse, Toreth thought. He would bet a great deal of money on it being the socioanalyst's idea in the first place. "So why pick me out?"

"Because I selected you to be the first to receive an offer of re-employment. I abused no rules to do so—I'm confident that you have no personal loyalty towards the old Administration, and that you will ply your trade just as efficiently for us. Beyond that, I know you and I know your strengths. I need someone to persuade the rest of those selected to remain at I&I to cooperate with us. You can fulfill that role superbly."

Flattering. From anyone else Toreth might've considered believing it. "'Personal fucking liaison' again, right?"

"An accurate description of the post, yes." Carnac's voice held a "clever boy" edge that made Toreth tense his arms against the cuffs. "The new Administration is operating under martial law, and in any case Int-Sec is technically a military organization, so I could merely order you to comply, should I so wish."

But obviously he wouldn't—he wanted Toreth to ask him for it, to accept the offer. Let me fuck you, and I'll let you live. Simple choice. No choice at all, really. "What about Sara?"

"Sara is free to go."

She looked between them. "Free to go?"

"Yes. The excesses of the first few days were regrettable, but the administrative staff are not officially included in the purges. Sorry—in the 'reforms.' Most of the admins will be released over the next day or so. We are currently verifying identities to ensure that none of the larger fish slip through the net. If you also wish to return to work here, that would be your decision. I merely thought that your presence here would be . . . a demonstration of goodwill and authority on my part."

Toreth nodded, believing that at least. Sara was safe. "In that case—"

"No!" Sara stepped forwards.

"Shut up. In that case, Carnac, you can go fuck yourself, and your job, and your fucking treacherous, murderous new friends, and if you want to have me, you'll have to get someone to hold me down while you fucking well rape me, if you can manage to get it up, because—" He ran out of breath, spoiling the effect, but never mind. "Because I never thought I'd say this, but I'd rather fucking die."

Carnac raised an eyebrow. "Have you finished?"

"Yes."

"Good. Melodrama aside, is that your final answer?"

"Toreth, don't! Please don't."

He ignored her. "Yes, it is."

"I see." Carnac shook his head, mock regretful. "I have to admit, it wasn't the answer I expected. I had thought that you'd be sufficiently intelligent to say yes, and wait until you had the chance to run."

Toreth blinked. Oh, yes. Well, we can't all be geniuses, can we? "Try spending four days in the pitch dark with your ribs kicked in and then see if you feel like playing fucking games afterwards." Not a bad save, but he doubted Carnac believed it.

"In that case, I believe our business here is concluded." Carnac straightened his sleeves. "I shall be—"

"Can I have a word with Sara? Alone?" Much as he hated to ask Carnac for anything, this might, he realized, be the last chance.

Carnac took a few steps away, making it clear that that was all he would offer.

She had started crying again, and it was getting on his nerves. "Sara? Do you think you could possibly shut the fuck up and listen for a minute?"

With an effort, she swallowed the sobs. "What?"

"A favor, that's all. Could you tell Warrick—" And his mind went blank. Fuck. What the hell kind of message were you supposed to send under these circumstances? Tell him I committed suicide because I couldn't bear the idea of Carnac shoving his cock down my throat and expecting me to be grateful for it? Tell him I'm going to miss him, for however long it takes them to kill me? Tell him I'm sorry that the last thing we did together was argue and not fuck? Tell him that he was the best fuck in the world?

"Tell him I . . . " And his eyes started to sting from looking at her, seeing her crying for him. No one else ever had. "You're the admin—just tell him something. Whatever you think he'd like to hear. Make it sound good."

She nodded, choking on tears.

“You can tell him yourself,” Carnac said.

Toreth turned slowly towards him. “What?”

“Keir is here to collect you—he’s waiting upstairs. Rather impatiently, I imagine.”

“To... collect me?” The bastard was lying. He had to be lying. Playing games.

“Yes. Public transport services are still suspended and I wouldn’t advise walking through the city. Certainly not in uniform.”

Beside him, Sara stared, too, tears dried by the shock. “But—but you said he...”

Carnac smiled at him with the most purely vindictive expression Toreth had seen in his life. “Toreth, did you honestly think that I would make your release conditional upon your providing sexual services? After your charming farewell last time I was here? Dear me. I think you have a somewhat exaggerated opinion of your own performance.”

Of course, Carnac hadn’t said anything of the kind, not specifically. Heavily fucking implied it, yes, and Toreth knew all about that technique. Fuck, but the man could hold a grudge. “Why?” Toreth said.

“I thought that I had explained. Shall I go through it more slowly?”

“No. Why the fuck are you letting me go?” If he was.

Carnac looked at him for a moment, then shrugged delicately. “I don’t suppose it matters if I tell you, although I doubt you will like the answer. I’m doing this for Keir. I have a lot to thank him for, and for some reason that I cannot begin to fathom, he decided my gratitude could best be expressed by extracting you from here and returning you to his safekeeping.”

“What the hell do you owe him for?”

“Ah. Now that, I think, he will be able to explain far better than I.” He paused. “If you wish to ask him. I would advise against it, but I’m used to having my advice ignored.”

“I’ll hear it from you.”

“Actually, no.” Carnac looked at his watch. “Now I do have to get along. Organizing a revolution is time-consuming work, but—” He shared one of his devastating smiles between them, leaving Toreth cold. “At least I’m not bored.”

Toreth had a ready response, but it wasn’t original. Let it go. Try not to hope too much that Carnac might be telling the truth.

Carnac started to turn, then paused. “The offer of a job, incidentally, remains open—it was the justification for your release, and I see no reason to complicate my own situation by rescinding the order. However, I doubt that anyone will have reason to chase it up, should you decide to disappear quietly. After you.” He gestured to the door. Still not believing, Toreth did as he was told.

A split second before it happened, he noticed that although Sara’s hands were cuffed, her legs were free. Just as he began to form the thought, “How sloppy,” she turned to Carnac as she passed him, smiled sweetly, and kicked him in the balls. Hard. Really, terribly hard.

Toreth cringed in instinctive empathy, even as he relished the high, choked scream. Carnac's expression was beyond priceless. He dropped like a stone, already doubling up before he hit the ground.

Sara stood over him, tears flowing freely, screaming hatred. She didn't kick him again, but it would have been utterly superfluous in any case—his nervous system was fully engaged. It was stupid, it might well get them both killed, but Toreth loved her for it. "Sara." He stepped back, out of the line of fire from the door. "Sara, leave it."

She didn't react to him in the slightest, utterly focused on Carnac, yelling obscenities with a passion and variety that impressed him, even under the currently stressed circumstances. "Sara, get away from him."

The door started to open. He took a deep breath, ignoring the fierce pain in his side. "Sara!" he shouted, desperately willing her to move.

At least she shut up. And at least the guards who entered seemed prepared to investigate before they fired. They looked between them, from Sara to himself to the writhing Carnac. What had happened was blindingly obvious, even without Carnac trying to gasp out something that might have been "Bitch."

To his surprise, Toreth recognized one of the guards. "Horley?"

The man caught his eye for a second, then turned away, towards his companion, who looked to Toreth like a civilian—a resister. "What do you think?" the civilian asked.

Horley shrugged. "We've already got our orders. I don't see that this changes them." And, briefly, he smiled. Actually *smiled.* They weren't looking at Carnac anymore, not even a glance. He had a sudden feeling that Carnac's talent for making himself unpopular had been manifesting itself again.

Horley nodded at them. "Get a move on."

Toreth went over and nudged Sara with his shoulder. He wasn't leaving her, whatever happened. "Sara, come on. Before they change their minds." Before Carnac got his voice back, which fortunately wouldn't be for a good while yet.

She looked up at him blankly, then nodded. "I'm sorry," she whispered, her voice raw.

"I'm not. But we have to go. Please."

To his relief, another nudge got her moving, with only a brief backward glance. Once they were out of the room, Carnac's anguished moans fading behind them, Horley stopped them. "Take the cuffs off them," he said to the other guard.

"What about—"

"Forget what the spook said. They're going home, what the hell does it matter? Besides, it'll take forever to walk him up there with the leg restraints."

He recognized all the corridors, every lift, every door. He'd worked there since the building had been completed. And still everything seemed strange; every person was a stranger, even the few he recognized. Yet at the same time he was aware all his colleagues (or at least the surviving ones) were there, somewhere, locked up. In coffee rooms, like Sara had been, or in cells like Chevril, cuffed and in pain. And alone now, except for poor fucking Sedanioni.

They passed bodies, and Service troopers bagging them for removal. He recognized some of the corpses, but most of the faces were made unfamiliar by death. Bloodstains marked places where other bodies had already been cleared, making it plain that on the interrogation levels the killing had been extensive.

So much blood.

Sara walked beside him, tears falling steadily as if she was no longer aware of them, averting her eyes from the dead. But Toreth didn't feel anything beyond a sense of wondering disbelief, or even find it strange that he didn't. His body still hurt, but even that seemed distant. It was simply too much for him to take in—his world fallen apart around him. How could this have happened? How could the Administration have allowed it to happen?

Eventually, they reached the ground floor, coming out of a lift that stank of blood into the long corridor leading to the interview rooms near reception. Through a glass door he saw a dark-haired man, with his back to them.

"It's him," Sara said in a low voice. "Oh, God—it really is." Clearly she'd put as much faith in Carnac's promises as he had.

The guards halted them in the corridor and opened the door to the room, and it *was* Warrick. Unbelievably, wonderfully Warrick, arguing ferociously with a man in a Service captain's uniform. "I *have* authorization from the socioanalyst. I have all the fucking paperwork. Hand him over or let me see Carnac, *now*."

Toreth took a step forwards, unable to help it, then stopped at a warning gesture from Horley. The captain looked up, over Warrick's shoulder, and his face lit up with relief. "They're here."

Warrick stopped in midexposition and spun around so fast he was in danger of whiplash. Toreth had no idea what to say, but luckily Warrick didn't seem to want a major reconciliation scene. "Toreth. Thank—Sara?"

She stepped up beside him. "You don't sound too pleased to see me."

"I wasn't—never mind. Come on." He turned back to the captain. "Everything is in order? Yes?" It didn't sound like much of a question.

"Yes, everything. Just take them away and get out of my office."

"Thank you very much for all your help," Warrick said with tremendous insincerity, and picked up a pile of papers and scannable IDs from the table. "I think this is all mine."

He brushed past the guards as if they didn't exist and came out into the corridor, stopping beside them. "Which way to get out?"

"Depends which exit you want," Toreth said.

"The main one. I left some things there."

"That way, then, but—"

Warrick had already set off, walking quickly. "Questions later. We need to leave, now."

Reception was oddly normal—he didn't recognize the guards, nor the people at the desk, but it looked like business as usual. He rubbed his wrists where the cuffs had scraped the skin raw. Half an hour ago, he'd been in the cell, sure he was going to die. Now he was ten meters away from freedom.

Desperately wanting to keep going, Toreth was still glad of the chance to rest while Warrick collected a bag from the main desk. Adrenaline buoyed him up, but the brisk walk had left him breathless and dizzy. Something touched his arm, and he looked down to find Sara gazing at him anxiously. "Are you okay?" she asked. "You're sheet white."

He took a breath, keeping it shallow, regretting it even so. "I'm fine."

Warrick opened the bag and handed him a bundle of clothes. "Get changed."

"Here?"

"I had to leave the car some way off. They're not letting anything into the Int-Sec complex—there was an explosion not far from here yesterday, although no one seems to be sure who did it, or why. But if you walk around dressed like that, you'll get lynched—Int-Sec uniforms are a death sentence."

"Right." He started to strip, gritting his teeth against the pain from his ribs and aching shoulders, ignoring the glances from the guards.

"What about me?" Sara asked. "Am I okay?"

Warrick smiled suddenly, nerves temporarily vanished. "You look as gorgeous as ever. As do you." He turned the smile on Toreth, who found himself genuinely dazzled, before Warrick sobered again. "But we aren't clear yet, and it would be stupid to make a mistake now." He studied Sara more closely. "I think you should be all right. There is the badge on the jacket, unfortunately, but it's not too obvious. I didn't bring anything for you, I'm afraid. I only expected to collect Toreth—Carnac said they were releasing the admins anyway."

Her eyes narrowed. "I'm a gesture of goodwill and... don't mention his fucking name again."

Warrick stared. "Sara—"

"Look," she said. "If I take my jacket off, and you lend me your pullover, then my skirt isn't too much of a mess. At least I won't look so much like I've been stuck here for four days, with just a wash in the toilets to keep me going."

"Very well—that sounds reasonable." Sensibly, he seemed willing to drop the question of Carnac.

Toreth dressed as quickly as he could, given that every movement hurt. The new clothes—not his own but in his size—felt wonderful, although they made him uncomfortably aware of how badly he needed to wash. He knew he must stink, although after so long in the cell he could barely tell. He rubbed his face, feeling the four-day growth of beard. The prospect of shaving and showering, soon, was so wonderful that it brought back the fear he'd felt in the interrogation room. If they had everyone else locked down, could Carnac really have arranged to set him free? It would be just like the bastard to let them get this far before snatching him back.

While Sara stuffed his old clothes into the bag, Toreth donned the clean jacket. Anxiety made him rush, and the pain stopped him with it only halfway on. "Ah, *fuck.*" Everyone looked around at the exclamation—Warrick and Sara, the receptionists. The guards. Toreth shoved his other arm into its sleeve, ignoring the knife twisting in his side. "I'm ready. Let's go."

Right up until the moment the guard opened the main doors and they walked out, he wasn't sure. The rush of relief when the doors closed behind them was tinged with disorientation—he'd expected it to be morning outside, for no good reason other than he'd just woken up. In fact it was afternoon, the pale winter sun low in the sky. Warrick checked his watch. "We need to hurry, if you can manage it. There's a curfew. In theory we have plenty of time, but if we're delayed, I don't have a permit to be out after dark. We'll be arrested—if we're lucky."

Toreth looked at Sara, and saw his own thoughts mirrored on her face. He'd rather be shot in the street than taken back to that cell.

The walk to the car seemed to take hours, instead of thirty minutes or so. To his annoyance and embarrassment, Toreth had to stop three times to recover his breath. There were plenty of people around, most of them heading in the same direction as themselves, away from the complex. Official-looking groups, troopers, and what seemed to be random citizens exploring the Int-Sec grounds. But although they attracted a few curious glances—probably due to Sara's tear-stained face—no one tried to stop them.

"Where now?" Toreth asked, as the car started to move.

"We're going to my flat. It will be best if you both stay with me for a while—it should be safe enough. There's been looting and riots all around the city, but I have SimTech security there, as well as the building guards."

"I need to get some things from my place."

Warrick shook his head. "I collected everything yesterday. What I could find—a few clothes and one or two bits of the exercise equipment that didn't look too badly damaged. There are lists of names out of Int-Sec employees, and their addresses. It's been a free-for-all."

"Fuck." Toreth didn't particularly care, not about possessions in general, except—"What about the gear? What about the chains?"

"Gone." Something must have showed on his face, because Warrick added, "It doesn't matter—we can always buy some more."

Not like those ones. And even if they were identical, they wouldn't be the same. If he ever laid his hands on the vermin who'd done the looting...

Warrick turned to Sara. "After I saw the mess at Toreth's I went round to your flat. I'm sorry—when I got there, there was nothing left. The whole building was burned out."

"Bastard?" she whispered.

Warrick looked blank, until Toreth said, "The cat."

"Ah. I don't know. Was he locked in the flat? If he was, then I'm afraid he's gone."

"He had a window. He got in and out through the bathroom window. I don't—" She sniffed, then wiped her eyes angrily. "It was raining that morning. I don't remember if I left it open."

"I'll send someone to look for him tomorrow, I promise."

"Thanks. And...I have to call mum and dad. They'll be going out of their minds."

"Yes, of course. That is, you can try as soon as we get back to the flat. The comms network has been intermittent at best, but I'll set something up to keep trying until you get a connection. If you can't get through, give me the address and I'll make sure they know where you are. But it would be safer to wait until the morning for that."

"Thanks again. I should call my sister, too—but Fee's probably at mum's anyway." Sara frowned. "How's Dillian? Wasn't she off-world?"

From Warrick's sudden stillness, Toreth guessed the news wasn't good. "I haven't heard anything from her, and nor has Cele. Comms to Mars have been out since it started. I hoped there might be something today, but regrettably not. But on the other hand, there is no definite bad news either." His voice was as carefully expressionless as his face.

"Oh. Well, there might not even have been any trouble there."

Warrick shook his head. "I hoped the same thing, at first. But there have been one or two reports suggesting that isn't the case."

"I'm sure she's okay. I mean—" She looked across at Toreth, obviously hoping for a contribution to the conversation.

"What about Kate?" he asked.

"Fine. She's fine." Warrick seemed as grateful for the change of subject as Sara did. "And the rest of the family. Cele's there with them. The trouble hasn't been so bad that far out. I managed a connection for a few minutes this morning and she said it was all quiet."

Toreth looked out of the window. Everything seemed surprisingly normal, except for the odd damaged car, buildings with broken windows and, here and there, squads of Service troopers on the streets. "It looks quiet enough here."

"It does now, yes. However, the troopers only appeared in numbers the day before yesterday, after the Service senior command put out a broadcast pledging their loyalty to the new council."

"Took them long enough to make up their minds," Sara said.

"Indeed. I expect they were extracting concessions from the new Administration before they decided whether to back them or not."

"Treacherous fucking scum," Toreth muttered. He wished he had the energy to be as angry about it as he ought to be. The fucking Service was supposed to be on the same side as Int-Sec, and instead they'd left their colleagues to twist while they made their power plays. Four days in that fucking cell, because the Service wanted shinier toys.

There was a brief pause before Warrick said, "It may not be over yet, either. The new council has far from universal support. No one really knows about departments other than the Service, and a few members of the parliament are still calling for the new council to wait for formal ratification before they start exercising power. It was as quiet as this during the day yesterday, and then there was a hell of a lot of trouble last night, all across the city."

Then there could be trouble again tonight. "Will it be all right for us to stay?" Toreth asked.

"Of course. Why shouldn't it be?"

"You know why. People know we're together. They know what I do. Someone in the building might recognize me. Take Sara, and I'll find somewhere safer, somewhere no one knows me."

Sara started a protest, but Warrick overrode her. "You're both coming back to the flat with me. The question is not open for discussion."

Toreth stared at him. Not a tone of voice he often heard from Warrick—certainly not directed at him. A glance out of the window showed them to be in a quiet street, somewhere he recognized. He touched the control panel. "Stop."

The car continued smoothly along. "You're wasting your time," Warrick said. "I cleared your voiceprint from the system. And I activated the iris scan for the manual controls so there's no point in your trying those, either."

Of course, he would have done. Toreth hated being predictable. "And you're going to lock me in the flat as well, are you?"

"If I have to. In fact, if you make me do it, I'll chain you to the bed. I think we have one long enough to let you reach the bathroom. If not, I'll padlock a couple together."

Jesus, he was *serious.* "All right," Toreth said. "I'll come quietly."

Warrick smiled. "I should hope so."

Chapter Two

❖

Toreth could've stayed in the shower until he fell asleep on his feet, but he kept it short because it was obvious that Sara desperately wanted one, too, and she insisted he went first.

With the blood and filth washed away, he assessed his injuries in the bathroom mirror. A short but deep cut on his right browbone had been the source of most of the blood, and would probably scar—too late to have it properly bonded. At least there was no obvious sign of infection. The skin over his cracked ribs was an ugly Technicolor display of black, purple, yellow, and green. Plenty of smaller bruises and abrasions—far more than he wanted to count. Then he thought of Sedanioni and Chev, and decided things could be a lot worse.

He opened the medicine cabinet and smiled at the stock on display. The occasional advantages of fucking a masochist. It took a third of a bottle of liquid skin repair to paint over all the scrapes within easy reach—Warrick could do the rest for him later. His ribs hurt badly, but Warrick's increasingly sophisticated stock of painkillers came into play, and by the time he sat ensconced on the sofa in the living room, mug in hand, things seemed weirdly normal. In the familiar surroundings, he found it hard to believe that the last four days had been anything more than a nightmare. He kept having to touch his side, fingers pressing lightly into the flesh, so that the drug-muted pain felt real enough for it all to be true.

I&I gone. Or at least finished for him. It simply wasn't possible. He felt cut adrift, lightheaded, although that was probably hunger. Warrick was cooking—he'd feel better once he'd eaten. He settled back into the sofa, burning his tongue with an incautious mouthful of coffee. Everything would be fine. He was where he'd so badly wanted to be when he was lying in the cell with Chevril. Funny that he hadn't consciously noticed at the time. He'd wanted to be here, in Warrick's flat. Maybe he'd subconsciously realized that corporate-grade accommodation would be safer than his own, apparently looted, place.

Things weren't entirely ordinary, of course, even here. There was a SimTech guard inside the flat, with others stationed elsewhere in the building. More guards belonging to other residents and the residential complex itself patrolled the corridors. Toreth was willing to concede that his earlier worries seemed unjustified. Here did look like being the safest place, even for him.

Sara came in, her dark hair damp and disarrayed, wearing a borrowed dressing gown that looked ridiculously large on her. "What have you got there?" she asked him.

"Coffee, with a splash of brandy. It's all the alcohol Warrick's letting me have until I've eaten." He smiled at her, and she returned it, a little wanly. "Ask him, if you want one."

"In a bit." She sat on the sofa beside him, folding her legs up under her. "How are you?"

"Okay, all things considered. You?"

"About the same. Tired, mostly."

"Did Warrick show you the spare room?"

"No. I don't think I want to sleep—not on my own." She glanced down, fiddling with her belt. "Would it be all right if I had a nap here? With you? Just until the food's ready."

"Of course it would. Hang on." He shifted, making himself as comfortable as he could, then patted his thigh. "Come on, then."

"Thanks." She lay down, her head light in his lap, and he took the opportunity to run his fingers through her hair, brushing damp strands back from her face.

"Feel better for the shower?" he asked.

"Much. I *hate* being dirty. I don't think I'm going to feel properly clean for a week."

"I know exactly what you mean." He'd run the shower near scalding hot, but he could still smell the cell on his skin. "But we're out of there now. Dinner and a good night's sleep, and you'll be fine."

She shivered. "God, it was horrible."

"I know. Why the fuck they couldn't have let the admins go before, I—"

"Not that. Well, yes, that was, too. But I was thinking about Carnac."

"Oh. Yes." Scratch Carnac's charming surface and you'd find the bastard underneath. "I'm sorry about that. You remember when he was at I&I, doing his poxy report?"

She nodded.

"I pissed him off. Actually, I told him he was a lousy fuck, which he is. That was payback." Payback with interest.

"I know."

That was news. "How?"

"Oh. I—" She hesitated, then smiled. "I'm your admin. I know everything."

"Not anymore."

"I don't know everything?"

"No, you're not my admin. I'm unemployed, remember?"

She smiled again, already drifting off to sleep. "Right. Of course you are."

Right. Of course he was.

He put his arm over Sara's shoulder, and thought about unemployment and Carnac.

The offer of a job remains open.

Never, was his first reaction. He never wanted to see the man again. The humiliation knotted his stomach. He'd nearly cried, for the first time since—fuck, the first time since the Retraining Center. Never mind that it had been because of Sara—that's not what Carnac would've thought. He never wanted to see Carnac again. But that meant never having the chance to settle the score. The bastard *had* made Sara cry. On its own, that was enough to make him want to take the job and then make Carnac pay, and pay over again for what he'd done.

He took a sip of the cooling coffee. He shouldn't even want to think about that, after the last four days. However unreal it all felt, he'd have to get used to the idea that everything had changed. It would be stupid to go back to the I&I building when Warrick had taken so much trouble to get him out. And Warrick... Warrick would have a fit at the suggestion.

Leaning his head back against the sofa, he closed his eyes, just to rest them. He wasn't going to sleep yet. He'd wait until they'd eaten.

A firm touch on his hand startled Toreth out of a dreamless sleep. Opening his eyes, he found Warrick trying to remove the mug from his fingers.

"Sorry," Warrick said. "It looked somewhat hazardous, under the circumstances."

Sara still slept in his lap, and the mug in question balanced on the arm of the sofa above her, half full of the now-cold coffee. He surrendered the mug to Warrick, who took it and then touched Toreth's cheek briefly with his other hand.

"You shaved," Warrick said.

"And it felt great. I hate beards."

"I thought it looked rather good, as far as one could tell through the grime. A slight reddish tinge to the blond. Very attractive."

"Yeah? Well, maybe I'll grow one for your birthday. I'll get Sara to remind me, or—" He stopped, the strange feeling of disconnection triggered again. Sara wouldn't necessarily be there to remind him. Warrick looked at him inquiringly, and he shook his head. "Nothing."

"I don't think I've ever seen you not finish a drink before," Warrick said after a moment. "Would you like something else?"

"Food. I'm fucking *starving*."

"Ready in a few minutes. That's why I came in." He sat down in the chair opposite.

"I thought you might've had it on the table for us when we got here," Toreth said.

It wasn't a serious complaint, and Warrick smiled. "I would have, except that I was at I&I since first thing this morning."

Toreth blinked. "All day?"

"Yes. Most of that was occupied with getting to see someone in the first place, or waiting while they said they were trying to find you. I didn't dare leave in case they wouldn't let me back in. In the morning there was some shooting inside the building." He shook his head. "In the distance. I don't know what it was. But after that it seemed best to stay."

Another lot of interrogators experiencing mob justice. Or possibly Carnac's rabble being encouraged to go enjoy their freedom somewhere else. He could always hope. "Thanks, anyway," Toreth said. "For getting us out. I knew you would."

Warrick raised an eyebrow. "Really?"

"Well, no. But I did know you'd try."

There were a few seconds of silence, then Warrick said, "How's Sara doing? And what was that about Carnac?"

He shrugged, carefully. "She'll be fine. Carnac pulled something not at all funny to get at me. Sara got caught in the crossfire. Except... no, she didn't. The bastard did it deliberately, to her as well."

Warrick nodded. "I have to say, I worried it might be something like that. But he was the only resource I had available to try to get you out."

The idea of being grateful to Carnac stung him, and also reminded him of something else. "Carnac told me he helped us because he owed you. What for?"

Warrick closed his eyes briefly. "Oh, hell."

"Warrick, what was it?"

"If I said it was Carnac causing trouble, and that it was better that you didn't ask, would that work?"

More or less what Carnac had said himself. So if Carnac didn't want him to know, then obviously Toreth had to. "No. I want to hear it."

"I thought as much. Let me get a drink."

Warrick took a long time about it. When he sat back down, he still didn't say anything.

"Well?" Toreth asked.

"Do you remember when Carnac came to SimTech? When he did the report?"

How could he fucking forget? "Yes."

"I spent some time alone with him. In the sim."

Oh God, no. Not like that.

Warrick looked up and shook his head at the unspoken question. "Nothing sexual. Although that might've been better, in the long run. He was having doubts about the Administration. About his role in it. He mentioned an interrogation you showed him. He wasn't sure if such things were justifiable simply to maintain the stranglehold of the Administration on Europe."

Toreth stared at him, open-mouthed. That was treason. Blatant, concrete, inarguable treason. From a socioanalyst at that, although it was ridiculous that he should be shocked when he'd seen the man at I&I, working with resisters. "What did you *say* to him?" he asked eventually.

"I told him that I thought he was probably right." Warrick's gaze didn't waver. "And that whatever he wanted to do about it was up to his own conscience."

Treason again. "So he went away and started a fucking revolt?"

"It does look that way, yes."

"Because of what you said to him?"

"If you want an immediate cause, perhaps." Warrick ran his hand over the arm of the chair, then picked off a speck of fluff. "Or one could equally well say that it was because of what you showed him. I imagine that the situation is too complex for either of us to take the whole blame."

"Fucking hell." My fault, Toreth thought. In some small way, my fault. Carnac had come to I&I to check them for subversive tendencies and left with the seeds of his own subversion sown.

He laughed, once, the sound escaping before he could get his hand up to his mouth to stifle it. If he started laughing, he knew he wouldn't be able to stop, and he didn't want to wake Sara or aggravate his ribs. He bit his lip, fighting down the hysteria by thinking about Carnac, the fucking hypocrite. It proved highly effective. "He offered me a job, you know. Back at I&I. Doing the unjustifiable."

Warrick sipped his drink and nodded. "He's nothing if not a pragmatist. He said the system couldn't simply be undone overnight. It would take time, even after the heart of the problem had been torn out. The offer was a formal condition for your release, as I understood it. He said you wouldn't have to accept it."

"Yes, I know." He thought of Carnac telling him he could walk away and leave it all behind. Fine, in theory. In practice, it meant that Carnac had won. He had I&I and he could do whatever the hell he wanted with it—and from his tone of voice in the interrogation room, that was nothing good. What Warrick had told him only made him more certain of that.

He made a decision. "Warrick, I'm sorry about this, I really am, but I have to go back." If Carnac would let him, after Sara's excellent piece of footwork.

Long silence, then Warrick said, "Are you sure?"

"Yes. Whatever—" Whatever Carnac's plans are, I'm going to fuck them over as thoroughly as he fucked with me and make him eat every word he said. However, that sounded petty, or at least an inadequate reason for going back to I&I. Nor did he want to take the risk of voicing it out loud. Best not to take chances where Carnac was concerned.

What else could he say? He could call it loyalty, and that would, surprisingly, be partly true. As far as he'd ever belonged anywhere, it was there, and if I&I survived then he wanted to be a part of it. Warrick wouldn't understand that, though—

he'd said so himself. He thought about I&I in the same way as the people who'd gone from room to room and killed admins, medics, and interrogators without bothering to find out who was what: as something that ought to be eliminated.

Finally Toreth fixed on something. Something that might do as an explanation, without getting into a discussion of the rights and wrongs of I&I. That was an argument they somehow managed to avoid having too often, and he was far too tired to have it now. "Do you remember Don Chevril? I think you met him a couple of times."

Warrick nodded.

"He was in the cell with me. He's a mess. In fact, he might be dead by now if they've had another go at him, but if he's not, I can get him out. If I take the job." And if Carnac meant what he said. "There are all the others, too. I've worked with them for a long time. They're—"

"You don't have to justify it to me. If it's what you have to do, then do it."

Warrick delivered the statement so unemotionally that Toreth had to rerun it through his tired brain several times before he was sure he'd heard it right. "Really?"

Warrick smiled slightly. "Really."

"I thought you'd be pissed off about it."

"I knew you'd take it—or I guessed you would. I would've preferred it if you hadn't, of course. However, as I am occasionally required to remind people, I fuck you, not your job."

"Oh." Toreth felt peculiarly unbalanced, ready for a fight that hadn't materialized. "Well, thanks."

"Nothing to thank me for, in this instance."

Toreth slipped out from under Sara with the ease of long practice, laying her head down gently onto the sofa. Warrick watched him, sipping his drink.

"Are you thinking about going now?" Warrick asked. "Because the curfew—"

"No. But I'll call Carnac and tell him I'm accepting. He's probably just about able to stand up by now. That'll get things rolling. And then..."

"Then?"

"Then you can fuck me, not my job."

Warrick smiled. "I thought you might want dinner first."

It was a testament to how incredibly hungry he was that he actually agreed.

Sara woke up in a cold sweat, struggling against the clutch of the sheets, still hearing screaming and smelling the blood. Then the room came into sharp focus around her and she almost sobbed from sheer relief. The realization that she was safe didn't banish the choking tightness in her throat, though. Sick. Oh, God, she was going to be—

She made it to the bathroom just in time to bring up the remains of her lovely, expensive dinner into the sink. She ran water into the bowl, trying to decide if that was it, or if the feeling was coming back. At least she hadn't thrown up all over Warrick's lovely, expensive carpets.

She heard a tap on the door and a male voice she didn't recognize said, "Excuse me? Are you all right in there?"

It had to be the security guard. She clutched the edge of the sink tightly and closed her eyes. "Fine," she said, trying to sound it.

"Okay. Sorry to disturb you."

She rinsed her mouth out and splashed water on her face. Much better. It had been the nightmare, that was all. Or maybe the fact that she'd eaten too much after three days living on coffee and biscuits.

Drying her hands felt strange, with no need to be careful of her rings. She wondered when she'd get used to it. The indentations around her fingers were still there, but fading. Well, she hoped whoever had the rings now was enjoying them. Bastards.

How long had she slept? However long it was, she felt barely less exhausted than when she'd gone to sleep. Still, she might go and sit in the living room for a while. Find a news feed—and her stomach knotted again at the idea. Well, perhaps not that. But not go back to bed just yet.

She was about to open the door when, in the nick of time, it finally registered that she was completely naked. Oh, hell, again. She wondered if the guard had seen her on the way here. She hadn't spotted him, but she'd had other things on her mind. A quick hunt around revealed only hand towels. Oh, hell in spades. Maybe he'd gone away and she could make a dash for it. She knocked quietly on the door. "Um, hello?"

"Yes?"

Right outside. Well, where else? "Look, could I possibly ask you a favor?"

"Of course."

"Could you . . . could you go to my room—the spare room—and get my dressing gown? It's over the back of the chair."

"Certainly. I won't be a minute."

She waited until she heard returning footsteps and then opened the door a crack. He handed the dressing gown through without comment, and she put it on, feeling her cheeks start to burn. It was tempting to wait until he went away and then run for her room. Instead, she took a deep breath and stepped outside.

She found herself looking at the SimTech logo on the shoulder of a dark gray uniform. It took her a moment to force her eyes upward to meet his. "Er, hi," she said, unable to think of anything more face-saving.

He offered his hand, as if nothing untoward had happened. "Rob McLean. You must be Ms. Lovelady." He said it with a perfectly straight face as well, which she always appreciated.

"Call me Sara, please."

He nodded. "You can call me Rob, or McLean, whichever you feel most comfortable with." He looked at her more closely. "Are you okay?"

"Um, actually, no. I had a... a really, *really* bad day. Four days."

"Why don't you go sit in the living room, and I'll bring you a drink. What would you like?"

"Tea, please. I'll come with you."

They went through into the kitchen and Sara sat and watched him while he made her tea. She didn't remember noticing him at the AERC, and she thought she would have done. He was certainly easy on the eye: tall, with dark brown hair and eyes to match it. Looked after his own body as well as other people's. Not very expressive, but that was probably professional veneer. Semiseriously, she wondered whether Toreth had seen him yet, or if she could put a claim in first.

He set the tea down. "Here you are."

"Join me?" When he hesitated, she added, "Please? I'd appreciate the company."

"Of course," he said. "Let me get a cup."

After he sat down, there was a short silence.

"Have you worked for SimTech for long?" she asked. "Only I volunteer for sim trials and I don't remember seeing you."

"You wouldn't. Normally I do personnel security assessments. Advice for the mid- to high-risk staff—home security, helping them plan their lives to make them safer, that sort of thing. Screening new employees. They reassigned me here when the trouble started."

"So what's been happening out here? I've been stuck in a coffee room at I&I for the last four days."

A hint of a frown creased his brow, then he shrugged. "I'm not entirely sure. I doubt anyone is except the people who organized it. And it *was* organized—well organized."

It would be, if Carnac had anything to do with it. "Go on."

"From the news I've seen, it happened all across Europe at about the same time. Administration buildings occupied, the comm networks taken down, mobs out on the street. The Parliament of the Regions put out a statement condemning the 'lawless rioters'—of course, now they're mostly supporting the new council."

Sara laughed shortly. "I expect they're worried about their expenses and their pensions."

"Probably." Rob smiled, too. "I've heard rumors of new elections being called when order's fully restored. Still, I don't think the revolt would have stuck, except that the Service sat it out to start with. Now they're out on the streets, dealing with looting—there was a lot more shooting last night than there has been. And tonight as well. You can hear it now, if you listen."

When she listened, she could. A faint background noise, different from the usual sounds of New London. But whatever was happening was going on a long way from the security of Warrick's well-guarded flat in his exclusive residential area. She wondered how her parents were—she hadn't got through to them, but maybe that was just the comms. No need to start worrying yet, she told herself firmly. As if she could help it.

"Warrick said the Service is on the side of the new Administration," she said.

"Yes. Or that's what it looks like. I wouldn't put money on how it's going to turn out in the end, myself. Not when there's so much trouble still going on. There are more buildings burning tonight, if you go into the living room and look out."

"I'd rather not." She closed her eyes and shivered. Buildings burning, like her building had burned. Bastard, trapped in the flat, not understanding what was happening, yowling for her until the smoke and heat became too much for him. She knew where his body would be—he'd have gone to hide under her bed, where he always went when he was frightened. If he was dead, please let the smoke have got him before...

"Sara?" McLean touched the back of her hand, and she opened her eyes to find him looking at her with concern.

"I'm fine. Just thinking about... something."

His hand lay gently on hers, his eyes warm and very expressive indeed. "Is there anything I can do?"

"Well—"

Then the door opened. Of course. She took her hand away and picked up her tea, sitting back in the chair.

It was Toreth, also wearing one of Warrick's dressing gowns and looking exhausted. Better than he had when he'd said a rather incoherent good night after the meal, though, and a thousand times better than when she'd first seen him in the interrogation room.

McLean didn't react to Toreth's entrance. Of course, he'd know who Toreth was even though he'd come on duty after they'd all gone to bed. She'd still seen McLean first.

Toreth was opening cupboards. "God, you can tell when he's been stressed out—he reorganizes every bloody thing. Where the hell—ah."

He produced a glass, filled it with water and downed it in one long drink before refilling it. "Couldn't sleep?" she asked him.

"Still dehydrated." He opened the freezer and helped himself to ice. As he straightened up he winced, putting his hand gingerly to his side. "Fuck. And the painkillers wore off. Fucking resisters." He turned around, leaned on the fridge, and looked between them. Then his body language altered, sending a message Sara was all too familiar with. "Aren't you going to introduce me?" he said.

She wished Toreth wouldn't *do* that. He'd always done it, to some extent, but ever since Jon Kemp had hospitalized her it was like having an overprotective older brother. One who could unconsciously give the impression that he would break the limbs of anyone who laid a finger on her. He had scared off more than one boyfriend—these days she tried not to let them meet him, and warned them first if it was unavoidable. If he met them at the "interested" stage, she usually wrote them off as a bad job.

To her surprise, McLean didn't look even faintly intimidated. Of course, that was his job. "Rob McLean," he said. "I work for SimTech."

Toreth nodded. "I guessed that. You must be night shift."

"First half. Six 'til two." He looked between them. "Should I go and guard somewhere else?"

"No, that's fine," Sara said before Toreth could say anything. She'd be damned if she'd let him interfere with the only nice thing that had happened in the last five days. "McLean, this is Val Toreth, my boss. Toreth, we were just talking about what's been going on."

"Going on where?"

"With the revolution," McLean said.

Toreth's lip curled. "'Revolution'?"

McLean shrugged. "Call it what you like. Sara said you didn't know anything about it."

Toreth's expression now bordered on open dislike. "No, I don't. Because I've been lying in a cell for the last four days, in the dark, with a lovely set of broken ribs that I got from the 'revolutionaries.' So frankly, I don't *want* to hear about it."

McLean nodded. "Of course," he said with professional coolness.

Sara sighed silently. "Are you still planning on going back?" she asked Toreth.

"Yes. I'm not giving Carnac free rein at I&I."

McLean looked surprised. "Jean-Baptiste Carnac?"

Sara stared at him, which was exactly what Toreth was doing. "Do you know him?" she asked.

"Not know him, as such, but I've met him. He stayed here, before you arrived."

When Sara was a child, her family had holidayed in Switzerland. They'd stopped for a picnic by a mountain lake and, after her mother had checked that it was marked as safe for swimming, Sara had jumped into the inviting-looking water—only to discover that it had come straight from a melting glacier. The shock then was like the shock now.

"I beg your pardon?" Toreth said quietly.

"He was here—Carnac. I assume it's the same man. Tall, blond, a bit effeminate?"

Shut up. Just shut up, now. Sara tried to force the words out, but every instinct was telling her to keep as quiet and still as possible.

"He stayed here?"

She almost wished Toreth had shouted, because then she would've known what would happen next. McLean glanced at her, realizing that something was wrong but unable to back out now.

"Yes. He was here for the first couple of nights we were. He left yesterday." He checked his watch. "The day before yesterday, rather. Monday morning."

"Monday morning." Toreth nodded. "Excuse me."

He put his glass down hard, and walked out.

His departure released Sara from her paralysis. "Oh, *shit.*" She jumped up and dashed to the kitchen doorway. McLean followed her.

"What?" he said, bewildered. Warrick's bedroom door slammed. "He stayed here, that's all."

"Where did he *sleep*?" Sara asked.

"In the guest room, at least while I was here."

"Couldn't you have *said* so?"

"I didn't know it—"

"Shush. Let me listen."

"Was he here?" Toreth's voice came from behind the closed door, furiously loud and clear. "Well, *was* he?"

She waited anxiously through a minute or so of quieter voices, words indistinct but the edge of anger still audible. Then the bedroom door opened again, and Toreth reappeared, heading for the outer door, mostly dressed, his face set and flushed with fury. Warrick was only a pace or two behind him. "Toreth, be sensible, please. Housekeeping, cancel all accesses."

At the last moment, Warrick managed to get in front of Toreth and turned around, blocking the path to the door. "There is a curfew. They are *shooting* people. For God's sake, be reasonable and—"

"Get out of my fucking way."

"I'm not going to let—"

"You lied to me."

Warrick looked past Toreth, catching sight of the audience. "Do we have to do this here?"

"No we don't, because I'm leaving. Curfew or no fucking curfew, I'm going back to my own flat."

"You leave this building over my dead body."

As she waited for Toreth's response, Sara reflected that people didn't usually sound so serious when they said that. Moreover, you didn't usually think there was a chance it would happen. Toreth stood absolutely still in the corridor, and even though she couldn't see his face, she was awfully glad she wasn't standing where Warrick was. Warrick looked as imperturbable as ever.

McLean started to move, and she grabbed his arm. "Jesus, don't even think about it," she whispered.

Silence, seconds stretching out, then Warrick stepped aside from the door. "Very well." He did something to the security system, and then turned back to Toreth. "I'm going back to bed. You're—" He looked up, towards them, then stepped closer to Toreth and said something too quietly for Sara to hear. Then he walked past him and went back into the bedroom, leaving the door ajar.

Toreth hesitated, reaching for the front door, and Sara prayed that she wouldn't have to stop him from leaving. Just as she was about to take the first step into the corridor, Toreth slammed his hand against the wall and swore, making her jump. Then he turned and followed Warrick. If he saw the two of them in the kitchen doorway, he didn't acknowledge them.

After a long moment of silence, McLean said, "Excuse me? Could I have my arm back, please? Only—"

"Shit, I'm sorry." She let McLean go, only realizing as she did so how tightly she'd held him. "Are you okay?"

"Fine." He rubbed his arm. "Although I don't usually have to worry about the people I'm supposed to be looking after bruising me."

"I'm sorry. Would you like something else to drink? Something with a bit more kick than tea?"

"I'm on duty."

And on reflection, something alcoholic might not be good for her stomach. "There's soda if you want some. Fruit juice. Coffee." Out of the corner of her eye she saw him step into the doorway, looking up the corridor. "I wouldn't go looking for them, if I were you."

"I'm fine, thanks." He hesitated. "I think I should go and check on them. Your boss sounded pretty angry back there, and I am responsible for Warrick's safety."

For a moment she was tempted to say "go ahead," but it wouldn't be funny. Not really. "They'll be fine. They do this a lot."

"But that doesn't mean I'm any less responsible for anything that happens." He sighed. "I *hate* this job sometimes."

She looked at him in surprise. She'd never heard him express an opinion, never mind such a vehement one. (Never being, of course, all of half an hour.) "Come and sit down. I honestly don't think there's any urgent guarding that needs to be done."

With a last look up the corridor, he came back and took a seat. She poured herself a glass of soda water, then sat down opposite him. "What do you hate about it?"

"Intruding in people's lives. I'd rather be patrolling the building, to be honest."

"So why aren't you?"

He shrugged. "I'm good at this role. I'm presentable and fairly unobtrusive. I get on with people. But I still don't like it—that's why I switched to consulting. Although at least I don't have to stay here off shift."

"But what about the curfew?"

"Oh, no, I meant here in the flat. We're sleeping in the building—most of the private security people are." Seeing her raised eyebrows, he said, "There are break rooms and a canteen down in the basement, for the building guards and the maintenance and other staff. The building supervisor's opened up her flat and another couple of unoccupied ones. It's pretty crowded, but I shouldn't complain." He looked at his watch. "I really ought to show an interest."

"No. It's only been a few minutes—not long enough to start worrying."

"How long do you recommend?"

"Don't worry at all. They haven't killed each other yet. The worry is what kind of a mood they'll be in when they reappear, and you can tell that by how long it takes. If it's five, ten minutes, then they've argued, so stay out of the blast radius. If it's more than fifteen, they've argued and made up, and they're safe to approach."

He laughed. "Are you sure you should be telling me this kind of thing? What if you don't know when it started?"

"Ah, that's easy. If they're both smiling, then it's okay. If neither of them is, then it's bad news. If Toreth isn't smiling and Warrick's doing that...have you seen it? The thing that isn't a smile but uses the same muscles?"

"Oh yes, I've seen that one."

"That's a good time to start looking for cover until one or the other of them clears out." She shrugged. "Except right now there's nowhere for either of them to go. Better hope they make up."

Toreth closed the door behind him. Closed this time, not slammed, because Warrick was playing cold and reasonable and Toreth didn't intend to lose at that game.

Warrick had already sat on the sofa under the window, looking so calm that Toreth barely restrained himself from going over and hitting him harder than either of them would enjoy. Safer to stand by the bed, his hands clenched behind his back, even though that made him think of I&I. He'd been lying in that fucking cell while Carnac was *here.*

Finally Warrick said, "The answer to the question is no."

"What question?"

"No, I didn't fuck Carnac. That's what you want to know, isn't it?"

"I don't—" He couldn't say that he didn't believe him, because Warrick would only point out that *he* wasn't the one who bent the truth on a regular basis. "If you didn't fuck him, why did you lie about him being here?"

"I didn't do that either. I will freely admit that I omitted to mention it, but that's not the same thing."

He ignored the attempted diversion into an argument over semantics. "So, why?"

"Because I knew that if I said anything about it you would react precisely like this."

"I'm not reacting like—" He took a deep breath and clenched his teeth at the stab of pain. When it subsided he said, "I wouldn't have done, if you'd told me to start with."

"Yes, you would. You can't honestly expect me to have forgotten the last time?"

Warrick shook his head. "I don't understand why you have this... persistent idea that I find Carnac the slightest bit attractive."

In a way, Toreth didn't either, other than that it was Carnac and the man *was* attractive, even when you knew what a bastard he was. Plus there was the other thing, the important thing. "You fucked him before."

"I slept with the man three or four times, more than fifteen years ago." Warrick breathed out, short and exasperated. "For God's sake, Toreth, you've fucked him more often, and considerably more recently, than I have. And, may I point out, you're proposing to go and work with him, back at I&I, presumably in the same office where you had your previous little liaison."

The open jealousy—and touch of anger—from Warrick canceled out some of his own. "I wouldn't fuck Carnac again if my life depended on it," Toreth said, which he knew for a fact, although he hadn't told Warrick the details of the encounter.

"And neither would I." Warrick sighed, and scrubbed his face with his hands. "So what the hell are we arguing about?"

"I have no idea." The anger drained out of him, like water through a sieve, leaving the ache in his ribs and a bone-deep exhaustion. "Just give me some more painkillers, tell me what he was doing here, and then let's get back to sleep."

Warrick found the tablets while Toreth undressed again, then joined him in bed, sitting up a little way away, watching him.

"So what happened?" Toreth said.

"He called the day it started. All he said was that he needed somewhere to stay, and with the trouble going on in the city, of course I said yes. He didn't tell me then that he had anything to do with it." Warrick shook his head. "I assume he didn't trust me, although I suspect he didn't entirely trust his revolutionary friends, either. Neither to manage things right in the first place, nor to keep control of the general uprising if it did succeed. I was a safe house that none of them knew about. By the time he told me that he was involved..."

"Yes?"

"By then I knew what had happened at I&I. I didn't think it would be helpful to antagonize him by throwing him out onto the street. Once the troopers appeared and it became obvious things were going his friends' way, he left. He's at a hotel near the Int-Sec complex."

He had to ask again, even at the risk of pissing Warrick off even more, as well as sounding pathetic. "And nothing... happened?"

"Not a thing. He didn't even offer. I expect that even if he might still be interested under normal circumstances, he had other things on his mind. He slept in the spare room, and when he was here during the day we discussed the sim, when I wasn't busy trying increasingly improbable ways to get access to an active comm network." Warrick smiled slightly. "Ask the security guards if you wish. I expect they would've noticed anything else, given my propensity for noise."

Toreth nodded. He believed him, really. It was just that it was Carnac, and he didn't trust the man a centimeter. The fact that Warrick didn't want to fuck him didn't necessarily mean that it would never happen. The important thing was that it hadn't happened, not this time.

"So can we go back to sleep now?" Warrick asked. "If you're really intending to return to that place in the morning, you'd better get *some* sleep."

"Sounds great." He slid down between the sheets, relaxing into the embrace of the mattress. Despite his assorted aches, he'd never felt anything so comfortable in his life. "God, I dreamed about this, when I was in that fucking awful cell with Chev."

"Yes?" Warrick switched the light out and the bed shifted as he lay down.

"I thought I told you about it already, when we got to bed the first time?" Toreth asked.

"You must've dreamed that, too—you were asleep by the time I'd undressed."

"Was I? Probably. It's all a bit hazy from halfway through dinner, to be honest. So much for fucking me, not my job. Pity."

Warrick laughed and touched his shoulder. "Is that a request?"

Toreth thought about it, and the idea definitely appealed, but his body was already mostly asleep, with his brain fast catching up. "No. Making offers I can't live up to. Sorry."

"Don't be." Warrick's hand closed over his arm. "Having you here, and in almost one piece, is more than enough."

"Funny, that's exactly what I was thinking." He turned onto his side, careful of his ribs, and pressed his face into the pillow, breathing in the scent of clean cotton and Warrick. "Mmh. When I was on the floor, in those bloody handcuffs. Don't know how you can get such a kick out of the fucking things."

"The circumstances are somewhat different."

"Yeah, 'course. I know. Anyway, I was dreaming about this—except it feels even better than I thought it would. Fucking fantastic. Clean sheets. You."

Warrick moved across and kissed him gently, exactly as he'd imagined. Soft cotton and warm skin against him, soothing and luxurious. Hand on his back, touching carefully. He had a moment of fear that *this* was the dream, that soon he would wake up in the cell. Then a noise distracted him: distant firing in the city. He tensed, and Warrick's hand stroked a circle over his shoulder blade. More firing, but it was nothing to do with him. Nothing to worry about, even if he could manage it. Safe, here.

He recaptured the tail end of a thought, before it disappeared into sleep. "Just you. 'S enough."

If Warrick said anything in reply, Toreth didn't hear it.

Chapter Three

❖

In the morning, Warrick insisted that he borrow the SimTech car, and Toreth accepted gratefully. He certainly wasn't up to the walk, even if it had been safe. He'd hoped to slip out of the flat before Sara woke, but she must have set an alarm, because she came out of her room as he was leaving. She looked hollow-eyed but determined. "Wait for me. I'll be two minutes. I just need to grab something for breakfast."

"No. Go back to bed—you're staying here."

Before the rebellion in her eyes could get any further, he put his hands on her shoulders. "Sara, listen. They were shooting people there a couple of days ago—maybe yesterday, too. Let me go and check it out, make sure it's not going to start up again. I promise you can come in tomorrow if it's safe."

Maybe by tomorrow, they'd have finished clearing the bodies away. He wouldn't have time today to cope with her crying all over the place.

Eventually, she nodded. "I could do with finding some new clothes." She smoothed her jacket. "It'll be a nuisance to have to wash everything every night."

Thank God she was going to be reasonable. There would doubtless be enough stress today without kicking off with a scene here. "Good idea."

"And I have to collect Bastard. If he's alive."

"Don't be stupid, of course he is. He's far too fucking evil to die."

She glared at him, although her exhaustion was evident in how poor an effort it was. "He'll be so scared, poor baby, not knowing where I am or what's happened to the flat."

He'd long ago given up trying to shake that particular delusion. "Yeah, he must be terrified." And so must everything he's met. "But you won't go on your own, will you?"

"No, of course not. Rob said he'd help me look—he went off shift at two but he's going to come back up for me at lunchtime. We're going to get Bastard, and then we're going to mum and dad's to check that they're okay."

"That'll be fun for him." Rob, was it? Toreth gave it a moment's thought, then decided that it wasn't worth taking Sara in to I&I just to keep her away from McLean. Anyway, Bastard would be in a fouler temper than usual if no one had been feeding it—an encounter with the psychotic monstrosity should be enough to put anyone off. The idea of McLean trying to entrap an irate Bastard improved his mood no end. "You'd better take some antiseptic with you."

"What? Why?"

"In case Bastard's been hurt, of course."

There was a moment of, if not precisely fear, then certainly unease, as he presented his ID to the guard on the main door. Evidently the automatic internal security systems were out or had been switched off until the new occupants of the building could be authorized. The guard looked to be Service and as he examined the ID his face showed a flicker of surprise. Probably wondering what a para was doing loose and trying to get *into* the building. Carnac must have arranged things, though, because the man opened the door without comment.

It felt strange, crossing the foyer, nodding to the receptionists, none of whom he recognized. Walking through the building, surrounded by more strangers, was even odder. The difficulty of the job he'd accepted began to sink in. He had not only to persuade the I&I staff to work with and for the people responsible for the revolt, but also the reverse—to make at least some of these outsiders into part of the division. Replacement staff would have to come from somewhere.

He remembered how difficult it had been simply to integrate the Investigation and Interrogation Divisions into one, and the disruption now was on an entirely different scale from the old reorganization. Justice, he thought sourly, would be delighted by the turmoil at Int-Sec in general and I&I in particular. Departmental politics could turn out to be a bigger headache than the damage to the building.

Carnac had taken over the director's office. The previous occupant's effects had been cleared away, leaving the room rather spartan. The only personal touch was a small but expensive-looking chess set on the wide desk. Toreth wondered if Carnac enjoyed playing, or if he just liked the image. Carnac himself looked uncomfortable in the generously sized chair, probably due to Sara's parting gift rather than any defect in the upholstery.

"'Morning. How are you?" Toreth asked.

Carnac shifted and winced. "I'm taking a sufficient quantity of anti-inflammatories and painkillers to make the answer to that question at least publishable."

"Glad to hear it." Toreth smiled in satisfaction and hoped it looked at least a little like sympathy. "Well, I'm here, as promised. What's the plan?" Carnac was bound to have a plan, probably several, and Toreth wanted to make sure he knew what they all were.

"The main priority is to return all facets of I&I to operational status as quickly as possible. Interrogation has been given a higher priority than Investigation. I have a great deal to accomplish elsewhere, so I shall be leaving the organization to your good self."

"Suits me. I need the authority to do it."

"You have it. I have given you operational authority over all the division's sections. And security clearance to match, although I must warn you that the security and various other systems are suffering assorted problems."

Yeah, your bastard friends trashed them on the way through. "I'm sure I can work round it."

"I have every confidence in you. That only leaves the question of what you ought to be called. How does Acting Assistant Director sound?"

Toreth gave it five seconds' consideration, which was four more than it merited. "No way."

Carnac affected surprise. "Wouldn't you like a promotion?"

"To Assistant Director? As in 'Head Scapegoat' when this blows over and everything gets back to normal? Thanks for the offer, but no thanks."

"The circumstances of the appointment might be slightly irregular, but there is no reason that it should not become permanent. You will need a title of some kind."

"I've already got one. Senior Para. It means something around here, at least to the people you want me to drag into line."

"I'm afraid that the Service people will not find it so impressive."

"Then I'll have to keep sending them to you to get it sorted out, until you get sick of dealing with it and issue them an order to do what I tell them. Or you could save a lot of aggravation by doing it now. It'll make them happy—they like orders."

Carnac smiled and shook his head. "Did I ever tell you how much I enjoyed working with you?"

"Probably. But I'll bet I didn't say that I believed you."

Brief, tense silence, then Carnac glanced down at his screen. "I have a lot to do."

"Me too, so I'll go and get on with it, shall I?"

"Don't do anything yet. There is a substantial Service presence in the building, as you may have noticed. I have yet to spread news of your arrival in all the appropriate quarters, and it would be unpleasant for you and inconvenient for me if someone took it into their head to reincarcerate you. I need to appoint you a Service liaison to make sure that your position here is understood and you are not obstructed in your endeavors."

"Thanks." Something between a bodyguard and a watchdog—just what he needed.

"Wait until he arrives before you start, ah, throwing your weight around." Carnac smiled again, his gaze flicking over Toreth, whose skin tried to crawl away.

"Okay, I'll wait for him. But don't take too long."

On his way out of the office, Toreth looked around the mainly Service personnel waiting to see Carnac, and wondered which lucky soul had been selected as his "personal liaison" this time. There might be someone out there who would enjoy being used as Carnac's private fuck toy, but he couldn't imagine who.

Toreth gravitated naturally to his own office. For one thing, it was far enough away from Carnac's that if he stormed off there in a temper he might've calmed down by the time he arrived. Moreover, the idea of Carnac being able to drop in on him casually was unappealing to say the least. It was also familiar, and he knew where everything was, which helped him keep a grip on what *he* was: a senior para-investigator. He mustn't let Carnac's promises tempt him.

The first thing to do was to sort out the mess. Nothing much seemed to be seriously damaged—even the screen was still functional—but furniture had been overturned and the contents of drawers scattered. Oddly, his spare uniform jacket still hung in its usual place, neatly creased amid the chaos. His chair had a broken wheel, so he took an admin chair from the main office. There seemed to be no one in the whole office except him, and he wondered what had happened to his team and to the others in the section. Sara would know about the admins. With luck, he'd be able to find out about the rest down in the cells.

Once the office was tidy, he was tempted to go down to the detention facility straight away and try to get things moving. However, there was no point antagonizing Carnac unnecessarily. There'd no doubt be plenty of necessary opportunities later. In any case, he needed to prepare before he went down there. The first part of this project would be the trickiest, and if he messed it up he might as well resign today and beg a job from Warrick. He sat down (back at his desk, after five days) and started work.

He'd just completed preparations when someone tapped on the door. "Come in."

A man in a Service lieutenant's uniform opened the door, and hesitated briefly before entering—presumably the promised liaison. Younger than Toreth had expected, or possibly Toreth was feeling old today. Brown hair, slightly gangly, unfinished-looking body that he still seemed to be trying to grow into. Nice arse, when he turned around to close the door behind himself.

"And you are?" Toreth asked.

"Lieutenant Payne, sir." Toreth must've stared, because the man spelled it out, then said, "Lieutenant Jay Payne."

"Jesus. Someone with a sense of humor sent you here, then."

The lieutenant didn't smile. "Possibly, sir. I just do what I'm told, where I'm told to do it."

"Good. Then we should get on fine. What did Carnac tell you to do in this case?"

"To report here and place myself under your orders, until told otherwise."

"Did he explain my position here?"

"Yes, sir."

"Well?"

"You have operational authority over I&I, which I'm to make clear to anyone who questions it."

Well, if that was true then Carnac had been as good as his word. Of course, there were undoubtedly other orders that the lieutenant wasn't mentioning.

"Right. We're going down to Detention first, and if that goes all right we'll have a look at a couple of other places. Then you can take over one of the offices up here—no need to share since there's so much space—and you can help me find out what we've got to work with. Does that sound okay to you?"

"Yes, sir."

The personnel in the main detention facility control center were a mix of Service, civilian (meaning resister), and a handful of I&I. The latter, even the ones he didn't already know, could be distinguished by their generally nervous demeanor. The ones who didn't look nervous Toreth marked down as probably treasonous. Not that it mattered anymore, of course—it was purely for personal interest.

The facility itself was in a better state than he'd expected. Many of the control officer desks had been damaged and jury-rigged repairs were evident everywhere, but lights and some screens were on. Most importantly, the main cell monitoring screen, running the length of one wall, was active.

Blood still in evidence, he noticed. Plenty of splashes here and there, and dull swirls over the gray plastic of the floor where more had been cleaned up. The smell of it thickened the dry, processed air, inadequately hidden by the usual underground levels' mask of disinfectant.

"Excuse me." He raised his voice. "If I could have everyone's attention over here."

He waited until the occupants of the room had gathered loosely around. "Who's in charge here?"

As he'd feared, there was a pregnant pause. "In that case, who's in charge and *isn't* here?"

One of the Service personnel stepped forwards. "Major Bell took personal command of the detention operation."

"Where is he?"

"As far as I know, er—" He glanced at Payne, and Toreth saw the lieutenant nod. "As far as I know, sir, *she* is away from the building."

Good start. "Fine. I'll speak to her on her return." It made things easier in a way, but he'd have to make sure Carnac put the Service major in her proper place (i.e., somewhere else) as soon as possible. "My name, as some of you might know, is Senior Para-investigator Val Toreth."

That drew a reaction, not a friendly one, among the majority of the crowd, and he felt glad that he'd waited for Payne before he came down here. "Carnac—Socioanalyst Carnac—has now put me in charge of getting things sorted out down here. If anyone has a problem with that, I'm not interested. Waste his time with it, not mine." He gave them a brief space for objections, but no one spoke. "For now, I'd like a few questions answered and a few things done. The first thing I want to know is who's in which cell, and what condition they're in."

This time he let the silence stretch out. He knew they wouldn't be able to do it, but he wanted someone to say so. Finally one of the men he'd pegged as I&I and probably loyal stepped forwards. "I'm afraid we don't have the occupancy status available, Para."

He affected surprise and disappointment. "An approximate status will do...?"

"Senior Security Officer Adams." Adams shrugged, spread his hands. "I can only tell you what I've seen during searches for named prisoners. The occupancy is probably thirty to forty percent paras and interrogators. The rest is mostly investigators or security officers, but there are medics, admins, technicians, maintenance—anyone who openly sided with interrogation staff or put up resistance. We were told that they're all to be considered political criminals, regardless of occupation."

For fighting for their lives? He kept his voice coolly professional. "Numbers?"

"There's nothing, Para. Not even a bad guess."

"Then I suggest you organize cell-to-cell monitoring and count people. While you're doing it, you can make medical priority estimates."

"I'm afraid I can't do that, Para. The building surveillance was the first thing knocked out in the takeover. Among the first things, anyway." Adams pushed his hair back, revealing an impressive bruise on his temple. "Selective damage, but very thorough. The maintenance techs are restoring it piecemeal as best they can, but it's going to be a long job."

"I understand." Well, selective system damage confirmed his guess about inside traitors. "Moving on—lights in the cells. Why aren't there any? I assume the systems are down?"

No answer. Eyes began to slide away from his as he looked slowly around the room. The I&I staff were the first to look down. He took a deep breath, and the stab of pain from his ribs helped diffuse the anger. Grabbing the turncoat bastards by the throats and smashing their faces into the nearest desk wouldn't achieve anything, beyond immense personal satisfaction.

"Then switch them on again, right now." He waited until Adams activated the systems. "Good. Put them back on the fourteen-ten in every cell, unless there is a damn good reason for an exception. Short-shift the first light period to get it on schedule. How about water and food? Heating?"

More silence. "Is anyone even looking at the systems? No? Okay—who are the technical officers here? There must be some."

Half a dozen men and women stepped forwards, moving to form a small, nervous group. Toreth looked them over, picked out a woman he recognized and whom he hoped was loyal. "Wheeler—" He glanced at Adams, caught a slight nod. "Tell me what's going on."

"We were told to concentrate on the surveillance, Para. The major's orders."

"How long before it's restored?"

"Down here, days. All over the building, it could be weeks."

"Then a delay won't matter. Wheeler, you're now in charge of restoring the cell systems. This is what I want: water, heat, food, surveillance, in that order. We can worry about the rest afterwards. I also want daily progress reports, and I want to see progress in them. Now—" Toreth took a hand screen from his pocket and paged through until he found the version that best matched the circumstances. "I need a volunteer to read this over the cell comms. Assuming we have cell comms."

The nearest technician nodded. "They're functional, as far as we know. If you'd like to read it yourself, Para..."

He'd been hoping someone would ask. "No, I wouldn't. Because the first voice they hear is going to be identified with the bastards who kicked the shit out of them, locked them up in there, and left them in the pitch dark for four days, cold, frightened, hungry, thirsty, and in pain. And it'll also be the voice that tells them that the same bastards aren't going to open the doors right now and let them out."

He looked around the crowd. A few of them were angry or insulted, but most were looking uncomfortable again at the idea that there were real people out there, really suffering. Good. He knew all about prisoner depersonalization theory. "For obvious reasons, that voice isn't going to be mine. You." He picked out one of the civilian types. "You're going to read it."

The woman shook her head. "Not me."

Perfect. He smiled at her, and without looking around said, "Payne."

"That's an order. Senior Para-investigator Toreth has been granted operational authority by Socioanalyst Carnac."

"It's a simple choice—you can do what you're told, or you can get the fuck out of I&I." She flinched slightly, and Toreth looked around the room, then back to his selected victim. "That applies to you, and to everyone else in here."

He'd almost been hoping for a couple of walkouts, but no one moved. Spineless fucks. The woman he'd chosen took the screen from his hand and glanced around. "Where do I read it?"

"Over there," Adams said.

She sat down and scanned down the screen. That showed some independence, or at least something of a sense of self-preservation. Adams activated the systems, and she coughed. "Er. Attention, please. As you may have noticed, the lights have been switched on again. They are now on a normal schedule, and other services to the cells will be restored as soon as is practicable." She looked over at Toreth, and he nodded at her to continue. "I&I is now under the control of the new Administrative Council, represented by Socioanalyst Carnac. The policy of the Administration is that there will be no summary executions and no further illegal ill treatment. The Administration requires the continued services of I&I and procedures are being put in place to expedite your release from detainment. Further announcements will be made to inform you of progress."

That provoked a murmur in the room, particularly from the civilians. Clearly Carnac's policy wasn't general knowledge. "If you or someone else in your cell is badly injured or requires urgent medical attention for any other reason, please activate the cell alarm system, and someone will be sent to deal with you as rapidly as possible. Please, I ask you to call for assistance *only* if your need is genuinely of a high priority. Thank you."

Toreth watched on the large overhead screen as the cell indicators started to light up. They'd all scream for help, of course, injured or not—loyalty to colleagues went only so far. At least they *would* scream, though, when a simple request for people to identify occupied cells would have created suspicion. Some sections remained blank, suggesting that either the comms or the alarms were malfunctioning. In general, though, it wasn't a bad start.

"Right, everyone. Thank you for your attention and get back to work." He watched the group start to break up, conversations beginning to hum. "Adams. A word, please."

The man stopped and came back, looking wary. "Para?"

"You're in charge of Detention for the moment—I'll make that official as soon as I get back to my office. You're also responsible for getting me the occupancy and status reports. I'm sure you can find some Service people hanging around to start cell-to-cell checks. Tell them to get names and medical status, and to offer to pass on one message per prisoner to someone outside. And make sure they get the messages right."

Adams nodded. "Yes, Para."

"Clear the corpses out as well, and get names for them, if you can. DNA samples for any unknowns, store them for processing when someone has the time. I want the status reports first thing tomorrow. Don't bother making them look nice and official, just tell me what's going on. If you have any trouble, with anyone but especially with Service people, don't argue with them—tell them to take it to Carnac or me. I'm in my usual office: level five, General Criminal. And send me a suggestion for a night shift supervisor before shift change. That's all."

Adams nodded again, looking unutterably relieved. "Yes, Para. It's good to have someone who knows their arse from their fucking elbow in charge again." He glanced at Payne and lowered his voice. "Watch out for Bell when she gets back—she's going to throw a fit over this and she's got plenty of clout."

Toreth watched as Adams went off to start work, a distinct spring in his step. Well, at least he'd made someone's day. "Come on, Payne. No point hanging around down here."

Next they went to the medical section. Even at I&I, medics tended towards the community spirited, so he wasn't entirely surprised to find that the handful of staff he saw when the lift doors opened were I&I.

A senior medic sat behind the desk in the reception area, a woman he vaguely recognized. She had her chin in her hands, staring across the room. She didn't react to their arrival until he and Payne were a couple of meters from her. Then she blinked at him, and her eyes widened with surprise. "Toreth!"

The voice was more familiar than the haggard face. "Yeah, 'fraid so. Dr. Mandelson?" He was unsure enough of her identity to make it a question.

She straightened up. "Good Lord, do I look that bad?"

"You're a sight for sore eyes, Mandy, I swear. How are things here?"

"Not so bad now, since the Service people showed up." She nodded to Payne. "Even though they haven't been down here much. But it's infinitely better than the last few days, I can tell you that."

"Have you been here all along?"

She nodded.

The first chance he'd had to talk to someone who'd been in the lower levels during the attack. "What happened?"

"When?" she asked.

"During the revolt. From the beginning," he added.

"The beginning?" She shook her head, then looked down at the desk, composing herself. "The short version is that it was terrifying. Gunfire everywhere."

"They shot at the medics?" Payne asked, sounding shocked. Of course, Toreth thought, the lieutenant had only arrived in the building this morning.

"No," Mandelson said. "Just the security guards, not anyone unarmed. Not at first, anyway. Most of us didn't even try to fight, although if we'd known what was going to happen… They locked people in rooms, with a guard on the door. Which made it easier for them later when—" She stopped and cleared her throat.

The brief hope that Sara's ideas about casualty rates in Medical had been exaggerated by fear and rumors faded. Beside Toreth, Payne shifted. Didn't he fancy hearing what the Service's allies had been up to? "Go on," Toreth said.

Mandelson took a deep breath. "When the security defense collapsed, the resisters made it down to the detention levels. They opened the cells and after that it was hell down here. Chaos. Medical was on the edge of it, but you can't imagine what it was like." She glanced at Payne. "You just can't. The prisoners tore apart everyone they could find and the resisters didn't try to stop them—they joined in." She paused, wiping her eyes, although he saw no sign of tears. Reflex, perhaps.

"Do you have any idea how many survivors there were?" Payne asked quietly.

"I don't know. More than I thought at first. It's a big place—people hid. Some people played dead. Or switched sides quickly enough in the confusion. I don't blame them. And there are so many lifts and stairs that once they'd disabled the security systems they couldn't seal off the lower levels." She pointed across the room to a closed door. "Victor was treating a prisoner down on level D. He got out in one of the service lifts with three interrogators. He told me he saw the resisters herding people into rooms and throwing grenades inside. I heard bangs, but I didn't see it myself."

Toreth shook his head, appreciating even more how lucky he'd been to have met organized resisters concentrating on taking control of the building, not a mob bent on immediate slaughter. Leisurely vengeance might be unpleasant, but it beat a grenade. "What happened to you?" Toreth asked.

"I was in one of the stores all the first night. When the noise started, some of us locked ourselves in a back room. Then on Saturday, a group came through the level and broke the door down. We thought... but they were looking for medics to patch up the resisters hurt in the fighting. Then they kept us segregated, but we could hear what was going on." Without looking over to it, she pointed towards the corridor leading to the medical level detention cells. "That's where they kept some of the people they brought down from upstairs."

Now Toreth was the one who didn't want to hear it. This was too close to his own fun-filled four days. He tried to interrupt but she was speaking quickly, stumbling over the words.

"It went on until the Service arrived. Not all the time. Maybe killing people in cold blood doesn't come naturally, not even to bastards like that. They'd stop for a while and we'd pray it was the end and then they'd work themselves up into another righteous fury and go back to the cells. We could hear it. Some people tried to fight back—we had a few of the resisters brought in here injured. But they wouldn't let us help the others."

Her eyes were fixed on him, pleading for understanding, or maybe forgiveness. "We tried, but they wouldn't *let* us. The cells are empty now—on Monday, before the Service arrived, they took everyone who was still alive down to Detention."

"Well, you'll get a chance to help now," he said. "They're starting cell-to-cell searches, pulling out the wounded."

Mandelson shook her head. "Do you want the truth? Once the Service arrived I just wanted to go home, but I was too afraid to leave. Do you know what it's like outside?"

If he didn't tell her, someone else would soon enough. "There's no transport, but if you leave in daylight you should be safe enough." He put his hand on her arm. "But we need everyone we can get."

She looked down for a moment, then nodded slowly. "I'll stay. If there's anyone left alive to help."

Toreth grinned and squeezed her arm gently. "I'm alive, aren't I, Mandy?"

That got a faint smile. "Yes, well. You would be."

Toreth looked around. More medical staff were assembling, clearly wondering what the hell a senior para was doing here.

He gathered reports on personnel (scanty), damage (extensive), supplies (low), and mood (bleak). He didn't make any promises, but he hoped he'd at least managed to impart enough cheer to stop them from fucking off in the next couple of days. At any rate, the atmosphere seemed more positive by the time he'd finished. There were even offers to call in colleagues known to have escaped or not to have been at work during the attack.

Bell didn't seem to have appointed anyone to take control of Medical. As far as he could discover, she hadn't visited the place at all. Treatment for the injured obviously rated a long way below being able to keep an eye on them. From the most loyal-seeming I&I staff available, Toreth picked a few people to take charge, which seemed to be a source of relief once more. He also warned them that they could expect injured staff to arrive, starting any time, and that if they experienced any obstruction in their duties they should take it up directly with Carnac. Time for the bastard to do some of the work.

When they had finished, he checked the watch he'd borrowed from Warrick, and decided they had time for one more visit. "Have you met the head of security yet?" he asked Payne as they set off back up towards the office levels.

"No, sir. I haven't met anyone. I was called in here first thing this morning."

Interesting. "Why? I mean—why didn't Carnac pick someone who was already here?"

"Couldn't say, sir." After a few seconds, he added, "I met him the day before yesterday at headquarters. One of my wife's relatives works here, and I think I mentioned that to him then."

Interesting again. Toreth filed it under "think about it later."

"Well, to get back to the point, Head of Security Bevan is one of the most important people in the building. Nothing goes on here that he doesn't know about. He's been HoS here ever since the reorganization. He runs the surveillance, the security systems, the security guards, the external and internal access, and a lot of other things he's maneuvered under his control. If Carnac's managed to piss him off—which in Bevan's case he'll be able to do by walking into the building—then it'll make my life a hundred times more difficult. So don't you do anything to make it worse."

"Are you sure he's alive, sir?" Payne asked.

"*Bev?* Of course he is." In fact, Toreth had no idea whether he was or not, and he worried about it all the way up to the Surveillance offices.

His first view wasn't reassuring—it took him a minute to spot even a couple of I&I staff among the Service uniforms in the main office. An inquiry as to where he might find the head of security produced directions to Bevan's usual office, but a glance through the door showed only Service once more, including an officer behind Bevan's desk.

Eventually, as he passed a workroom, he caught sight of an I&I uniform. A man with thinning dark hair sat with his back to the door, alone except for a truly staggering amount of surveillance equipment which covered the benches, shelves, and most of the floor. Much of it was obviously badly damaged and being stripped for parts. "Bev?"

Bevan looked around, then stood up, his long, sour face knitting into a scowl. "I wondered how long it'd take before *you* showed up." He had a vivid black eye and an assortment of other cuts and bruises.

"Really?" Toreth asked.

"Bad news travels fast, so I've heard all about it. To start with, I've heard that your head's stuck so far up that bastard spook's arse that you can kiss his fucking tonsils. If you think that means you can order me around now, you can fuck off."

Toreth grinned. At least in here everything was business as usual.

However, before Toreth could say anything else, Payne said stiffly, "Senior Para-investigator Toreth has been granted operation control over the division."

Bevan looked Payne up and down, then shook his head. "Fuck, *another* one. And I thought the rats down in recycling were bad."

"Yeah. It followed me back to my office and now I can't get rid of it." Toreth turned to Payne. "Why don't you go and have a word with your colleagues out there, see what's going on? I'm sure they'll be happier talking to you than to me." Payne hesitated, so he added, "What I mean is, piss off while I'm talking to the grown-ups. I'll come and find you when I'm done."

Payne stared at him, then said, even more stiffly, "Yes, sir."

As he watched Payne go, Toreth considered how to handle Bevan. It was important—probably essential—to get him on Toreth's side and back in his office. If Carnac had Service people running Security under his direct control, then working against him undetected would be impossible.

Since Bevan didn't seem inclined to say anything, Toreth opened with, "Bev, how long have you known me?"

“Since you started in Interrogation, back at Justice. And you were an arrogant tosser then.”

“I won’t deny it. But did I kiss arse to get onto the para program? Or to get to senior? Have I ever fucked over my team because Tillotson wanted me to?”

Bevan seemed to think it over for a while, then shook his head. “No. For a para, you’re all right. Used to be all right.”

“I didn’t suck up to management before, and I’m not going to do it now. I was down in those bloody cells for four days. I’ve got five cracked ribs and no fucking reason to love Carnac or his resister friends. More than that, I’ve got no reason to be here at all. Carnac gave me a free pass out of here, and I didn’t take it.”

Bevan snorted, plainly unconvinced. “Why should you? Seems to me you’re doing very nicely out of all of this.”

Toreth paused, checked the door. Open, and no one visible outside. “I came back because I wanted to make sure Carnac doesn’t do whatever he’s planning to do. I don’t know what it is, but I do know he’s lying when he says he wants us to survive.”

“Us?”

“Yes, us. Although *I’m* not going to lie—it’s not got much to do with loyalty to I&I. It’s very fucking personal. I’m not going to tell you why, but I am going to make him regret ever setting foot in the building.”

Bevan nodded. “Now that’s a motive I can believe.”

“Have you met him?”

“Of course I have. He’s as bad as that prize bitch Bell.”

“Bell?” What had she done up here?

“Major bloody Bell—if you haven’t met her, you’ve been lucky.”

“What’s she like?”

“Brunette, with one of those bloody awful pinned-to-death hairdos. Makes her look like the most fucking sadistic primary school teacher you can imagine. Face like someone set it on fire and put it out with a shovel.”

Toreth laughed, although Bevan sounded thoroughly pissed off. “No, what’s she *like?*”

“She knows what she’s doing.” His voice held a grudging—and worrying—respect. “She had me dragged up here half an hour after she arrived in the building, and told me to start pulling in technicians to get the surveillance running again. And she left a bunch of Service so-called security officers to keep an eye on me. Waste of fucking time, because they wouldn’t recognize a decent security system if it fucking saluted them.”

Bevan poked through the pile of components beside him, then sighed. “She took all the security codes with her, all the call IDs for the guards—not that there are many left, poor fuckers—and every other sodding thing that would be any use.” He shrugged. “I wasn’t arguing with that many guns, and it was better than being locked in that fucking cell.”

Toreth nodded, and wondered if this was why Bevan had been so irate about his own apparent defection. "Nothing else you could do. So what about Carnac?"

"When I'd just about got used to the idea of her running the place, that bastard turned up and started giving the orders. The first one being that I was out and Captain Clueless was in. He's behind the whole bloody awful mess, you know. Carnac." Bevan's lip curled. "The bent fucking shirtlifter should've been strangled at birth—it would've saved the whole world a lot of grief."

Toreth blinked at the antique insult. "Bev, you do know that *I'm* a bent fucking shirtlifter, don't you?"

Bevan snorted. "Of course I do. I edit the New Year party recordings. But you don't come in here, acting like you own the fucking place, and kick me out of my own sodding office so some know-nothing wanker can sit in there and fuck up whatever bits of the poor bloody systems are still managing to struggle on. And then expect me to fucking *thank* you for it."

Carnac certainly had a winning way with people. "Point me at the know-nothing wanker in question and I'll get you your office back. Payne-by-name wasn't kidding about the operational control."

Bevan still looked skeptical. "And in return?"

"And nothing in return. I want to get I&I back for *us,* before Justice comes round to pick up the pieces, or Carnac lets Bell and her friends run it into the ground and suck it into the fucking Service for good. But, hey, if you want to spend the rest of your career polishing screens and saluting Captain Clueless, I won't bother."

Bevan shrugged. "All right. I'll say yes, if for no other reason than to watch you have to come good on it."

"Piece of piss. Come on, then."

They returned to Bevan's former office, picking Payne up on the way. When they arrived, Toreth was relieved to find that the crowd had dwindled to the captain behind the desk and two women who looked like something technical. He wasn't so absolutely confident of his authority that he wanted a large audience.

The captain looked less than delighted to see them, which Toreth ascribed to Bevan's presence. He doubted the man had taken the loss of his job and office quietly. "I'm busy," the captain said curtly.

"Not anymore." Toreth turned to the women. "Excuse us, but we need to speak to the captain urgently."

They glanced at the captain, then left on his nod. Toreth went over to the desk, but didn't sit. He almost asked the man his name, but it was too appealing to keep thinking of him as Captain Clueless. Besides, with any luck he wouldn't be around long enough for it to matter. Instead, he said, "My name's Senior Para-investigator Val Toreth."

The captain nodded. "I've heard of you."

No "sir" from this one. "Good. That's going to make things a lot easier. Who put you in charge of Security?"

"Socioanalyst Carnac."

Too late to back out now. "Well, I'm rescinding that appointment. Thank you for your time and effort."

Captain Clueless stared. "Don't be ridiculous. You can't do that."

"Payne."

Toreth walked away and leaned on the wall, watching while Payne explained the situation, and then while the captain called Carnac and tried, politely, to persuade him to overrule Toreth's order. The conversation went on for some time, until the captain canceled the connection and looked over to him. His expression suggested that Carnac's parting words had been firm and clear in the extreme.

"I apologize for questioning your authority, sir," he said, virtually choking on the title.

"No problem. Everything's a bit confused at the moment. Take as long as you want clearing out, as long as it isn't more than twenty minutes."

"Yes, sir. What about the other Service personnel?"

"Oh, leave them." Toreth smiled. "HoS Bevan can decide what to do with them later."

"HoS—?" The captain shut his mouth abruptly. "Yes, sir. If you'll excuse me, sir?"

"Of course." Toreth led the other two out of the office. There was no point in rubbing it in excessively, and besides, Bevan was so flushed with the effort not to laugh that Toreth was mildly concerned the man might have a stroke.

Back in the parts room, Bevan threw his head back and roared with laughter, pausing occasionally to draw breath and pound his fist on a bench, rattling the jumbled equipment. Toreth watched, fascinated. Bevan never laughed and rarely even cracked a smile—he was famous for it.

After a minute or so, Bevan managed to get himself under control. "Oh, God. Best fucking thing I've seen since those Service twats first turned up. You should do the same to the whole treacherous lot of them. Worse than the resister scum." He paused, turned to Payne, and said with unexpected seriousness, "No offense to you, son."

"I, er—" Payne coughed and started again. "None taken, sir."

"Call me Bevan." He turned back to Toreth, still serious. "And the next person who tells me you're kissing Service arse gets their canteen access canceled for the rest of their life."

"Thanks, but it was my pleasure. If there's anything else, let me know. You know where my office is. Keep as many of the so-called security officers as you need, although if it was me I wouldn't want too many of them hanging around."

Bevan shook his head, grinning again. "No. I'll throw the fuckers out as soon as I can get our people back."

"Our people." The risk had been more than justified by getting those two words.

"I owe you, Toreth," Bevan said as Toreth and Payne left, and those were four more words Toreth was extremely pleased to hear.

On the way up to his office, he turned to Payne. "What do you think?"

"About what, sir?"

"Anything at all would make a change, but I meant about the state of things down there."

"I, er…to be honest sir, it's a mess."

"Yes. Yes, it is that. What did you think about the speech for the prisoners?"

Payne hesitated, then said, "I thought it sounded nothing whatsoever like you, sir."

Was that a glimmer of a sense of humor? "Good." He looked at his watch. "Lucky us, it's just time for coffee."

"Coffee?"

"Brown stuff? Caffeine?"

"I know what it is, sir, we just don't usually, er…"

"Well, you're working for I&I at this precise moment, so you do now. If there is any, that is."

Toreth tried his usual coffee room, but it was clearly one where they'd held the admins—filthy and coffee-free. The second one proved to be the same, and he was about to give up when he hit on the idea of trying Tillotson's office.

Tillotson's coffee machine had survived intact, which made him wonder for the first time about the head of section himself. Toreth didn't seriously think anything had happened to him, unfortunately. If there'd been a tactical nuclear strike, Tillotson was the sort who'd slither out from underneath a rock afterwards, unharmed, flickering his tongue to find new opportunities.

"Milk? Sugar?"

"Er, yes, sir. Both, please, sir." Payne seemed to be twitching on the spot, which Toreth guessed was caused by watching someone he seemed to feel compelled to "sir"making him a drink.

"Here you go. Enjoy it, because once they get the mess sorted out we'll be back to the usually revolting crap they put in the section machines."

"Thank you, sir."

The novelty had worn off. "Call me Toreth."

There was a strained silence, as Payne clearly tried to construct an agreement to the order without using the word "sir" and couldn't force himself to do it.

"Let's go back to my office, shall we?" Toreth only made it a question out of sheer evil fascination.

"Yes..." The uncompleted statement hung in the air.

They started to walk back. "Payne, I'm not doing this for fun. Pretty soon we're going to be talking to a lot more very fucked-off I&I staff. Fucked-off and frightened. If you go around sirring me all the time, they're going to think one of two things. The first is that you're some Service tosser who thinks I&I is a collection of undisciplined thugs and wants to make a point of it. The second is that you're an arse-licking little creep, because that's the only kind of person who makes a big deal out of saying 'sir' around here. Neither of those things is going to make my job any easier."

"Oh."

"See how easy that was?"

"Yes, s—"

Toreth sighed. "Just work on it. If you have to call me something that isn't my name, call me Para."

Back in the office, they sat and drank coffee in silence for a while, as Toreth tried to think what he might've done wrong so far and what, if anything, he could do to fix it. On reflection, he decided things had gone as well as could be expected under the circumstances. In fact, he was amused to find that he was in a good mood—he'd expected to be throwing furniture by this point in the day. If only his ribs didn't hurt so damn much, he'd even say that he was enjoying it. Whatever game Carnac was playing, he seemed to be serious enough about letting him take charge. Not that that made him any less sure there was a game, and that he'd been designated the part of loser. All he had to do was remember to be careful, however well things *seemed* to be turning out.

That out of the way, he turned his attention to Payne. Might as well try to generate a slightly coffee-time mood. "You're married, then?" he asked. Idle curiosity, really, because he had better things to do with his time than look for a passing fuck.

"Yes. *Happily* married, sir."

The emphasis made him pause. "Carnac?" he said after a moment.

Payne nodded.

"What did he say?"

"Um. Nothing, as such."

"Make your mind up."

"He said that, er, that you were keen on getting to know your staff."

You had to admire the nerve of the man, even as you wanted to kill him. "You should be careful believing what he says. He has a very peculiar sense of humor."

Payne looked surprised. "Really, sir? I didn't think sp—socioanalysts had one at all."

"Debatable. He thinks it's funny, anyway. However, you can relax. I'm not after your honor, your virtue, your arse, or anything else."

He watched Payne carefully, and caught all the signs. Open relief, and hidden disappointment—so well hidden that he might not even be aware of it. Yet. Typical of Carnac to send him someone so tempting, then warn them off. If Carnac believed that would distract him from the job in hand, then he obviously didn't know Toreth half as well as he thought he did.

By the time he'd had painkillers and more coffee for lunch and spent half the afternoon gathering status reports on exactly how fucked the building was, Toreth found himself badly missing Sara.

He'd sent Payne around to make sure the admin releases were happening speedily, and to make equally sure that the departing staff were being asked (or preferably begged) to return to work in the very near future. However, he wanted to take a look at the cell-to-cell inspections in person, on the grounds that if they were fucked up it would be ten times harder to get people to cooperate later. At the same time he couldn't leave his office unattended, since he'd already told several people he'd be there to deal with problems. He felt a brief, unlikely kinship with Tillotson.

Payne proved unexpectedly useful by purloining a Service admin from somewhere. The man seemed competent enough to sit at Sara's desk and take messages from visitors while Toreth was absent. After ensuring his personal comm was functioning, he set off again for the detention section.

The main information from the tour was that his previous "personal liaison" with Carnac had caused more widespread gossip than he'd guessed at the time. He gathered a variety of sarcastic comments, questions, and plain insults themed around the general idea that he was taking it up the arse from spooks. He noted down some of the more imaginative ones. Carnac might get a kick out of them, and Toreth needed him in a good mood.

The horrified reaction of Payne amused him no end. Either the Service was improbably virtuous, or Payne had led a staggeringly sheltered life, or he was upset by the lack of sirring that went with the inquiries as to whether Toreth had to salute while he was bending over for it. Probably the latter. "They're angry, that's all," Toreth told him. "And who can blame them? I would be, too, watching some twat stroll around in a nice clean outfit while I'm nursing my bruises in the filth down here."

He found the team searching the block he thought he'd been imprisoned in and tagged along with them for a while. It wasn't long before they found the cell, and Toreth was mildly surprised by how pleased—or at least relieved—he was to find Chevril alive. Sedanioni was still there, of course, and it occurred to him that in some of the cells the restoration of the lights would be a distinctly mixed blessing.

The cell stank worse than Toreth remembered, even though he'd been down in the detention level long enough for the edge to wear off, but he went in anyway. He took the cuffs off Chevril while the Service people organized a trolley to Medical. Chevril had managed to work one boot off; his allegedly broken ankle was unpleasantly swollen and an eye-catching purple. More bruises dappled his body. His skin felt icy, but he was still coherent. "How are you?" Toreth asked.

"About fifty times worse than the last time I saw you," he croaked. "Or didn't see you. Got any water? Or a bloody great big gin and tonic?"

A paper cup lay on its side by the wall. Toreth picked it up, remembering the awkward struggle to drink out of it from Chevril's cuffed hands. The dispenser delivered half a cup before it started hissing air and spurting water, splashing over his hands. He gave up. Too much too quickly and Chevril would only throw it back up anyway. Didn't bode well for the inmates of the rest of the cells, though.

"Here you are," Toreth said as he knelt beside Chevril.

Chevril struggled into a sitting position, with some help, and leaned against him while he drank. When he'd finished, he nodded weakly towards the door, where Payne stood watching. "What the bloody hell are you doing with *them*?"

Toreth sighed and his ribs twinged. "I'm working for Carnac."

"Carnac? The socioanalyst?" Chevril raised his eyebrows. "*Again?*"

"That's what I said. And if you have any comments about it you'll have to try hard to get an original one."

"No comments at all." Chevril rubbed circulation back into his hands, moving his injured shoulder gingerly. "I'm just bloody grateful to be getting out of here, whoever you're working for. Why's he back here?"

"Didn't you hear the announcement?"

"I heard something. I wasn't really paying attention. Busy freezing to death."

"Carnac's in charge of I&I now."

"Great. A bloody spook. Just what we need."

Toreth lowered his voice. "More or less what I thought. I'm trying to make sure we don't end up too thoroughly screwed at the end of all this."

"Yeah?" Chevril nearly sounded as if he believed that, or at least as if he was too exhausted to care. "Look, Toreth, I'm sure you're busy, but do you think you can find a couple of minutes to tell Elena that I'm okay? Or at least alive."

"Of course, if I can get through. The comms are a mess." Toreth heard the trolley in the corridor. "I'll come down and see you later when I've done it. Don't forget what you said before."

"What?"

"You said that if I got you out of here, you'd fuck me. For free."

"Oh, hey!" Chevril's voice strengthened. "I didn't mean it."

Toreth grinned, standing up and moving away as the medics took over. "Don't worry—I'll wait until you're patched up."

He rejoined Payne, and considered whether to catch up with the search party. On reflection, there were probably more urgent things that needed doing.

As they went back up to the office, Payne said, "May I ask a question, sir?"

"Of course."

"Did you know the woman in the cell?"

"You mean the dead woman? Yes. Carla Sedanioni. She was a senior investigator. She worked for Chev—that was the man in the cell with her—not for me. But I've known her for years, ever since she joined, in fact."

"Why was she killed? If she was an investigator, I mean?"

"From what she said, she tried to get between a bunch of your friends and some interrogator they were busy kicking to death." Out of the corner of his eye, he saw Payne open his mouth at the phrase "your friends," then close it again. "She didn't know who he was. All she could recognize was the uniform—they'd been working on him for a while. She told them to leave him alone." Toreth shrugged. "She was like that sometimes. Lippy. They finished him off, then started on her."

"It's a shame, sir," Payne said, with apparent sincerity.

"Yes, it is. She was bloody good at her job. I can think of plenty of people we could've stood to lose, but she wasn't one of them. Every one like that who's dead will make it harder to get things running again. If Carnac had got here a day or two earlier, we probably could've done something for her. There'll be a lot like that."

Something about the idea bothered him unexpectedly. Maybe it was because people were dying in the cells, right now, despite his best efforts. He'd always felt protective towards his own team, and now the feeling seemed to be spreading to encompass his new responsibilities. He shrugged the feeling away. It wouldn't help him or them to dwell on it.

It was early evening by the time he left Payne in the office next to his, collating the incoming reports, and caught up with Carnac. By then he had the outline of a rough plan. Carnac probably had his own, and it would probably be better, but at least Toreth felt as though he was making a contribution. Whether that was a good thing was another question. Once he made the suggestion, even though it was something Carnac would have had to have done anyway, it was his idea. His responsibility. And, best of all, his fault if it went wrong. Still, he'd taken the job, ulterior motives or not, so he'd better do it.

It took fifteen minutes of hanging around before he was allowed into Carnac's office, so he didn't waste time on pleasantries. "Carnac, the tribunal system isn't going to work, not in the current scheme, anyway. There are too many prisoners down there and not enough people to do the processing. Plus, the whole system is shot to hell. There isn't even water to all the cells, and the medics are struggling already."

Carnac pursed his lips, looking as though he wanted to disagree. In the end he said, "What do you suggest?"

"Honestly? Open the cell doors and let everyone who can, walk out." He held his hand up, even though Carnac hadn't started to speak. "I know. Impossible. So, at the minimum, we need to release the investigators and all the non-interrogation staff as they're found in the search. Get the injured ones out to hospitals if they're too badly off to go home. Offer them their jobs back, tell them to come in when they feel up to it. Every one of them who does come back will help speed up getting the system running again."

"That won't be popular," Carnac said. Clearly he wasn't going to put up a fight about it.

"They aren't political criminals by any fucked-up definition. All they did was their job, within the letter of the law." Which is all any of us did. "If your friends have a problem with that, they should take it up with the people who defined what the law was."

"Very well." Carnac tilted his head. "You have the authority to make that decision yourself, Toreth. There's no need to involve me."

"I thought it would sound better coming from you." And I'm not getting all the shit shoveled on me, no matter what you think. "For something that important they'd only come up here to double-check it, anyway."

Carnac smiled, clearly understanding the real motive. "Very well. Was that all?"

"Yes, thanks." He stood up. "I'll stop taking up your valuable time."

"One moment, please." Toreth stood and waited, and Carnac gestured to his chair. "Sit."

He obeyed what was clearly an order, not a request. Carnac came around the desk and sat on the edge of it, still moving cautiously. Having him so close set Toreth's teeth on edge. He'd never hated someone so physically attractive before—in fact he'd rarely hated anyone to this degree—and it was a peculiar feeling.

"The Service has been invaluable to our cause," Carnac said. "Without their cooperation, the revolution would have failed. Failure is still not out of the question, should they withdraw their support. At least, it is unlikely, but possible, and the degree of risk is unacceptable. I would prefer not to have them antagonized unnecessarily."

It took him a moment to realize what Carnac was getting at. "You mean by reinstating Bevan as HoS?"

"Quite. A small incident, in itself, but shift enough pebbles and one can create a landslide."

"Is that a socioanalyst saying?"

"It's an observation, and one I am being highly paid to make."

"I'm surprised you didn't let Captain Clueless tell me where to shove my orders, then."

The corner of Carnac's mouth twitched slightly, but his voice remained serious. "Under other circumstances I might've. I backed you because you made it necessary for me to do so. You chose to test the extent of your authority in front of someone whose bad word would destroy your credibility with the entire staff of I&I."

He hadn't considered the situation in that light, although once Carnac pointed it out it was obvious. Well, he deserved the occasional piece of luck.

"Bevan is a dangerous man," Carnac continued, "strongly opinionated, set in his ways, and impossible to control, which is why I followed Major Bell's recommendation to remove him in the first place. Possibly I should've followed her other recommendation and had him shot, but it was one of those annoying and paradoxical situations where that would've been a show of weakness, not strength."

Toreth ignored the tactical digression, implied threat and all. "Your friends want I&I running again. Bev can do that a lot better than some," know-nothing wanker, "Service officer who isn't familiar with the building or the systems."

Carnac nodded, looking faintly irritated. "I understand your reasoning. Nevertheless, you placed me in a difficult position. Bell has no operational authority in the building, beyond the Service personnel, but she has the ear of several officers in the Service Command and I cannot be seen repeatedly to ignore her opinions."

"I'll try to make sure it doesn't happen too often."

"Thank you." Carnac returned to his chair, and Toreth wondered if this was a glimpse into his real plans for I&I. When he'd told Bevan that Carnac intended to hand I&I over to be swallowed up by the Service, he'd been spinning a worst-case scenario. Had he been closer to the truth than he'd imagined?

As he was leaving, Carnac's voice stopped him in the doorway. "Just a point regarding the investigators: the reinstatements can only be probationary."

"What?" He turned back, wondering what the hell Carnac was up to now.

"Without the authority of a tribunal, an offer of re-employment can only be probationary. I'm sorry." He shrugged. "It's out of my hands. It was the decision of the Administrative Council when they approved the plan for I&I."

Fuck. "I'll do my best with that, then."

Back in his office, he sat and worried at the problem for a while, then gave up. Clearly there was to be no way around it, even if Carnac was lying through his teeth about whose decision it was. Toreth would just have to live with it, and so would the investigators. Since it was long past curfew, there was no point starting the releases today, anyway. Maybe they'd be so glad to be free that they wouldn't notice the wording.

Yeah, right.

❖❖❖

By the time Toreth left I&I, it was past nine. He should have stayed longer, but after the third time he found himself staring at the screen, with his eyes open but asleep for all practical purposes, he decided he had to call it a day. His ribs ached, his head ached, and hunger had begun to give way to nausea. Time to go, while he could still manage the walk out of the building.

He was stopped five times on the way back, but the curfew pass got him on his way with nothing worse than suspicious glances at the uniform jacket folded on the seat beside him. He passed the guards in Warrick's building on autopilot; fortunately building security recognized him without his being required to string together a coherent explanation of who he was. When he opened the door to the flat, wondering whether he could manage to eat anything before he fell asleep, the first thing he noticed was the cold draft blowing down the hall. The second thing was Sara peering anxiously around the living room door.

"Oh, thank God, it's you," she said.

"Could be." He closed the door and mildly impressed himself by managing to reset the security. "What's going on?"

"Jesus, Warrick is going to kill me." Then she disappeared back into the room.

Tempted to head for the kitchen, he went to see what was wrong. He found Sara standing over McLean, who was on his hands and knees, scrubbing the carpet and the side of the larger sofa. All the windows were open, which explained the cold. There was a sharp smell in the air, of disinfectant and something else it took him a few moments to identify. "Ah, you found Bastard, then?"

Sara nodded and McLean looked up. He had a beautiful set of scratches that ran from the corner of his right eye to the angle of his jaw. If Toreth hadn't been so thoroughly exhausted, he might have laughed.

"Can you still smell it?" Sara bit her lip. "It wasn't Bastard's fault. He's upset, that's all. I made him a litter tray, and it's in my room, and I was going to keep him in there but I thought I'd let him out for a bit of run around. Who on earth buys cream-colored carpets, anyway? Even oatmeal would be—"

The cold draft was stirring a headache behind Toreth's eyes. "Sara... tell me tomorrow. When there is a tiny chance that I will give a fuck."

"God, I'm sorry." She came back over and took his arm. "You look like shit. Can I get you anything?"

He stood for a moment, letting himself lean on her shoulder, trying to focus. "Is there any food going?"

Sara nodded. "Rob made something. Things from the fridge with tomatoes and rice, but it's a lot better than I could manage."

The absence finally registered. "Where the hell is Warrick?"

"Still at SimTech. He called to say he had to stay until after the curfew, so he wouldn't be back. When you arrived I thought he'd found a way to get a pass."

"Fuck." Or rather not. Not that he had the energy anyway, but God, he'd been looking forward to seeing him. Suddenly he couldn't face the idea of food. "I'm going to bed."

"Did you have anything to eat earlier?"

"I'm not sure." It felt like an unnecessarily complicated question. Earlier than when? "I had breakfast."

"Then you're eating now. For Christ's sake, you were in that bloody cell with nothing to eat for however long. You'll kill yourself. Sit down."

Sit down where? Looking around, he found they had somehow made it into the kitchen. He sat and ate whatever it was that Sara put in front of him, because it was easier than trying to argue with her, and then let her put him to bed.

Chapter Four

❖

The Int-Sec complex had been reopened to cars, provided they had the proper clearance, so they were able to drive right up to the main I&I entrance. When it came to it—getting out of the car and walking up to the doors—Sara began to wish she hadn't been so insistent about coming back. Part of her acknowledged that the longer she left it, the harder it would be. Part of her said it was too hard already and she should've stayed at the flat. Carnac had said it, though: it was her decision, and she'd made it now.

Even so, at the doors she almost bottled out and called the car back. And again when she saw the Service guards, and again at the lifts. They walked through the building, and she felt her stomach churning with every step. She tried to distract herself by looking at Toreth, wondering what he was thinking.

It didn't seem to bother him at all. He was happy to be here, where he belonged. He nodded to the Service guards as they passed them, and one or two even returned the greeting. He'd said in the car that he'd been down to the cells yesterday and found Chevril. The same cell where he'd been held, the same places where he'd been beaten up and threatened. He must have been frightened at times, when it was happening, but now that it was over the unpleasant memories seemed to have faded more quickly than the bruises. Part of his general disconnectedness from the things normal people would feel, and something she envied right now. She'd be all right, though, as long as she could stay upstairs. She couldn't face the idea of the interrogation levels. Nor could she think of a way of explaining to Toreth that she couldn't.

He could manage to be sympathetic enough, when things weren't too busy and it was a case of taking her out for a drink and some ego-restoring flirting after she'd been dumped by a boyfriend. Even then she was sure he wasn't listening to her complaints most of the time, although he always seemed attentive. That was one of his tricks, handy for pickups, but she appreciated that he cared enough to do it for her, time and again, without expecting anything in return.

That was outside work, though, and this was inside. He'd expect her to cope because he wanted and needed her to, and as far as he was concerned that was what mattered. After the fuss she'd made about coming in, she'd just have to brave it out and hope she'd be kept busy at her desk.

The first thing she discovered, when they reached the office, was that her desk had been looted and presumably had also been in use the day before. Someone had had a stab at tidying it up and she didn't imagine Toreth would've done it. Most of her remaining possessions had been cleared and piled in a box beside the desk. On top lay her coffee mug, crushed flat. She picked it up, feeling suddenly and stupidly tearful. It had been a present from her sister when Sara had first started work here.

Toreth would have a fit if he came out if his office and found her sniveling over a mug. She should have thrown it out before anyway—the heater in it had been broken for years. She dropped it into the recycling, wondering as she did so whether the system was even functional.

It took her fifteen minutes to get her desk straightened out and scavenge around the office to find replacements for the lost and broken items. She borrowed Kel's coffee mug, deciding she could give it back to him when he came in. If he... she put it back on his desk and started looking for unbroken pencils. Once she felt that her territory was her own again, she set to work. Despite Toreth's warnings on the way in, the systems were partially functional. She found his messages—which he clearly hadn't had time to deal with yesterday—and started sorting through them. Many had been rendered redundant by the events of the past few days, and some of them were... unusual.

While she worked, she managed to forget the emptiness of the office, but when she'd finished and looked up it hit her all over again. She could have called through to his office, as she normally would have done, but she fancied seeing another person. She tapped on his office door and opened it.

Toreth was leaning back in a chair at an alarming angle—it was one of the admin chairs and they weren't designed for that kind of abuse. He had his feet on the desk and was throwing a pencil up into the air and catching it one-handed. He held up his other hand and she stopped on the threshold.

"Yes, Major. Yes. Yes, naturally I understand. Ah... one moment, please." He caught the pencil and muted the comm. "Get me a coffee, would you? Use the machine in Tillotson's office—it's the only working one I've found." As she left, she heard him sigh, then the conversation start up again. "Sorry about that, Major. You were saying?"

She found the coffee, took Tillotson's official I&I-logoed visitors' mugs, and liberated the biscuit supply from his desk. When she returned, Toreth was still talking.

"Yes, of course. Major, I'm terribly sorry, I have to go. Yes, it is urgent. I'll keep you informed."

He cut the connection and took out the earpiece. "Jesus, that woman can *talk.*"

"Who was it?"

"Major Bell. Service liaison stroke officer in charge stroke pain in the neck. Next time she calls, I'll connect her through to Carnac and maybe they'll talk each other to death." He took the coffee and waved for her to sit down as he took a sip. "Mmm. Thanks. Anyway, I managed to piss her off yesterday without even meeting her—now she's giving *me* grief without even being back in the building. All because I made her Service troopers get off their backsides and help down in Detention. What did you want?"

Company. "There's a pile of messages in the system. I've shoved all the ones from . . . well, everything that was to do with cases and so on from before, I've put aside. I've had a look at all the ones which have come in since, sorted them by priority and left them for you. And . . ." She hesitated.

"What?"

"Well, there are some messages from your mother."

"Very funny." Not that he looked as if he thought it was.

"No, seriously. There are. Half a dozen."

"Did you read them?"

"Of course not!"

"Well, read them now and let me know if it's anything important."

She briefly thought about suggesting he read them himself. It wasn't as if either of his parents sent messages every day. Or, in fact, ever. "Fine. And Carnac," the bastard, "wants to see you at ten thirty, about the start of the tribunals. That's all."

"Good. I've got things to do first. I'm going down to Medical to—" His eyes widened. "Damn, I forgot to call Elena. Okay, I'm going down to Medical as soon as I've got hold of *her.*"

Back at her desk she called up the messages from Toreth's mother and read them. They weren't long, but they were interesting. The first one, which must have slipped through during a brief period of comms function the day after the coup, was a cold couple of lines asking him to get in touch. By the last one the tone was more urgent; she must have heard about the disaster at I&I from somewhere. Sara wondered why she'd kept sending them here after that, then realized it would be the only contact they had for him. Nice of them to worry, she supposed, but it was probably a bit late in the day to show that they gave a shit.

She'd been with Toreth on probably the last occasion he'd seen his parents. Years ago now—nine, maybe. Even back then they didn't know his address, as he'd warned her on the way over. "So don't fucking tell them," he'd said tightly. "Either of them. Otherwise I'll have to move again."

Only curiosity stopped her from finding an excuse to back out at that point.

The odd thing was they weren't even that *bad,* at least not while she was there. Cold, distant, and unloving, but nothing like the ogres in the picture she'd drawn for herself from his occasional cryptic comments and obvious loathing. They'd introduced themselves by their first names—Glynis and David—but Sara had felt oddly reluctant to use those in front of Toreth.

As she remembered it the visit had been for his birthday, but after so long she couldn't be sure because there had been no kind of celebration. No cake, no other family or friends. The four of them sat in the silence of the ferociously neat flat, where cups were whisked away as soon as they were empty. The only homelike touch was half a dozen photographs on the walls of a golden-haired child, from a few months old to three or four years. She'd wondered if they were of Toreth, but hadn't dared comment on them. The largest, over the mantelpiece, had a vase of fresh, expensively real flowers beneath it.

His mother asked Sara about herself, then seemed to quickly lose interest once she mentioned I&I. His father said virtually nothing. She remembered Toreth sitting beside her on the sofa, so tense that she could see the pulse beating in his temple.

Clearest of all was the departure. Toreth stood up suddenly, looked at his watch, and announced that they were leaving. His parents hadn't seemed in the least surprised. Only his mother came to the door with them. No kiss, no goodbye hug, both omissions unimaginable to Sara. He opened the door, hesitated, and turned back to look at his mother, smiling for the first time. "Bitch," he said, absolutely calmly. No inflection at all. "Fucking bitch."

He didn't wait for a reaction, but Sara saw not a flicker of emotion on the woman's face as she watched her son stride away. Sara had never been able to decide whether it was iron control, or genuine indifference, although she preferred to believe the former. Too shocked to move, Sara stayed frozen to the spot in the hallway, until she came to her senses, muttered something she couldn't recall, and fled.

She caught up with Toreth outside, walking quickly, his hands in his pockets. He didn't look around or slow his pace. She had to skip every few steps to keep up with him. It took her a few minutes to think of something to say. "You don't have to go there."

He stopped dead. "What?"

"You don't have to go and see them. They can't make you."

It was the first time that he really frightened her. His face twisted with fury, his shoulders jerking back as if raising the fists still in his pockets, before he regained control and all expression vanished. "It's none of your fucking business," he said in the same dispassionate tone he'd used at the flat.

She remembered the hot silence in the sunlit street around them, noticing that there was no one in sight, and how badly she wanted to run. Instead, scraping together all her courage, she took a deep breath. "No, of course not. Sorry. I just—I just thought I'd say, because I . . . because you . . . " The sentence dried up under his icy stare. "Sorry."

After a moment, he shrugged and turned away. "Doesn't matter."

He started walking again, much slower. She fell into step beside him, and eventually slipped her arm through his, trying to work out why the hell he'd wanted her to come with him in the first place. A shield, maybe. How might things have gone at the flat if she hadn't been there?

He didn't say anything else until they reached the train station. Before they went through to the platform, he bought her an ice cream, without even asking her if she wanted one. Three scoops, chocolate sprinkles and little pink marshmallows on top, the whole thing slathered in toffee sauce. As he handed it over, he said, "You're right—they can't." That had been that—the end of the conversation and, as far as she knew, of his contact with them.

Sara thought about her own parents and her sister, who'd been almost embarrassingly happy to see her yesterday. Her father had cried, holding her so tight that she could hardly breathe, and his tears had set first her off, and then her mother and Fee. Everyone crying and laughing at the same time, so much noise and fuss. Even Rob had been dragged into it, hugged firmly by her mother in his role as savior, despite his protests that all he'd done was drive around with her and be scratched by Bastard. That had led into the (edited) story of Warrick's heroic rescue mission to I&I and—and she didn't want to think about that too much. However hard she tried, she couldn't imagine hating her parents, not at all.

She was debating whether to pass the notes on or just let him know what they said, when Toreth's door opened. He stood in the doorway, hands braced against the frame, and glanced around the room. There was no one else there. "Well?" he asked, expressionless.

"She wants to know if you're all right." Should she say anything else? Probably not. "She sounds worried."

His face didn't alter. "Does she really. Well..."

"Shall I let her know?"

"No." She waited. "Yes. Or...look, you can tell her whatever the hell you like."

I don't want to tell her anything. "I'll take care of it."

"Thanks." He disappeared again.

First person or third? she wondered, as she started the reply. First might encourage a response, and she didn't intend to spend the rest of her life impersonating Toreth. She made several false starts, distracted by something she couldn't put her finger on, before she realized what was wrong.

The silence. There should be dozens of people, at desks and going in and out of the senior paras' offices. The mess made it worse, a constant reminder of what had happened. She abandoned the note and started around the office, tidying desks, throwing out everything that couldn't be salvaged. People would appreciate it when they got back.

She'd been here when it had started—the alarms had rung and she'd tried to leave along with the others, only to find the way blocked by I&I security, frantically ordering people back to the offices. She'd heard the firing then, distant but closing quickly as she'd turned and tried to fight her way back against the flow, and her first assumption had been a breakout from the cells. The security doors should have taken care of that but she'd noticed, vaguely, that they weren't closing.

She'd tried another way out, along with some of the other admins. The security doors there had been locked when they shouldn't have been because it was a fire route. So they'd gone back to the section and waited. Everyone milled around, making suggestions as to what might be happening, lost and unsure. She couldn't remember exactly who had been there. Whom she had seen there for the last time. Nor did she know how long it had lasted. People had left, alone or in groups; some had returned, some hadn't. Maybe if she'd gone then, she might have found a way out.

It had seemed impossible, though—absolutely unthinkable—that whatever was going on wouldn't be brought under control. The idea hadn't even occurred to her until there was firing, suddenly, right outside the door and then, before anyone had had time to do more than scream, they'd been there.

In a weird way, it had been a relief, because she hadn't thought through the implications. All she had thought was that, thank God, it wasn't the prisoners after all. They'd been thorough, searching the offices and driving everyone into the main section office—this office. They'd been restrained then. Only sensible, in retrospect, when they were trying to control so many people with a relatively small force.

The resisters had ordered them to split up, and that, too, oddly, had felt better—that there was someone in charge, someone giving orders. Some of the paras and investigators, quicker on the uptake than the others, had stayed with the admins. It hadn't helped in the end, when they'd...

Movement across the office caught her eye, thankfully distracting her from the memory, and she recognized the man immediately from Toreth's description. "Lieutenant Payne?"

"Yes, ma'am."

Also part of the description. "Sara Lovelady. Call me Sara."

"Ah! You're Toreth's irreplaceable admin."

The familiar tone threw her slightly and she must have looked surprised, because he smiled. "Your name came up yesterday. About every ten minutes, when he was cursing the fact that you weren't here."

Whether Payne had any deliberate intent to flatter or not—and she thought not—Sara couldn't help smiling. "Serves him right. I did want to come in, but he wouldn't let me."

He nodded. "He said you were—"

Unfortunately, she didn't get to find out what she'd been, because Toreth's door opened. "There you are, at last." He turned to Sara. "I'm going down to Medical. I'll be about an hour, I expect—I'll send a message if it's going to be longer. Sort out everything you can yourself, call me if it's absolutely urgent, but I'd rather you didn't. There's a list of things to do."

She nodded and they left. Normally she wouldn't even notice it, but the confidence he clearly had that she *would* be able to handle things up here cheered her. She knew he trusted her to make decisions for him, but just now the reminder was welcome. In a more positive frame of mind, she turned back to the problem of how to reassure Toreth's mother, preferably while convincing her that she didn't have to reply.

Toreth shared the lift down to Medical with Payne, a couple of maintenance techs, and several of the low, upholstered chairs from a coffee room. He wondered what they were for, but the question was answered as soon as the doors opened and the noise hit him. And then the smell.

The reception area was packed with people who had until recently been locked in cells with inadequate water and erratic sanitation. Apart from the region immediately by the lifts, the only visible floor was narrow corridors through the mass, kept clear by tape barriers and security guards. He moved out of the lift to let the techs unload, and stood by the wall, surveying the chaos.

To his relief, it became apparent that it wasn't quite chaos. There was clearly a triage system in operation, even if some of the assessors were people he knew for a fact had no medical qualifications beyond the most basic first aid. Screens partitioned sections of the area, and he guessed they were to give some privacy to the worst injured and the dying.

People still dying, despite everything he could do.

Service personnel were still thin on the ground down here, and he wondered whether he should have left Payne behind. Better safe than sorry, though, for the time being. The first time he lost a confrontation with Service people was the time he'd lose whatever reputation he was accruing, beyond being Carnac's pet. However, just now he needed to talk to I&I people alone.

He turned to Payne, who was standing quietly beside him. "Could you, um—" And he couldn't call up an excuse. There were no immediately visible Service officers for him to talk to. Maybe sending him back upstairs would be easier.

"Piss off while you're talking to the grown-ups?" Payne inquired, deadpan.

Toreth blinked. "Actually, yes."

Payne turned obediently to go, and Toreth stopped him with a hand on his arm. "Listen, I'm sorry about that. I meant to apologize yesterday, but it slipped my mind. It was nothing personal."

“Don’t worry about it, sir. Para.” He smiled slightly. “I understand that you needed to show Bevan who was in charge. I’ll hang around and look busy until you want me.”

Toreth watched him go. Definitely a sense of humor under there somewhere.

He picked his way gingerly through the injured, glancing at people as he passed, assessing. Broken bones and infected wounds were popular, as was dehydration. There were also a lot of unpleasant-looking bruises, although the good news was that they were all at least two or three days old, which meant that the Service people and resisters were behaving themselves.

He was oddly surprised to find how many of the injured he recognized. He ought to, of course. Even given the size of I&I, he’d worked there for fifteen years and had worked his way around before settling in General Criminal. He made mental lists, of jobs rather than names. Lots of investigators and guards, fewer paras, even fewer interrogators. The number of investigators puzzled him until he made the connection—they also wore black uniforms. Probably the mob hadn’t been that selective.

Halfway through the crowd he heard a voice he knew at once. “Para!” Mistry ducked under a barrier and hurried over. She looked tired but uninjured. “Para,” she said again, then stopped, suddenly awkward.

Taking care to keep her away from his injured ribs, he put his arm around her shoulders and hugged her briefly. It felt like the right thing to do, and it obviously was, because when he released her she was smiling.

“I’m sorry,” she said. “I heard you were in charge, and I meant to come up to the section. But when they opened the cells they asked anyone with any medical training to report here first. They haven’t let go of me since.”

“That’s fine. Are you okay?”

“Yes. I was locked up and mostly ignored.” She gestured to herself, short and slender in her investigator’s uniform. “I’m lucky I don’t look like an interrogator.”

Neither had Sedanioni, and it hadn’t done her much good. On the other hand, Mistry would have had the sense to keep her mouth shut.

Mistry smoothed her hair back. It had lost its usual gloss, suffering more than the rest of her from the days of confinement. “I’ve seen Andy—Andy Morehen,” she said suddenly. “He’s the only one from the team, except you.”

“Is he okay?”

She grimaced. “He’s not dead. They brought him in yesterday evening. One of his legs was—” She waved her hand helplessly. “Smashed. I mean, just really… And there’s an infection in the bone, so the medic said there was no point even trying to save all of it, not with things the way they are, here. He’ll need a graft. I spoke to him for a couple of minutes, but he wasn’t making any kind of sense. He came out of a cell full of PC interrogators, though, so I think someone must’ve recognized him from back when he worked in Political. How about you? Is there news of anyone else from the team? Or the section?”

"Not a lot. Chevril's alive, Sed—" Suddenly he couldn't be bothered to go on. "Listen, I'm in a hurry. Sara can give you the news when you get up there. Other than that, keep working down here until things straighten out. I don't think we'll get many Investigations In Progress filed soon."

"Yes, Para." Then she startled him by taking his hand in both of hers, a brief squeeze and release. "It's good to see you, Para."

Feeling surprisingly buoyed by the encounter, he left her to get back to her work.

Reception was mobbed, despite the efforts of security guards to keep people back. He'd need to send more people down here to ensure order. The place was loud but the atmosphere was calm enough at the moment. He knew that could easily change. Pain didn't improve people's tempers.

Showing his ID to the guards, he worked his way through to the right-hand end of the reception desk, where the crowd was slightly thinner. He collected sufficient elbows in his tender ribs that, when he reached the desk, he had to pause to catch his breath.

The receptionists looked harried, but in control. There were more pieces of paper and squares of card piled on the desk than he had seen in his life. A long table had been set up behind, covered in more paper and cards filed in an eclectic assortment of small boxes. He remembered a note saying that the systems were down in Medical, but he hadn't thought through the consequences of that.

He recognized the admin working closest to him from his first visit yesterday, when the place had been virtually deserted. He tapped the desk in front of her. "Excuse me," he said, loud enough to be heard over the bedlam.

"There is a queue," she said without looking up, and in the face of considerable evidence to the contrary.

"Not for me there isn't."

"I don't care—" Then she did look up, recognizing him at once. She flushed slightly. "I'm sorry. What can I do for you, Para?"

"I'm looking for Don Chevril. Senior Para, General Criminal. Brought in yesterday afternoon about fourish. Dehydration, hypothermia, dislocated shoulder, probably a broken ankle, maybe broken ribs." About most of which Chevril would doubtless whinge for the rest of his life.

Toreth waited patiently while she sorted through cards. It took a surprisingly short time before she found the right one. "Yes. Nothing life-threatening enough to warrant a bed. He's been returned to the cells . . . oh, except that he had concussion. Detention is delaying taking anyone recommended as requiring surveillance until they get the cell monitoring back on-line."

She didn't sound at all happy about that. Something else to look into. "So where is he?"

"Let me check the list."

Eventually, she directed him to the high-waiver interrogation suites—the next section along from Medical—which appeared to have been taken over by patients. He found Chevril in an interrogation room, dozing on a couple of coffee-room chairs that had been pushed together into something too short to make a comfortable bed, even for Chevril. He had a molded plastic cast on one ankle, so it looked as if he'd been right about the break. At least he'd managed to get some clean clothes, even if it was only an interrogator's oversuit. That was something else for Toreth to add to the list—fresh clothing for the detained staff. It was a list that was growing with depressing speed. Well, at least he'd managed to complete one task on it.

Chevril had his arm over his eyes to block out the harsh lighting, and the marks from the cuffs still showed on his wrist. Toreth leaned on the back of the chair and shook Chevril's shoulder. "Wake up."

"Uh?" Chevril lifted his arm and blinked at him blearily. "Oh. You."

"Great to see you, too. How are you?"

Chevril moved over to give him space to sit and grimaced as the chair shifted under Toreth's weight. "I'm better than I look, or so the medic said."

"How's the ankle?"

"Hurts like bloody hell. But a lot less than when they straightened the damn thing out."

"They're out of painkillers?"

"Unless you're making enough noise to be a nuisance. And I wouldn't *want* to have most of the things they're shoving into people to get them to shut up—the pharmacy's being very creative. They seem to be out of more or less everything. I got a half-strength dose of bone accelerant and told I should be bloody grateful to be alive at all. Which I am," he added. Toreth grinned and Chevril rolled his eyes. "Not *that* bloody grateful. Did you get through to Ellie?"

"Yes—that's what I came to tell you. When she got over the disappointment of missing out on the widow's pension, she said to tell you she's fine, and the flat's fine, too. No torch-wielding mobs in your part of the city. I said that if you were up to it, I'd drop you off there tonight on the way to Warrick's." As he finished speaking, he heard a scream from somewhere not too far away—someone, female at a guess, in a great deal of pain.

Chevril's leg twitched, and he winced. "Up to it? God, yes. I'll be glad to see the back of this place, I can tell you."

"I bet you will."

The scream came again, higher, more desperate. A familiar sound in these rooms, except that it was a colleague, not a prisoner. He made a mental note to chase up supplies in the pharmacy—he didn't imagine that whoever was responsible for that noise would be keen to get back to work soon, if ever.

"I'm putting you at the top of the list for the tribunals," he said to Chevril.

"We're starting them today so I'll send someone down to fetch you when it's your turn. Once that's done you're free to crawl out of here as soon as you like, if you don't want to wait for a lift."

Chevril frowned. "What the hell are you talking about?"

"Tribunals. To assess whether you're the kind of person the new Administration wants working for them. Probably Carnac's bloody stupid idea, although he says not. There's going to be an announcement about it. Basically, all you have to do is turn up, answer a few questions, and they'll let you out."

"Hang on, what happens if I'm *not* the kind of person they want working for them?"

"It's just a formality, I promise. Don't worry about it."

"Don't bloody *worry*?" Chevril took hold of his sleeve. "Toreth, what happens if they say no?"

"Carnac's threatening executions."

Chevril sat up abruptly, then went pale.

Toreth disentangled himself, then patted Chevril's arm. "There's nothing to worry about, I promise. Listen—I'm putting the paras through first. We need the senior staff desperately, so they won't reject anyone to start with. And I'm going to get the system scrapped, somehow, before we get too far down the list."

Chevril lowered himself carefully back onto the makeshift bed, wincing. "If I end up in front of a firing squad, Elena won't be happy."

"All you have to do is turn up, be a bit cooperative, and you'll be out—and don't mention that I warned you about it. I'll be there anyway, keeping an eye on things. It'll be fine."

"Easy for you to say. I bet *you* didn't get a bloody tribunal, did you?"

No, he hadn't. Which meant, according to what Carnac had said last night, that his own re-employment was "purely provisional." Not a happy thought.

Before he could reply, a woman's voice broke in on the conversation. "Para Toreth? Someone said you were here. I need to talk to you."

Toreth turned to find one of the senior medical officers in the doorway. He recognized her at once—he'd put her in charge of coordinating medical supplies only yesterday, but his mind blanked completely on her name. Even by the current standards of the medical unit, she looked harassed. "Is there a problem?" he asked.

"Yes, Para. There are Service people in the medical stores, taking things."

"What things?"

"Everything, more or less."

He stood up, instantly dismissing Chevril and the impending tribunals. "Show me."

In the stores he found a dozen troopers, busy crating up supplies under the supervision of a lieutenant.

"What are you doing?" Toreth asked, with what he thought was admirable politeness.

The group looked up, then went back to their work, dismissing him. Toreth straightened his jacket; as soon as he'd finished here, he had to get the rest of the uniform from the stores. "I said, what the hell are you doing?"

The lieutenant sighed, and came over. "I've already explained everything to your colleague," he said.

"And now you can explain it again to me."

For a moment, the man clearly weighed up the advantages and disadvantages of simply telling him to mind his own business. Then he said, "We have orders to requisition surplus supplies for the use of the Service medical units."

Bastards. "Well, they're not surplus, so you can put them back and leave."

"Major Bell gave us permission to search the stores here."

"Major Bell doesn't have the authority to do that." Then, just too late, it occurred to him that Major Bell very well might. Carnac had mentioned martial law, and he hadn't had the time to look up exactly what that meant. Nothing to do but continue with confidence. "My name is Senior Para-investigator Toreth, and I have operational authority at I&I. If you don't believe me, you can check with Carnac. You do know who *he* is, don't you?"

The lieutenant shrugged slightly. "The order applies to all nonessential medical stations. I suggest that *you* confirm that with the major."

"I don't need to talk to the major, I need you to stop what you're doing, put everything back, and leave. Look outside—does this *look* bloody nonessential?"

"It's designated as such. The major will tell you that as well."

Was punching a Service officer mutiny, or was there an exclusion that said it was okay if they were being an infuriating tosser? He was seriously considering the merits of finding out, when someone spoke.

"Excuse me, sir?"

It took him a moment to realize he was being addressed. Then he turned to find Payne behind him. He wondered how long he'd been there. "What?"

"There's a message for you. An urgent message."

He followed Payne a little way off. "Well? What?"

"Let me have a go," Payne said, in a low voice.

Toreth blinked. "What are you—you mean, with him?"

"Yes. You don't have a rank he recognizes; he probably hasn't even heard about you if he's from out of the building."

"Well..." Toreth thought it over. He certainly hadn't been getting anywhere. "Okay."

"Thanks." Payne waited for a moment, then added, "If you could..."

"Piss off while you're talking to the grown-ups?"

"That's the one, sir."

Once outside the stores, and somewhat to his irritation, he found himself smiling. Payne was turning out to be less of a bore than he'd looked set to be. Not to mention, if he could pull this off, a lot more useful. Maybe he'd try some light flirting later and check exactly *how* happily married the man was.

In the meantime, Toreth's dry run on Chevril had given him some idea of how the seniors would take news of the tribunals. He went back to the reception area, pried a receptionist away from the mob and told her to check the whereabouts of four dozen paras, mostly seniors, whom he'd known long enough that they'd be willing to believe him when he said he wouldn't play tame executioner for Carnac. Some of them were bound to be in Medical and also well enough to be released. For the rest, he could get cell locations from Adams. While he waited, he wondered how many of the names would turn out to be on neither list. The list of dead was too patchy to be useful yet, so he'd just have to see how many on his list couldn't be found anywhere.

In the end, the receptionist located less than a quarter of them. Toreth took the paper list, almost reluctantly, then scanned down it. Mike Belkin in the medical unit with a fractured collarbone and a serious concussion—not bad, since Toreth would've bet on the resisters killing him. Perhaps, like Bevan and unlike Sed, when the pinch came, Belkin had known when to fold. Christofi back in the cells with only minor injuries—lucky bastard as usual. Tom Hepburn had been a recent transfer into General Criminal from Political Crimes. He wouldn't be fascinating the office with his tirades at the junior members of his team in the near future, if ever: fractured skull, coma, another paragraph of injuries Toreth didn't bother reading. Scratch him from the tribunals.

Turning a page, he found Chris Doyle's name. The junior had left Toreth's team more than two years ago, but Toreth still felt a proprietorial pleasure at seeing him listed as a survivor. Doyle seemed to have suffered almost as badly from the systems failures as the resisters, being brought up to medical with severe dehydration to accompany a selection of broken ribs and fingers, and heavy bruising. Doyle was tough, though, and smart. He'd see the necessity of cooperating with Carnac's charade.

A cough distracted him from the list. He pocketed it and turned to find Payne looking pleased with himself. Toreth waited for a moment, then asked, "Well? Did you sort it?"

"I explained the situation, and he agreed to clarify it with Socioanalyst Carnac before continuing. Until then, he'll put everything they've already taken back."

"Good. Excellent, in fact." Toreth didn't believe in stinting praise when it was due. "Well done."

Payne glowed quietly. "Thank you, Para."

Toreth decided to test him out a bit further. "Now I need you to go up to the office and do the same trick with Major Bell. Make it a courtesy call. You're not asking permission, you're explaining the misunderstanding so she doesn't get embarrassed later. I'm unfortunately unavailable, that sort of thing."

"Yes, sir."

Payne always slipped back into bad habits when there were senior officers involved. "I'm going to call Carnac from down here, so when Bell calls *him* about it, he's forewarned. Off you go."

Personal comm frequencies had gone down again, so he found an office with a working comm and tracked down Carnac in another part of Int-Sec. Carnac sounded less than thrilled that Toreth had probably managed to upset Bell again so soon, but he nevertheless conceded that having half the staff die of untreated injuries would impair the efficiency of the division. That done, Toreth went off to pay a few more visits to the sick before the tribunals began sitting.

Toreth hadn't raised much objection with Carnac to the idea of tribunals, because he'd suspected what would happen. The interviewees were suspicious, frightened, and therefore angry; most of them would say nothing at all. Meanwhile, faced with actual people, people they could sit and talk to (or at least talk at), most of the tribunal members lost their enthusiasm for authorizing executions. And the bruised, limping prisoners escorted in and then eventually out of the tribunal room made for a particularly sorry sight.

Toreth had decided to give it most of a day before tearing up the procedure and starting again, so that no one could accuse him of not giving the system a fair trial. It was so clearly a disaster, though, that he had to make an effort to let the tribunal stagger on until late afternoon. They'd done less than half as many people as they'd hoped to; it would have been only a quarter without his unilateral decision to send back to their cells anyone who hadn't said anything after fifteen minutes.

The tribunal had agreed to that without hesitation, frustrated and possibly embarrassed by the lack of cooperation. Of course, they weren't to know he'd picked the most paranoid bastards he could think of to interview first, for exactly that reason. When he finally called a halt, the sense of relief around the table was all he could have hoped for.

He walked around the table and faced the panel. Nine members in total: a majority of civilian resisters, two Service officers, a Justice rep Carnac had dragged in, presumably to give the thing an air of respectability, and an empty chair for the senior para fraternizing with the enemy. No wonder the I&I staff weren't keen to talk—he didn't much like the view himself.

"Right," he said. "I think it's fair to say we're getting nowhere." Nods and murmurs of agreement. "With your permission, I'd like to try a different scheme. The first thing I suggest is to cut the panel from nine to three. We can do more cases, and people will be less intimidated. Secondly, effectively telling people that they're here to answer questions and you'll kill them if they get the answers wrong isn't the best way to conduct an interrogation. Trust me on that." He smiled, and the tribunal looked suitably uncomfortable. "So I suggest that we start with the offer of re-employment—set out why they're here, and make it sound positive. If people refuse, let them go anyway."

One of the resisters shook his head firmly. "You're saying that we should allow the guilty to escape punishment. While it's understandable you might have some loyalty towards—"

"I'm sorry to interrupt, but nothing is further from my mind. I'm being practical. We lack the resources to keep people here indefinitely. Most of the ones who go will change their minds in a few days anyway, and those who don't can be rearrested later when we have a clearer idea of the final number of surplus staff. The more it looks as if we're keeping our promises, the more willing people will be to consider the proposals. News of what's going on here *will* get back down to the cells, believe me."

There was no necessity to explain or suggest. He could simply order them to run the tribunals any damned way he wanted. After Carnac's warning, though, he thought tact was in order. In the end he didn't have to sell it very hard.

The first new interviewee in was Chevril, and he proved such a model of eager cooperation that Toreth felt sure the tribunal would smell a rat the size of the Justice statue. They didn't. Nor did they as he sat with them through the list of prebriefed interviewees, and onto the beginning of the list of paras, graded by Sara from most to least likely to play along. He decided that they were simply delighted to have some progress to report to Carnac. Sometimes he wondered where the socioanalyst found idiots of this caliber.

In the car on the way home that night, Sara slept next to him all the way, and he practically had to carry her up the stairs and into her bedroom. Bastard hissed furiously, then retreated under the bed as Toreth aimed a kick at him. Sara was too wiped out even to protest. To the accompaniment of a perpetual low growl from Bastard, Toreth helped her undress, amused by the role-reversal from last night.

As he left her room, he met McLean in the corridor. Toreth knew he must be missing Warrick, because he caught himself thinking that McLean wasn't unattractive, from the point of view of fucking him from behind in a darkish room. That was just his cock feeling lonely, and besides Sara had staked out a definite interest. From the way McLean frowned when he saw Toreth coming out of her room, she probably wasn't wasting her time.

"How's the face?" Toreth asked.

McLean touched the fading scratches. "Fine. Injured almost in the line of duty, so I picked something up for it yesterday from the SimTech stores."

Toreth wondered idly what else SimTech had, and whether he could commandeer it to take to I&I's medical unit. "Speaking of which, shouldn't you be at SimTech, keeping an eye on Warrick?"

"Normally, yes." The frown had disappeared, replaced by professional politeness. "I was told to stay here."

To look after himself and Sara, no doubt. "How long are you lot going to be hanging around?" Warrick, should he ever reappear, didn't like an audience.

"Until the risk assessment program decides we're no longer needed. My guess is weeks rather than days. There's still trouble in the city and besides, in the current climate, there's an upgraded risk of corporate sabotage."

"In the current climate" meaning, among other things, while I&I was out of commission. Something he hadn't thought of, and which he ought to have done. "Is it a serious risk?" He headed for the kitchen, and McLean followed him.

"Well, that depends on how you measure it. The absolute danger is still small. But from SimTech's point of view any threat to Doctor Warrick is serious, and worth paying for the security to reduce to as close to zero as possible. He's worth a lot of money to us." He paused, then shook his head. "I'm sorry. That sounded rather cold-blooded, but it's true. In lots of ways, he's absolutely vital to the company."

Toreth must have been more tired than he'd realized, because as he opened the fridge he caught himself thinking, "And to me." Christ, he *did* need a fuck.

Chapter Five

❖

Carnac was good at not listening. It was an approach based on the general truth that most people only want to listen to themselves; all that was required to make them happy was to sit and nod, making agreeable noises, until they had talked themselves to a standstill. At that point, if one simply told them what they were going to do, nine times out of ten they would agree and think it had been their idea in the first place, since you had listened to them so carefully.

He'd expected this conversation with Major Bell ever since Toreth had arrived in the building. As it was, it had taken until the third day after Toreth took up his new duties. Of course, Bell had been regrettably called away from I&I for the first two days; she wasn't the only one with friends at headquarters.

Carnac had come to I&I with a detailed, well laid-out plan—that was his greatest strength. In the normal way of things, he worked at a distance, analyzing and preparing, and leaving the interpretation of his reports and the execution of his proposed plans of action to be bungled by others. The current task was different, and he enjoyed the variety it offered, even though his tolerance for dealing with his subjects in person was not an infinite resource.

Bell hadn't been part of his original plan, but on discovering her here, he had been obliged to work her into it. She had her own petty agenda, naturally, but it was of no importance or interest to him. As far as his plans went, she had proved to be moderately useful so far—she acted as a minor distraction and irritant to Toreth, spurring him on in his efforts on behalf of I&I. Not that Toreth hadn't proved himself up to the task in hand without Bell's intervention. With Toreth, though, it was a good idea to provide opposition and secondary motives for him to uncover, both of which the major supplied in abundance.

The major talked a great deal, and said little. Without a doubt, she had missed her calling in life—law would have suited her a great deal better than the Service. However, she had a politician's mind that would assuredly see her in the senior ranks at the end of her career, if no one had felt compelled to plant a knife in her back before then.

He'd been looking at the insignia on the major's uniform as the woman talked. Now, at a suitable pause in the nonconversation, he lifted his gaze and looked her directly in the eye. "Are you questioning the fundamental correctness of the decision to maintain I&I?"

Bell looked startled. "No, of course not. It's a dirty job, but it has to be done."

No, it doesn't, and if people like you were capable of seeing that, things never would have come to this. "Then what, precisely, is your problem?" he asked.

"The senior para-investigator you've placed in charge. Whether you are aware of it or not, he's riding roughshod over my instructions, and refusing to acknowledge my authority."

Careless of her. He smiled gently. "Authority?"

There was a pause, then the major said, "I am well aware that I have no official authority here, at least not over the I&I staff."

Implying, "but over the Service I do." Not insignificant, since the Service currently made up a substantial minority portion of the occupants of the building. That was partly his own fault—it had been, he acknowledged, a gamble that had failed to pay off. Now he had to work around the consequences.

"I do regret that my choice of deputy has caused you inconvenience. However, I appointed him based on my instructions from the new Administrative Council, with which you are familiar. Do you have any specific instances where he has acted against those instructions?"

She hesitated. "I've been away from the building. But he has removed Service personnel from the posts to which I appointed them, without consultation. And he seems to feel that he can commandeer the services of my people without bothering to seek permission."

"And have those incidents harmed I&I in any way?"

"They . . . not directly, perhaps, no. But they are contrary to discipline and good order."

"His manner can be a little abrasive, I grant you. I'll ask him to moderate it and respect your authority over the Service personnel here." Not that it would have any positive result, but it would annoy Toreth delightfully. "In return, I would ask you to remember that he's dealing with a difficult situation, and that I&I is not a part of the Service, and has never been."

As he'd expected, that drew a sharp glance. He kept his expression neutral, and after a moment she nodded reluctantly. "I'll agree that culture clash may be responsible for *some* of the problems."

"Quite so. Consequently we must all practice a degree of understanding and tolerance. For the good of the new Administration." Carnac touched the comm. "Send Lieutenant Payne in here, please." He turned back to Bell and smiled again. She seemed to be learning, because she looked at him warily. "Despite your apparent conviction that I am permitting Toreth to create havoc unsupervised, I asked

Lieutenant Payne to keep an eye on him. To assess his suitability for the post from, as it were, a position of closer contact."

The major frowned. "I wasn't told about that."

"No. Ah, Lieutenant. Come in. Over here, please."

Payne glanced between them, professional caution evident. "Yes, sir." He stopped at the indicated place, saluted, and waited.

"Lieutenant Payne. I would like your impressions of Senior Para-investigator Toreth."

"He's a capable and dedicated officer, sir."

Bell sneered silently at the word "officer." Carnac ignored her. "Expand on that, if you would be so kind. Do you feel that he's carrying out his assigned orders, for example?"

"Yes, sir. I'd say that he places the execution of his orders above all other considerations. In the time I've spent with him, I've never seen anything to suggest that the restoration of I&I services isn't his highest priority."

"Do you think he's suited to the job? Capable of it?"

Payne tried to glance at Bell, but Carnac had carefully positioned him so as to make cuing impossible. In the end, the man nodded. "Yes, sir. In my opinion."

"In your opinion, of course. And we thank you for sharing it. Major, do you have any questions?"

"No."

"You may go, Payne."

Carnac hoped the lieutenant didn't catch the glare Bell sent in his direction as he left.

"Major?"

"In *my* opinion, Toreth is dangerous, and a potential troublemaker."

Well, at least her judgment was sound. "I am not interested in your personal assessment of his character. I am interested in what you will say to your superiors about his ability to execute the task in hand—the restoration of I&I to full function. I'm sure that's how the question will be phrased when you speak to them. Well, Major?"

"In that regard, his performance is adequate, yes." There was no other reply possible.

"Excellent."

Carnac waited until the door had closed behind the major before he allowed himself a smile. Really, she ought to have spoken to the council first, rather than approached him, but she didn't want to appear incapable of handling the situation. She was ambitious, and not unintelligent, but she was no match for him. In due course he would get rid of her, but for now she would do very well.

Toreth's day had not so far gone well. The medical unit was filled far beyond capacity, with staffing levels that would have struggled to handle a normal workload. The plan to move injured investigators and support staff to outside hospitals kept coming up against the stumbling block that they, too, were badly overstretched. To compound the problem further, medical supplies were low and deliveries fitful and inadequate.

Similar difficulties beset the restoration of all the other services. After a morning of listening to a string of problems he could do nothing to resolve, Toreth canceled his remaining appointments, switched off his comm, and settled down in his office to work out some alternative plans.

Behind every problem, large and small, was the lack of people to do what needed to be done. So, he first had to find his missing staff. It should have been easy to tell who was present and who not when the building was attacked, but the security logs had been lost in the general chaos. Nor were there complete records of the support staff released piecemeal once Carnac had taken control.

Some of the missing hadn't been inside I&I on the day of the takeover, and hadn't called in since, like B-C and Nagra. They were presumed, or rather hoped, to be in hiding somewhere, although records of lynchings were still slowly filtering over from Justice—the upheaval had turned Justice's normally torpid information processing into something best measured in geological time. Justice itself had suffered some damage during the revolt, although reports had it far better off than I&I. For one thing, no one had imprisoned a substantial portion of their surviving officers.

At I&I, the task of identifying bodies was also proceeding far too slowly, because—once more—there weren't the people to do it. It was a vicious circular problem: they needed more staff, so that they could get more staff. Even if it meant efforts suffering in the short term, he needed to reallocate resources so that they could spare the necessary personnel to track live people down. The trick would be doing it with the least damage possible.

He'd been working for an hour, and was beginning to make some progress, when he heard the door open, then close. Toreth didn't look up. "Sara, I told you I wanted some peace and quiet. Whatever it is it will have to—"

"I'm afraid I talked my way past her."

Startled, he looked up. Warrick stood by his desk, smiling at his surprise. "Warrick? What the fuck are you doing here?"

"Well, that makes me feel welcome, I must say. Shall I go?"

"No, I didn't mean it like that." With his own late nights here, and the curfew trapping Warrick at SimTech, seeing him anywhere was a pleasure. Although Warrick didn't look as if he was serious about going. In fact, he looked rather—

The thought vanished as Warrick leaned down and kissed him firmly. "Mmf?"

Warrick pulled back. "I beg your pardon?"

"What was that?"

"A kiss. I'm surprised you've forgotten what one feels like in just three days."

"No, I know what it was, but—" What the hell are you doing here, in the middle of the day, in my office, in a building you hate, acting like you're in charge? But if he said it, Warrick might go, so he shut up and sat back.

Warrick smiled again. "Good." He started to strip, briskly. "As a matter of fact, I came here to see Carnac. It seemed a pity to waste my contact within the new Administration, so I asked him to assist in obtaining curfew permits for a few key SimTech personnel. It's going to take him a little time to finalize all the approvals, so I thought that, since I was in the building anyway, I might as well come and see you." Warrick's shirt joined the rest of his clothes in the neat pile, leaving him completely nude. "I hope you don't mind?"

At some point during the explanation, Toreth had lost the power of speech. He settled for shaking his head.

"Excellent." Warrick opened the top drawer of his desk, rummaged through the contents, and produced a tub of hand cream. "I thought I remembered that you kept something suitable in there."

He straddled Toreth's thighs and sat, facing him, reading the label. "Mm. Hypoallergenic, unscented, dermatologically tested." One eyebrow arched. "How very convenient."

That was, Toreth felt, a touch unfair. He *did* use the cream for its intended purpose, because the overprocessed air down in the interrogation levels was extremely drying and the gloves made his skin... but Warrick didn't look as if he'd be in the least bit interested.

"Hold this. Thank you." Warrick gave him the jar, and turned his attention downwards, unfastening Toreth's clothes with the same concentrated efficiency. Toreth watched, still speechless but admiring the contrast of Warrick's pale skin against the black of his own uniform.

Next Warrick opened the lid of the jar, took out a generous portion and smoothed it between his palms. "Mm. Very nice." He reached down and began massaging Toreth's cock, long slow strokes that rather distracted him from Warrick's monologue. "But then I assume it cost a fortune. Even Dilly spends less on her skin than you do. I suppose I ought not to complain, since the end result is so appealing. Vain, but irresistible."

Leaning down, Warrick kissed him again. Toreth opened his mouth to him, unresisting, letting him do whatever he wanted. At any moment, he thought vaguely, he was going to wake up at his desk and find he'd missed an important meeting. But if he had dreams this vivid, this hot, then he'd never bother getting out of bed to come to work in the first place.

Eventually, Warrick pulled back, eyes opening slowly. "Hold the edge of the desk and keep the chair still." His voice had lost some of its cool, but it was still commanding.

He reached around Warrick, depositing the jar on the desk, and as he did so, he thought about the door. It wasn't locked. Had Warrick asked Sara to make sure they weren't disturbed? Warrick wouldn't be doing this if he thought there was the slightest chance they would be caught, but at the same time he had trouble imagining him saying...and then he gave up imagining anything at all as Warrick lowered himself slowly down.

The last of the idea that this might've been a sudden impulse on Warrick's part was banished at the same time. He was prepared and open enough to take Toreth all the way in. Toreth arched back against the chair, the protest from his ribs swamped by the pure physical pleasure. *God,* it felt good. Distractedly, he tried to remember how long it had been since they'd last fucked, then gave up. Too long, anyway. Far too fucking long.

"The desk," Warrick said.

"What?" He opened his eyes, and found he had his hands on Warrick's hips, pressing him down. "Ah. Sorry."

A moment of stillness, Warrick's hands shifting their grip on his shoulders, before Warrick began to fuck him. A few slow thrusts to start with, then faster, hard and deep and utterly wonderful. Not an experience designed to last long, but if that was what Warrick wanted, then it was fine—more than fine—with him. He had to fight to stop himself from thrusting back up, because if he did the chair would surely go flying.

The whole situation, the weird reversal, only magnified the excitement. Warrick, fucking him in his office. The door *wasn't* locked and whether Sara was there or not, someone could walk in. He imagined Carnac's expression, seeing this, and he almost laughed out loud. He tightened his grip on the desk and braced his feet, his eyes closing as he concentrated on other senses. Warrick's mouth on his throat, teeth grazing the skin as Toreth drew in a deep breath, smelling him, still tasting the kisses.

Being fucked—being taken.

Warrick leaned against him now, breathing hard, one arm around his shoulders, the other moving between them. For once, he couldn't tell how near Warrick was to coming, couldn't tell anything at all, disoriented by the strangeness and desperately close himself.

"Warrick—"

"Yes. Don't hold back."

He'd managed to keep quiet until now, but at the end he couldn't help it. Muffled, thankfully, by Warrick's shoulder, he cried out, ecstasy mingled with delighted disbelief that this was *real.* Just a few seconds, and Warrick's fingers dug sharply into his shoulder, and he moaned, surprisingly restrained, as he also came. Toreth let go of the desk and held Warrick in place as he relaxed against him and until, eventually, they were both breathing normally again.

Over Warrick's shoulder, Toreth caught a glimpse of the screen waiting for him. He closed his eyes and wished he could stay like this forever, or at least until someone else had sorted out the whole fucking mess for him. Then Warrick sat up, obscuring the screen, and shook his hair back. He studied Toreth's face for a moment, and said, "Very nice."

Me or the fuck? Before he could ask, Warrick held his hand up, the gesture more an order than a request, and Toreth obediently licked it clean. Not that he minded doing it, despite the taste of the cream. When he'd done, Warrick stood up, wiped his hands on a handkerchief from his pile of clothes, and started to dress, at a more leisurely pace than he had stripped.

Toreth watched him, bemused and thoroughly enchanted. How often had he thought, "it can't ever be better than this," and been wrong? There seemed to be no upper limit on how good fucking Warrick could be. In the grip of the warm glow of well-fucked contentment, he almost wished he could think of a way of saying that to Warrick that didn't sound…

Tell him that he was the best fuck in the world.

When he had nearly finished dressing, Warrick said, "Assuming that Carnac has finished processing the applications, I shall be able to get back to the flat tonight after work. So I will see you there?"

"I—yes." His voice sounded strange. "I'll probably be late."

"I expected you would be." Warrick pulled on his jacket and smoothed out the creases, looking as if nothing at all had happened. For a moment, Toreth had the weird sensation that nothing *had* happened, and then he licked his lips, tasting hand cream and come. Tasting Warrick…

Who was already leaving. "See you," he said from the doorway, and was gone.

He gave him twenty seconds to get away, refastening his own clothes as he waited, then tapped the comm. "Sara. In here."

She opened the door, grinning. "Yes?"

He'd hoped to manage at least an unconvincing presence of a reprimand, but his smile must have been wider than hers. "I told you not to let anyone in."

"I'm sorry." She managed to fight her expression down to a smirk as she came over to the desk. "He can be terribly convincing."

"What did he *say*?"

"He asked me if you still had the hand cream in your drawer."

Toreth blinked, then started to laugh. "Fucking hell. So you said yes?"

"I said I thought you might. And I must've been right."

"Why?"

"Because it's on the desk. But also because you've got it all over your shoulders, some in your hair, and a blob on your cheek."

"Shit." He wiped his face and discovered she was absolutely right. Warrick hadn't had a spot on him, the bastard.

"I'll find you something to get it off your clothes with, shall I?" She left the room, still grinning.

After the door closed behind her, he leaned back in the borrowed chair, which had suddenly acquired a set of very fond memories, and briefly thought about being annoyed with Warrick for leaving him like this and not saying a word. He could've walked out into the office and been seen by anyone. Except, of course, that Sara would've stopped him, and Warrick knew that she would. When Warrick planned, he planned carefully and comprehensively. So instead, he put the top back on the hand cream, dropped it into the drawer, and settled back again to wait for Sara to return. His fingers ached from holding onto the desk and he rubbed them absently, working in the cream that had somehow ended up there, too. In the middle of all the stress, and mess, and impossible problems, he was suddenly having an extremely good day.

Sara left I&I early—she still didn't have a pass of her own, so the choice was to go before curfew started, or wait until Toreth was ready to go, and she was too tired to do that.

To her surprise, Warrick was already at the flat when she arrived, sitting in the kitchen with a SimTech guard she didn't recognize. They were discussing something with serious expressions, but when she came in, Warrick looked around and stood up, smiling. As it couldn't possibly be her presence that generated something so brilliant, she knew there had to be good news of some kind.

"What is it?" Even as she asked, she guessed, because there were only two people she'd ever seen him smile like that over.

"I heard from Dilly—about an hour ago."

"Really?" She hadn't even realized that she'd been worrying about Dillian, but she felt the load lift from her mind. Without thinking she threw her arms around him and squeezed him tight. "Oh, God, that's fantastic!"

He tensed, then returned the embrace briefly before he stepped back. "Yes. Yes, it is."

"Is she hurt? What about Mars? What did she say?"

"Not much. The connection lasted for about twenty seconds. But she's fine and she's trying to get a shuttle back as soon as she can. She didn't say anything about the base."

"But they must be okay, if she's alive and there are shuttles." She grinned. "We should celebrate."

"Why not?" He smiled again, seeming amused by her enthusiasm. "I'll see what I can find. Do you want something to eat?"

"Please. I don't know how long Toreth's going to be, though."

She left him to it and went for a long, hot shower. The smell of I&I, which she'd never noticed before, seemed to stick to her hair and skin these days. It reminded her of a hospital, something she'd always found depressing. Perhaps it was still the imaginary residue of the four days' imprisonment.

When she returned to the kitchen, the scene was much the same, although the cast had changed. This time Rob McLean stood up as she entered, looking gratifyingly pleased to see her. The food was beginning to smell delicious, and there was an open bottle of wine on the table. Rob poured her a glass, and the three of them toasted Dillian's (hopefully) safe return. Then she joined Rob at the table, and listened to Warrick and him discussing security at the AERC. The situation in the city still seemed to be improving, if slowly, which was something. After the difficult day at I&I it was nice to hear good news.

Toreth came in earlier than she'd expected him. When she'd left, he looked to be settling in for the night. In fact, it was only nine when she heard the door open. He whistled his way down the hall and into the kitchen, and out of the corner of her eye she noticed Rob wince. Obviously a music lover.

For a moment, as he came through the door and saw Warrick, Toreth had exactly the same smile he'd worn in the office, only without the hand cream. Then it modulated into something less obviously sex-induced. "Hello, all." It was almost disturbing to see him in such a good mood after work. "I'm starving," he said, as he went over to join Warrick by the cooker. "I had a snack earlier, but it only made me hungrier."

This time, Sara winced. That had the ring of a conversation heading rapidly downhill. Warrick obviously thought the same thing, because all he said was, "Really," in a chilly tone.

"Uh huh. And this looks nice. Smells nice." Toreth put one hand lightly on Warrick's shoulder, and reached for the pan with the other. "But how does it taste?"

"Be careful, it's hot."

"I know that." He licked his finger. "Mm. Nice—spicy. And creamy."

Warrick's shoulder twitched. After a few moments he said, "It's nonspecific curry, I'm afraid. All I could do with what I had. If I don't manage to get some fresh things in, we're down to packets for tomorrow."

"Oh, I'm sure you'll be able to find something in a drawer."

This time the twitch turned into a coughing fit. Toreth patted his back with mock solicitude. "Are you okay? I'll get you a drink." Humming happily, he went to fetch a glass. Sara tried desperately not to catch his eye, because she was millimeters away from developing a cough of her own. As she looked away, she saw Rob staring fixedly at the table and clearly in professional deaf mode. She felt fleetingly sorry for him, but not enough to dispel the happiness. It was surprising how quickly Warrick's flat had started to feel like home.

Toreth's good mood lasted all the way through dinner, and he even managed to be civil to Rob. Afterwards, he declared, suddenly and improbably, that he was tired, and went to bed. For about ten minutes, Warrick managed to keep going the thin pretense that he wasn't desperate to follow him, then he muttered a carbon copy of Toreth's excuse and departed.

It should have provided a good opportunity to spend some more time with Rob but, to her annoyance, Sara discovered that she seemed to be the only one in the flat that evening who genuinely was exhausted. Leaving Rob in the kitchen, she went to the spare room. All was quiet from Warrick's room, but she would've put a large bet on that not lasting for long. She didn't care, as long as they didn't keep her awake.

They didn't. Instead she was awoken a few hours later by thirst, and the fading fragments of a dream—another nightmare, she suspected. The still-strange room disoriented her, and for a moment she couldn't find the clock. One in the morning. No wonder she felt so tired during the day if she couldn't manage to sleep through the night.

Heading for the kitchen, she hesitated in the hallway. She didn't know what prompted her to go into the darkened living room—a movement, a noise, just a feeling—but when she switched the light on she saw Warrick, sitting with his back to the door. As she came around the end of the sofa, she saw him slipping a folded handkerchief into his dressing gown pocket. Even without that clue, it was obvious—when he looked up his eyes were red and his lashes damp.

She sat down beside him and asked the ridiculous but necessary question. "Are you okay?"

"Perfectly, thank you. You?" He checked his watch. "It's late."

"I got up for a glass of water." He'd closed the conversation, but she felt compelled to try again. "Are you sure you're all right?"

"As I said, yes. I couldn't sleep, and I thought that, rather than wake Toreth, I'd come in here."

"And sit in the dark?"

He shook his head. "Not particularly convincing, is it? Although I genuinely didn't wish to wake him up—seeing me making an idiot of myself would distress him needlessly."

He was right about that. Toreth wouldn't have the faintest idea of what to do or say. Although, to be honest, neither did she. She liked Warrick a great deal—he was kind, generous, and he made Toreth happy. Except for rare occasions, though, there was a distance between them that made her wary of him. She was never sure what he was thinking.

After a moment, Warrick cleared his throat and said, "I apologize, incidentally, if I embarrassed you at work today."

"Not a bit. Really. Any time you want a reminder of the contents of his desk is fine with me."

He raised his eyebrows.

"I mean, it only makes my life easier. He was as ratty as hell before you showed up, and after you'd gone I seriously thought about asking for a pay rise, he was in that good a mood. Not that he doesn't have plenty of reasons to be ratty," she added, in case he thought she was complaining.

He smiled slightly. "I doubt it will happen again in the immediate future. Or at least, I hope not."

"Oh?"

"No. It was . . . I went for lunch at work, and the screen in the cafeteria was showing the damage to some of the Int-Sec complex. It suddenly occurred to me that it was pure luck—or pure chance—that Toreth survived at all. I don't know why it should have come as such a surprise. He even mentioned it, if you recall, while we were eating on the first evening."

"He left Interrogation early, to go to the gym."

"Yes." He seemed to consider the problem for a while, then said, "I suppose it's that I didn't allow myself to dwell on the possibilities before you were released, and afterwards there seemed no point in thinking about might-have-beens."

"I was sure he was dead. Really sure. There was someone in with us who'd seen the interrogation levels and—" She stopped as the images returned, as clear as the instant the lift doors had opened and she'd seen it for herself. Warrick looked at her questioningly, and she shook her head. "It sounded bad. I knew he was down there, so I thought there wasn't much of a chance. Mind you, most of the time I was too busy worrying I was going to end up the same way to think about him, or anything much."

There was a pause, then he said, "I can't imagine how awful it must have been."

It sounded peculiar, and it took her a moment to realize why. It wasn't simply a platitude. In fact, it was closer to observation than sympathy—he'd tried to put himself in her place, and failed. "At least we had you to get us out," she said.

"Yes. I have no real grounds for complaint, do I? I was here and relatively safe."

She almost said, "sometimes waiting is the hardest part," but that *was* slipping into platitudes—she'd readily have swapped her four days at I&I for four days in Warrick's flat. And she vividly remembered Toreth in the interrogation room, bruised and cuffed, and stumbling with fatigue. Instead, she said, "So, you saw the Int-Sec stuff?"

"Yes. And then I thought a lot of terribly clichéd nonsense, and it suddenly seemed very important to see him. I'd intended to ask Carnac to help with the curfew permits anyway, so that was sufficient justification for indulging myself. Afterwards I felt a great deal better. I think I worked the last of it out of my system just now, before you came in. So I am, now, perfectly all right."

She wasn't entirely sure she believed him, but there was no point saying so. They sat for a while, then Warrick looked at his watch again. "I'm afraid I ought to be getting back to bed. Good night, and thank you for your patience."

"It's, um, no problem. 'Night."

When he'd gone, she sat on the sofa, hugging a cushion and feeling unexpectedly lonely. There was no one to be needlessly distressed if she woke up in the middle of the night and felt like crying. No one except Bastard, anyway, and he'd been banished down to the basement, where at least he'd been granted the privilege of a small open window.

She was almost ready to start sniffling, when she heard a movement behind her. "Warrick?"

"No, only me." It was Rob, standing in the doorway.

"Come in. Where've you been?"

"Keeping out of the way in the dining room."

The room furthest away from the main bedroom. She couldn't help smiling. "Were they loud?"

He stared at her, then his expression smoothed away and he said, "I have no idea what you mean."

"Oh dear. That bad? I must've been faster asleep than I thought."

Not a muscle in his face twitched. "Can I get you anything?"

Fun as teasing him was, she thought she'd better change the topic before she overdid it. "Something hot would be good. Without caffeine."

"No problem."

After he left, Sara sat and watched the city through the window. The shooting seemed more intermittent than on previous nights, and there were fewer of the fires that had kept her away from the window before. She wondered how many more people like her were out there, unable to sleep. Stuck remembering for the rest of their lives things they'd rather never think about again.

There must be hundreds, she decided, or probably thousands. She wasn't even that badly off. All the people she really loved were alive and safe. It was only people from work who were gone from her life. The still missing and the definitely dead. Parsons, who had—she closed her eyes, shutting out the distant fires, and forced herself to think about something else.

Rob returned a few minutes later, with a mug of herbal tea. "I'm not entirely sure what it is—most of the label on the jar is in some exotic alphabet, but it smells okay."

She took a deep breath and forced a smile. "Is it safe, do you think?"

He grinned. "I'll test it for you." He took a sip. "Seems to be. At least it's not instantly fatal. Tastes good. Lemony."

"Okay, I'll trust you."

He crouched by the sofa and offered her the mug. Instead of taking it, she wrapped her hands over his and leaned forwards as if to take a sip. She pulled gently on his hands, bringing him in closer. She couldn't have offered a much broader hint and, finally, he took it, leaning over their joined hands and kissing her.

Lemony, indeed.

It lasted only a couple of seconds, then he sat back on his heels and gently disengaged his hands. "Rob?"

"I'm sorry," he said.

Not the response she'd been expecting. "You're sorry you kissed me?"

"Something like that. Except for the part about being sorry. What I mean is—"

Ah. Daylight dawned. "You're on duty."

"'Fraid so," he said, relief evident at the understanding.

She smiled. "Well, that's easy. Because you're only on duty until two, and then, when you're not..."

"Yes?"

"I'm in the spare room."

He looked at her for a moment, still crouched by the sofa. "Just like that?"

"Just like that." She curled her feet up under her, and settled back into the embrace of the deep sofa. Warrick had great taste in furniture, even if it wasn't cat-proof. "I thought it would save a lot of time."

He stood up. "Sara, I, er..."

She took a sip of the drink and rested her head on the back of the sofa, closing her eyes. "'No thanks' will do fine."

"It's not that—not at all. But I'm working for SimTech. For Warrick. If anyone found out I'd done something like that, here, I'd probably get sacked for it."

"I understand. No need to say any more." Pity, because she could fancy it. Just a fuck, as Toreth would say. Not something she often wanted to do.

Even with her eyes closed, she could *feel* him hovering nearby. Eventually he said, "I, um..."

"It's fine, honestly." The sofa was too comfortable to get out of, but the atmosphere in the room was anything but. For a few moments she considered asking him to leave, but that seemed unfair. Besides, she needed to get back to bed or she'd be a wreck at work tomorrow. Even though it was Saturday, it seemed unlikely that she'd be getting in any later than usual.

They knew her name. They were going to kill her—the certainty of that knowledge paralyzed her with terror. They meant to take her away and kill her. If they found her, they would lock on the cuffs and take her through the door and through the door she could see the bodies. Smell the blood. Toreth was dead. She'd seen him dead in the interrogation levels and they'd handcuffed him, too.

They knew her name.

Calling her name and she thought, I can run, but there was nowhere to go, even if she could have forced her leaden limbs to move. Blood, everywhere, sticky and clinging. So she crouched in the center of the crowd, trembling, as they searched. Closer and closer. They were looking for *her.*

People creeping away, leaving her alone in the middle of the stinking, blood-slippery room.

They knew her name.

"Sara. Sara!"

Now she struggled for real, released from the paralysis of sleep and fighting the hands on her wrists, dragging her towards the door.

"Sara, it's me. McLean. Rob."

For a moment, caught between dreaming and waking, she knew it was real and she knew it was a trick to make her give herself away. Then her eyes opened and she saw him in the light from the doorway.

"I heard a noise." He let go of her wrists and touched her cheek, and she realized she was crying.

"I was dreaming about—" She couldn't say it.

He took his hand away and rubbed his thumb over his fingertips, then moved up the bed and she leaned against him, still shaking. He stroked her back, gently. "Shh. You're fine. You're safe. Everything's okay."

She swallowed, wondering if she was about to be sick again. Throwing up all over him would be a wonderful next step. "I'm sorry."

"Don't be silly." He pulled away slightly, looking down at her. "That is, it's no trouble at all. All part of the service."

There were a great number of replies to that, many of them highly suggestive, but all Sara managed was to look back at him, grateful and at the same time wishing he could be a little bit less professional. She put her hand on his shoulder and, gently, pulled him down towards her. He resisted for just a moment, before he kissed her lightly, like the first, brief kiss in the living room. Then he kissed her again, and it went on and on, warm and tender. While he kissed her he held her gently, almost impersonally, as though waiting for permission to do anything more. He kissed very nicely. Eventually he pulled back and looked down at her, seeming serious in the dim light. "I wouldn't want it to be... taking advantage."

"Me neither. Would I be?"

He smiled, a flash of teeth, then he went across the room to close the door.

"I thought you'd get sacked?" she whispered.

"I decided I don't care."

"You never know—if you get caught, maybe they'll let you patrol corridors."

There were footsteps, then a pause. "Well?" she asked.

Sara listened to him stripping in the dark. She felt tempted to turn the light on—there was no reason not to—but it seemed more fun to leave it off. As he slipped into bed beside her, she realized why. It was just like sneaking a boyfriend into her room at her parents' home. The idea of Warrick and Toreth playing the part of her parents almost made her laugh out loud.

Once in bed, he hesitated again, close beside her but not yet touching. She reached out, guessing, and found his mouth with her fingers. "Kiss me again."

Sweet. It was sweet; he was sweet. Also gentle, considerate, patient, and lots of other delightful adjectives, but mostly sweet. He even came sweetly, pressing into her, gasping softly into her ear, sounding almost surprised.

Afterwards, he didn't show any sign of rushing off, which was rather sweet, too. In fact he seemed happy to hold her, playing with her hair, murmuring compliments. She was terribly tired, but not so tired that she didn't mind staying awake with him for a while, until he finally had to go. He smelled lovely.

Eventually, he propped himself up on one elbow and looked down at her, a dark outline against the window. "Can I ask you something?"

She turned her face up to him and he kissed her. "Sure. Go ahead."

"Do you . . . do this sort of thing a lot?"

"What? Meet men, proposition them outright, and screw them?"

"Er, yes."

"No, not really." She ran her finger along his collarbone. "Usually I get references from friends, check them out, follow a strict dating plan and *then* screw them, if they look like a solid prospect for a reasonably long-term relationship."

"Oh."

"Don't worry. I felt like a change."

"So I'm what? Not a prospect?"

Oh, great. Just her luck to try casual screwing and get a stalker. Toreth would die laughing. "I'm sure you're lovely. But don't you have a girlfriend or something?"

He sat up. "No! Of course I don't! What the hell would I be doing here if I had a girlfriend at the moment?"

Even better—a faithful stalker. "Sorry. I didn't mean—"

"I don't cheat on my girlfriends."

Bloody hell, he sounded actually upset about it. "I'm sorry, honestly. I didn't mean to say I thought you would. Or I didn't think about it. Oh, hell." Too complicated, when she was so tired. "I think my standards are screwed—spending too much time with Toreth does that to you."

"I'm sure it would."

The sudden coldness drove her to sit up, too. "And what's that supposed to mean?"

Rob paused, then said in his professional voice, "Nothing."

"Yes, it bloody well is. What?"

"All I meant was that it's not exactly, well, moral. Working at that place."

Oh, of course. Bloody outsiders. "I work there as well, you know."

"You don't... do what he does."

"No, I just screw men I've known for five minutes. I suppose you think that makes me a whore, does it?"

"Don't be—I didn't say that."

"You didn't need to." She hated him, suddenly and absolutely. Ruining everything—all she'd wanted was half an hour's fun with someone she liked. Something to make her feel sure she was alive.

"Sara, I was talking about I&I, not you. What used to happen there was wrong. People knew that, and they were just too frightened to speak out. If it's the only result of all this, I think they did a good job when they started to clean the place out."

"You have no idea what happened at I&I, so you can—"

"And you might not like to hear this, but I'm sorry they didn't finish the job and close it down for good."

"Get out."

"Sara—"

"Get the hell out of my room and don't even *think* about ever coming back."

"I just—"

"Out!" She raised her voice. "Get out!"

"All right, all right, I'm going."

He jumped out of bed, and she heard him stumble. Then more noise as he tried to find his clothes. Angrily, wanting him gone, she snapped the light on and caught him, frozen, halfway into his trousers. She had to laugh. McLean frowned, gathering clothes. "Don't worry, I'm leaving as fast as I can." He pulled on his shirt and shoes and suited action to words.

When he had gone she switched the light out and lay back in the dark, still seething. The arrogant little worm. How dare he talk about Toreth like that? (She conceded the point about morals, but *he* had no right to say it.) How could he say that what the resisters had done at I&I was *good*? Of course, he hadn't seen it. He hadn't seen people he knew, dead in a pool of blood. Parsons, screaming as they'd dragged him out of the coffee room along with the other interrogators and the paras...

Think about something else. What the hell was with "Aren't I a prospect?" Men. They weren't happy if you tried to "trap them," and they weren't happy if you said you didn't want to. Well, he could go to hell. She wasn't going to think about him anymore.

She didn't think about him for fifteen minutes or so, until she finally fell asleep.

Chapter Six

❖

Working at the weekend was an annoyance made only marginally more bearable for Toreth by the knowledge that Warrick was also working, so he wasn't missing out on the chance of a long, leisurely weekend fuck. Nevertheless, leaving for I&I early on Saturday morning put him in a black mood even before he reached his office and found the stack of messages that had been left overnight.

As he plodded his way through them, he kept thinking of what he ought to be doing on a Saturday. A swim at the university gym first thing, then back to Warrick's flat for breakfast in bed and afters. One of the more enjoyable of the routines that normally made up his life. It would've been nice to have had *something* that hadn't been utterly disrupted by the revolt.

As far as work went, Saturday was hardly better than Friday. The water to the cells had failed totally overnight, and Toreth was ten minutes away from ordering the detention officers to open all the cell doors when the service crew called to say the pumps were working again. Once they were fixed, power breakers tripped and the air cycling went down. This time he'd already given the order to open everything when the cycling came back on. It was only yet another fault, this time in the cell security master overrides, that saved him from a building full of angry and uncooperative paras and interrogators.

The near disasters did nothing for his temper or his nerves. To top it all, Sara crept into his office at lunchtime, and he knew by her expression the news was bad. She offered a screen, hovered for a moment, then left without a word.

A fresh death list. He scanned down the screen and found the highlighted name. Starr, Joel, junior para-investigator, General Criminal. Starr had joined Toreth's team only last October, fresh from training, and Toreth hadn't been greatly impressed by him so far. Another blow, though, another part of prerevolt I&I that could never return to normal. Still no news from B-C or Nagra either, and the idea of having to build an entire team virtually from scratch depressed him.

Toreth opened the associated report file. By the look of the postmortem report,

Starr had been caught in the periphery of a grenade blast. Not discovered until today because he'd made it down to the waste recycling level where he'd crawled into a corner and eventually died a couple of days later of blood loss, dehydration, and injuries sustained. Toreth wondered for a moment if the body had been found by a repair team, which would be good news. No one had yet worked far enough down the list of critical systems even to send him a report on the waste recycling.

When Toreth ventured outside, he found Sara crying at her desk. He went straight back into his office.

By midafternoon, he was desperately hoping that Warrick would turn up again. Regrettably, he'd already put that down as a once-in-a-lifetime experience. Payne proved to be only a slight distraction from the stress. Direct flirting would probably scare him off, so Toreth amused himself by playing accidental touching whenever they were in the same office—not often enough to create suspicion, but enough to be sure that there was some spark of response buried down there. It wouldn't take many days before he'd have the lieutenant trained to lean back in his chair whenever Toreth walked past behind him.

Apart from that, the day was generally dismal.

Sunday brought no better news. For every problem solved, two more appeared. Unless things started to improve soon, he'd have to admit to Carnac that he couldn't perform as requested. God only knew what would happen then. I&I closed down and the remnants returned to Justice, or subsumed by another part of Int-Sec or the Service. Which meant Carnac winning. That thought kept him at I&I until past midnight, only finally forced back to Warrick's flat by sheer exhaustion.

On Monday, though, he began to see some results from his attempts to reallocate resources. Sufficient admin staff had been cajoled back that he could put together something approaching a skeleton personnel department. He sent Sara to brief them, and get them started on the task of tracking down the missing, checking the list of dead and presumed dead, and drawing a fuller picture of what the final staff complement was likely to be.

Wheeler sent a report an hour after Toreth got in, saying that the water, food, and heating systems in the cells had been completely restored. Toreth had read similar reports before, but this one used words like "guarantee" rather than "believe," so he was inclined to put more faith in it.

The cells had been emptied of all those who could walk out, except for the interrogators and paras, and the tribunals were beginning to nibble down the numbers of those. Medical was still a disaster, and people were still dying unnecessarily, but even there things were slowly improving. Some supplies had arrived—nowhere near as many as were needed, but enough to raise the morale of the medical staff.

A second pleasant surprise came midmorning, when someone knocked on his office door. "Come in." Toreth looked up from the screen in time to see Barret-Connor open the door.

"Morning, Para," B-C said. The sudden shock of normality left Toreth speechless.

"Sorry I'm late," B-C added as he crossed to Toreth's desk. "There's hardly any transport running, and then the Service people had trouble with my ID. I thought for a while they were going to throw me into detention."

His team. With Mistry and Sara, and maybe Morehen, who was still hanging on in the face of the shortages of drugs and decent facilities, that made five of them alive. Toreth cleared his throat. "Where the hell have you been? Why didn't you get in touch?"

B-C looked surprised. "Didn't you get my message, Para?"

"No."

"Oh. Sorry about that. I sent it on Friday, as soon as I got the general call for everyone to come back in."

"Must have been lost in the network problems." How many other, more important, messages were going astray?

"Does that mean you don't know about Nagra either?" B-C asked.

Six survivors? "No, I don't. Is she okay?"

"Yes. When it all happened, we started back here from Justice, but we couldn't get onto Int-Sec grounds and pretty soon after that we realized we didn't want to. We both laid low at my mother's place until the troopers appeared, then Nagra took off. She's gone up north somewhere, she didn't say exactly where. I got a note to say she was safe, though, and I sent it in the message to you."

Toreth realized he was grinning, but couldn't squash the delight. Six of them. God, maybe things *could* be normal again one day.

In the meantime, B-C provided a skilled and reliable pair of hands, although even he looked dismayed by the time Toreth had finished delegating. To make up for it, Toreth gave him Hepburn's office. The senior wouldn't be needing it—his name had shown up on the death list yesterday.

As the morning drew to a close, Toreth found himself with no desperately urgent life-or-death tasks to complete for the first time in four days. Given the chance to sit back and look at the situation as a whole, he found himself beginning to worry—not because things weren't now going better but, oddly, because they were. When Sara returned, sounding optimistic about the new admin arrangements, he left her in charge and went off to have a coffee and a think. As he reached the corridor he heard Sara's delighted cry of, "B-C!" followed shortly by, "Toreth, why didn't you *tell* me?"

Without looking back, he waved and walked on.

Toreth sat in Tillotson's office, with his heels scuffing the section head's desk, sipping section head-grade coffee, and thought about the bigger picture. He'd been too preoccupied by the chaos and problems to give much thought to Carnac's ultimate plans, and perhaps that had been part of them. Trying to second-guess

Carnac's motives was simply a waste of time, so he considered only what he knew had happened so far.

Carnac had stayed in Warrick's flat until Monday morning. That meant three full days after the start of the revolt and two and a half days after the resisters had control of Int-Sec. On Friday (and he smiled without noticing) Warrick had come here to see Carnac in his capacity as new Administration higher-up with special interest in I&I. And something Toreth had said to Payne on the first day back: if Carnac had made it to I&I a day or two earlier, Sedanioni might not have died.

Why had Carnac been hiding at Warrick's flat when he should have been directing the revolt and taking charge here? No doubt he'd laid his plans carefully, but it wasn't like Carnac to trust lesser mortals to carry out his directions unsupervised. Payne might know more, and seemed amenable to questioning.

Payne's presence was something else that might bear closer consideration. Carnac wouldn't have chosen him at random. The reason Payne had offered seemed a thin connection, but it might make sense if Carnac was looking for someone favorably predisposed towards I&I. He was reasonably certain that Payne was telling the truth as he knew it, but a chance conversation with Carnac had a ring of plausible coincidence that made him certain that the socioanalyst had set it up. The question was why, and he doubted he could find out from Payne. At least not directly.

When he left, he took Tillotson's chair with him. Handy as the armless admin chair had been for Warrick's surprise visit, he thought he deserved something more comfortable.

Back in his office he found Payne waiting for him with good news—he had somehow managed to divert some technical supplies to I&I from some unspecified alternate destination. There was a strong suggestion that it was better not to ask how or where, so Toreth didn't. Instead he said, "If only Carnac had pulled his finger out and got here sooner in the first place, we'd be a lot better off."

"Yes, there was some trouble about that," Payne said.

Had he struck gold on the first try? "Really? Where?"

"At headquarters. As I understand it, Socioanalyst Carnac decided to direct the operations at Int-Sec in person. There was some confusion, I believe, and the, uh, irregular forces involved in the original uprising were allowed to run out of control here for longer than planned."

He didn't say it, but it didn't take a trained investigator to spot the subtext: involving civilians in military matters was a mistake. "You got here before Carnac?"

"Yes—not me personally, but the Service. Not by long, but Major Bell took control on Monday morning and the socioanalyst arrived later in the day. This is all what I've heard since, though, so it could be wrong."

It certainly fitted in with what he knew. "Nice to know even Carnac can fuck things up."

"I know what you mean—he is a bit unnerving, isn't he? But it was a pity for

I&I. By the time we arrived, I'm afraid most of the damage had been done."

"I didn't think you'd care that much."

Payne looked slightly offended. "I won't pretend that there aren't some pretty unflattering views within the Service about the status of some Int-Sec departments, I&I included. But you're Administration, just like us. Or that's how I see it."

After Payne had gone, Toreth sat in his newly acquired chair and added his new witness statement to the case. It was starting to develop into something which needed its own IIP.

There didn't seem to be any doubt that Carnac had deliberately delayed getting to I&I. Maybe he'd been hoping that the mob would kill enough of the staff that the division would be destroyed at that stage. That made sense, because not rebuilding I&I would be politically easier than persuading the new Administration to eliminate it. I&I wasn't loved, but it was useful. It seemed sound enough, except that Carnac had then given Toreth operational authority and allowed him use it, knowing full well that he would never let Carnac close I&I if there was any way to prevent it. Carnac had backed him up against the Service, both over Bevan and over the medical supplies. He'd given him Payne, who was both useful and sympathetic to I&I. He'd appointed an embarrassingly soft-hearted initial tribunal panel. First, he'd left I&I to be torn apart, now he seemed to be doing his best to put it back together.

Over the last couple of days, the interview panels had been set up and trained, ready to start processing interrogators and paras at full speed tomorrow. If Carnac genuinely wanted to see I&I blood, then the tribunals were perhaps the strangest thing of all. Why go to the trouble of legitimizing the re-employment of the interrogation staff by the new Administration?

Of course, the tribunals also had the power to order executions. Four days ago, Toreth had stacked the interviewees to get the outcome he wanted. What if Carnac had done the same with the tribunal members? Had he chosen them so that Toreth would underestimate their willingness to schedule "surplus staff" for elimination?

Toreth pulled up the lists of names of tribunal members, and scanned through it. None of them were familiar, but that was only to be expected. Luckily, another one of Carnac's gifts was the authority to dig deeper.

To his surprise, he managed to get a connection to the security files on the first try. He called up the members' files and read a few at random. He found nothing in them to suggest they were of any higher caliber or any more ruthless than the members of the test tribunal. Reassuring, to a certain extent. Still, it remained a puzzle, and a worrying one, because the tribunals certainly weren't something Carnac had allowed by accident. He considered it for a while, then gave it up. It was only a matter of time before he'd find an excuse to scrap the tribunals for good, and it was highly unlikely they'd be started up again later. Once that happened, Carnac's plans, whatever they were, should be neutralized.

That thought was a worry, not a comfort, because it suggested that Carnac's plan to take down I&I—and he was still convinced Carnac had a well-hidden agenda—would have to come into play soon. There was something going on, something he knew nothing about, and with Carnac involved, that ignorance could be fatal. He had to find out, quickly. But how? "How" was the big question. He doubted that anyone at I&I besides Carnac was in on it. It wasn't as if he could simply take Carnac out for a drink and ask him what he was planning.

Toreth spun himself around in the chair, the beginnings of a smile mirroring the beginnings of an idea. It wasn't as if…

Sara had already gone to bed when Toreth finally let himself into the flat. He heard Bastard, scratching at the inside of the door to her room, no doubt hoping to be let out to wreak havoc. From that he deduced that McLean must be guarding bodies elsewhere—only the totally insane would try to get near Sara with Bastard in the vicinity. The animal was possessive to a disturbing degree.

Toreth was convinced that, given half a chance and a bit of cooperation, Bastard would be screwing Sara with the same enthusiasm he applied to stealing food and destroying furniture. When he'd mentioned as much to Sara, she had been unamused to say the least, which made him wonder if she thought the same thing.

He found Warrick in the bedroom, still awake, or almost so—he was sitting up in bed, a screen on his knees, his head nodding. "Warrick?"

He jerked upright. "Mm? Oh. I was wondering where you'd got to."

"Sorry, I should've called."

While he undressed, he thought about how bloody domestic that little exchange sounded. He needed to get his own flat back, soon, before he ended up imagining that he liked it. "You don't have to wait up for me."

"I wasn't." Warrick yawned and put the screen down. "I'm trying to work out how long we can keep paying our employees if our customers and sponsors use the current difficulties as an excuse not to honor their obligations."

Toreth hadn't even thought about how all this might be affecting SimTech. "Is it serious?"

"Not yet. Or at least Asher says not, and I trust her judgment. I was going over the numbers she gave me, just to double-check. Two pairs of eyes are better than one." He yawned again. "Although possibly not at this precise moment."

Toreth went to kneel beside the bed, still brooding about the idea of being waited up for. Being positive, at least it meant that he knew where Warrick was when he wanted him. "Warrick, I need a favor. A big favor."

"Ask away." Warrick ran his hand across his shoulder. "I'll do my best."

"I need the address of Carnac's hotel, and his medical records."

That woke him up. "Medical records? Why?"

"Warrick—"

"Yes, of course. And I very much doubt I want to know, in any case."

"Can you do it?"

There was a long silence, then Warrick shook his head. "The address I have, as you know, but as for the other—no, I don't think I can."

At first, Toreth thought he must have misheard. Then, briefly, that Warrick meant he wouldn't do it. "Why not?"

"They'll be in the Socioanalysis Division system somewhere, and I have no idea how to go about getting into that."

"You can get into Int-Sec, why not Socioanalysis?"

Warrick smiled. "You let me into Int-Sec originally, remember? Once you're part of the way in it's much easier. And I can access the less secure files—ordinary citizens' files, medical files from Central Medical Services. But it's unlikely that Carnac's file will be stored there."

"Fuck."

"If it's that important, I can try. But it won't be easy—or safe. I can't do it from here. I'd need to find somewhere to start that can't be traced back to me."

"No... no, if it's going to be that hard, don't do it." Carnac was too damn dangerous to risk attracting his attention.

"Is there anything else I can do to help?"

"No." That was it. He didn't *have* a Plan B, because he'd been so confident that Warrick would come through. "I'll have to think of something else completely."

"I'm sorry. Is there anything else I can do?"

Hadn't he just asked that? Toreth looked at him blankly, then focused on the smile in his eyes rather than his still serious expression. "Yeah, maybe." It certainly wouldn't hurt to stop worrying about Carnac for a while and there was no better distraction than Warrick. "What did you have in mind?"

"Nothing elaborate."

Suited him—he was too tired for games. "Just a basic fuck?"

Warrick laughed. "Sometimes you're so amazingly charming. Well, come on, then. Get into bed."

Ten minutes into nothing elaborate, Toreth had managed to forget I&I, Carnac, and everything else except the fact that Warrick really was better at this than anyone else he'd ever fucked. He wanted nothing more than to come in Warrick's mouth and then fall blissfully asleep before he even felt him stop swallowing.

He heard an indistinct exclamation from under the sheets. "What?" he asked, hoping it wasn't anything important. When Warrick lifted his head, Toreth bit back a moan of protest.

"I'm an idiot," Warrick said. Didn't look like blissful sleep was imminent after all. "I can't believe I didn't think of it straight away." Warrick threw the sheets aside and knelt up. "Does it have to be current?"

Did what? Then he realized what Warrick meant. "Not as long as it's not too old. No more than a few years."

"How much of it do you need?"

"Biochem and metabolism, known drug reactions, genetic predispositions—nothing fancy."

"Then I can do it. In fact, I can do it right now."

Eleven minutes earlier, that would have been music to his ears. Now he wished Warrick could've thought of it a bit later. "How long will it take?"

"A couple of minutes." He took Toreth's hand, licked the palm, and placed it onto his saliva-slicked cock. "Keep yourself amused and you'll hardly notice I'm gone."

"What?" Toreth sat up. "And I thought you said it would be risky?"

"Couldn't be safer." Warrick was already out of bed, pulling on his dressing gown. "Carnac's been in the sim, which means that his medical details will be in the volunteer archive at SimTech. I've got a copy of that here. Just the basics, but if that's all you need..."

Toreth started to follow him out of the room, remembered that they weren't alone in the flat, and went back for something to wear. By the time he reached the office, he found Warrick already working.

"All the medical records are anonymized. It won't take me long to undo it."

Toreth watched for a few seconds, trying not to ask the question. Then he said, "You were thinking about Carnac?"

"Mm?"

"You were thinking about Carnac while you had my cock in your mouth?"

"Not really." Warrick didn't even look around. "More along the lines of a sudden flash of inspiration."

"You must've been."

"Well, I suppose he might've been at the back of my mind. I can think about more than one thing at once, you know, especially when one of them is technically exacting but hardly intellectually demanding."

What were you thinking about him? Toreth decided to drop it. There was no point in asking questions until you got the answer you didn't want to hear; he of all people ought to know that.

"Ah. Here we go." And then Warrick paused. "Before I give this to you, I ought to ask you to promise me that whatever you want it for, Carnac won't be harmed as a consequence."

"I didn't know you cared about him that much."

"I never said that I did." Warrick's face, reflected in the screen, was utterly serious. "But in any case, I don't need a promise because it would be suicidally stupid of you to do anything to him, and I know you're neither of those things."

"Thanks for the vote of confidence."

Now Warrick did smile, slightly, as he brought the information up. "Is that enough?"

He scanned the details over Warrick's shoulder. It was indeed just the bare basics, but it held more or less everything he needed to know.

"Can I have a copy? On paper."

"Of course. I'll take the name off, shall I?"

"Please. And don't take too long." He rested his hands on Warrick's shoulders. "How strong is this chair, do you think?"

Warrick laughed. "Go back to bed. I'll be there in a minute."

After she closed the door quietly behind her, leaving the room pitch-dark, Sara nearly changed her mind. This was so stupid. But she couldn't bear to try to sleep on her own again, and she was almost ready to cry from sheer exhaustion. Even sneaking Bastard into her bedroom hadn't helped her sleep—he'd refused to cuddle, and spent his time scratching the door and sulking because she wouldn't let him out. The only other option was McLean, but after their disastrous night she couldn't think of anything to say to him. So it was this or nothing.

Her stealthy entry didn't seem to have disturbed the occupants. She'd heard them both in the hall outside her room the second or third time she'd woken up, but that was an hour ago. Now the only sound in the room was the quiet breathing of deep sleep.

It took a few minutes' careful groping in the dark before she even found the bed. It was only then that she realized she wasn't sure which side Toreth slept on. Mostly she only saw him asleep on sofas. The right side, she guessed.

Well, if she had to make a mistake, at least it would only be with Warrick and hopefully he'd understand.

"Toreth?" she whispered. No response, so she tried a gentle touch on his shoulder. "Toreth?"

"Mm?" Movement in the dark, then, "Sara?"

Oh, shit—it was Warrick. Well, it would be. She should think of something and leave. Exhausted as she was, though, should and could proved to be two different things. In the end, she said, "Sorry. I thought you were Toreth."

A pause, then he said, "Housekeeping, minimum lights."

Slowly, the lights came up to a dim glow, revealing Warrick lying on his back, propped up on his elbows, blinking up at her, with Toreth sound asleep beside him. He studied her face for a moment, then frowned.

"What's wrong?"

"It's…I had a nightmare, about I&I. Blood and people screaming and they were looking for me and…and then I went back to sleep, and it happened again. I'm so tired, and I just can't—" To her horror, she felt tears starting. "I'm sorry I woke you up. I wanted to ask Toreth to—" To make it all better, somehow. "To come and sit with me. Or something."

Warrick smiled slightly. "Or something?"

She blushed, hoping the dim light would hide it. "Let me sleep with him. Or, on the floor next to him, I mean," she added quickly, because it was Toreth.

"Would you like me to vacate the bed?" Warrick asked.

The kindness in his voice, and of the offer, brought the tears back.

"No! I mean, I don't want to throw you out, I just don't want to be alone and—" She couldn't carry on, so she looked away from him, blinking quickly until the tears subsided. This had been a stupid idea. "I'm sorry I woke you up. I'll be fine. I'll—"

"Please, don't worry about it."

Toreth moved, sighing in his sleep, then stilled again, and as Warrick turned away to look down at him, she caught a glimpse of a smile. Sudden envy chased the tears away. It wasn't fair. If Toreth woke up, Warrick would be *there*.

Then Warrick sat up. "Very well. Turn your back, please."

She did, wondering why, until she heard him get out of bed and cross the room. A drawer opened, and clothes unfolded, then he returned. When she looked around, she found him clad in a pair of dark pajamas, blue or green in the low light, made of something silky. Silk, very possibly.

After a moment she realized she was staring. Warrick looked quite unperturbed. "Best if you go first, I think," he said.

She probably ought to go through a few minutes of protestations and apologies. Instead, she climbed into bed and moved across, next to the still oblivious Toreth. Once she had settled in, Warrick joined her, keeping a discreet distance which must have placed him on the very edge of the bed.

"Do you want me to leave the light on?" he asked.

"No, thanks. I mean—I'll be fine without."

"Housekeeping, lights off."

Darkness again, but a different darkness. Not lonely, or full of lurking horrors. Toreth was warm beside her, his slow breathing almost a snore. Warrick's quiet breathing from her other side made her feel surrounded and secure, as if she were in the safest place in the city.

Suddenly, Warrick laughed—she felt rather than heard him. "What?" she whispered.

"I was thinking that this will give the security team something to discuss in the morning, should they notice you coming out of here."

Something she hadn't thought of. She turned to face him. "God, Warrick, I'm sorry. I'll go. I don't want to—"

"Shh. There's nothing to apologize for. Go if the idea makes you uncomfortable, of course, but not on my account. And I don't imagine Toreth will mind."

Before she could reply, a voice from behind her said, "Uh?"

"Nothing," Warrick said. "We have a visitor, that's all. Go back to sleep."

"Huh?" Toreth reached out and found her, his hand sliding over her, breasts down to waist, before she could react.

"Who the fuck... Sara?"

"Yes," she said.

Other people—normal people—would have wanted an explanation at this point. Toreth, falling outside that category, simply pulled her closer, and said, "Always wanted to fuck you. You and Warrick. Together. Do you think?"

Then, while she was still trying to come up with a reply, he apparently fell asleep.

Warrick laughed again. "What an educational night."

"I don't think he meant it," she said.

"Don't you? I find that if you catch him partly unconscious, he can be startlingly honest. However, I am sure that he won't remember saying it in the morning."

Which would be good enough. "I wouldn't do it, you know," she said.

"Certainly not without my cooperation."

The wry tone made her laugh. "No! I mean, I wouldn't screw him, on my own, with you, or with anyone else. I don't screw friends' boyfriends. Ever."

A pause, then he said, "And I'm honored to be considered as such. Now, Sara..."

"Yes?"

"Good night."

Giving up on the last shreds of reluctance, she snuggled back against Toreth, who tightened his arm around her and muttered something thankfully incomprehensible. After a minute or so, she felt Warrick moving across to reoccupy the vacant space. With the last worry removed—that he might fall out of bed at some point due to overconsideration—she finally fell asleep.

Voices woke her in the morning—voices talking about her. She drifted slowly up to consciousness from a deep and dreamless sleep, listening to the warm, male voices, matching the physical warmth surrounding her.

Toreth had his arms around her, holding her tight against the hard, reassuring strength of his body. She also couldn't help noticing his equally hard erection trapped between them, twitching against her from time to time. However, that was nothing more than bodies in contact, and the morning—it felt friendly, rather than anything else.

In front of her was the warmth of Warrick's body, still at a distance but closer than he'd been last night.

"If you move, she'll wake up." Warrick sounded concerned and slightly amused.

"I have to get to work." The low voice ran right through her from Toreth's chest. "And so does she."

"I don't think she ought to go." Abruptly, the amusement vanished.

"Well, good luck talking her out of it."

"Then you ought to tell her not to. She'll make herself ill if she keeps forcing herself back to that place. She has made herself ill. You didn't see her last night. She was nearly in tears."

"I need her," Toreth said in his "end of argument" voice.

"And getting your filing done is worth Sara's health?"

"It's not—" He lowered his voice. "It's not fucking filing, and you know it. I can't do my job without her. She runs the bloody place—all I do is go around kicking Service arse to get things moving."

"I'm sure that isn't true."

"Yeah, well, maybe not quite. But I don't have time to break in a new admin *and* work a sixteen-hour day. Which would be a twenty-six-hour day without Sara."

She ought to move, or to say something, and let them know she was awake. But Toreth didn't often bother to say things like that to her face, unless he was deliberately flattering her to get something. The rest of the time it wouldn't occur to him—it was simply taken as given. He needed her, and they both knew that. Still, it was nice to lie there and hear it. For one thing, it made the idea of I&I a little more bearable.

"You can't even do without her for a couple of days?" Warrick asked.

"I can't do without her for a morning. A morning I'm going to be late for already."

"Just for—"

"No. Just nothing. She's coming in to work, full stop." There was a pause before he added, in a softer voice, "Not that I'd mind staying in bed with her. And you."

After a moment, Warrick said. "I don't think Sara would concur."

"Oh, I don't know. If you don't ask, you don't get. And it was you she woke up last night, wasn't it?"

"Under the misapprehension I was you."

"So *you* say."

"So Sara said."

"And I bet you offered to go sleep in the spare room, didn't you?" A silence, and she could imagine Toreth's smile. "Talk about looking a gift fuck in the—"

"Toreth!" Outraged whisper. "Be quiet! What if she wakes up?"

"I'm only saying it because she *is* awake." He tapped her nose with his finger. "Aren't you?"

Flushing, she opened her eyes to find Warrick looking between her and Toreth behind her. He didn't seem to know whether to be relieved or shocked. Toreth released her and sat up, pulling the sheets back as he did so. She grabbed at her dressing gown, which had slipped in the night, and managed to wrench the front together before she had further cause for embarrassment. "Bastard!" she snapped.

He laughed, naked from midthighs up, still erect, and completely unconcerned. "Yeah, yeah, so I've been told. Now clear off and let me put your contribution to the morning to better use, since Warrick's going to be boring about it if you stay."

She scrambled out of the bed, not fast enough to avoid a slap on the behind as she passed him, and fled for the door before he could say anything worse.

Toreth whistled for most of the journey in to work and all the way up to his office, ignoring the pained looks from both Sara and the guards they passed. In his book, waking up to a bedful of Warrick and Sara was as near as damn it a perfect way to start the day. Even better, he had a plan with regards to Carnac. The atmosphere in the building seemed brighter than it had done since he returned.

When Toreth reached his office, he found Bell waiting for him, which took some of the shine off the morning. Worse still, she looked pleased to see him. "I'm sorry to disturb you, Para-investigator, but I wondered if you had time to answer a few questions I have about the restoration of interrogation services."

His instinctive reaction was to give nothing away at all. "You've seen the state of the place, you've got Service people everywhere. Why are you asking me?"

"Because you're in charge." A pause while they both acknowledged the unspoken "at the moment." "And progress seems to be slow. I'm doing my best to reassure my superiors, but questions are being asked."

"Everything's on schedule," he told her, trying not to sound too irritated.

"Unfortunately, the schedule's unclear. Do you have an estimate for when services will be restored?"

"No." Then, seeing the beginnings of a smile on her face, he added, "Soon, for a basic service." Time to shift the responsibility as far away as he could. "But that's only if the other departments can cooperate—we aren't the only place in chaos. You'd better go and talk it over with Justice and come back when they're saying something intelligible. If you can find anyone to talk to at all, that is—they're making the most of the damage they took."

"I'll talk to whoever's necessary."

"Good." As she left he called after her, "Let me know if you get anywhere."

He doubted she would, but with any luck it would keep her from reporting his supposed incompetence to her bosses. Wrestling with Justice was something he wouldn't usually wish on anyone, but for Bell he'd make an exception. With her out of the way, and hopefully harmlessly occupied, he set about the real business of the morning.

One advantage of Toreth's temporary promotion was that he had access to the security systems. A glance showed at once that Daedra Kincaidy was in residence at the pharmacy—no one else there wore their hair in hundreds of long, thin, bleached-blonde plaits. Better still, she was alone. Unfortunately, the check also demonstrated that the sound feed was working. He debated switching it off, but that left too obvious a trail when you were talking about Carnac. He'd have to work around it, and Bell had unintentionally provided him with an excuse.

Once he was sure Bell had gone for good, Toreth slipped past Sara without her asking where he was going.

Upstairs in the pharmacy, Daedra didn't look deliriously happy to see him, but by now he was used to that.

"Toreth? I heard you're doing very nicely out of all this."

"Great to see you, too."

At least she seemed to have come through the revolt unscathed—she looked unhealthily pale and thin, but then she always had. The only obvious change was that one of her plaits, hanging down by the left-hand side of her face, was now dyed jet black.

She must have caught his gaze, because she reached up and ran the plait through her long, bony fingers. "It's for Digger—Devon Eldridge. Did you know him?"

Toreth shook his head.

"Junior interrogator. Worked for Mike Belkin. I'd been seeing him for a few months."

"Ah." Belkin he knew well, but not all of his high-turnover team. "I'm sorry."

She shrugged, fingering the plait again. "It was this or get a tattoo, and we weren't that serious. What can I do for you?"

"How's the shop?"

She wrinkled her nose in disgust. "Looted to heck. I'm surprised the resisters running all over the place could even see straight, never mind kill anyone. If you've come to pester me about the medical supplies, we're still doing our best and we can't do any more. As far as I can tell, we're bottom of the list for deliveries in the whole of New London."

"No, I appreciate the problems—and I appreciate what you're doing to work round them. I came down to get some professional advice."

He took the paper out and handed it over. It held the outline of Carnac's medical records and a list of drugs beside it. He'd tried to provide as many alternatives as he could, but as he hadn't dared run it through the analysis system, he needed an expert human opinion.

"I'm trying to get a shell of an interrogation service running again," he said as she scanned the list. "I need to know if it'll be possible to do that with what you've got."

"Don't worry—I can see what you're trying to do." She hunted under the counter and found a pencil. Tucking a handful of plaits behind her ear, she started running down the list, moving between the drug names and the medical details.

After a while she said, "Nope, I can't fill this, I'm afraid."

In the margin she wrote, 'U'll kill him!!!' and underlined it a couple of times.

Good job he'd checked. "Are you sure?"

"Positive."

"Well, that's what I'm here for. Tell me what you've got and what we can use."

"Hmm... Oral dosing?"

"Yes. Ethanol compatible."

She tapped the bottom of the list. "Is that a requirement?"

"No point at all without it."

"Okay. Let me think." She started going down the list again, slowly, crossing out names and making substitutions. He waited, hoping that no one would turn up and interrupt.

Eventually, she handed the paper back. "This should provide approximately the same basic service. I've made a few notes; let me know if there's a problem."

He read the list. Bless her, she'd even written in the doses, which was good because a couple of the things on this list he'd never heard of. At the bottom of the page she'd written, "5-10% poss. bad react ?50/50 fatal. Can't do better."

A five percent chance of killing Carnac was practically a bonus. More worryingly, the last drug on the list was marked as injectable only, dosing four hours apart. That would drag things out. However, he didn't bother arguing—if Daedra said that was the best she had, he was willing to believe her.

"Thanks. That looks great."

"While you're here, do you want me to work up a sample kit? For a tryout?"

"That'd be great." He'd been wondering how best to phrase it. "You're a sweetheart."

She grinned. "It's good to see you again. How's Sara?"

"Fine." The sudden friendliness threw him slightly, but Daedra had never been one to hold a grudge, and she always enjoyed a professional challenge. "I'll tell her you were asking after her."

"And tell her we'll go out, when they get this flipping curfew sorted out." She disappeared into the stores, her voice fading. "I tell you, I'll just be glad when everything's back to normal."

Chapter Seven

❖

Toreth had expected to find it difficult to find a suitable opening with Carnac to implement his plan, but the very next day presented a perfect opportunity. It came about, ironically, as the indirect result of a blazing row.

When he arrived on Wednesday morning, he found Adams already waiting for him. Early morning visitors had begun to induce a sinking feeling; they never had good news. "Can I have a word, Para?"

The senior security officer looked nervous. Toreth was used to talking to nervous people, and this seemed to him like someone about to broach a subject they thought the audience wouldn't want to hear. "Of course you can. Sara, can you get a couple of coffees?"

Once in his office he sat down and offered Adams a chair. "Go on."

"It's the prisoners, Para. I appreciate your confidence in us, but I don't think we'll be able to cope."

He felt as though he'd walked into a conversation halfway through. "What's changed? Have more of the systems gone down?"

"No, Para. I mean the new prisoners. They're arriving now, and we—" Adams stopped dead. "I'm sorry, Para. I assumed you knew."

Bloody Bell—it had to be. "I don't know anything about any new prisoners and I'd appreciate it if you could fill me in." And then I'll go fill *her* in.

"There are fifty to arrive today and more scheduled. I'm afraid we can't accommodate them, never mind start the interrogations."

Interrogations as well. "Are they from Justice?"

"I don't think so, Para. There are Service troopers with them."

"Right. Don't take any prisoners—leave them in the transports, tell whoever's bringing them that you won't process them unless you see properly authorized transfer documents and arrest records, which they won't have. I'm going to sort it out."

On the way out of the office, he nearly collided with Sara. She took one look at his face, and said, "No coffee, then."

"Give it to Payne and B-C, if the lazy swine are in yet."

❖❖❖

By the time he reached Carnac's office, his temper had reached a nice simmering point. He ignored the protests of Carnac's admin, and the numbers of waiting visitors, and went straight into the office.

Carnac sat at his desk, discussing something with Major Bell. Whether that was good or bad, Toreth wasn't sure. They both looked up as the door opened. "I need to speak to you. Now," Toreth said, making an effort not to slam the door behind him.

Carnac frowned, then shrugged. "Very well. If you would excuse us, Major. We can finish this later."

Bell stood, but made no move to leave. "If there is a problem, perhaps I might be able—"

"I hear there are prisoners arriving," Toreth said, ignoring her.

Carnac nodded. "You hear correctly."

"Why wasn't I told?"

"The decision was made by the Administrative Council yesterday." His eyes flicked briefly towards Bell. "I wasn't informed until this morning—I left a message for you immediately I knew."

Toreth didn't believe a word of it, except possibly the implication that Bell had been behind it. "You're telling me you didn't know?"

Carnac smiled fleetingly. "Even I am not omniscient. Or omnipresent."

"Well, whether you knew or not, the decision will have to be unmade, because since you're not omnipotent either, it's not possible. And certainly not if you want us to do anything more than lock them up." Maybe Adams had been mistaken about the interrogations.

"It has to be done." Carnac glanced at Bell, who shrugged slightly. "Confidentially, there are still elements within the various resister factions who are not satisfied with the current progress of reform, and want to see more, and even more radical, action. In addition, there are people within the Administration strongly sympathetic to the old regime and hostile to the new. The council is nervous—justifiably so, perhaps, but the arrests are somewhat precipitous and against my advice."

Bell shook her head. "They are necessary," she said, with the calm confidence of someone who is supporting the official position.

Toreth addressed Carnac directly. "*If* we had the equipment and parts for all the systems, and *if* half the staff weren't dead or in hiding, and *if* people didn't keep interfering in things outside their authority—" he looked at Bell, who remained impassive, "—*then* we might be able to provide an interrogation service. We can't do it now."

Carnac frowned. "I thought that the interrogation levels were virtually ready?"

"That was the impression I was given," Bell added, sounding surprised.

After you maneuvered me into it. Toreth kept a firm grip on his temper, because the woman was trying to provoke him. "The levels might be ready, just, in a day or two. That won't give me the extra cells to keep the prisoners in, or the qualified staff to run the interrogations properly."

"Then run them any way you can," Bell said. "But the information must be obtained."

Carnac nodded agreement.

Toreth looked between them, judging his chances of succeeding in changing their minds with a reasoned argument, then said, "No."

Carnac stared at him. "I beg your pardon?"

"No." Toreth looked at Bell again, including her in the refusal. "If you want it done, one of you two can order them to do it. SSO Adams is in charge down in Detention, and I've told him not to accept any prisoners without the proper paperwork. I'm not changing that instruction."

"*Paperwork?*" Bell paced across the office and turned. "They're to be interrogated. They're resisters suspected of performing sabotage or otherwise trying to destabilize the new regime. What more do you need?"

Toreth sat down and crossed his legs. "How long a list would you like?"

Bell merely glared at him, so he carried on. "Prisoners brought in here ought to have been arrested by a warranted investigator or para, or arrested and processed by Justice. Then they need to be assigned Justice reps; some of them might have the right to independent representation, although not if they're political. Let's say not, to keep it simple. If, after assessment, there's a case for interrogation above level two, then we need a damage waiver from Justice."

All the paperwork which normally frustrated him so much, and he suddenly appreciated its value as a symbol of I&I's legality. This was what differentiated them from the mob that had been tearing interrogators into bloody pieces.

"Interrogations have to be carried out according to the P&P—that's the *Procedures and Protocols for Interrogation,* if you didn't know. They need to be recorded, and assessed for evidential value by qualified staff, and then sent back to Justice with the prisoner for trial and sentencing, assuming the rep doesn't object."

Bell snorted. "I think, in this case, we can dispense with all that. There won't be any trials—all we require is information."

Toreth shook his head, secure in his own territory. "Ah, well, if you want information, then you're looking at witness interrogation authorization and that's a whole different game. You'll need to—"

Carnac lifted his hand sharply to cut him off. "I have no interest in further legal discussions. Take the prisoners, interrogate them. That is an order."

He'd changed his fucking tune, Toreth thought sourly, from when interrogations were a regrettable necessity.

"No." Toreth took a deep breath, realizing that his preparations with Daedra might not be needed now. "Sack me, have me arrested for mutiny or whatever the hell you want to call it, but I'm not doing it. Because if I do, then I'm breaking the law."

"The *law*?" Carnac's voice rose, for the first time Toreth could ever remember. Even the imperturbable Bell stared at the socioanalyst. "For *torture*?"

"Interrogation. The technical definition is, 'Using legally sanctioned methods, including but not limited to verbal, pharmacological, and physical persuasion, to obtain proof of guilt or innocence by questioning.' It's at the front of the P&P if you'd ever bothered to look."

Carnac paled, then flushed, his hands clenching. The outrage, Toreth was convinced, was utterly genuine, which made it all the more interesting that Carnac was so keen to accede to the council's demands to have interrogations started up again. Yet another glaring contradiction in Carnac's behavior—Toreth wished to hell he knew what it meant.

"If you don't want to sack me," Toreth said, "calm down and we can talk about it sensibly."

Bell was clearly hoping Carnac would accept Toreth's implicit offer to resign, but after a moment, Carnac nodded. "Do you have anything sensible to say?"

"I want I&I back on its feet as much as you do," or almost certainly more, "but I'm not going to turn it into something else."

He turned to Bell. "You want unlawful interrogations, let your troopers have a crack at it and you can find out why it takes so long to train an interrogator. Or take your prisoners over to Justice. I'm sure they'd love to help. There's nothing they like more than holding someone's head under water until he confesses to something he didn't do."

Why was it always that example that sprang to mind? He could see the scene in his mind's eye, as clear as the day he'd stood aside and let them do it. And, earlier memory, he could feel the water filling his lungs as he struggled; he could hear the I&I instructors and other trainees laughing in the endless few seconds before he blacked out and it stopped being funny. He swallowed down the feeling, the cold panic. Not now.

Fortunately, Carnac didn't seem to notice. He waited for Toreth to continue, then said, "You are a member of a professional, legal body. I understand this. Nevertheless, as the major says, present circumstances make the matter urgent."

He sounded serious about that, anyway. "It can be done, and it can all be done legally, if you release the paras and interrogators."

Bell started to protest, but Carnac beat her to it. "No. Out of the question."

"It'll free up the cells for the new prisoners, and there'll be the staff to handle the interrogations. God knows, they won't all stay, but a lot of them will, if you'll let me offer them the same incentives we're giving at the tribunals."

"The Administrative Council made the tribunals a condition of I&I's continued existence," Bell said.

"We all know that," Toreth said. "And we know that you can get round it with provisional pardons. You can still run the tribunals retroactively, because we simply don't have the spare staff for you to execute in order to keep the rabble happy. So far they've passed everyone, including a few of the interrogators who *I'd* happily see dead. There's no damn point keeping people in cells until there's a slot free to rubber-stamp their release."

After a moment, Carnac said, "It is politically impossible for me to do that."

It's all in the phrasing. "I'll do it on my authority. I'll take responsibility for it."

Carnac steepled his hands, considering. "On your authority?"

"Yes."

Bell leaned down to Carnac. "Socioanalyst, I urge you to consider the consequences of this. I cannot recommend this course of action to my superiors."

Carnac looked up at her, his expression suddenly cold. "No? You recommended to the council that the interrogation service could be resumed. Without consulting either myself or Para-investigator Toreth."

"I—" Bell stared. Obviously, she'd thought that her name had been kept out of it. "Yes, I did. That was the impression I had been given."

"Well, it appears that your impression was incorrect. I realize, of course, that it was merely a careless mistake and not an attempt to embarrass myself or the para-investigator."

"Of course not."

Carnac continued as if he hadn't heard her. "Nevertheless, embarrassment will result if we cannot complete the required interrogations. Unless you wish to take up Toreth's suggestion that your men familiarize themselves with the P&P, then I'm sure you would wish to do everything you can in order to correct your error, yes?"

She nodded, reluctantly.

"Then you will support my decision, whatever it is?"

A moment while she looked for a way out, then she nodded again. "Of course, Socioanalyst."

"Excellent."

It was nice, Toreth thought, to see someone else in Carnac's field of fire for once. Another few seconds' thought, then Carnac looked back at him. "Very well, Toreth. I agree to your proposal."

Bell stepped back a little, distancing herself from the decision, but said nothing. That was the beauty of the Service—for ninety-nine point nine percent of the time, they did what they were told. Of course, in the other point one percent, the treacherous bastards jumped into bed with fucking resisters.

Toreth sat up straighter and uncrossed his legs. "For the first batch of prisoners, you can look at the charges—or whatever the hell kind of information they've got with them—and set an interrogation level. Then make a special director's order for each one and I'll get the processing done retroactively by Justice. They'll make a fuss but they always do. But from tomorrow onwards, they go through Justice first, okay?"

"Very well."

"The council will have to be told about this," Bell said, clearly hoping to get to do the job herself.

Carnac shook his head, answering her unspoken question. "I will explain the legal necessity to the council in person. I'm sure they will be delighted by our adherence to the letter of the law."

Toreth ignored the sarcasm. "Great. And you can make out release orders for all the paras and interrogators. Individual clearance, so they can walk out of the cells and go wherever the hell they want to."

Carnac frowned. "That will all take time and I have other things to do."

"I'll help. Do it this way and I guarantee I'll have the place running smoothly by the end of next week." When Carnac still hesitated, he added, "Do you want these bloody prisoners interrogated or not? Because, frankly, I don't give a shit about them. I have better things to do with *my* time, too."

Carnac closed his eyes briefly, then nodded. "Bell, you may deal with anyone waiting who absolutely cannot delay seeing me."

Toreth smiled, thinking about the busy room outside.

"Of course." Bell saluted, immaculately, and left.

Carnac moved aside to let Toreth sit next to him at the screen. "Let's get started."

As Carnac called through to his admin and canceled his appointments for the morning, Toreth reflected that it had been surprisingly—worryingly—easy. All along, he'd assumed that Carnac's real motivation was to stop I&I from recovering. And now he had simply handed the interrogators and paras over to Toreth on a plate. It was possible that Carnac might have seen the virtues of interrogation if his own neck was somehow on the block. He wasn't sure he believed that—it felt wrong, for no reason he could put his finger on.

Still, for the first time, he wondered if Carnac had been telling the truth to Warrick about his reasons for supporting the revolt. He didn't doubt that Warrick had accurately reported Carnac's words—he was an extremely reliable witness—but Carnac could have been lying. If so, then he had also been faking his anger a few moments ago, and Toreth didn't believe that either. Which left him with… what? Even less of an idea what Carnac intended for I&I and, for some reason, an even stronger conviction that it was nothing good.

❖❖❖

Sara had never really liked Parsons. Toreth didn't recruit people to his team based on personality, but on how well they did their jobs. Few of the interrogators were what Sara called likable; if they had more people skills, they'd be paras. Parsons had done his job efficiently and unemotionally—coldly—and that was all. He'd rarely joined the rest of the team in the coffee room and never on evenings out. She'd barely known him. She'd never wanted to.

There was a difference between not liking the man, and reading his autopsy.

Not that there was much there: a photograph of the body, a sketchy description of the injuries, and the cause of death, which she didn't need to read at all. Certainly not a dozen times, until she could virtually recite it from memory. At least Parsons was a corpse now, not one of the gradually dwindling list of missing. He was always known to have been in the building—she'd known, to start with. She'd seen the resisters take him away, and he hadn't shown up in Medical, so he'd been put on the "missing, presumed dead" list. Now that the body had been identified, she could fill in the notification to registered contacts form, write a personal note of condolence from Toreth for him to sign, and it would be finished.

It shouldn't bother her so much. Over the last few days she'd read dozens of similar documents. She'd seen countless more over the years, although they were only prisoners. Only a couple of days ago she'd dealt with the details of Toreth's second junior. Starr hadn't been bad, for a para. At least he'd understood that being polite to the senior's admin was a good tactic. She'd processed his death report and cried, but it had felt healthy. This was different. Every time she saw Parsons's unsmiling picture on the screen she wanted to throw up.

She finished the note—much like all the others because what was there to say?—and stared at the photograph. Parsons looked older than she remembered.

Who'd told them? She'd often wondered about that. Their captors hadn't scanned IDs, so someone must have given up the names. Someone had looked at the room full of frightened staff and picked out the paras, investigators, and interrogators taking refuge there. One of the people who'd been working for the resisters from the start, perhaps, or someone desperate and terrified enough for the betrayal. She might have done it herself, if it had come to that.

Parsons had been one of the few who'd made it up to level five from Interrogation after the initial attack, and he'd told her about it. In fact, he'd told anyone who was prepared to listen, as if repetition would turn the memory into something comprehensible. She couldn't remember, now, much of what he'd said. Only, "They opened the cells. They opened *all* the cells."

He was normally so cold, so reserved, that it had been strange to see him agitated. Shaken, like everyone else, by the enormity of what was happening. Not distressed, not crying, like so many of them were—angry, if anything, and simply unable to sit still. But he'd screamed. When they'd come for the interrogation staff, he'd screamed. He'd known what was going to happen. It wasn't hard for anyone to guess, but he was the only one who'd seen it.

She stared at the report on the screen, not seeing it through the tears blurring her vision, but not needing to.

That had been Saturday morning. The report gave time of death as 1800 (provisional) on the same day. Not even half a day, really, and he would've been unconscious for some of that. Quicker than many of the other reports she'd processed. Quicker than poor Joel Starr.

She wished that she'd done something. She had no idea what—rationally, she knew there was nothing that she could have done to save any of them, but that didn't change the feeling. She should have done something for Parsons. Liked him better, perhaps.

She wished even more that he'd shut up and gone with them quietly, like the others. She couldn't even remember who they were, because she'd been watching Parsons. If he hadn't screamed, she wouldn't have to remember him, either.

"Sara?"

She looked up, expecting Toreth or B-C, and found Lieutenant Payne. She sniffed hastily, wiping her eyes with her hand.

"What's wrong?" he asked.

"Nothing. I'm fine. If you want Toreth, he's with Carnac." The bastard. "And B-C's off somewhere chasing medical supplies."

"Hm. Would you like a coffee?"

"Coffee?"

He smiled, disarmingly, looking improbably young for an officer, even a lieutenant. "Brown stuff with caffeine. It seems to be the standard response to anything going wrong around here, so I thought I'd try it out."

"I'd love one, thanks."

She assumed he meant to fetch it, but instead he said, "Come on, then."

As they turned down the corridor, she realized he was heading for the room where she'd been held. She almost stopped, but she forced herself to keep going. It was impossible to avoid the place forever. Tillotson's office would run out of coffee or become out of bounds again before long. At the doorway, though, she found she couldn't follow him in. It wasn't that her resolve was any less, but her feet simply wouldn't move.

"—or take them back with us?" Payne's voice, disappearing with him into the coffee room. He'd been talking all the way from her desk and she hadn't heard a word until now. After a few seconds, he reappeared.

"Sara?"

"Sorry. I don't think I want a coffee after all." She meant to go back then, but her legs were shaking so much that it was all she could do to stay upright.

"What's the matter?" He took her arm, gently. "You're white as a ghost. Come and sit down."

"No!"

She pulled her arm away, and he let go quickly, only to catch hold of her again as her legs finally gave way. She let him lower her against the wall and waited for the tears to start, but her eyes remained dry. She was too terrified to cry, sick with the intensity of the fear, and she clasped her hands together tightly to still their trembling.

"Shall I get someone? Toreth?" Payne looked a little panicky himself, and she made an effort to pull herself together.

"No. I'm . . . that's where we were, that's all. In there. They put all the admins from our section in there. I've not been in since."

"I'm sorry—I had no idea. Look, let me help you back."

"No." She held out her hand and he helped her to her feet. "I can't hide from a bloody coffee room. Just . . . get ready to catch me if I do anything stupid, like faint."

He smiled. "Will do."

Three steps and she was at the threshold. The room had been cleaned, and it looked nothing like it had the last time she'd been there, but once more she couldn't force herself to take the next step.

When the guards had called her name, no one had reacted. No one had done anything, just as she'd done nothing when they'd taken Parsons and the others. Faces had turned away from her, pitying and frightened and so, so grateful that it was her and not them. When they'd locked the handcuffs around her wrists and led her out, she'd thought . . . she'd been sure . . .

She struggled to keep her breathing even. Hyperventilating herself into unconsciousness wouldn't help at all. It was only the coffee room. Birthday cakes. She'd eaten dozens—probably hundreds—of birthday cakes in there. She'd sat and dunked vanilla creams while listening to Toreth's improbable fuck stories. She'd fished for rumors and planted rumors. She'd bought tickets for sweepstakes on big-name prisoner interrogations. She'd held hands and listened to broken hearts being spilled out. One New Year she'd spent a drunken and ill-advised ten minutes on that exact chair over there with one of the accounts admins, until Toreth had pried her away from him. And she'd made enough coffees to float the building.

"Are you feeling like keeling over yet?" Payne asked.

"No. I'm *fine.*" Compared to all those memories, four days was nothing, and she wasn't going to lose her coffee room for that.

In the end, it was surprisingly easy. Being one step inside was just like being one step outside—horrible, but possible. Then it was only one step after another away from the safety of the door, until she reached the coffee machines.

Payne shadowed her, and she must still have looked awful because he all but had his hands out ready to catch her. "Here, let me get it for you," he said, "Mugs . . . oh, thanks. Milk? Sugar? Actually, there doesn't seem to be any of either, so that keeps thing simple. There you go." He handed the coffee over. "Do you want to go back now?"

Yes, she did, but determination made her shake her head. "Not yet."

She sat down, keeping a tight grip on the mug, holding it up near her face. The aroma of coffee masked the sting of disinfectant, and the faint smells beneath it that she had been trying to ignore. Looking at the door was the worst thing, because it was only a tiny step away from thinking about Parsons again. "Talk to me," she said. "Tell me something not about this bloody place. Are you married?"

"Oh. Um, yes, I am." He looked fleetingly uncomfortable, and she wondered why she'd never bothered to ask him before. "Would you like to see her?"

"Sure."

He opened his hand screen and brought up a picture. "There you go. Marianne."

"She's very pretty," Sara said, although in truth the woman was an insipid blonde she knew she'd forget the moment he put the picture away. "How did you meet?"

"We didn't meet, as such—we've known each other forever. Our families were friends, in fact, before we were born. Everyone always said we were meant for each other."

She'd always thought that kind of arrangement sounded creepy. "That's so sweet. Is she Service, too?"

"Oh, no. She's a teacher. Little kids." He grinned. "We're going to have one of our own. The conception license is being processed right now. It's just a formality really—I've got my commanding officer's approval and the preapplication genetics were clear." The smile switched abruptly to a frown. "God, I hope all this trouble doesn't mess it up."

"I'm sure it won't. The Department of Population wasn't hit anything like as badly as here."

"But if they've lost the records . . ." He shook his head. "Mary would be heartbroken."

"Why? How old is she?"

"Oh, it's not that. It's just that her sister had an application approved not long ago, and Mary wanted to have hers—ours—born around the same time. So they'd be able to play together. Do you have any kids?"

"No. I don't even have anyone to have them with." She thought, briefly, of McLean. He'd been so sweet, so unlike her usual run of rich, good prospects. Silly idea.

"Oh, that's—" He stopped, teetering on the edge of pity.

"I don't mind. I mean, I've always promised my approval to Fee, anyway. Surrender of rights to a sibling's routine enough and she's far more maternal than I am."

"I could never do that. I've always wanted kids." He ducked his head slightly. "I know it's not the kind of thing men usually say, but—"

"No, no." He was sweet, too—sweeter than she imagined a Service officer should be, anyway. "I think it's lovely that you do. And I'm sure everything will work out fine. You never know, maybe they'll abolish the system anyway."

He stared at her. "Abolish reproduction control?"

She shrugged. "Why not? For a while at least. For popularity. It's something that resisters press for a lot, isn't it?"

"I, er... I wouldn't know." Now he sounded distinctly uncomfortable. She'd forgotten, briefly, that he was still an outsider.

"Well, it is," she said. "I listen to a lot of interrogation transcripts."

"Ah, I see."

She grinned at the relief in his voice. "I don't know what you're worried about—I mean, you work for resisters now, don't you? Carnac and his friends."

He stiffened slightly. "I'm an officer of the Service."

"But—"

"No. I swore an oath to the Service and to the Administration. We all did. I haven't broken that oath. Service Command did what was best for the Administration."

He really believed in it, she realized. The novelty was vaguely charming. She felt tempted to tell him that loyalty to the Administration, like saluting and sirring, wasn't a big feature of I&I, but she didn't think he'd like to hear it. "Yes, of course," she said. "I'm sorry. I didn't mean to suggest... um, shall we go back? I've got things to do."

"Yes, good idea." He still sounded brittle.

After they had rinsed the mugs and started to walk back, he suddenly said, "Is Toreth married?" It had the sound of a question he'd been trying to think of a subtle entry for, and given up.

"*Toreth?*" Actually, her first instinct was to say, "practically," but Payne still worked for Carnac, whatever he said and however nice he seemed. She'd learned her lesson there—no mentions of Warrick, or anything personal at all. "No, he isn't."

"Oh." He sounded pleased, and her heart sank as the other possible motive for the query occurred. She shouldn't interfere in Toreth's plans, assuming he had any, but she felt she owed Payne for the coffee and sympathy. Instinct and caution warred briefly.

"He's—" He's a professional bastard who specializes in fucking married people, the more happily married the better. "He's anything but married. He's really not the type for fidelity." Maybe that would be a warning of sorts. At least she'd tried to do something.

❖❖❖

When Toreth had finished with Carnac, he went back to his office, intending to ask Sara to start organizing the releases. She wasn't at her desk and, to his surprise, he found Major Bell waiting inside his office. She was sitting at his desk, looking perfectly at home.

He didn't bother asking her to move. Instead he went over to the window and looked out, forcing her to turn to follow him.

"There was no one here, so I thought I'd wait," she said.

"Always a pleasure to see you." He turned and sat on the windowsill and smiled at her. "Is this a social call?"

"That was an impressive performance this morning, Para-investigator."

It hadn't occurred to him before how much the way she used his title annoyed him. He could hear the quote marks around it, the contempt for a non-Service rank.

"You can call me Toreth, or you can fuck off. We've got the staff now, so we don't need the Service around here anymore."

His deliberately aggressive tone didn't ruffle her in the least. "You might want to give that some thought. Carnac might feel he can ignore my concerns—the Service's concerns—but he has his place on the council. You don't."

"The Service doesn't run the Administration, it doesn't run Int-Sec, and it certainly doesn't run I&I."

She smiled, coldly. "No. But it has plenty of influence, especially right now. And it will have more in the future, when its traditional place in the Administration has been restored."

For a moment, he didn't understand her. "What? They're... Jesus! They're planning to undo the reform? Put the old Department of Security back together?"

"There is a feeling within the Service that a much closer, more fundamental, collaboration between the military and other security departments might be best for the future safety of Administration as a whole."

Which sounded like a yes. "It'll never happen. Service Command is tripping if they think the other departments'll stand by and let the DoS take over again. And Int-Sec and Ext-Sec would fight them every step of the way."

"Do you think so? I&I may be an exception, but you forget that the majority of staff at both Internal and External Security were in Department of Security divisions before the reforms. They'll be glad to get back where they belong—with the Service."

"Maybe ten, fifteen years ago, when everyone was still pissed off about being ripped out of there into new departments, but not now. It's too late. People are used to it. They like their independence too much to want the Service calling the shots again."

"I think those in charge of the divisions concerned will see that cooperation is in their best interests, as well the interests of Europe."

"People like me, you mean? And if you get my cooperation, you get I&I?"

She carried on as if he hadn't spoken. "Every division which cooperates makes the task easier. Don't doubt that the Service will reward loyalty—loyalty to the needs of the Administration."

Interesting redefinition of loyalty. Not that he had much, but if Bell thought he wanted to spend the rest of his life saluting people like her, then Service Command weren't the only ones on drugs. Still, he must be doing better than he'd thought if she was trying bribery instead of threats. Something else occurred to him. "Does Carnac know about this?"

"Of course. He accepts the inevitable. A private understanding, for now."

If Carnac was behind it, then I&I and the rest of Int-Sec were in deep trouble. But putting the military in charge of the Administration didn't feel like Carnac's style, not even to get at I&I. He had no real evidence either way so, with absolute confidence, he said, "You're lying."

He caught the flash of surprise and, yes, fear in her eyes. And then a classic, guilt-confirming response. "Why would I lie?"

"Because you think Carnac doesn't have a clue about it, and you don't want me to tell him." The odds that Carnac didn't know already were vanishingly small, but he didn't see any reason to tell her that. "Because you know that when he does find out, he's going to be with the civilians in the new Administration, not with you lot."

The major lowered her voice, unnecessarily. "*If* that were true, and if you stick with Carnac, you'll go down with him, and anyone else in the new Administration who doesn't fall into line."

"Yeah?" He'd back Carnac against the Service any day. "Well, it's all very interesting, Major. But not very concrete, is it? You can tell whoever's interested that I'm not sticking my neck out to give them I&I on a plate on the basis of some vague promises about rewarding loyalty. Mind you, if they pull it off, I wouldn't say no to staying on. I think I'll take my chances sitting on the fence, if you understand me."

After a moment, she nodded. "Are you going to tell Carnac about this conversation?"

"Fuck, no. I've got no love for that bastard. He isn't Int-Sec or Service. And I'm not political—never have been."

She smiled. "A healthy attitude, Toreth."

He watched her go, thinking that she really ought to take her own advice about that. On balance, he thought he'd handled it about right. From her point of view, buying his neutrality was a victory of a sort and there was always the chance he might be open to further persuasion. In the meantime, the conversation might provide some useful leverage for his own plans.

❖❖❖

Carnac leaned back in his chair and frowned thoughtfully at his visitor, more for effect than from genuine puzzlement. The only unknown had been exactly long Bell would take to make her move. "Why are you telling me this?" he asked.

"I thought you might be interested. Actually, I assumed you already knew. But in case you didn't—" Toreth shrugged. "I didn't think the idea of the Service running the Administration would appeal to you any more than it does to me."

"And you would be right, in all three cases. I am aware of their plan, I am interested in it, and I do not support it."

Toreth cocked his head, considering. "Are they going to carry it through?"

The obvious confidence in his ability to answer that definitively was mildly flattering. "Doubtful. Your assessment of the attitude of the other departments is accurate and, despite the major's presentation of the situation, the Service itself is divided over the question. The Administration's professional soldiers as a body shy away from overtly bold political moves, and my prediction of the most likely outcome is that they will procrastinate until the political climate makes success impossible."

"But they might make it stick?"

Was Toreth wondering which side to choose? "Lots of things are possible. For example, one exceptional individual may step forward and carry others with them, although given the available candidates that also seems unlikely. But I can only deal in probabilities."

"Fair enough. It all adds to the fun." Toreth yawned, and stretched, making Carnac remember why he'd picked the man as his liaison on his first visit. The effort required to keep his body in that kind of condition was, in Carnac's opinion, excessive and narcissistic in the extreme, but the results were exceptionally pleasing for onlookers.

The healing scar on his right eyebrow was an interesting addition to the look. A romantic might call it piratical. A realist such as Carnac would say thuggish—an external marker of the innate violence of Toreth's life which had otherwise left him surprisingly untouched. A useful reminder to the world at large of his true nature. Toreth stretched further, arching his back up out of the chair, then stopped abruptly and put his hand to his side, wincing.

"Are you all right?" Carnac asked.

"Fine." His expression showed a predictable flicker of irritation at having displayed weakness. "Leftover reminder of your friends' visit to I&I, that's all. Has anyone ever cracked any of your ribs?"

"Fortunately, no."

"You surprise me." The tone implied that Toreth himself was frequently tempted by the idea. "But in that case you won't know that they hurt like fucking hell."

"My sympathies."

"Thanks." Toreth looked at his watch. "God, I'm starving."

"I also. Fortunately, the restaurant at my hotel is excellent, even under the current circumstances."

"Really? Is that an invitation?"

Carnac smiled. "If you like. I didn't think that you would be amenable to the suggestion, after the opinions you expressed so firmly when we first met."

"I was in a bad mood."

"And I don't suppose I can blame you for that. Now that your temper has been restored by the idea of I&I back in business once more?"

Toreth shrugged. "I can bear to eat with you in the same room, if that counts."

Actually Carnac doubted that, but Toreth was clearly trying hard to make it sound true. The one-hundred-and-eighty-degree shift of attitude caught his interest. Transparent as it was, it might be entertaining to go along with for a while. It would probably be the easiest method of determining the motive behind it. "Then I would be delighted to extend the invitation," Carnac said.

"You'll have to give me the address."

"No need." And no need to compound any risks by letting Toreth know in advance where the meal would be. "I can take you back in the car when we finish this evening."

"Yeah, okay." Toreth stood up. "Why not?"

A number of reasons sprang to mind at once. However, he doubted that even Toreth was stupid enough to attempt a simple assassination. A kitchen-cooked dinner with wine in sealed bottles was harmless enough.

Carnac had never believed in heaven. Not until now.

Heaven was being fucked. Heaven was being fucked by Toreth, right now, here, every second of it drawn out into what felt like an hour, diamond sharp, glittering and exquisite. Only his vision was blurred, turning everything in the hotel room into restless shadows. But who needed sight, anyway? Better to keep his eyes shut, and feel.

Oh yes. Feel.

Everything was perfect, except that at the back of his mind, persistently annoying, was a voice. It seemed to have a lot of comments about his current situation, none of which he wanted to hear. However, he couldn't shut it away because it was inside him.

Inside him.

Toreth was inside him. Inside him, above him, everywhere around him. He normally found fucking face-to-face uncomfortable. Physically...

Well, we're not as young as we used to be.

...and emotionally. Unpleasantly open and vulnerable, to be on your back, with someone lying between your legs—he'd always thought that women must hate it. It was embarrassing. Not now, though. Not with Toreth.

Toreth moving slowly inside him, so slowly, never stopping, not a millimeter of movement wasted. Arms around him—he liked to be held, although he'd never given much thought to it before. Lips against his throat, on his mouth, whispering in his ear. You could fall in love with someone who could make you feel this good.

You're pathetic. Pull yourself together.

He had a vague, hazy memory that Toreth had hurt him. Once. A long time ago. This didn't hurt. This was ecstasy—endless, warm waves of bliss washing over him. He'd never felt anything like it before. Fuck of his life.

Never let it stop.

This is heaven.

This is drugs. *He drugged us. He put something in the wine, somehow.*

"Carnac?"

Voice near his ear. Beautiful voice.

"Yes?"

"Why did you come to I&I?"

Oh, come on. He's asking us questions. Does that sound like a man having the fuck of his *life? Don't tell him anything.*

Some sense in that, perhaps. He tried his best. "Toreth, just... keep doing that. Don't..."

"Carnac, I know there was a reason behind it." Lips brushed his ear, right against it now. Every word fired nerves he'd never felt before. "You didn't pick us at random for special attention, out of all of the divisions at Int-Sec. You don't do anything without a purpose. So why us?"

Not trusting himself to speak, he shook his head.

At last. Now keep your mouth shut and we'll be all right.

Toreth stopped moving inside him, and he moaned. "No, please. I can't." He had to explain, because he desperately wanted Toreth to keep going. He just desperately wanted Toreth. Had he ever wanted anything more? "Voice. Won't let me."

Oh, for pity's sake. Tell him everything, why don't you? No—forget I said that.

"Like that, is it?" Low laugh, thrilling him. "Well, don't worry. It won't keep talking for long. I'm not relying on my overrated performance alone. But let's see what I can do to shut it up."

Toreth's weight shifted as he took it all on one arm. Carnac knew what would happen next and he tightened his arms around Toreth, trying to prepare himself. Hand on his hip. Hand brushing over his stomach. Hand...

Too much. The feeling was too much. He should have come the moment Toreth touched his cock, but miraculously he hadn't.

If you don't stop him, I won't be held responsible for the consequences.

Hand. He moved his own hand. It was the most difficult thing he had ever done in his entire life. Closing it around Toreth's wrist. He couldn't bear to try seriously to stop him from doing the incredible thing he was doing, but it was a gesture to go with the words. "Stop. Please."

"You don't mean that. I know you like it."

Words like warm honey and treacle, flowing down his spine. And true. So very, very true. Where had he heard them before?

You said it to him. When you were trying to get him to trust you. When you were trying to break him. For God's sake, get your brain out of your prick and think.

Somehow, his hand was no longer where he'd ordered it to be. After a moment he found it again, wrapped around the bedpost, holding on as he thrust up into Toreth's hand.

It was too good to last and he found himself wishing it would end, wanting it to finish. It was going to be so... oh, yes, if it felt like this now, what would it be like when he came? But it wasn't enough—fingers too loose around him. He needed more. "Toreth, please—"

"Tell me." Tongue in his ear, nearly making him scream. "If you want me to finish it, you'll have to tell me what I want to know."

Listen to him. He's interrogating *you. Don't you remember how much we hated watching him work on that poor bastard? Don't you remember why we're doing this?*

He remembered. He really did remember, although he had to fight to hang on to the fact that the same man who'd done that was the man now coaxing such mind-blowing sensations from his body. He arched his back, whimpering helplessly as Toreth's mouth abandoned his ear to brush across his nipples.

What do you remember? Think.

He remembered the interrogation. He remembered the prisoner: his voice, his body jerking against the restraints, his overwhelming fear and pain. He remembered the stench of shit and sweat and fear. He remembered fighting down nausea as he watched Toreth's hideous, professionally detached handiwork. And he knew the memories wouldn't help for long. For now it gave him the strength to clench his teeth, shake his head.

"Tell me, lover." Voice in his ear again.

Compromise. Maybe that would be enough. "After. I'll tell you after."

"Come on. That last glass must be kicking in about now. You want to tell me, don't you?"

If you tell him about I&I, we're dead. Is any fuck so good that you want to die for it?

Yes.

Yes to both—he didn't care if he died here and he did want to talk. It was taking every gram of willpower he could summon to keep his lips closed, the words piling up in his throat. The voice in his head still talked to him, berating him, but the words grew increasingly indistinct. He couldn't even remember why it mattered anymore. Nothing mattered, except Toreth.

Well, that's it from me. You're on your own.

"Why did you come to I&I?"

"In order to—" Last hopeless effort, and then his control slipped away. "In order to destroy I&I, I had to be inside it, in charge."

"Go on."

"They think it can be reformed. Morons. You can't change psychopaths. It has to go. It's everything that was wrong about the Administration. Pure evil, if evil exists."

"That's very good." Kisses. Angel's kisses, rewarding him. "Now tell me how."

"By letting them see what it's really like. They don't know. I didn't know, until you showed me. When you broke that prisoner, just to demonstrate how it was done."

How could he speak so clearly? He should be panting, writhing, begging for more of the indescribable caresses he could still feel. But he wasn't—he talked on, telling Toreth what he wanted to know.

"That's why I gave you that pathetically repressed lieutenant. I knew you'd charm him, and he'd back you up to the Service. I could stand back and let you run, bring back all the horror, and then in the end, they'd all see there was no choice and it would finally be destroyed."

"So why me?"

"Because I love you." Some distant part of him knew it wasn't true, but he felt it.

"Of course you do. But that wasn't the reason, was it?"

"No. I knew you'd get done what I needed—you were the perfect tool. You'd destroy the tribunals, you'd manage to get all the interrogators and paras reinstated. You'd insist on the damage waivers. You'd make certain that they saw the whole obscene structure, because you're proud of it. You disgust me—you and all of the rest of the animals there. I'm sorry."

"No need to be, love." Sunshine voice, stroking him like the hand on his cock, pushing him closer towards orgasm. It was all right—Toreth understood. Silly of him to think that he wouldn't. He could hear himself panting now, the strange detachment slipping away, everything becoming too real.

"Is there anything else I need to know about? Who's the 'they' who're going to see I&I?"

Speaking faster, trying to get it all out before it was too late.

"There's going to be a report, an inspection. Weeks. Two... two weeks. That's when it'll be decided. And then they'll be... executed. Everyone. Paras and interrogators. Investigators. Eradicated. I'll make it happen. Toreth, please make it—"

"And is that everything?"

“Yes. Everything. Everything.” Everything falling apart. Holding on to Toreth, holding him close. Soon… God, please, soon. “Everything.”

“Good.” Even through the blissful haze, he heard the voice change. “Then let’s get this over with.”

A sudden, hard thrust pushed him down into the bed, shattering the beautiful intimacy.

“No. Toreth, don’t—”

Hand over his mouth, pressing down, making him struggle for breath.

“Shut up, you worthless… lying… piece of shit. Just be grateful… that I’m going to finish it… at all. I should… break your fucking *neck.*” Short, vicious strokes, grinding deep into him. “Bastard. Treacherous… treasonous… *bastard.* I—*fuck.*”

Toreth’s weight bore down, as his hands tightened on him—mouth and cock—and that was enough to carry Carnac over the edge. Coming and coming, endless shivering spasms, jerking up against the body pinning him.

By the time he could think again, he was alone in the bed. Gasping for air, utterly spent. Knowing he’d failed. I’m sorry, he told the voice, wondering if it was still there. I couldn’t…

It doesn’t matter. We’ll deal with him in the morning. He won’t get away with this.

A cold touch against his neck startled him. Hiss of an injector.

Ah. Yes. Unless, of course, he makes sure that… we… don’t… remember…

Darkness reached up to swallow him.

Chapter Eight

❖

When Carnac awoke, the light through the window seemed unbearably bright. He made the mistake of rolling away to shield his eyes, and the nausea and pounding headache that awakened made him moan out loud. Too loud. It took him a moment to make sense of his condition, because it was something he experienced so rarely. Hangover. He had the most horrendous hangover of his life.

Carefully, he turned over onto his front and pushed his face into the pillow. Dark. That was better. Not much better, but without the glare of daylight—painful even through his eyelids—he could just about manage to think.

Hangover. Which meant drinking. He was on assignment, on an *important* assignment, so why would he be drinking at all, never mind to the extent that he must have done to cause this? He couldn't remember. He absolutely couldn't remember, and that was far worse than any of the physical symptoms.

Theoretically, he knew that the consumption of a sufficient quantity of alcohol could induce memory loss. It was theory only, because the Socioanalysis Division didn't permit the brains of their young charges to be affected by anything other than carefully controlled chemicals. By the time he had been old enough to be within reach of temptation, the lessons had been thoroughly absorbed.

Two glasses of suitably expensive wine was the maximum he ever permitted himself. He loved clarity of thought too much, feared the idea of damaging himself, and above all, he hated the loss of control. Not last night, clearly. Last night had been different. How, and why?

Something familiar distracted him from the exploration. A small pain, more of a discomfort and insignificant beside the monstrous pain behind his eyes, but nagging at him, insisting on its importance. He directed his attention down his spine and shifted carefully, assessing.

Well and truly fucked, by the feel of it.

He backtracked, looking for a point where the darkness became memory, until he found it. A single, horribly clear scene. Himself, leaning against the wall of a corridor, needing the support, and pulling Toreth against him. Toreth's mouth on his, demanding. His hands on Toreth, fondling him through his clothes. The sharp, dizzying excitement at finding that Toreth was hard.

He'd said something then. Something to Toreth, the words thankfully blurred. However, he remembered Toreth laughing, kissing him again. "I'll do it here if you really want me to. But wouldn't you rather wait until we get back to the room?"

Staring into the pain-filled blackness behind his eyelids, Carnac sincerely hoped that he'd said yes, because Toreth had certainly fucked him somewhere.

He should, perhaps, have tried to remember more, but right now he couldn't bear it. He struggled up to sit on the edge of the bed, almost sobbing as the headache intensified, setting the room spinning around him.

Managing a painful squint around the room, he found no sign of his presumed lover, and no clothes other than his own. Toreth must have left already, last night or this morning. Of course, he had far more practice at this sort of thing.

After he'd showered and dressed—everything taking at least twice as long as normal—Carnac discovered that he'd missed breakfast at the hotel. To be honest, he felt relieved. He felt obliged, on medical grounds, to eat something, but his stomach was not impressed by the importance of replacing lost salts. Black tea, perhaps, might be acceptable.

Before he left the room, he searched as carefully as he could, looking for any kind of note from Toreth. He found nothing, which was another relief, but also pointed to a tiresome scene ahead. No doubt Toreth would have a great deal to say about the night before. He had appointments elsewhere that day, but he decided to detour to I&I first. Better to clear things up than to let the situation disturb his concentration during the day.

Toreth wasn't in his office, but Sara was outside, and she directed him downstairs to Security. Carnac searched her face but found nothing. Interestingly out of character for Toreth not to have told her everything at the earliest opportunity. He held little hope that Toreth had learned some discretion since their previous encounter at I&I.

In the Security offices, Toreth was in earnest consultation with Bevan. When Carnac asked to speak with him for a moment, he expected Toreth to delay, to make him wait. However, he excused himself at once and followed him out. Carnac found a quiet corner, and decided to tackle the problem head on. "Toreth, last night—"

He smiled. "Enjoy yourself?"

There was no point in pretending. "In all probability, yes. The latter part of the evening is a little unclear."

The smile widened. "Really? Want any reminders?"

Perhaps he should have left this until later, when he felt more in control. "I believe I have an idea of the main points of the evening."

"We should get a coffee and compare notes."

"No, thank you." And suddenly, he saw a potential escape route from this tedious, childish confrontation. The hangover really was slowing him down. "I hope Warrick wasn't unduly inconvenienced by your absence. I must remember to apologize for detaining you, the next time I see him."

Toreth froze, the smile turning into a mask. "What the fuck does Warrick have to do with anything?"

A button so reliable that pushing it was hardly even amusing anymore. Not at this trivial level, anyway. "You were going to tell me what happened, I believe?"

A brief, visible struggle, then Toreth said, "Nothing happened. We had dinner, we got pissed, and I put you to bed. End of story."

The pleasing realization that he might be able to come out of this ahead on points did a great deal to dispel the misery. "Very much as I recollect it."

Toreth nodded sharply. "Right." He waited, looking distinctly uncomfortable, then said, "Was there anything else?"

"No. Just to let you know I shall be out of my I&I office today. I'm sure you'll be able to manage splendidly without me."

As he left, he heard Toreth mutter something under his breath. He couldn't hear the words, but the tone was perfectly clear, and kept him smiling all the way back to the car.

When Toreth went back into the office, Bevan was still behind his desk, looking sourer than ever. "What did that tosser want?"

"Morning after the night before." Toreth considered sitting down, and decided pacing would feel better. God, he hoped Carnac had bought it, because if his suspicions were aroused now—

"Sit down and stop panicking."

Toreth stopped dead. "I'm not fucking panicking."

"No? Well, maybe you should. I'd be giving it serious fucking consideration if that bastard was gunning for me."

He forced himself to sit down and not fidget. Bevan was the last person he needed thinking he couldn't handle things. "I wouldn't look so bloody smug about it if I were you. He's very fucking thorough and he likes you about as much as you like him."

Bevan opened his desk drawer, produced an unlabeled bottle of something clear and a couple of paper cups, and poured them each a generous measure. "Here you go."

The first, incautious mouthful burned down his throat like acid, sending him into a coughing fit that lasted a good minute. When he managed to stop, eyes watering, he asked, "What the fuck is that?"

"Friend of a friend of a friend makes it."

"Where does he work, a chemical factory?"

Bevan took a sip himself. "It's good for the nerves."

"I bet it is. As a solvent." The second sip went down more easily. There wasn't much of a flavor, although that might be attributable to unconditional surrender on the part of his taste buds. "Thanks."

"Pleasure." No one could say that less convincingly than Bevan could. "So, to get back to business, how did you find all this crap out?"

"I fucked it out of Carnac last night. With some pharmaceutical help."

Bevan snorted. "Talk about devotion to the bloody cause."

"Yeah." Toreth rubbed his temples, and wondered how Carnac felt. "I've had better nights. He had a lot more fun than I did. I bribed the waiter to doctor the wine with a needle before he opened it, so I had to drink the fucking stuff as well, at least until Carnac was well gone—I spent five hours afterwards throwing up from the antidotes and blockers." His ribs hadn't enjoyed that one bit. "I can't believe you can put most of that shit into prisoners on a level four."

"You're sure he was telling the truth?"

"Give me some credit for knowing my job."

Bevan nodded. "So why the hell are you in my office?"

"Looking for advice."

"No, I asked why the hell you're in *my* office."

"Collecting favors owed. And I trust you." He shrugged, deciding to go for all-out honesty. "Or at least, I don't trust anyone else here any more, and I've got no chance of stopping him on my own."

"You can cut and run." Bevan said it without any particular inflection, just offering an option.

"Like I said before, this is personal. I won't let him win, if there's any way to prevent it."

"Giving your life so that we might live?"

Toreth didn't recognize the quotation, but he could spot irony. "Fuck, no. If it comes to that, you won't see me for dust."

"Just checking. I'd hate to be thinking about throwing my lot in with someone who's completely fucking insane."

"So you'll do it?"

Bevan drained his cup, coughed, and stared down into it. "I said I was thinking about it."

Toreth waited while Bevan considered the proposal, or pretended to. He didn't have much doubt as to the outcome. Bevan lived for his job here, for the considerable personal power he'd hoarded over the years and the niche he'd cut for himself. Without his post as I&I Head of Security, and with the people he knew so much about dead or dispersed, he'd be nothing more than a late-fifties bureaucrat with a string of ex-wives who according to rumor got together once a year to burn him in effigy, and a CV that wouldn't endear him to anyone in the new Administration.

Prompting seemed to be required, though, and persuasion. Bevan liked to feel that he was being obliging. Toreth moved to the edge of his chair and spoke quietly. "I need your help, Bev. If you say no then I might as well start running now, because I can't do this without you."

Bevan looked up and shook his head. "I can see how you got that fucking spook bending over for you. Switch it off, for Christ's sake." He waited another few seconds, then said, "I can't say as I give a shit for many of the interrogators, or most of the paras come to that, but it'll be my fucking pleasure to screw Carnac over. I'm in."

Toreth grinned, not hiding his relief.

"So what's the plan?" Bevan continued.

"I haven't got one yet. I wasn't kidding about needing you. If you'd said no, I'd have been booking tickets out of here by now."

Bevan nodded, looking even more morose than usual, which meant he was pleased. "Well, yell when you want me."

"Before I can do anything or talk to anyone, I need to know about the interior surveillance. What can Carnac see?"

"Everything that you can see from your office—you've got all the clearance there is."

"I know about all the official surveillance. But I don't know about whatever else is out there."

Bevan's eyes crinkled in what was nearly a smile. "Well, I've got a few little tricks. I had feeds from the director's office, from—"

"*Carnac's* office? Fuck. Can you put that through to me?"

"I said 'had.' About the only positive thing Captain Clueless managed to do was rip it out. From there, and a few other offices the Service people are in now."

Toreth bet he knew exactly where the orders to remove those feeds had come from. He also had the acutely uncomfortable feeling that Carnac had seen this moment, this conversation, coming a long time ago and planned for it. If he closed his eyes, he'd see black and white squares all around him and feel Carnac's hand, moving him across the board. It was paranoia. Nothing but stress and paranoia. Right now, though, "cut and run" didn't seem like such a bad option. If Carnac would let him go, which was a bloody big if.

"Toreth?"

"Sorry. Thinking. What about senior paras?"

"Office surveillance was on the original plans, but the tight-arsed bastards cut it for cost. So they're all clean, except a few I keep a special eye on—you don't rate that, by the way. Not before today, anyway. I'll have to put something in."

Possibly a joke, but as Bevan's expression didn't change he couldn't be sure.

"A few other places," he continued. "Nothing important for this. All the comms are monitored, obviously—and that's unsecured personal comms used in the building as well. It's automatic, and the system can't pick out every dodgy call, but you might get caught by saying something stupid. If there's anything more, then it's nothing to do with me. There could be an office somewhere in Int-Sec that has us on screen right now, and the bastard upstairs could have a link to it, considering the friends he's got. But if that's true, then it's bloody well put together, because I've never found any evidence. And, believe me, I've looked."

Toreth nodded. That would have to be assurance enough. At least it set out the parameters of where was safe.

"Who else are you going to tell?" Bevan asked.

"I don't know. Probably no one, until I've got something sorted out. Except Sara, of course."

"Jesus, you could just tell everyone straight away."

He pushed down the sudden surge of anger. "She won't say anything."

"Are we talking about the same bloody admin here? Gossip queen of I&I? I didn't get my regrettably graphic knowledge of your sex life from wiring up your bedroom."

He waved the point aside. "That sort of thing doesn't matter. For the important stuff she can keep her mouth shut." Usually.

"Okay. Who else? Carnac's going to be watching you, you know. You'll need someone to get things done, and people will notice if I start running your fucking errands."

Toreth considered. Sara was his first choice, but Carnac would be watching her, too, and besides, she was already too busy. B-C and Mistry might attract less attention, but while they were good investigators he wasn't confident of their skills as conspirators. "What about Chevril?"

"Don Chevril? Senior Para? He's a pillock."

"True. But he's a pillock I've known for a long time, and he owes me. He's a senior, he's got the rank to get things done. Besides, he's still on the sick at the moment, so he can limp back in and potter around for me without it looking suspicious."

Bevan shrugged. "If you think you can trust him. Prat. At least don't tell him until you absolutely fucking have to. When you've got a plan and you need some help. No point going out of our way to make sure Carnac hears what's going on."

"Fair enough." Toreth looked at his watch, surprised by how much time had passed. "I've got things to do. Work hasn't stopped just because Carnac wants to kill everyone."

"Yeah." Bevan leaned back in his chair, and looked thoughtfully at the ceiling. "It all makes sense, you know."

"What does?"

"I've been shoving screenfuls of requisitions and orders across that wanker's desk and he's signed off every sodding thing without a murmur. I've been tempted to try putting a case of scotch past him, see if he notices. But of course he isn't going to care about the bloody budget, is he, if his major future expense is fucking cremations?"

Carnac must be getting a huge kick out of that. Laughing at the lot of them as they went about their doomed lives while he counted down the days. Well, the bastard was going to regret it, that was for sure. Knowing about Carnac's plan was the first step towards stopping it. Now he just had to work out what the hell he was going to do.

"So?" Sara asked, following Toreth into his office. "What's going on?"

She'd been waiting for him to get back ever since Carnac had been and gone. From the socioanalyst's manner—unusually readable—she'd known that something was up.

Toreth paused, halfway into his chair, then sat down. "We're in shit, that's what's going on."

"Carnac?"

He nodded. "Short version: he's planning to drive a pack of his traitor friends through here and bounce them into taking I&I apart while they're still throwing up from the shock of seeing how the real world works."

The short version was too short for her to handle in a single piece. "Taken apart?"

"Yes. We're going to be shut down, dismantled, and—this is the good part—executed. Paras, interrogators, and probably investigators. Basically, it looks like anyone who's done the interrogation intro course is for it."

Her first instinct was to say it couldn't happen. That only lasted long enough for her to remember her walk through the bloodstained interrogation levels. Judicial murders, with Carnac's hand guiding them, would be just another facet of the hatred that had fueled the slaughter there. "What about the admins?" she asked.

Toreth shrugged. "Don't know. He didn't say anything about any of the support staff."

"But that doesn't mean—" Then her brain caught up with his words. "He didn't *say* anything?"

Toreth nodded. "It's all straight from the horse's mouth, courtesy of Daedra and a far more enjoyable fucking than he deserved."

"So that's where you were last night. Warrick did wonder, and so did I. Why didn't you tell me what you were doing?"

Toreth shrugged. "I don't take chances where Carnac's concerned. The fewer people who knew about it beforehand, the better."

"I wouldn't have told him."

He didn't say anything. She wanted to say it wasn't fair, but she couldn't. She'd talked to Carnac before, and told him things about Toreth that only she knew. Even though it had been three years ago, and although it had happened before either of them had appreciated what Carnac was, Toreth wasn't interested in excuses. He had a long memory for betrayals of his trust. "I wouldn't have told him," she repeated. Then, seeing him start to frown, she added, "It doesn't matter now, anyway. What're we going to do?"

"I'm still working it through. But I know one thing—he's not going to get what he wants. When he walks out of here for the last time, I&I is going to be as rock solid as ever. I'm going to fuck him a lot more thoroughly than I did last night."

Her heart sank at the determination in his voice. She'd been thinking more about how they could get away. "Are you... sure that's the best thing?"

He stared at her, surprised. "What the fuck else can we do? Let him execute everyone?"

"No, of course not!" Blood. Blood and bodies—people she knew. Friends. "But maybe we should be thinking about the longer term than just screwing up Carnac's plans."

His eyes narrowed. "Such as?"

"Toreth, if we survive this one, what's to stop it all from happening again in a few years? Next year? Give Carnac what he wants. Shut I&I down before his inspection and that'll be the end of it. He said we were an anachronism and maybe he was right about that. Nobody wants us, not really—they were just too frightened to speak out." Not her words. They sounded strange, even to her own ears. She'd been angry when Rob had said it but now, through the filter of fear, it made a lot more sense.

"Well, well, well." Toreth leaned back in his chair, appearing interested rather than annoyed. "Where's all this coming from? I can't see you being suddenly struck with revolutionary fervor. Or spontaneously joining Carnac's crusade, not even given his usual wet-knickers effect on you. So it must be something else. Some*one* else, maybe?"

Oh, hell. He was too good at this. She must have given something away, because he smiled. "Am I getting warmer? How about... Rob? Rob, with his safe, clean corporate number? Putting in a hard night's work, sitting on his arse, drinking Warrick's coffee and fucking his guests. Rescuing pussycats."

She wasn't going to rise to the bait. "It's got nothing at all to do with R—with McLean. I'm—" I'm frightened. He wouldn't want to hear that, and wouldn't care anyway. "I'm just trying to be realistic. This isn't section politics with Tillotson, or fighting Psychoprogramming over budgets. This is Carnac we're talking about. Do you really want to play against him for those kinds of stakes?"

Toreth ignored her question. "Does McLean think his nice little world would stay safe if we all packed up and went home? Or maybe we should let the resisters go around blowing up re-education centers and inciting discontent? That sort of thing isn't going to go away just because Carnac and his friends are in charge now. All it comes down to in the end is that McLean is too fucking gutless to accept what has to be done. He's no different from Carnac."

Although she had no obligation at all to defend him, she couldn't help it—not for that. "He's nothing of the kind. Just shut up!"

"Hey, you're the one who wanted to talk politics. Now you see why I never bother discussing that kind of bollocks with *my* fucks."

It was far too late, but she tried for icy dignity. "For your information, I'm not screwing him."

"Really?" He put his hands behind his head. "Well, maybe you should be. It might put you in a better mood, at least. I see I see?"

ICIC. Insufficient Cock In Cunt.

After that, the choice was between hitting him, and leaving. The problem with Toreth, one of the many problems with him, was that he was too damn fast to land a punch on. So she left.

She'd been at her desk for five minutes when Toreth came out of his office. For a moment, she thought he would apologize, but of course he didn't. "I'm going to see Warrick. If anyone turns up..." He frowned. "Just tell them something. B-C's in charge while I'm gone. I'll be back later."

It was only after he'd gone that she realized he was frightened, too. She should have seen it in the office, hidden behind the taunting. Or at least, if he wasn't scared in the same way that she was by the mere idea of Carnac wanting them dead, then he was deeply unnerved by the scale of the threat. And he hadn't suggested a single thing they could do about it.

Carnac had declined to travel to this session of the New Administrative Council in person, something for which he was now profoundly grateful. A flight or train journey to Brussels first thing that morning would have been insupportable; a comm link was quite bad enough.

Over the course of the meeting, the proportion of Carnac's attention devoted to listening to his esteemed colleagues slipped from ninety percent to somewhere around five. Mutual congratulation was the order of the day, and it always pained Carnac to see people who had so little justification for it feeling pleased with themselves.

He had half an hour's entertainment flicking the view away from the current speaker to watch the rest, picking out the beginnings of bitter rivalries and backstabbing emerging among the participants. In many ways, the New Administrative Council was not easy to distinguish from the old, and the comparison both amused and disgusted him. He'd set out with grand plans for reform, and he'd ended up here, with his achievements constrained as ever by the inadequacies of others.

Still, with these tools, however blunt, he would at least achieve something. The more idealistic resister networks he had found and investigated were pathetically ill-organized. Worse, they were so out of touch with political and social reality that examining their so-called "plans" was nothing short of depressing. He'd been forced by circumstances to turn a number of them in to Int-Sec—many of those had no doubt ended up at I&I. Cruel as that seemed, it had been necessary to keep his reputation intact and above suspicion, as well as to unify and strengthen the overall resistance movement. While he deeply regretted it in one way, from another perspective he couldn't help feeling it had only improved the net intellectual quality of the human race.

He'd settled on this uninspiring coalition of dissatisfied corporates and dissidents within the Administration and Service because they were at least marginally competent. More importantly, they appreciated the role he had played in the coup and understood (as he had made a point of ensuring they did) that without him they would have got nowhere. They were manipulable, and currently grateful enough to him that they would serve as his instrument of destruction. Not, regrettably, sufficiently grateful that they had been willing to eliminate I&I straight away. There was simply too much inertia in favor of the status quo. Hours of debate and weasel words had boiled down to the summary that they might not like the idea of torture, but they accepted it as a useful and necessary tool. The ends justified the means, so long as they didn't have to think about them too much.

Well, he'd damn well *make* them think, and see, if he had to drag each one of them into an interrogation room with his own hands.

When it was all over, he might go, or stay on, depending on how much longer he could stand their self-interested hypocrisy. Not long, he suspected, since they were beginning to bore him already and that always lowered his resistance. Nor was he so certain of their stamina in power that he was willing to tie his name to theirs irrevocably. For now, he would participate in their interminable meetings, and keep an eye on them while he thought about other things.

Today, it was his current star pawn that occupied him. Toreth.

With the hangover an unpleasant fading memory, he reassessed the encounter at his hotel. The sex itself wasn't entirely surprising, given the starting point of the evening. Buoyed by the excellent progress of the plan so far, by the nearness of his final goal, he had allowed himself to become careless. Toreth's newly acquired scar had clearly failed in its role as reminder of that man's dangerous nature and violence. Why it had done so was something he felt compelled to think about, although he doubted he would like the answer.

"Hated" was perhaps too strong a word, or perhaps not, but at the least he deeply disliked Toreth. He despised him, for what he represented and for his unpleasantly damaged psyche. At the same time, he recognized that, physically, Toreth was extremely attractive, and he was, when he chose to be, a skillful lover. In all honesty, Carnac was forced to admit that under the right circumstances the latter considerations might outweigh the former. He was accustomed to sex with men he despised, because there were so few who fell outside that category.

Keir Warrick was one of those few. He almost regretted now that he had let the days in Keir's flat go past without any attempt at greater intimacy, but it had been painfully obvious that Warrick was caught up with the fate of his paramour and family. Trying to seduce him then would have been tactless and counterproductive. He smiled, unconsciously. There would be time enough to remedy that omission later. For now, he disciplined his mind back to the hotel.

He had been drunk—extremely drunk. Although it was probably too late to have a screen done, it was likely that Toreth had found a way of administering some kind of drug or drugs as well. That would economically explain both the alarming degree of memory loss and the fact that he had been induced to drink as much as he had.

He did wonder why Toreth had bothered. "Pathologically unfaithful" might be an acceptable working description of Toreth's sex life, but he was by no means out of control. It was a pathetic defensive mechanism to shield him from feelings he feared, and to that extent it was compulsive in the extreme. However, he was certainly capable of choosing who he fucked, and when, and in what condition. So why had he chosen Carnac, and gone to so much trouble to have him? A desire to rub his face in it the next morning was the most obvious explanation. The combination of revenge and physical gratification would certainly appeal to Toreth.

Fortunately for the peace of his remaining time at Int-Sec, the plan had been fatally flawed. It surprised him that Toreth hadn't realized that he was placing power in Carnac's hands by setting up the encounter. However, he knew from previous experience that Toreth was accomplished at banishing Warrick from his mind while he perpetrated his serial infidelities. In any case, a more pressing problem was what he might have said to Toreth. He hoped that, even drunk, he had had the sense to keep his mouth closed about his plans for I&I. What if he had let something slip?

The most likely outcomes were that Toreth might run, or he might plot against him. Running would be an irritation, although not a major one, because the work of restoring I&I was well underway. It would disturb his plans, but not damage them significantly. Besides, he doubted that Toreth would do anything of the kind. The man was psychologically incapable of it, unless absolutely convinced that he had no other choice, and his native arrogance made that unlikely.

That left the second option. Carnac smiled again, at the idea of Toreth trying to outmaneuver him. He almost hoped he had been a little indiscreet. At least it would in some small way alleviate the current stirrings of boredom.

The sim room wasn't one Toreth had been in before—a clearing in a forest, which fuzzed out a few yards into the trees, suggesting that the room wasn't completed yet. They stood in a tangled garden of vivid flowers crammed into tiny beds. Narrow paths, paved in multicolored pebbles, wound between them. A grassy orchard held a few apple trees, bearing an improbable mix of blossom and fruit. In the center of the garden stood a small house—cottage, he thought the correct term was. The building was as colorful as the garden, its shiny brown walls patterned and painted. The warm breeze carried a strange smell, out of place in a countryside setting. He couldn't identify it—something sweet and spicy.

"What do you think?" Warrick asked.

The most tactful thing he could think of was, "It's a bit... twee."

Warrick laughed. "Special room for a well-paying customer. It's adapted from a children's story."

"Never read any."

"Here, try this." Warrick bent down and broke off one of the more lurid flowers. "Go on, taste it."

Toreth took the flower and tried it dubiously. Then he spat into the flowerbed. "Oh, God. That's revolting—it's like neat sugar. Pink-flavored neat sugar."

Warrick gestured around the garden and the cottage. "It's all flavored. The house is gingerbread, which wasn't easy, texturally speaking. At the moment, it's just a shell, but when it's finished the interior will be edible as well. Silis is trying to generate something to make furniture from that's strong enough but still behaves sufficiently like toffee to satisfy the spec, without simply cheating and putting in a hard form-function override."

A fat bumblebee droned past and Toreth wondered what it would taste like, and if it would still sting. "Jesus, some people have more money than sense."

"I wouldn't dream of saying that about any of our clients." Warrick led the way over to the tiny orchard and they sat down under a tree. On closer inspection, the apples were coated in toffee and the trunk proved to be slightly sticky to the touch, but at least the grass felt normal enough.

"Well, what's so urgent that it can't wait until this evening?" Warrick asked.

"We're not on record?"

"The session is being wiped as it goes. There'll be nothing."

"Good. Right. I need to tell you something." Concise and straightforward would be best. "I didn't make it home last night because I was seeing Carnac—

outside work. I put something very relaxing in his drinks, then I fucked him, and got him to tell me what he's planning to do at I&I."

Warrick looked at him for a long moment. "Was the fuck absolutely necessary?"

"Yes."

He smiled wryly. "Technical reasons?"

"Something like that."

"So why are you telling me?"

"Well, for one thing, because I expect that Carnac will try to find some way to mention it, and if I hadn't told you first, you'd be thoroughly pissed off about it when he did."

Warrick said nothing. Well, it had been a fifty-fifty bet which way around would prove more hassle in the end.

"Warrick, if there'd been another way—"

"No, no. I understand. I was merely contemplating the fact that informing me that you had sex with someone else last night—after drugging him—falls under the heading of your being unusually considerate."

God, he hoped this wasn't going to turn into an argument. "And?"

"And I came to the conclusion that I have a strange life. Not at all how I once imagined it would turn out. However, on balance, it's not unsatisfying. Was that it?"

"Er, no." For a moment, he wondered what Warrick had really thought about it. Then he dismissed the speculation. There were more important things than Warrick being difficult. "I need you to come up with a bloody good idea. Probably several."

Warrick smiled. "I'm flattered by your confidence in my abilities."

"At the moment they could be all that's standing between the staff at I&I and a busy execution schedule."

Warrick stared, eyebrows lifting. After a moment, he said, "All the staff?"

"Paras, interrogators, and investigators. And I wouldn't put it past Carnac to include everyone down to the maintenance staff if he can get away with it."

"This is what you got from your... from last night?"

"Yes. He's going to do to the new Administration what I did to him—show them high-level interrogations. Then he's going to persuade them to give him carte blanche in stopping them."

"And carte blanche means executions?"

"Yes. I'm serious, Warrick."

"I can see that."

"He wants I&I destroyed. Finished for good. And I haven't got the first fucking clue what I'm going to do about it."

Warrick raised one eyebrow slightly. "You're asking *me* to help you save I&I?"

"Yes." Put like that, it did sound unlikely. He'd hadn't thought about—

"No. I won't do it."

Won't. No apology along with it. Clear enough this time. "Why?"

Warrick sat up straighter, considering his response carefully before he spoke. "I've never made any secret of how I feel about some of the functions of I&I. If I help, then I'm perpetuating something fundamentally wrong. Everyone who is subsequently interrogated, everyone who dies there—it would be my responsibility."

Toreth didn't believe it. No—he did believe it, he just didn't want to hear it. He clenched his fists, suddenly aware of his real body, lying in the sim couch.

"Responsibility? You fucking hypocrite." Warrick started to protest, but Toreth carried on over him. "What about all this? I remember that first fucking lecture—some stupid bastard who probably ended up on level D asked you about the applications. 'Tool for oppression' or the usual bollocks like that. I know the Administration keeps sniffing around; Psychoprogramming is still drooling for a chance to get at it once they can scrape up the budget. You're happy enough to make money off it, and you won't help me?"

By the time he finished, Warrick was pale with anger. "That is not the same."

"No? I knew what you could do with this thing the first time you showed it to me. I could reel off a dozen interrogation scenarios for the sim right now, but you know what? I don't need to, because you already know, don't you? You can pretend all you like that it won't happen, but it will. It started as an Administration project, for Christ's sake. Do you think they wanted it for fucking children's stories?"

"'All this'—" Warrick waved his hand to indicate the clearing, "—is what *I* do with the sim. I am not responsible for the uses others may wish to put it to. I can only make it as difficult for them as possible, which I also do." He was over-articulating, every word sharp with anger in the way that usually started Toreth looking forward to the make-up fuck. Not this time.

"You made it, you're fucking responsible for it, right? For everything that happens with it afterwards. Seems simple enough to me."

"No doubt. But if you cannot, or will not, see the distinction between helping to invent a technology which may have undesirable applications and helping to protect a collection of—an organization whose sole function is destructive, then I think the discussion is over."

He was right about that, anyway. He could recognize Warrick being insufferably, infuriatingly stubborn when he saw it. "'Sole function is destructive'? That could be considered seditious, you know—defamation of the Administration or a part thereof."

A childish, spiteful threat, which didn't impress Warrick at all. "Really?" He smiled faintly. "Apparently not under Carnac's new definitions."

No, now Toreth was probably the treasonous one. "So…what? You make a fuss over us annexing a few resisters, but you're happy to let that bastard kill everyone?"

Warrick looked at him sharply. "No, I'm not happy about that, and if it had to include you, I'd be very unhappy indeed. But it doesn't."

"You mean I should walk away and let the fucker win?"

"Yes. He gave you the chance before, he'll do it again."

"No. No fucking way. No fucking way in hell. Clear?"

"Admirably." Cool and precise.

That left only one important question. "Are you going to tell him that I know?"

Warrick looked down at the grass, pulling virtual blades between his fingers, releasing a faint scent of mint into the already sickly air. Eventually, he shook his head. "No. But it's not necessary. Not where that place is concerned."

"What the fuck do you know about us?"

"I'm not claiming a comprehensive knowledge of I&I, but I do know that if you try to implement any kind of plot again Carnac, he will find out about it. There will be too many people involved. And—" He began placing his words carefully, like fragile crystal, which was always a bad sign. "Someone told me once about the psychological profile of interrogators and para-investigators. I can't provide a citation, but it's not one conducive to successful conspiracies where personal danger is involved. Someone will betray the plan in the hope of saving their own skin."

Toreth stared at him, speechless with fury.

"If you still want my opinion and advice, then—" Warrick shrugged. "You know what it is."

Fuck you, basically.

Warrick lifted his hand, his fingers moving to click for the control panel. Toreth leaned forwards and grabbed his wrist. "I'm going to stop him," he said quietly. "I'm going to think of something, and I'm going to make it work, and you're going to take back every fucking word of that and apologize for it, before I fucking touch you again."

Then he let him go.

Warrick snapped his fingers and the control console appeared in the air beside him. Toreth noticed distractedly that it had acquired a pink sugar trim. "Ending the session now," Warrick said.

Back at the flat that evening, Warrick wasn't surprised to find only Sara there. She was in her room, packing. Bastard sat in a carrier cage on the bed, ears flat, growling intermittently. "What happened?" she asked. "I've never seen him in a mood that bad."

It was obvious that she didn't mean the cat, which seemed to be in a perfectly normal state.

"We had an argument, that's all. Nothing more exciting than that. Has he gone already?"

"Yes—back to his flat. He said to tell you he's borrowed a few things and thanks for all the hospitality. Well, that's not how he phrased it, but it's what he meant."

Nothing more than he'd expected, but it still caused a tiny twinge of something. Irritation at Toreth's utterly predictable reaction, or possibly regret. He'd enjoyed having Toreth living here more than he ever imagined he would, even though they had both been exhausted for most of the time and had, in fact, seen surprisingly little of each other. Perhaps that had helped.

"You're welcome to stay, of course," he told her.

She shook her head. "I don't think that would be a good idea. You know what he's like."

"Jealous, irrational, demanding, and utterly unreasonable covers most of the relevant attributes."

She grinned. "Just about. Do you want me to tell him anything tomorrow?"

"Thank you, but no. I think a cooling down period is in order. Do you have somewhere to go?"

"My sister said I could stay for a while. Have you ever met her?"

He shook his head.

"She's great—you'd like her." She smiled again. "And she'll let me creep in bed with her if I need to. Only problem is she's miles from work. Closer than Mum and Dad, but still a pain. I put in a housing request, but I bet it'll take forever. I might be back yet."

He wondered how much she knew about the events at I&I—everything, he guessed. Toreth hadn't specified that the admins were in danger. "You are always welcome. And..."

She put down the clothes she was holding. "What?"

"Should you wish to consider a change of employer, I'm always interested in talented administrative staff."

"Oh." She sat down on the bed. "So that was what you were arguing about. He asked you to help?"

"Yes. It seemed to come as a surprise to him that I declined."

"'Course it did. Oh, fuck. He's going to be..." She sighed. "It's always me who suffers for it, you know."

She wasn't entirely joking. "I'm sorry for that, at least."

"Forget it. I understand. I mean—I even think you're right. In a way, anyway—mostly the way that Carnac scares the shit out of me, to tell the truth. You know what he was like before, and that..."

"Was for his personal amusement, yes."

"He's going to enjoy this, too. God, in that interrogation room, he was so..." She shook her head. "I told Toreth we should shut the place down. At least that way everyone gets to live."

"And?"

“He said no.” She frowned slightly. “And a few other things. Couldn’t you talk him out of it?”

“I didn’t really try.”

“Why the hell not?”

A good question. “For one thing, I was sidetracked into, ah, losing my temper somewhat. For another, I don’t see that it would have helped.”

After a moment, she nodded. “Probably not. Carnac’s got Toreth wound up so bloody tight about it, there’s no way he’s going to let it go. *I* don’t want the bastard to get away with it either... but not enough to get killed trying to stop him. But as long as Toreth stays, I’ve got to stay with him.”

He was, selfishly, glad. If he couldn’t keep an eye on Toreth himself, he trusted Sara to do it for him. “The offer of a job remains open indefinitely.”

“Really?” She smiled. “I’ll think about it—not just because of Carnac. It’d be fun, I bet, working at SimTech.” She looked down at the bed, briefly, and he wondered whether to ask, because he suspected he knew the reason. In the end he didn’t need to, because she said, “Is McLean here?”

“I think he’s off shift.”

She sighed. “Oh. Figures.” Before he could say anything she stood up, and continued folding clothes. “I ought to get going. I’ve got a pass, but it just gets worse later and the taxis will stop soon.”

“Stay for dinner, at least. You can use the car.”

“Yeah? Thanks.”

While she was still there, he should try to get as much as he could out of her regarding Carnac’s plan. He ought at least to know what Toreth was getting into.

Dinner had been as good as Warrick’s cooking always was, although it had been a little spoiled by his subtle but unmistakable fishing for information. Since Toreth hadn’t told her that much yet, she was saved the difficulty of not knowing what to pass on. Afterwards, he helped her carry her things down to the garage and made her promise to come back, if she needed somewhere to stay. To her surprise, as he left, McLean appeared and joined her in the car.

“Warrick asked me to go with you,” he said, as he closed the door. “Just to be sure you get there safely.”

A typically Warrick way of going about interfering in someone else’s business—set up the situation, then retire from the scene and let them make of it whatever they would.

“Okay. Thanks.” She moved across the seat, letting him sit beside her and thereby provoking a growl from the fortunately caged Bastard.

After giving the car her sister’s address, she sat back. She wasn’t sure whether she was grateful for Warrick's initiative or not. She'd avoided speaking to McLean since she'd thrown him out of her room, with the vague idea that she would talk to him again at some point, when things were calmer, but they never had been. Certainly she had regretted the idea of leaving the flat without saying goodbye to him, which must be some kind of a hint.

He sat in professionally shielded silence, so to break the ice she said, "I hope you don't mind—Warrick said it was your night off."

"There's not a lot to do down in the staff accommodation, if you don't like playing cards."

"There's not a lot to do here, either."

"We could talk," McLean said. "If you don't mind."

"What about?"

"Well, to start with, the things I said before."

She waited, not prompting him. If he said he hadn't meant them, she would tell him to forget it. If people were going to have opinions, they should have them. An honest change of mind was all right; lying to get another fuck most definitely wasn't.

"Well, what I said before wasn't exactly tactful, considering where I was and what you'd been through. I'm sorry."

Honest enough to be going on with. "Good. I mean—thanks. It's okay."

He smiled. "Thanks. So . . . what now?"

Honesty in return seemed like the best policy. "I don't know. There's too much going on, with everything, and . . . I don't want to rush into any decisions."

That was designed to sound optimistic without promising anything, and it seemed to work because he nodded. "I understand. If you'd like to get together again, dinner or something, once the curfew's lifted, let me know? You can do your dating plan the wrong way round."

She smiled. "Yeah, sure. When everything's back to normal."

The rest of the journey passed in pleasant enough conversation, leaving her in a good enough mood that when they reached her sister's flat, she invited him in to say hello to Fee. However, he declined and, after walking her up to the door of the building, he left her there.

She lingered, watching him get back into the car and be driven away. She hadn't been sure before that he'd been serious in her bedroom. He really wanted there to be a "what now" that wasn't simply another night or two. What did she want?

It felt too complicated for right now. Something else that could satisfyingly be blamed on Carnac, the bastard. If it hadn't been for this morning's bombshell, she might have been able to think things through sensibly. The idea crossed her mind that Rob would probably get on well with Carnac—they certainly shared the same opinion of I&I. On the other hand, so did Warrick, and somehow things worked out for him and Toreth. Not that they were much of a pattern for a normal relationship. She found herself envying them again, though, because despite all the fights and difficult compromises and, okay, the plain *weirdness* of what they had, they still had it. All she had was the cat grumbling in the cage at her feet.

Now she was feeling sorry for herself again. She had family, and plenty of friends, and her job at I&I, which she loved—or had loved. The idea that she might seriously be thinking about changing her life because of the opinions of a one-night stand didn't appeal. Had she liked the sound of Warrick's offer because of Rob, or because of the fear she still felt every time she walked into I&I, every time she stepped into the lifts there—even every time she made a bloody coffee?

Or was it the new awareness of how fragile things were? A consciousness of time ticking past, brought on by four days of believing that it had nearly run out? Abandoning I&I could give her freedom from the fear, a new job, a new relationship. As Fee kept pointing out, she was getting older and... leave it. She'd think about it again, when imminent execution occupied less of her attention.

Picking up the cage, she pressed the comm. "Fee? Yeah, it's me."

Chapter Nine

❖

The next day, Toreth had hoped to take some time off from I&I to devote to Carnac's threat, but he was tied to the building by the influx of prisoners. It didn't help that he now knew his response to the problem had played right into Carnac's hands. Every arrival reminded him of how beautifully he'd been manipulated—used—and brought another distracting surge of anger.

The newly released paras and interrogators presented a fresh set of headaches. A surprisingly large number of them had accepted the re-employment offer—or not that surprising, factoring in the common rumor that refusal was a shortcut to arrest and execution. After careful consideration, he hadn't tried too hard to dispel it. He needed the staff and the truth of the situation would become clear with time. One way or another.

Interrogations had begun already, bringing still more trouble. He dealt with problems with the interrogation levels, with the cells, with the scarcity of drugs, and the fact that the medical section had no space for prisoners. He'd even had a few people make it past Sara with complaints about broken furniture and missing admins. He told them, as politely as he could manage, to fuck off and tell someone who cared.

In his office, between work and interruptions to work, he thought about Carnac's plan. He talked it over briefly with Bevan, and later with Sara, but he didn't want to show either of them exactly how uncertain he was; Sara was frightened enough already, and he couldn't risk spooking Bevan. He wished he could discuss it with Warrick, but Warrick had made it absolutely clear what he thought about the situation and Toreth's own heat-of-the-moment declaration about apologies had destroyed any remaining possibility of a truce.

Briefly, he even considered whether Bell could be brought into play against Carnac. However, she despised I&I as much as he did—if she couldn't guarantee its loyalty to the Service, she'd happily let Carnac destroy it. Besides, once he told her anything, he might as well write what he knew in five-meter letters on the side of the building.

During the day, the new Administration announced that the curfew would move back to ten. So, after leaving work as early as he could, he went out and tried thinking about the problem over a drink in one of the bars that immediately reopened at the news. If he didn't find inspiration, his reasoning went, he might at least find a distraction.

Other customers were thin on the ground, though, and the atmosphere dead. People were probably too scared to come out. He turned down a couple of offers without thinking about it, and went home when the bar closed at half past nine.

Back in the flat, he tidied up, or at least moved the debris around. He stacked broken furniture in the corner of the living room; he could throw it out some other time, although there wasn't any reason not to do it now. There weren't likely to be complaints about the noise, because the building was half empty—most of the tenants had been Int-Sec staff. His neighbors on both sides seemed to have gone—dead or not he had no idea.

Pity Warrick wasn't here—for once, Warrick could be as loud as he liked without generating tedious notes from the building administrator.

The gear was indisputably gone. He checked around the bedroom, knowing Warrick would've searched, but hoping anyway. All that remained were the leather straps on the bedposts, and even they somehow looked wrong. Everything out of place, everything damaged in some way.

The heating was barely functional and the place was freezing. At least building maintenance had repaired the door, or tried to, and the broken windows had been sealed over. The looters had left the bed and the sofa, although most of the kitchen was gone. He'd have to get a new fridge, if he was going to stay. Not that he had anywhere else to go.

Living at Warrick's had been... convenient. Being able to walk in at night and not have to worry about anything had meant more than he'd thought. It had been fun having Sara around. Then there'd been the good food, laundry service, a warm, comfortable bed... and when he caught himself thinking about what else he'd be missing, he put his mind firmly back to the problem at I&I.

Tomorrow morning he would be buried once more under mundane but important tasks that would only distract him. Carnac would still be there and the deadline would be another day nearer. Toreth sat on the sofa and drank beer, and thought his way through a dozen dead-end plans, all of which served only to highlight what a good idea it would be to run like fuck. Carnac would love that. He'd watch Toreth scuttle back off to hide under Warrick's protection, then he'd tear I&I to pieces. Compared to Carnac triumphant, execution didn't seem so bad.

Eventually, since there was nothing else to do and he was tired, he went to bed, without undressing. Lying in the chilly darkness, shivering, anger stirred—directed primarily at Warrick. He'd been utterly unreasonable yesterday. He should've helped because... and Toreth ran up against a dead end. There was a sense of obligation he didn't care to examine too closely, and also the fact that Warrick hadn't—apparently—felt the same, which was even worse. Whatever it was, it was entirely Warrick's fucking fault.

Then, somewhat to his surprise, he discovered it was one o'clock in the morning and he still couldn't sleep.

"You're drunk," Chevril said, two seconds after he opened the door. He wore only a pair of pajama bottoms, slit at the side to accommodate the cast on his ankle. He stayed blocking the doorway, leaning on his crutch and looking less than pleased to see Toreth.

"Not much, but well spotted. I suppose that's why they made you a senior in the end." He heard a laugh from behind Chevril and looked past him to see Elena standing at the far end of the hall, dressed in a startling red silk nightdress. "Hi, beautiful, how're you?"

She came to stand behind Chevril, almost a head taller than her husband. "Very well, thank you," she said, unruffled as always. "You?"

"Go back to bed," Chevril said to her, over his shoulder. "And *you* can just go. What the hell do you want at this bloody time of night?"

"Well, either I've come to declare my undying love for Elena, or I've come to talk to you. Which do you think?"

Chevril didn't move to let him in. "Come back in the morning, sober, and try again."

"Don't be rude, Don." Elena moved Chevril gently aside. "Come in, Toreth. What's wrong?"

He slipped inside quickly, closing the door behind him. "I need to talk to Chev about something. Something important."

He heard a strangled protest from Chevril, but he and Elena both ignored it. "Come through to the living room. Would you like something to drink while Don's putting on some proper clothes?"

"No, thanks. I think I've had enough already."

They sat on the sofa in the living room, and made small talk while Chevril grumbled off to dress. Toreth liked talking to Elena, or at least listening to her, because she had the kind of soft, low, amused voice that it was easy to imagine hearing in bed. The view wasn't bad either—flawless olive skin, hair like a black waterfall and a beautifully proportioned body, tall and slender. Shown off to perfection by the nightgown, too.

"Toreth?"

He blinked. "Sorry?"

"I said, how is Warrick?"

They'd only met once, but she always asked after him. He felt a flicker of irritation. "Fine, probably. We had a huge fucking row and I'm not seeing him until... well, sometime. If ever."

She smiled, amused or sympathetic, he couldn't tell. "I'm sorry to hear that."

"Right, I'm here." Chevril limped back into the room, dressed but clearly not in a better mood.

Toreth smiled at Elena. "I hate to say it, but I need to talk to Chev alone."

"Of course." She rose gracefully. "Don't keep Don up too long."

He watched her leave, thinking that she looked ten years younger than she must be.

Chevril lowered himself carefully into a chair. "If you've finished eying up my wife, do you think you could get on with whatever it is so I can get back to bed with her?"

He'd had practice at summarizing Carnac's plan, but Chevril proved the hardest to convince so far. The way he'd obtained the information was, surprisingly, the thing he had the least difficulty with.

"Everyone? Executed as in *dead*? Are you sure?" he asked, after Toreth had run through it for the third time.

"Yes. Absolutely. Listen, if I had the drug list, I'd show you what I gave him. He's got beautiful genetics for that sort of thing—you couldn't ask for anyone more susceptible. He was well gone, but he wasn't hallucinating and he wasn't making it up for me. Textbook confession, if you don't include the fucking. I almost wish I'd taped it, if it wasn't too dangerous to have around."

"Oh, God, no." Chevril shuddered. "Jesus, talk about an image I don't need. Okay, say I believe you. What next?"

"That's what I don't know. I can't see a way of getting rid of Carnac, short of killing him, and he's the kind of forward-thinking bastard who'd have a plan in place to cover that. I can't see a way of stopping the inspection, either. But if I don't think of something soon, it'll be too fucking late to matter."

"Um. I see." Chevril frowned, sucking his teeth thoughtfully. Eventually he looked up and said, "Can't we make sure there's nothing for them to see? No interrogations?"

Toreth had thought of that himself. "He'd just bring the inspectors back. Or show them recordings—there are plenty of those around."

"I didn't mean just for the morning. I meant, change the whole system completely. Stop interrogations. You've got the authority to do it, haven't you?"

"Stop interrogations?"

"That's what I said. Bloody hell, it's not that complicated, is it?"

"No, it's..." Extremely simple, actually, although he hadn't thought of it. He turned the idea over, examining it. "I&I without Interrogation?"

"Well... no. I didn't mean that. There'd have to be some. We'd have to rewrite the P&P, that's all. Let's see." Chevril leaned back in his chair and stared at the ceiling. "Level one, level two stay in, of course. No one can have a problem with verbal only, can they? Levels three and four...may be okay, if we tighten up the medical guidelines for the level four drugs. Level five if—no. Cut all the neural induction—better to be on the safe side. And definitely nothing with tissue damage, so that leaves us with nothing level five or higher. Keeps it simple, anyway." He looked back at Toreth. "What do you think?"

It would never work. "What about the prisoners who won't crack for one to four? We let them go, drop the charges?"

"Why not? If the new Administration doesn't like unsolved cases, then they can come up with something. Not our problem. And anyway, I don't know about you, but I won't miss all the screaming. Gives me a migraine."

"It's..." He hunted for reasons, trying to work out why the idea felt so wrong. "It'd be unprofessional."

"And we'll be able to do a good professional job from the crematorium, will we?"

There was that. "Okay. Maybe. But Carnac won't like it. Not one little bit."

"I thought it was high-level interrogations he had the twitch over?"

"He thinks we're dangerous animals that need putting down. He really believes it. You had to hear it."

Chevril grimaced. "No, thanks. So this isn't going to do the trick for him?"

"No. He wants everyone *dead,* it's that simple. Classic resister obsessive, in fact. The Socioanalysis higher-ups would go into spasms if they heard him—their psych screening must be shot to shit. But he'd put a stop to everything as soon as he got wind of it."

"Yeah, you're right. Sorry. Stupid idea."

He was about to agree, when it struck him that, stupid or not, at least it *was* an idea, which was more than he'd managed to come up with. Why else was he here? He sat and thought it over, while Chevril watched him.

There were problems—a lot of problems. But fundamentally, it seemed sound. If there were no interrogations for the inspectors to see, and no reason to think there would be again, then Carnac's plan was sunk. He thought about Sara, suggesting that they shut I&I and give Carnac what he wanted. This was much better—it would be exactly what Carnac didn't want and he'd have to swallow it anyway, because the new Administration would love it. Comprehensive reform of I&I, something he'd heard dozens of prisoners mewling about.

"You're a genius, Chev."

"Am I?" He looked pleased, but wary. "What about Carnac?"

"We don't tell him. It can work. The hard part is going to be rewriting the Protocols, just because there's so much of it. And then putting it all into the computers for when the inspectors start nosing around. I'll have to have a word with someone in Systems." He ran through it again, looking for critical flaws that would sink the whole idea. "We don't know the date—that's going to make it harder."

"I thought he said two weeks?"

"Yeah, but not exactly two weeks. Could've been two weeks to the day, or a couple either side. It was no use asking for a date at that point—my fuckup. I should've pressed for it when he was sharper. But once it's done we can have everything ready to go, and brief the teams the day the inspection turns up."

"Or the day before—that'd be better. And even then we'll need to bring a few more people in beforehand. Some of the seniors, so it'll all happen smoothly. And the bloody interrogators." Chevril shook his head. "It'll be a bloody miracle if Carnac doesn't twig."

"Doesn't matter, if it's too late and he can't do anything. He'll have to bite his tongue and let it go."

Chevril looked at him dubiously. "Carnac?"

"If we do it right, yes." He grinned, savoring the words. "We'll have him and there won't be a fucking thing he'll be able to do about it."

They talked for a while longer, and then Chevril started looking pointedly at his watch. To Toreth's surprise, Elena reappeared to show him out of the flat. On the doorstep, she stopped him, with her hand on his arm. "Warrick," she said, then stopped. After couple of seconds, he nodded, uncertain.

She seemed to take that as permission, because she glanced over her shoulder, then said, "Call him tomorrow. Whatever you fought about... these things can be always be mended." She smiled slightly, mysteriously. "Always. I know."

He nodded again, surprised that she'd said anything at all. There was a last flash of red silk as she closed the door, and he shook his head. She was wasted on Chev, she really was.

He didn't call Warrick, of course. He had far too much to do, and anyway he'd made a promise. No way was he crawling back before he'd done what he said he'd do—he might as well buy a new collar, put it on, and hand Warrick the chain. Instead, as soon as he arrived at work on Saturday, Toreth explained the plan to Sara. She seemed approving and (to his relief) unfazed by the prospect of rewriting the Procedures and Protocols.

She called it up on her screen, and a depressingly large document it looked. After she'd skipped through it, she said, "If all you want to do is cut the top levels, it won't be too hard."

"It needs new guidelines for when to finish interrogations, that kind of thing—happy, fluffy resister stuff. Then it needs going through with a fine-tooth comb to make sure there aren't any references in there to high-level procedures. You could split the remaining levels on the old upper level/lower level divisions, and then we'll be back to eight. Should make it easier to keep things consistent."

She nodded. "Good idea. B-C and I can do most of it, if you or Chevril check the procedures afterwards." She paused. "B-C doesn't know about any of it, does he? Do you want to tell him?"

He'd recited the story too many times already. "You can do it. Don't forget to tell him it's confidential information. It goes no further without my say-so, and make doubly sure he understands that includes Nagra if she gets in touch."

"Can I talk to Daedra about the drug sections?"

He considered. This was a problem he knew he'd have to face over and over again: who was safe? With Carnac involved, the answer was "no one." So the question became: who had to know? The new contents of the P&P had to be convincing, if they were going to sell them to the inspection as the result of careful thought and consultation.

"Yes. And call Mistry up from Medical—she's better than B-C on interview techniques, anyway. No one else, though, not without asking me first."

She nodded. "No one. I promise."

"The P&P's got to look good, Sara." He knew that she knew, but he couldn't help it. "If they think we're faking it, Carnac wins."

"Don't worry, it'll be great." She grinned. "I'm looking forward to it, actually. Make a change from running this place single-handed. I can delegate most of that—I don't know if you saw, but now that the curfew's later there are more people back in. A few in our section."

He'd been too preoccupied to notice. "Anyone else on the team?"

"Not yet, but Kel's back and a few more admins called to say they'd be in on Monday. Enough to take some of the load, anyway, while I do this." She stood up. "I'll get started with it."

No arguments this time about whether shutting the place down would be the best thing. It was reassuring—he trusted Sara's judgment, and if she thought the plan was workable, that gave him a lot more faith in it.

When she had gone, Toreth walked over to the window and looked out, considering the list of "must knows." Bevan, and soon, because he'd guess something was up and Toreth couldn't risk pissing him off. The Systems people, because they would need as long as possible to get ready. They always did. And Chevril was right—some of the seniors would have to be told, if not yet, or there would be no chance of implementing the changes at short notice. Sara was dealing with Daedra. B-C could handle the technical investigative sections in the P&P, with Mistry's help if necessary, but they'd probably need to talk to one or two of the interrogation specialists soon. Far too many already.

Much as it annoyed him, Warrick had been right. Eventually, they would pick someone willing and probably eager to sell them out, and the senior paras and interrogators were the most likely candidates. I&I had never made any secret of the criteria it used to select its staff. They'd been open with him when they'd offered him a place on the interrogator training program. Psych assessments were mostly bollocks, but still...

Across the enclosed courtyard, the building was still scarred by broken, boarded office windows. One of the remaining reminders of the troubles. However, the important thing was that there were prisoners in the cells and people at work. Worries aside, for the moment he was winning; I&I was coming alive again. All he had to do was make sure Carnac didn't kill it.

Chapter Ten

❖

Trying to fit the planning around the rest of his workload proved to be a nightmare. On Saturday and Sunday, he didn't leave the building until well after midnight, and he was back in at six, with Sara keeping the same hours. Chevril was in less, but complained a lot more. Monday was no better.

It was necessary but exhausting, and potentially suspicious if Carnac started to take note. He tried to cut back on legitimate duties where he could, but that was suspicious again, and he wasn't sure which was worse. The only thing that gave him hope, as well as worrying him slightly, was that Carnac had pulled a vanishing trick. He was out of his I&I office almost all day, only putting in brief (and irritatingly unannounced) appearances in the building. It made it easier that he wasn't around, but it also made Toreth wonder if the inspection might be closer than he'd thought.

Further evidence for that was the fact that Bell was also out of the building. She had been recalled to headquarters for an uncertain length of time and, from the rumors he heard, was not at all happy about it. It had to be Carnac behind that as well, pulling in favors to prevent her from interfering during his absence. Clearing the decks, ready for the inspectors.

The remaining Service personnel were a nuisance to work around. Payne in particular had moved from being useful, slightly annoying, and mildly amusing to being, well, a pain. Keeping him away from anything important took up more time, but Toreth was careful not to let his irritation show. The indefinite promise of sex he'd carefully built up and maintained might be all that stood between them and disaster, if Payne became suspicious.

On Monday evening, he answered the comm and found himself staring at his last missing team member.

"Wrenn?" he asked, wondering if the long hours were finally causing hallucinations.

"Yes, Para." She smiled sheepishly. "I'm sorry I didn't get in touch before."

"So am I." Wrenn, with her talents for handling computers, would be a godsend for the plan. "You're still down as missing. Where the hell are you?"

"At home, Para. I made it out of the building when it happened and..."

He nodded. "Kept your head down. Good for you. But we sent a call out days ago. Didn't you get it?"

"Yes. I—I'm not coming back."

And now he was hearing things. "Well, there's no hurry, but—"

"No, Para, I mean I'm not coming back. I wanted to tell you before I sent my official resignation. And I'm not working out the notice. If Tillotson doesn't like it, he can whistle for it."

"He isn't back yet, either. All the spineless bastards are still in hiding."

She winced a little, but her expression of resolve didn't flicker. "I'm sorry, Para, I really am. I've got family to think of."

What the fuck did that have to do with him? "Fine. Good luck."

"Para, I'm—"

He cut her off in midapology. Years. Wrenn had been on his team for bloody years. He couldn't believe how much the betrayal hurt, even though he knew she certainly wasn't alone in having cut and run. Admins and investigators had been the bulk of the nonreturners. More paras and interrogators had stayed because, really, where the fuck else could I&I's broken employees go? Corporates wouldn't be so keen to flaunt their ex-I&I bodyguards and security now.

Fucking Wrenn. Much good it would do her when Carnac rounded up the escaping rats and had them exterminated with the rest of the vermin.

On Tuesday morning, there was a tense meeting in Bevan's office. The three Systems staff in the know disagreed violently with each other about the best way to implement the changes, with irreconcilable, highly technical and, in Toreth's opinion, probably irrelevant viewpoints.

When that had been sorted out to their dissatisfaction, the techs left and he, Chevril, and Bevan discussed the question of when to tell the other seniors about the plan, and who should be told. After a long and increasingly heated argument, they ended up agreeing to draw up shortlists and choose people included on two or more lists.

When he returned from the meeting, in a simmering bad temper, he found Payne waiting in his office. In fact, he was pacing across the room, and Toreth got the impression that he'd been doing it for a while. When he entered, Payne stopped and turned towards him.

"Toreth, there's something going on, and I'd like you to tell me what."

Well, it had taken him nearly a week to work out what Sara had spotted in a morning, which probably said something about the intellectual standards of Service officer admissions.

"There's nothing going on that you don't know about already."

"I had someone from Systems up here half an hour ago. They wanted you, and when I said you weren't here and I'd take a message, they started talking about system changes. Then when they realized I didn't know what was going on, they shut up and went away quickly."

"So? That's all? Someone wanted to talk to me?" When he found out who'd been so fucking stupid, he would make sure "they" never had the chance to talk to anyone again.

"No, that's not all. Captain Shoen was looking for you because you'd canceled a tribunal sitting without warning him. And you've been away far too many times, with Sara claiming not to know where you were, for it to be nothing. What is it?"

"Have you been to Carnac?"

"No. No, I haven't. And I should've, but I wanted to give you a chance to tell me about it first."

Somehow he kept the relief out of his voice. "I'm making some changes to operations, that's all. Nothing for Carnac to worry about."

"So it won't matter if I tell him?"

Damn him.

"Yes it will. It will matter a great deal." He went over to sit on the edge of his desk, getting the story straight in his mind. "What I'm doing is something Carnac doesn't want to happen. But it's something that needs to happen—for I&I and for the whole of the Administration. I can only ask you to trust me and not to tell him."

"Toreth, I'm sorry. Believe me, I do trust you, and I don't want to do this to you. But I have my orders, direct from Carnac, requiring me to report anything like that. If you can't explain, I have to do it—I should do it anyway."

So Carnac had told him to spy. Fair enough—he'd expected no less and he certainly didn't blame Payne for it. That was the problem with the Service: ninety-nine point nine percent of the time, they did what they were told. He could only hope this would be the other point one. "Will you let me show you something first?"

Payne hesitated.

"It'll only take a few minutes, and I can do it here. Then if you still feel the same, you can go and tell Carnac. I won't try to stop you."

Payne nodded. "All right."

"Sit down," Toreth said, indicating his desk.

Payne sat, and Toreth moved behind him, leaned across him to get to the screen and brushing against his shoulder. He could have done this part before Payne sat down, but it seemed wise to take every chance he could get to improve his position. Despite his determined, dutiful expression, Payne wasn't leaning away from him. "Right. Watch this." Toreth took a step back, and let the recording play.

It was one of the late-stage interrogation habituation recordings. Shown cold, out of sequence in the program, it was famous for cracking even the cockiest of new recruits. He'd picked it up in the middle, at about the point when the darkened training rooms would start to fill with the sound of vomiting and the thuds of the fainters. Toreth had no idea what Payne's wife looked like, but the female prisoner was generically young and attractive enough to add an extra edge to the experience for him.

To his credit, and somewhat to Toreth's surprise, Payne neither threw up nor fainted. He did, however, go pale and still. After five minutes, he said, "How much longer?"

"Thirty-five minutes until she breaks. Two hours and twenty until the end of the session."

"I've seen enough."

"Sure?"

"Yes." He turned his face away from the screen. "Absolutely sure."

Toreth leaned past him again and killed the sound, leaving the picture running. He crouched down beside Payne, resting his arms on the arm of the chair. "That's what I want to stop," he said, keeping his voice quiet. "If Carnac has his way, that will keep happening, over and over. I've been here for nearly fifteen years, seeing things like that." Doing things like that, in fact. "I'm tired of it. Do you think we all enjoy what we do here? Do you think we get some kind of sick kick out of interrogating prisoners?"

"Well, I... no." That clearly was what Payne had thought, at least at some level. "My wife's cousin works here, you know—she's a medical technician. I know the people here aren't inhuman." He hesitated, eyes flicking down and back, then he added, "I know *you* aren't."

The best sign he'd had so far. "No, we aren't. We do our job, and we get despised for it—by people like Bell, to start with. But the Service doesn't have clean hands, either. Haven't you ever worked special actions?"

"A couple of times. That's not the same."

"Really? We get the survivors in here sometimes."

"It's not the same," Payne repeated firmly. "Riot suppression, breaking up illegal meetings, that's necessary for public order. That—" He waved at the screen. "That's..."

"Yes?"

"That's *cruel.*"

Clearly, the idea that interrogations might be cruel had never occurred to him before. It still stunned Toreth sometimes that people could delude themselves so comprehensively about what other people did to keep them safe. He nodded, serious. "Yes, it is."

Payne glanced at the screen, then looked away and swallowed heavily. "Turn it off. Please."

When the screen went black there was a brief silence, then Payne asked, "Have you tried to persuade Carnac that things need to change?"

"No, and there's no point trying it, either. He knows what goes on here. He did a report on I&I, a few years back, praising our good work—I can show you a copy if you like."

"Has he seen that?"

"More than that—he's been in a live interrogation." Fragments came back of his own early days, before the reflexive responses to the stench of shit and vomit had been trained out. He let the memories through to color his voice. "And let me tell you, that's nothing like sitting in an office and watching it. What the microphones don't pick up, what you can smell... Carnac knows what it's like. If you asked him, he'd tell you it disgusted him. But he chose to come back here and get I&I running again, didn't he? Do you think he'd be here if he didn't want to be?"

Payne shook his head. "Toreth, what you say might be right, but I've got my orders." Now it was an excuse, not a statement of fact. He wanted to be persuaded.

"You want me to find you a way around the wording? I could do that—there'll be something, if you look hard enough. What did he tell you to look for? Something against the orders to get I&I up and running? Something against the best interests of the Administration?"

Payne started to speak and Toreth cut him off. "But if you're going to do this, I need you to do it because you want to. Because you believe it's the right thing to do. I don't want you using some excuse that means I don't know if I can rely on you tomorrow."

He waited out the seconds while Payne pretended to himself that he was thinking it through. Then he nodded. "All right. Yes."

He put his hand on Payne's arm—friendly grip, nothing more. "Thanks."

"No, don't. I'm going to pretend that I haven't seen anything at all."

"I won't mention anything about it again, I promise." He stood up and leaned on the desk, studying Payne. Only ninety percent convinced, and that was an optimistic estimate. If he changed his mind and went to Carnac, everything would come crashing down in ruins. He needed a stronger hold over him. "Do you play squash?" Toreth asked.

Payne looked up, frowning. "Do I what?"

"Play squash. I heard a rumor that the gym was open again today."

"Yes, I do. Or I used to, a bit. I'm pretty rusty, I should think."

"We can take an hour or so—get away from this damn place for a while. I'm beginning to feel like I live here."

"I don't know. I mean..."

"I could make it an order, if you like."

"No." Payne smiled, although he was still a touch pale. "No need. I haven't got any kit, though."

"I'll find you something."

❖❖❖

The gym was open, as Toreth well knew. He booked a court, and a sauna for afterwards, and paid the usual little extra to make sure no one would disturb them in there. They borrowed kit for Payne, and Toreth was pleasantly surprised to discover that his own locker had survived the troubles undamaged.

If Payne was rusty, it didn't take long to flake off. He was fit, talented, and young enough for it to make a difference. Toreth's early lead slowly disappeared, and by the time he was eight points down he was breathing heavily, and more than a little irritated. He felt he had legitimate reasons for not having made time for the gym lately, but that didn't make him feel any less unfit. It was amazing how quickly the edge could wear off.

He should've made the time to go to the university gym with Warrick—and then he remembered that he hadn't seen Warrick for nearly a week, and wouldn't see him for at least another nine days. The burst of annoyance that produced won him the next seven points in a row, and then Payne called it a day, claiming a strained calf muscle. He did have a genuine-looking limp, so it probably wasn't entirely due to the prospect of losing.

They showered, with Toreth trying not to look too obviously. What he could see in casual glances made the prospect of the fuck seem less like a chore. It was, he realized, days since he'd fucked anyone at all, never mind Warrick. Far too much work and not enough play.

He'd thought Payne might balk at the sauna, but he seemed willing enough to delay going back to I&I. When they'd made themselves comfortable (respectably clad in towels, sitting on the same bench, close, but not too close), Toreth said, "I thought you said you didn't play much."

Payne looked slightly embarrassed. "Well, I haven't for a while. I was first year champion at the academy, though. Then I didn't have time for everything, so I gave it up for football."

"Jesus. No wonder I'm fucking knackered."

"You're good."

"I play a lot. I enjoy it. Personally, I'd have given up the football."

"Oh?"

"Yes. I don't get on with team sports. Too much fucking around waiting for other people to do things. Too much like work." He smiled at Payne, making it an invitation. "I much prefer one-on-one." He waited for a moment, but subtlety was clearly not going to be enough to do the trick. "How's your leg?"

Payne stretched his leg out and bent forwards, rubbing his calf and incidentally providing a delightful view.

"It's fine, I think. Or, ouch, mostly fine. I tore the muscle once, playing football as a matter of fact, and it's been a bit off ever since."

"Should've stuck to squash. Let me have a look at it. I'm good with muscles."

If it had been Warrick, Toreth would've said, "I'm good with pain," and watched him react, disgust and desire, infinitely exciting. As it was Payne merely hesitated, albeit for longer than the request merited, then shrugged. "Sure. Thanks."

"Thank me later. Lie down."

Payne nodded and lay down on his front. A few seconds of awkward shifting suggested that the idea of being touched was enough to get him going all by itself. With luck, this wouldn't require too much in the way of dancing around before they got to the point.

The bribe to keep the room free of interruptions also provided a bottle of oil, which Toreth had already spotted in its usual place under one of the benches. He fished it out, lightly coated his hands, and set to work on the calf. He didn't waste much time there before he let his hands wander, further up Payne's leg, across his back and shoulders, slipping his fingers under the edge of the towel and hearing his breath catch.

Still sticking to the thin pretense that this might go no further, Toreth had plenty of time to study Payne. He wasn't at all unattractive—more muscular than he appeared when dressed in his uniform. He also smelt agreeably of hot skin and fresh sweat, but all that said, it was still a massage, and it was still boring. He could just about tolerate doing this to Warrick, but here it was nothing more than a necessary preliminary. After ten minutes, he said, "Turn over."

"Mm?" Faux sleepiness—from the tension he could feel under his hands Payne was very much awake. But if that was what it took to get him to play along, then he wasn't about to shatter the deception.

Toreth nudged his hip. "Turn over."

Payne complied, the towel loosening as he did so. He lay with his eyes closed as Toreth started on the front of his thighs, working upwards, pushing the towel aside until it slipped away—like unwrapping a present, Toreth thought whimsically. If New Year had more presents like this, he'd hate it less.

He slid his hands up over Payne's hips, down his stomach. His breath caught slightly but he didn't protest. He repeated the maneuver, closer every time, until Payne's hips started twitching under his hands, and the final sweep took his thumbs up the underside of Payne's cock. No protest, no faked shock. Good, because he wasn't in the mood for gentle persuasion. Abandoning all pretense, he moved further up the bench and concentrated his attention on his groin, easing Payne's legs apart a little, stroking and fondling, trying to judge his response from his breathing.

That part wasn't easy. He'd been hoping for a bit of acknowledgment by now, but Payne, eyes still shut, was desperately trying to keep his breathing somewhere near sleep. Jesus, it was hardly worth pretending at this point. Besides, he wasn't a bloody charity. He took his hands away, and after a few seconds, Payne's eyes opened.

"Val—"

Tell him that wasn't his fucking name, or let it go? "Yes?"

"Don't . . . I mean . . ."

He smiled. "Don't worry, I won't. I just wanted to make sure you were enjoying it."

"Oh. Yes."

"Good."

He lowered his head slowly, keeping eye contact for as long as possible, watching Payne's eyes widen in anticipation. As he slid his mouth down around him, Payne gasped. "Oh, *Christ*."

That was the only thing he said, which was fine with Toreth. The last thing he wanted to do with casual fucks was talk to them, or even listen to them, since talking wasn't an option. In this case, though, he'd known he might have to, given the necessity of keeping Payne sweet. Out of the corner of his eye he could see Payne's hand clenched in the towel, knuckles whitening. He slowed down, stretching things out, listening to Payne's ragged breathing.

Finally, Payne grabbed his shoulder, fingers digging in. "I'm going to—" Then he did, thrusting up hard as he came, making one brief cry.

Toreth pulled back expertly, holding him, swallowing, then finally sat back on his heels. Warrick had told him once that he should take this up as a career. He'd chosen to consider it a compliment, despite the unspoken corollary of "since you're doing it to half of New London, anyway." He hoped that in this case it was good enough to tie Payne to him, to keep him away from Carnac. The added dimension certainly gave more of an edge to the proceedings.

After a minute or so, Payne sat up, reaching automatically for the towel to wrap around himself.

"And?" Toreth asked. Payne didn't say anything, so he added, "I said you could thank me later."

"Oh. Yes." Payne grinned, making him look ridiculously—enviably—young. "Well, then—thanks."

"My pleasure." Let's see if he could take a hint now.

Apparently he could, because the grin faded. "What next?" Payne asked, and there was an irresistible hint of reluctance in his voice, more trepidation than unwillingness but still exciting.

Toreth smiled up at him, reassuring. "You don't have to do anything you don't want to. But you do want to, don't you?" There was a silence. Thinking about his happy marriage, maybe. He was about to do, not be done to, and that was always a decision Toreth enjoyed watching them make.

"Yes," he said finally. "Yes, I do."

"All right then, what?"

Payne stared at him.

"Come on, what do you want to do? Your choice. I can fuck you, you can suck me, or whatever else you want." Might as well make the bribe a good one and he didn't care which.

"I don't know," Payne said, and licked his lips.

Toreth laughed. "Liar. Go on, tell me."

"I'd like to..." He nodded towards Toreth's lap. "With my mouth."

Toreth shed his towel and sat down on the bench, leaning back against the wall, not saying anything. Waiting for Payne to take the last step and come to him.

Afterwards, Toreth stayed leaning against the wall, eyes closed, enjoying the endorphins. It had been far too long since the last time. For a complete beginner, Payne hadn't been bad. At least he'd been eager to please and willing to take directions, which went a long way to make up for a lack of technique. It hadn't been good enough that Toreth would normally bother to fuck him again, not when he'd given up so completely this time. After a long chase, the kill was often a disappointment. But, like scratching an annoying itch, the encounter filled a need. Tiresome, though, if he had to do it too much over the next week. Still, as sacrifices went, it wasn't the worst he could imagine.

He opened his eyes to find Payne back on the bench, watching him. After a moment, Payne looked away, down at the floor between his feet. "I wasn't going to tell Carnac, you know. You didn't have to do that."

It took Toreth a moment to frame a reply, before he sat up and moved along the bench, up beside Payne, touching thigh to thigh. "You think that was... what? A bribe? Jay?"

Payne wouldn't look at him. "It's a bit of a coincidence."

"Coincidence? This is the first time we've been out of I&I together. I was hardly going to fuck you in my office, was I?"

Payne glanced around, then looked away again, but the tension in his shoulders eased a little. "Well, no, I suppose not. But—"

"Jay, to be perfectly honest, I wanted you from the first day you walked in. But I didn't think you were interested—in fact you said you weren't—so I didn't push. If this is a way of saying you want that to be it—" He shrugged. "Then I'll accept that. I won't be happy about it, but I'll accept it. Is that what you want?"

"No!" Payne flushed. "That is, it would be great to do it again. If you don't mind."

He laughed. "Don't be such a bloody idiot." He turned Payne's face towards him, looking into his eyes—a lighter brown than Warrick's, with guilt in them, but also wanting more. Toreth gave him a moment to pull away, then kissed him. Payne's lips were still slightly sticky. "Of course I don't mind."

Payne smiled slightly, accepting the reassurance as Toreth had known he would, because he wanted it to be true. "Sorry. You're right, that was idiotic."

Toreth kissed him again, then released him. "It doesn't matter a bit. Come on, let's have another shower and get back to work."

They'd finally decided on Thursday as the best day to tell the senior paras. It was the latest day Toreth would accept, and the earliest Bevan would even consider. Bevan wanted to leave it until Monday, but that was within Toreth's estimate of the window for the inspection. In the end Bevan had agreed to Thursday, with very bad grace. Toreth was beginning to see Carnac's point about Bevan. Captain Clueless might have been more cooperative.

As Toreth waited at the front of the seminar room for the latecomers to straggle in, he couldn't remember a time when he'd felt more nervous. Speaking in public didn't bother him, and never had. It was the consequences of screwing this up that set off the queasy anticipation in his stomach, like looking down into deep water. There was always the possibility that, if he wasn't persuasive enough, they would simply say no. Everything he'd done would be for nothing, and he'd have to start running. It was probably already too late for that.

He looked around, assessing the mood. Cautious was an optimistic way of putting it—suspicious might be more honest. At least everyone they'd approached had agreed to come, and they had a good spread of sections represented. He nodded to Doyle, seated near the front, and the Political Crimes junior nodded back, relaxed and apparently comfortable despite the splints still on a couple of his fingers. Doyle was one of the ones they had argued over. Toreth had forced his inclusion, even though neither Bevan nor Chev had listed him. Doyle might only be a junior, but he was respected—popular, even, for a Political Crimes para—and if the division survived, Toreth expected to see him get an early promotion to senior. To pull this off, they needed not just the old guard but people with a long-term stake in I&I's continued existence.

Finally, they were all present, except Bevan. He was watching the section of building around them from his office, ready to break up the meeting if anyone came along. Sara sat to one side, with an open comm link to him. B-C provided backup watch in the corridor outside.

Toreth stood, waited until they quieted, and began. "When I went round the cells here a fortnight ago, a lot of people made it pretty clear what they thought about me. And I'd have said the same in your position. I told a few of you then what I'm going to tell you now—I work for I&I, not for the Service, and certainly not for Carnac."

No comments about spooks now, although he'd rather hoped for some. Piss-taking was what they did with peers. Silent attention was for senior management and other untrustworthy bastards.

"We do a good job here—a necessary job. And people like the results. They like being able to live their lives without the Administration being crippled by riots and strikes and sabotage. But I&I isn't popular, and it never has been. Some people hate us. Most people would just rather not have to think about what goes on here. That's their fucking problem. Or it was. But right now the outsiders have control over us. Carnac wants I&I destroyed, and he can do it."

That certainly had their attention, if not their trust. He gave it a second or so, then carried on. "There's going to be a review of the division in a few days' time. If I know Carnac, he'll pick the most spineless, weak-stomached resisters he can find and walk them through every high-level interrogation going on—and he'll make sure there's plenty for them to see. Then he'll see that they recommend shutting I&I down for good and that they give him a free hand as to the method."

He took a deep breath. The risk was that they wouldn't want to accept it, as Chevril hadn't. "Carnac wants us—all of us—executed. Everyone here in this room. All the paras, investigators, and interrogators. No exceptions, no survivors. And he can do it. He'll have the Service ready to move in as soon as the council gives the word. We've been set up and if we don't do something about it, we're dead. It's that simple."

He shut up and surveyed the room, letting the conversations buzz up for a while. Consternation. Anger. Fear, hidden to various degrees. At least they looked as if overall they believed him—or felt they couldn't risk not believing. At length, when the noise started to die down, Chevril caught his eye and he nodded slightly.

"Okay," Chevril said, loud enough to quiet the remaining voices. "What the hell do we do about it?"

Right, this was the tricky part. "Carnac's plan hinges on the fact that I&I hasn't changed. And since we were ordered not to change, he's right. So, the plan is easy—change. End the high-level interrogations." Pause, but no interruptions yet. "If Carnac sees it coming, he'll find a way to stop it, so we have to do it carefully. We've already worked out new interrogation protocols, and we'll be able to get everything in place so long as we get a few hours' notice. Carnac's not been in for the last couple of days—and my bet is he'll make himself scarce now until the review." And if I'm wrong about that, we're fucked.

"He'll want to be horrified right along with the rest of them when he sees what's going on. And he will be." Pause, smile for effect. "Because the day before the review starts, we roll out the new P&P, and by the time Carnac's resister friends turn up there won't be anything happening here that would upset a corporate's virgin daughter. Comments?"

"Will that be enough?" Voice from the back—Mike Belkin, who had plenty of clout. If he didn't go for it, the plan was sunk.

"I think so. I hope so. I can't guarantee it will work, and if anyone has another idea, I'd love to hear it. But if they still want blood afterwards . . . well, I can't see a way to stop them having it. There'd be no point in fighting it. All we could do is limit the damage to the minimum that will satisfy them."

There was a silence, then a man nearer the front gestured for his attention: Doral, an interrogator who'd taken the para conversion course a couple of years ago. Potential trouble, but they'd needed some people the senior interrogators would be willing to take orders from.

"Yes?" Toreth asked, dreading what he was going to say.

"You're saying we'd hand the interrogators over and let Carnac kill them."

The bald statement didn't produce as large a murmur of outrage as he'd feared. The prospect of general executions was obviously having a salutary effect on priorities. "No, I'm not saying that." Not exactly. "We can warn the people with the riskiest files, a few at a time, and they can take off and lay low. If it's controlled, it shouldn't be obvious, not until it's too late to matter, anyway. Movement notification's been suspended, so they'll have a good chance. If everything works out, they can come back."

"That relies on people keeping it quiet, Para," Doyle said.

"Yes. That means that we can't warn everyone. And, to get down to the fundamentals, if it does come to executions it'll be the interrogators first. And then, if there aren't enough of them around to make up the numbers . . . then it'll be us."

Glances were exchanged around the room, then shrugs, and then nods.

"We'll sacrifice as few of them as we can get away with," he said, and that seemed to clinch it. Sometimes, they were wonderful people to work with.

"What *about* us?" Doral asked. "Do we run, too?"

"No. We stay, and we forget—for now—that we ever trained in interrogation. Everything level one. And then, when Carnac's plan gets shot down and he goes away, we wait until someone from the new Administration turns up with a prisoner they desperately need to talk, and we'll get back to business as usual. We're not giving in, we're just . . . adapting."

The discussion continued for a while after that, with more questions and problems raised, some of which they hadn't considered before. But he knew it was settled already. Everything would go ahead as planned, provided that Carnac didn't pull out any surprises between now and the inspection.

That evening, he decided to give himself an early night off and offered to take Payne out for a drink, and then to a hotel afterwards. Rather to Toreth's surprise, he agreed. He thought about asking what his wife would think about that, but decided against it because, after the day he'd had, a nice, easy, certain fuck was exactly what the medic ordered.

Although the bar was on the way from Int-Sec to his flat, Toreth hadn't been there before. He sat at the bar while Payne bought them drinks. It was busier than most places he'd seen recently, with a lot of Service people in. Not a bad hunting ground, by the look of it, although probably somewhere you stood a better chance with the women than with the men. He'd have to try it sometime when he wasn't lumbered with Payne.

"Is this your usual place?" he asked, taking his drink and looking back at the crowd.

"No. I've been here a few times. I oft—"

His voice simply stopped dead in midword. By the time Toreth turned back, Payne had gone so pale as to be moderately interesting, from a medical point of view.

"What?" Toreth asked.

Payne gave a strangled squeak, cleared his throat and tried again. "My wife!"

"Really?" Toreth looked around the bar again. "Where?"

"We've got to go."

"For fuck's sake, you're only having a drink. Do you fuck men from work often enough that she'd be suspicious?"

Payne shushed him frantically. "Come on."

He caught himself just before he said something he'd probably regret. "Sure, if you'd rather." God, being agreeable was wearing thin.

He downed his drink and followed Payne out of the bar. "Do you want to go somewhere else?" he asked, when he caught up with him.

"No." Payne looked nervously over his shoulder. "I should go home."

"Why bother? She isn't going to be there, is she?"

"I know, but..."

"Did you know she was going out?"

"No. I mean, yes, because it's Thursday and she goes out every other Thursday with some of the teachers from her school. But I didn't think."

"Do you think she'll be long?"

"She usually gets home about eleven, so I expect she'll be back at curfew."

Toreth checked his watch. "Good. Then you can go home, take me with you, and I'll fuck you there—we'll be saving the division's expense account."

Payne stared at him with wide, hungry eyes. "I couldn't."

Oh, yes, he could. "Why not?"

"Because... I couldn't." He shook his head, trying to convince himself. "Not in our *home*."

Toreth put his arm around Payne's waist, and he didn't resist. "Yes. In your home. In the bed you fuck her in, if you like." He slid his hand down, around over Payne's buttocks, pressing between them. "At my age you need a bed for proper fucking."

Payne's eyes had closed, but he made a last, valiant (and entertaining) effort. "Val, I love her. I couldn't do that to her. Even if she doesn't know. I couldn't do some—some casual thing there."

So transparent that Toreth had to smile. "Does this feel casual to you?"

Payne shook his head slightly, his eyes still shut tight.

"Nor to me." And he kissed him, gently at first, then hard enough to satisfy Warrick. It was far too easy to be fun. Payne's resistance lasted barely long enough for Toreth to get his other hand up to bury in his hair.

He'd never taken candy from a baby, because he disliked both sweets and kids, but it had to be something like this.

Chapter Eleven

The Mondays weren't getting any better, Sara reflected. With B-C's help she had finished the P&P revisions over the weekend and thankfully handed it over to Systems. B-C's reward had been an all-day visit to Justice to discuss prisoner processing, a chore delegated by Toreth with great delight. Her own was to start on the ton of work that had been put off over the last week. She was afraid it had reached the critical point at which, by the time she had gone through it, as much or more would have accumulated again. And that was only the genuinely urgent things.

Not long after nine, Toreth stuck his head around the office door, scanned the room, and asked her, "Have you seen Payne?"

"No. Not so far this morning."

"Damn. If you see the lazy sod around, send him in here, would you?"

He disappeared again, slamming the door. Sara spent a couple of minutes staring at her screen but she had been distracted from work.

Payne.

He'd been different over the last few days. As pleasant and friendly as ever, but preoccupied. Also prone to turning up to Toreth's office with notably flimsy excuses, which took some doing when there were so many good excuses around. Toreth had started taking him to the gym on most days, and to lunch, leaving herself and B-C in the office. Considering that Toreth had barely been remembering to eat lunch lately, that was enough by itself to make her suspicious.

She hadn't caught them doing anything, but she was ninety-five percent sure that Toreth was screwing Payne and, since it had gone on for nearly a week and he hadn't said a word to her, there had to be more to it than his usual happy-marrieds compulsion. She didn't know what, exactly, but she was certain that it wouldn't be good news for the lieutenant. Maybe Toreth was simply substituting for his absent regular fuck, but she doubted it. She went to collect some bait for a fishing expedition.

Armed with two coffees, she entered Toreth's office, put his mug down and waited. After a few seconds he picked it up and drank, without looking up. "Thanks."

She'd been hoping for an invitation to sit down. "Toreth, what's going on with Lieutenant Payne?"

"Going on? Nothing, I hope."

"You're not screwing him?"

"Yes, I am." He looked up. "So?"

"Well, doesn't that count as something going on?"

"Not usually."

"Does Warrick know?"

He looked at her measuringly. "No, Warrick doesn't know. But then there's no way for Warrick to find out, is there? Not unless someone shoots her big mouth off."

"*I'm* not going to tell him. I haven't even seen him since I went to Fee's."

"Good." He looked back down at the screen, dismissing her.

"Why are you doing it?" she asked.

She'd half expected him to lie, for no good reason other than most people would. She ought to know him better than that. "He got suspicious. Not bright, but he made it there in the end." Toreth scrolled down the page. "Luckily he asked me for an explanation before he went to Carnac."

"And you turned up the charm and screwed him into being quiet for you?"

"Got it in one." He frowned. "And it's working nicely so far, thank you very much, so I don't want you saying anything to him. About anything."

"You could've explained things, and asked him not to tell Carnac."

"That was the last-ditch backup plan. If I'd 'explained things,' and he'd gone running off to Carnac with that to tell him, we'd have been up shit creek with no paddle and no fucking canoe. You and I'd both be in cells now, probably over at Internal Investigations—if Carnac hadn't had us shot out of hand. Anyway, I told him the general principles. I dressed the motivation up a bit, that's all."

"Well—" Annoyingly, he was right. She didn't even know why she cared; she'd seen it happen plenty of times before. But Payne had been kind to her, when there was no percentage in it for him. She owed him for that at least. "It's... not nice."

"*Nice?*" Finally, she had his complete attention. "Sara, let's try to concentrate on the important things, shall we? Carnac's planning to execute the entire staff and you're worried about me being *nice* to some little shit from the Service?"

"But it isn't nice. Service or not, he's a sweet bloke. He showed me a picture of his wife. They've got a conception license approval pending."

"What the hell does that have to do with anything? He was keen enough to get a cock in his mouth, married or not. Anyway, he'll be gone after the inspection. It's no big deal—it's just a fuck."

God, Warrick must get sick of hearing that. "Does Payne know it's 'just a fuck'?"

"I don't know." He shrugged, scanning down his screen again. "Never bothered to ask him. If he doesn't think so, that's not my problem, is it?"

He clearly knew perfectly well that Payne thought it was nothing of the kind, and he'd probably gone out of his way to make sure of it. "It's . . . immoral."

This time, Toreth frankly stared at her, blankly uncomprehending. "*Immoral?* Jesus, you're expanding your vocabulary."

"I've got morals. You're trying to keep I&I going, Carnac's trying to destroy it, and poor bloody Payne's just a casualty in the crossfire between you, isn't he?"

"I didn't pick him. Take it up with Carnac, if you think it'll do any good." His voice hardened. "After everything's settled. Until then you keep your mouth shut. Understand? Why the hell are you getting so wound up about him, anyway? He isn't even I&I. And it's not like I particularly wanted to fuck him in the first place."

She stared back, genuinely outraged and knowing that she shouldn't be, not after all this time. "That's supposed to make it better?"

"It means I'll be glad when that fucking inspection finally turns up. He's boring the arse off me. Prissy, self-righteous little twat. If you want to feel sorry for anyone, try his fucking wife. She's the one who has to suffer it the rest of the time."

There was no point in trying to argue it out any longer. If she explained for a week, he wouldn't see her point. He wasn't capable of seeing it, although knowing that didn't put her in a better mood. So she left, without further comment.

As she sat down at her desk, the subject of the argument passed her, heading for Toreth's office and looking harassed. If she hadn't learned better than to do things in the grip of a bad temper, she would have stopped him and told him exactly what Toreth thought of him.

When the door opened again, he expected Sara, having thought of some parting words too good to waste. In fact it was Payne. He stopped inside the doorway and looked around the office.

"Have you seen my comm?"

"No. Where were you? I've got things for you to do."

Payne shook his head. "'Fraid not. Carnac called me down to his office as soon as I got in—he's sent me back to headquarters for a couple of days." He frowned. "Didn't he tell you?"

Carnac shouldn't even be here, which probably meant that the inspection was starting. How the hell had he managed to keep it so quiet? And if it wasn't the inspection . . .

He forced his attention back to Payne. "No, he didn't say anything. When was it?"

Payne was hunting through the controlled chaos in the room. "I should be gone now, but I've put my comm down somewhere and if I don't take it with me I'll be—"

"Payne, *when* did you see Carnac?"

"Oh, just a few minutes ago."

"Did he say anything about me? Was there anything going on down there?"

"No." Payne stopped his search and looked around. "What's wrong?"

"I don't know. Was there anything going on?"

"There were a few more Service people down there than usual, I suppose. Just ordinary troopers doing guard duty—they passed me on my way out. Carnac said—" Payne hesitated.

"Yes?"

"As I was leaving, I heard him say 'fifteen minutes.' That's all."

"Did you come straight here after that?"

"Yes."

Fifteen minutes, say five minutes ago, which meant that he had time—not much, but enough. He could've kissed Payne, and on reflection, decided that he might as well. Payne fended him off, briefly, then gave in. "Don't do that," he said eventually. "Not here."

"There's no one watching." Toreth kissed him again, just because Payne didn't want him to, then let him go. "I owe you a huge fucking favor, and I'm going to ask for another one."

Now the lieutenant looked wary. "What?"

"Don't go to headquarters, not yet. Go hang around in one of the offices and wait for me to come and get you."

Wariness turned into horror. "That's disobeying a direct order! I could get—"

"I know, I know. I promise it won't be for long—you can tell HQ that you got delayed on the way over. No one will ever know." He put his hand on Payne's arm, still standing close enough to kiss him again if he had to. "Jay, I wouldn't ask if it wasn't important. Please."

Squeeze of Payne's arm for emphasis while he hesitated. Finally, he nodded reluctantly. "An hour. That's the most I can do."

"No longer, I promise. Use Narr's office, he's in interrogation." As he was about to open the door, a sudden, clear premonition stopped him. Guards. Lots of guards in Carnac's office. "No, hang on—wait in the toilets. The ones down the hall and left."

He watched Payne go, gave him long enough to get away from the door, then went out, too.

Sara was staring across the office at Payne's retreating back. "What's wrong with *him*?" she asked. "I suppose it's too much to hope that he's seen sense at last and told you where else to stick it?"

"I don't have time to talk about Payne."

She looked around, instantly attentive. "What's the matter?"

"I need you to get onto everyone on the list. Tell them to put the plan into action now—whatever's ready. Start with the systems changes, then notify the others. Anyone you can't get on comms, go round afterwards and tell them in person. But everyone has to know."

She nodded. "I'll get started."

"No, not here. Carnac's on his way any minute—the inspection might be starting. And if it's not that, then I think someone's spilled the plan." Her eyes widened. "Yeah. In fact, if anyone looks guilty when you're calling round, make a note of the name." Then I'm going to nail their testicles to the wall. Or whatever else I can get hold of, if they don't have any.

She began gathering things up. "Where should I go?" she asked.

"Ah...down a level and find somewhere quiet in Systems. The surveillance is still out down there and you can tell them in person to start the changes. Tell everyone not to accept any orders changing anything unless it comes through me or you. And don't come back here afterwards. I'll call or come looking for you if I need you. If you don't see me, I'll leave a message with your sister this evening and let you know how it went."

"Jesus." She stared at him for a moment, but she didn't say anything else. She didn't ask if he was sure he wanted her to go, or if he would be all right on his own, or any other time-wasting rubbish. If Carnac didn't sack both of them, he'd get her the biggest bonus in the history of I&I when this was all over.

"Go on," he said.

"I'm going. Good luck."

She left her desk as tidy as it always was when she wasn't there, so he messed it up to make it look as if she was in residence. Then he went back into the office to wait for Carnac.

It took him another ten minutes to show, ten precious minutes while Sara got into place and started making calls. Carnac brought two of the Service guards into the office, and Toreth could see a handful more outside. A show of muscle to intimidate, he hoped. There weren't any legitimate grounds to arrest him—as if that would help.

"Toreth, what's going on?" Carnac sounded as if this was any other visit.

Start with the formal denials, to buy time. "With what?"

"You know perfectly well what I mean."

"Sorry, I'm afraid I have no idea. Could you give me a clue or do you want me to guess?"

"You're making major changes to I&I policy without my authorization."

"Am I?"

Carnac stationed the guards by the door and came over. He planted his hands on the desk and leaned across it. "You're wasting your time and mine. I know that you're planning to alter interrogation procedures. I know what the new procedures are. And I know why you're doing it."

"It's taken you long enough to find out."

Carnac shook his head. "I've known for days that you'd try something like this. Ever since I woke up and wondered why I'd suddenly become irresistible. More irresistible, rather." Dazzling smile, which didn't touch his eyes. "It seemed easier to let you run and allow you to occupy yourself with your little plans until the right time to put a stop to it. That time is now."

For a moment Toreth felt sick. This was why Carnac pulled in the kind of fees he did. Why the hell had he ever thought he'd be able to outplay him? But the fact that Carnac had known all along didn't matter, as long as the plan worked. "You gave me operational control. I'm doing exactly what you told me to do—getting I&I up and running again."

"Changes on that scale require my authorization."

"I'm terribly sorry, you didn't make that clear."

Carnac glared at him. "I'm making it clear now. Those plans go no further, no one else hears about them, and they will not be implemented. Is *that* clear enough for you?"

He spread his hands. "I'm sorry, it's too late. The order to make the changes has already gone out."

That stopped him dead. After a moment, Carnac said, "You're lying."

Somehow he kept the smile off his face. "The orders have gone out. The system's been changed."

"In that case, you will change it back. Quickly and quietly."

"I'm afraid not." He leaned back in his chair. "If you want me to do that, then I want an order, in writing, with your name all over it."

There was no way out of that. Carnac would have to let it slide, or he would have to put his own name on keeping the old I&I. Checkmate.

To his horror, Carnac smiled. "Do you know, Val, I thought you might say that." He stood up and pulled a hand screen from his jacket pocket and dropped it in front of Toreth. "Read this."

A quick scan through showed it to be the security file of an Int-Sec undercover agent. Interesting to consider how Carnac might have laid his hands on it, but not… and then he saw the agent's cover name.

Kailynna Avens. Known as Kate. Warrick's mother.

As much as seeing the name shocked him, it immediately made sense. He'd known for years that Warrick's supposedly late father had been an Int-Sec agent, and this new fact filled in a dozen tiny gaps and inconsistencies in the story that he hadn't even noticed until now. However, Warrick didn't know, about any of it, and the most cursory consideration of what Carnac could do with the knowledge chilled him.

After a few seconds he closed his mouth, then handed the screen back with his best attempt at nonchalance. "I don't see what difference that makes." At least he somehow kept his voice level.

"Oh, *good.*" Carnac's pleasure was undoubtedly genuine, and the fear tightened. "Then let me spell it out for you. You will rescind this order of yours or Kate will be exposed, arrested, tried, and executed as an agent of the old Administration responsible for multiple deaths."

Blackmail only worked if the victims showed they were afraid. "That would be a shame for Kate, but I don't see how it changes anything."

Carnac stared at him, briefly and impressively speechless. Finally he spoke in a venomous whisper. "Someone once said to me that no one deserves to die. But then, I suspect, they had never been to this place."

"If you say so." He shrugged. "I'm not the one threatening to kill Warrick's mother, and the entire staff of 'this place.'"

Carnac flushed crimson. "It will be a *pleasure* to put you all down. You and the rest of the treacherous vermin."

He'd never seen Carnac come so close to losing control, which offered an opportunity to catch him off-guard. "So that's how you found out."

Carnac's lip curled. "You didn't expect loyalty from the scum who work *here,* did you? You disgust me, all of you."

Point to Warrick. He'd have to tell him, if he saw him again. For now, he smiled at Carnac, wondering if he could tip him over the edge and what the guards would do about it if he did. "Disgust you? That's not how I remember it." He ran his hand along the desk, not bothering to keep his voice down. "I remember you bending over here, telling me you wanted it harder."

For one blissful moment, he thought Carnac might hit him. Then the socioanalyst caught hold of himself. "You two," he said, without looking away, "wait outside. Immediately outside. Leave the door open." His voice was all icy control and anticipation.

When the guards had obeyed, Carnac picked up the screen. "Before Kailynna is questioned, she will spend a day or two with a psychoprogramming team who have unwisely accepted my assurances that they will escape execution if they perform a small memory adjustment for me."

He paused, obviously savoring the moment. "They will give her the memory of recommending to Int-Sec that an agent be appointed to keep a close watch on her younger son and his small but valuable corporation. The sim provides so many opportunities for resisters, you see."

Toreth didn't need to hear the next sentence—his mind was already racing past it to the implications.

"She will also gain the clear and convincing memory that the agent is you. Since so many Int-Sec files were lost in the recent misfortunes, the lack of corroborating evidence will be unfortunate, but hardly fatal to the prosecution." Every word came sharp and crisp, as Carnac explained the inevitable progress of events. "You will be arrested, imprisoned, and possibly executed. This time, there will be no pleas from Keir to save you. In fact, I doubt he would cross the street to spit on you, once he has been fully appraised of your appalling betrayal."

It took him a few seconds to manage any response at all. "What the hell happened to 'I have a lot to thank him for'? Some fucking repayment."

"Keir will be devastated, naturally. A regrettable side effect, should you remain intransigent. But in the long run, his psychological profile indicates that he will recover with limited damage." The vicious, vindictive smile again. "Perhaps I will be able to bring a little, ah, comfort to him—I've always admired him, you know."

Now he knew why Carnac had brought the guards, because for the rest of his life he couldn't understand how he managed to stop himself from lunging across the desk and breaking the bastard's neck. Somehow he did stop himself. Somehow he managed to force himself to shut out the idea of Warrick and Carnac and try to react intelligently, try to keep the plan intact. But the truth was that he couldn't see a way out. Buy time, that was all he could do.

"It will . . ." He swallowed. "It will take time to undo everything. If you want me to make it look as if it never happened. Two days." If Carnac had acted, then the inspection must be close.

"You have until this afternoon. Or let us be generous—you have until nine tomorrow morning. You will sleep here, since you doubtless have much to do." He gestured to the guards outside. "These gentlemen will act as your escorts until then."

Fuck. "Fine."

"Cooperate fully, and I give you my word that you will be permitted to resign from I&I and no further action will be taken against you. You may ask what guarantee I can give of that." He smiled thinly. "All I can say is—what alternative do you have?"

Toreth didn't dignify that with an answer.

"Where is Sara?" Carnac asked.

Toreth had expected the question, so even when it was asked so abruptly he didn't hesitate. "No idea."

"Really, you are the most—" Carnac sighed. "No matter. She will be found and returned here. If you require assistance from her then she can perform her functions from your office. Now I suggest you get to work. Goodbye."

There must be something he could do. To start with—

"Oh, one more thing." Carnac paused in the doorway. "Kailynna was arrested this morning, so don't think that you could get to her before I did."

Fucking spook mind reader.

Carnac shut the door, leaving a deafening silence in the room.

He tried to think about what Carnac had said. To think it through carefully, looking for a flaw in the plan, unlikely as it seemed that there would be one. Carnac wasn't a magician. He did what he did by understanding people and organizations, and predicting reactions, and so far Toreth had obviously been too fucking predictable by half. Just think about the damn problem. Go through it carefully—there had to be something he could do.

Even in small pieces, his mind shied away from it. All he could think was that Warrick would believe it.

Warrick would believe it. The coincidental way they'd first met at a public lecture, the investigation at SimTech . . . God, he'd been the one who'd initiated things, pursued things. It was all too fucking convincing. He'd be in detention, unable to tell him the truth, and Warrick would watch him die, hating him. And then afterwards . . .

Easy to say Warrick would never touch Carnac, but that supposed Carnac was stupid enough to let his name be connected to the arrests. He imagined Carnac assuring Warrick he was doing his best, then taking him the news. Kate betrayed you. Toreth—no, Val, he'd call him Val. Val betrayed you. Here's a fucking shoulder to cry on.

Forcing the image away, he circled the problem for a while, looking for a solution, and found nothing. He could run, or try to run, and at least he'd leave a hell of a mess for Carnac to clear up. But it was scant comfort. The socioanalyst would win—had already won, during all this time when Toreth had thought he was being so clever.

Maybe Sara could come up with something; he wished now that he hadn't sent her away. Calling her back was a risk in itself, because the only slight advantage he had was that the changes had already happened. That was about the only thing Carnac hadn't had perfectly mapped out, the only thing that had surprised him, and that had been down to blind luck.

He couldn't risk leading the guards down to Systems in case there'd been a delay and Sara hadn't put the changes in place. On the other hand, it was safer to have her back up here than to leave Carnac's people hunting for her and stumbling over God knows what. He'd just have to use the building comms and be careful.

It took four transfers between offices before he found her. "Sara? When you've got a moment, I'd like to see you in my office."

To his relief, she merely said, "I'll be another couple of minutes, if that's okay?" She sounded as calm as if she was doing nothing more clandestine than chasing up errant files for him.

"That'll be fine."

A couple of minutes to finish, and the time to walk back up again. In an absolute sense it meant little, but every second wasted felt desperate. However much he tried, he couldn't stop playing and replaying scenarios in his mind. They all led to the same place, with variations in the details but never in the essentials.

Carnac and Warrick. Warrick and Carnac. Would Carnac play the game? Probably. He liked games, and he'd seemed interested in the gear the time he'd seen it. He'd know what Warrick wanted, what he needed—that was his job. He imagined Warrick kneeling for Carnac, obeying his velvet voice, shivering at his touch, begging for him . . . and somehow none of that was as bad as the idea of weekends, Sunday fucks, Carnac and Warrick in bed and happy together and—

The door opened, and Sara entered, looking over her shoulder at the guards, who thankfully stayed outside.

"What's the story?" he asked when the door closed.

"Everything went off without a hitch." She sat down, looking so pleased with herself that it seemed a shame to tell her the bad news. "If you look at the screen, the new systems are in place and running. The seniors are telling their teams. Chevril says the interrogators are taking it pretty well, considering. The only thing is—" She looked at him more closely. "Oh, shit. What's wrong?"

He outlined Carnac's blackmail plan to her. By the time he'd finished, her eyes were the size of teacups. "I don't believe it," she said finally. "It's just . . . and Carnac meant it? He'd really do it?"

"Looking forward to it. There's probably a damp patch on the floor by the desk where he was drooling at the thought of me in prison. Practically came on the spot when he started talking about telling Warrick all about what I'd supposedly done." The thought froze him again. Warrick would believe it. Warrick would—

"Jesus." She rubbed her arms, as if trying to get rid of something unpleasant stuck to her skin. "Jesus Christ. I can't believe it. Warrick's *mother?*"

"It's true. Carnac had the fucking file. And I never told you, but his father was some kind of Int-Sec agent. Citizen Surveillance, probably, but I don't know for certain. I am sure it's true about Kate—it makes sense."

She shook herself, then said, "You've got to tell Warrick."

"Tell him? What, you mean . . . ?" The one thing that simply hadn't occurred to him. Everything he'd considered had been about making sure Warrick never found out. "I can't."

"It's blackmail, and that's the only way to beat it." He'd never heard her sound so determined, which was saying something. "Tell him everything about Kate and about what Carnac's going to do. I know it'll upset him—okay, more than upset him—but he might be able to do something, out there. He won't believe Carnac's story about you now, but if Carnac gets to him first with Kate's file and an m-f'd confession . . . " She shrugged.

"I can't tell him." And he meant "can't." He couldn't imagine saying the first word. The breath knotted in his throat at the idea of even seeing Warrick now. "If you can't think of anything else, I'll have to do what Carnac wants—cancel everything."

"Don't be stupid," she said flatly.

He stared at her. "There's nothing else I can do."

"Then you might as well go over to his office and shoot yourself. Save him the trouble." She pulled her chair closer. "Toreth, he's going to do it, anyway. If he wants you dead, if he wants Warrick—what's to stop him? Think about it."

He did think about it, unwillingly and with increasing horror. She was right. There was nothing to stop Carnac from simply going ahead with his plan. There was nothing, in fact, to stop him from adapting the plan to use any other Int-Sec agent, but it only mattered because it was Kate. She would make it convincing: her relationship to Warrick, her existence as a deep cover agent. The indisputable evidence in her file would damn Toreth by association. The more he thought about it, the more sure he was, because if Carnac wanted Warrick there would never be a better opportunity to get him.

Which all left him with only one course of action, impossible as it was. "I can't do it. I mean... he won't fucking believe it, anyway."

"Yes, he will. He'll believe it from you. He trusts you."

That was almost funny, even at this moment. "Trusts me?"

She rolled her eyes. "For God's sake, of course he does. For the important things, anyway. He trusted you with Marian Tanit, didn't he? That was back when all you were doing was fucking. And what about the chains and all the other stuff? What about the cabinet? Dillian might think he's mad, but he isn't. He has to trust you, to let you do that to him."

He shook his head, although he couldn't deny there was some truth in it—he'd said the same thing himself. "It's not the same. Not at all. It's... what the hell would I say to him? I can't even think of how to start."

"Well, you've got until you talk to him to come up with something. You don't have any other choice."

Toreth closed his eyes, forcing himself to look at the problem with as much detachment as he could muster. She was right, of course. Even if Warrick reacted in the worst way possible, he'd still be in no more trouble than he was right now. Just do it, don't think about it. His hand was on the comm before he thought of the guards. Outside the door, for now, probably to encourage him to do exactly what he was about to do. The comms would be monitored, and he was willing to bet there was a human, not a computer, ready to call Carnac the moment they heard anything amiss. There was another way—Payne. Payne would take a message, with suitable encouragement. Unless Carnac had left him Payne deliberately, in which case he was as dangerous as the comm.

Thinking about it like this would leave him paralyzed in his office for the next day and a half. He made a snap decision—trust Payne. Carnac had tried (or had seemed to try) to get him out of the way. Not the best grounds for trusting Payne, but he had to do something. Time was ticking away already.

Sara was looking at him questioningly. "I'll do it," he said. "But I can't risk the comm. I'll send Payne."

Relief turned to concern. "What if he goes to Carnac this time? I'll do it."

"Carnac will have you trailed as well as me. Bevan should be able to help, but I have to do it straight away." Before I have time to think about it.

"What about B-C?"

"Over at Justice, which Carnac must know about. I doubt they'll let him back in the building until Carnac gets what he wants." And then Barret-Connor would be arrested along with the rest of them. "Anyway B-C's still one of the team which means he's no safer than you. Payne isn't even supposed to be here. He's perfect."

She shook her head. "I hope you remember this when you're giving him his cards."

What was this thing she had for the little tosser? "What about who ratted us out? Did you get any ideas?"

"Doral," she said, with absolute confidence.

"Fuck. I knew we shouldn't have trusted the shit. Why do you think it was him?"

"Nearly everybody said Doral had spoken to them, sounded them out about what they thought of the plan. Coming up to people on their own, asking whether they really thought we could put one over on Carnac. Whether there might be another way to talk Carnac into dropping it all. Everyone told me that same thing. 'I didn't think anything about it at the time but now you mention it gosh, yes, it was a bit funny.' You know the drill."

"Yeah, I know." They'd been sitting on any suspicions about Doral until finally forced to decide which way to jump. Thank God they seemed to have chosen him—so far. "Nearly everyone?"

"He didn't speak to Chevril. Not at all." She paused. "At least not according to what Chevril says."

Which meant either Doral had thought Chevril was too closely involved to risk even hinting to, or it was the other reason. It was obvious enough which of the two Sara thought, and he tended to agree.

"The stupid bastard. Just what we need, on top of everything else."

"We can work round it, though, can't we? Now that we know who?"

"Yeah. Yeah, we can. In fact, it might not even be a bad thing, if—" He shook his head. Jumping too far ahead of himself. "I'll get it sorted. I need to set up the meeting with Warrick, and see if I can shift those bloody guards so that I can talk to people."

"Shall I stay here?"

"Yes. Use the comm, just be careful—assume Carnac's hearing everything. Get hold of Chevril, Christofi, Doyle, and a couple of the others. Anyone Doral's pissed off in the past will do, which doesn't narrow the field much, given what a bent bookie he is. Set somewhere up—you know what I need." Carnac wouldn't interfere. He'd assume it was Toreth taking his anger out in revenge. "And for fuck's sake, don't breathe a word to anyone about Kate. I don't want any more people thinking that maybe they'd be better off with Carnac than with me."

She set to work, while he took out a pencil and paper and nearly lost his resolve. Listening to Sara with half an ear, he stared at the blank sheet, pretending that he was thinking about what to write. A minute passed, then two, and then that excuse lost the last shred of plausibility, leaving him with the fact that he was afraid. He was afraid of what Warrick would say, of what he would do. That, in the end, he would believe Carnac and—

He cut the thought dead. Sara was right. It was the only way. He didn't have a choice. Keep repeating that and maybe it would help. He wrote the note, folded it, and slipped it in his pocket. As he walked outside, two of the four guards fell into step beside him.

He ignored them until they reached the toilets. Then he stopped and turned. "I'm going in there. You can come in with me if you have to, but I don't perform well with an audience."

There was a brief silence, then one of them held out his hand. "Comm, sir."

"Fuck, it talks." He handed the comm over with a show of reluctance. "Whoever would've thought it?"

As the door shut behind him, he had an awful moment when the room looked empty. His main fear had been that Payne would realize what a stupid thing he was doing based on nothing more than a few quick fucks, and would run.

"Payne?"

The door of one of the cubicles swung open, and Payne emerged.

"Jay, guess what?"

He smiled wryly. "Another huge favor?"

"Yes. I need you to take this for me. Go over to the university campus, as fast as you can, and find the AERC building. That's the Artificial Environments Research Center. Give this to Doctor Keir Warrick at SimTech—in person. Don't give it to anyone else. Get a reply straight away."

And pray that Warrick was there.

Payne frowned. "That's a long way, there and back. Can't I just call it over?"

"No. There's too much risk in doing it over the comms."

"There's no reason for anyone to be listening to me, surely?"

Staggeringly naive—but handy right now. "None at all, except that they'll be listening to everything and if this gets overheard I'm fucked. Please, Jay."

Long silence, then Payne nodded quickly and grinned. "Okay. Give me the note."

"Give me two minutes to get away, then go out." He handed over the paper, knowing that if Carnac was playing him over this one it was the end. "When you've got the answer, come back up. Don't go to the office—leave a note in here, and then clear off."

"Right."

Payne caught hold of him as he turned to leave and kissed him. Danger and desperation spiced it up into something rather good. Pity there wasn't time for anything else because a fuck would do wonders for his nerves right about now. "Thanks," Toreth said, when it broke off.

Payne shook his head. "I'm only doing it because it's you, Val."

"I know." He touched Payne's cheek briefly, more than satisfied with the warmth of the smile he got in response. "I know."

Chapter Twelve

❖

While Payne went off on his errand, Toreth set about arranging the rest of the plan. His timing was perfect—he caught Carnac just as he was leaving the building.

"I can't do what you want me to do with these missing links trailing my every step. Everyone will panic at the sight of them."

Carnac considered. "Very well. Here is the alternative: I will remove the escort, for the time being. In their place you will wear a surveillance bracelet. In addition, you will report to my office by comm every thirty minutes, and in person to my admin every two hours."

The tagging he'd expected; the reports were an unwelcome surprise. "Carnac—"

"Don't waste my time. If that is not acceptable it is because you are planning to leave the building. The exits are all monitored in any case, so I will be aware of any attempts to escape."

Escape. So that was what it had come down to. "That'll be fine."

Carnac checked his watch. "Time is pressing, and I have places to be. I suggest you continue your good work."

The Service guards took him down to the cell level to have the bracelet fitted. It was less humiliating than he'd expected—the thin band was light enough that he soon stopped noticing it, and it was a relief to leave the escorts behind. Of course, everyone he spoke to mentioned it at once.

"He's fucking tagged you," Bevan said, as soon as Toreth walked into his office.

"Yeah. You should've seen the size of the ones I traded in for it."

"Someone grassed us up?" He didn't sound that surprised by it, and Toreth wondered briefly if he'd somehow known in advance. The more likely explanation was that Bevan wouldn't allow himself to appear surprised if God Almighty and the angelic host manifested in his office.

"It was Doral," Toreth said. "How did you know?"

"Some Service wanker called me into his office for a load of time-wasting crap. When I got back here, Carnac had been through the building like a dose of salts, and everyone was scurrying around like someone kicked the ants' nest. Cohen said Sara called to say everything was emergency go, so I guessed we were rumbled."

Toreth shook his wrist. "I need the tag scrubbed from the system, or frigged somehow so I can get outside."

"Sorry, no can do," Bevan said with finality.

"What?" Toreth ran his little finger around under the bracelet, which had suddenly become a lot more of a problem than he'd expected. "Can't or won't?"

"I mean I can't—it's too late in the day to be playing silly buggers. I can deactivate the bracelet, I can authorize it to leave the building, but if I do any of that then Carnac sees it, if he's watching. If you're lucky, maybe he's having a nap."

"Fucking, fucking hell." Of course, Carnac wouldn't place any trust in the system if Bevan could override it so easily. "There's nothing at all you can do?"

Bevan shrugged. "The whole system's a black box. It came in from outside and it's pretty fucking bombproof, so I never bothered with it—who gives a shit about prisoners? I don't have any access to it except the standard interface."

"I have to get outside—only half an hour. If I don't, everything is shot to hell."

"I can open a door to get you out—any door you like—but I can't stop the system from tracking you, or screaming blue fucking murder when you leave the building. Except…" He stopped, frowning thoughtfully.

"What?"

"One thing. I can get you outside, *if* you're not going to be away long."

"Like I said, half an hour's all I have. I've got to report by comm to Carnac's admin. Maybe a few minutes either way, but not more than that."

"Okay." Bevan fished a pair of pliers out of the desk drawer. "Give me your wrist."

Bevan turned the bracelet around, then put the pliers around it. He adjusted the positioning and squeezed gently. After a few seconds, he repeated the maneuver, then again. Then he put the pliers away and sat back.

"What did that do?"

"Activated the tamper sensors, with any luck."

Toreth choked. "It'll trip the fucking alarms!"

"Yes, it will. And any time now there'll be a couple of guards steaming in here to see why."

So there had to be more to it than that. "Okay, go on."

"The system trips all the fucking time. It's practically antique. Fifteen years old, anyway—I keep telling them to replace it. Should've got Carnac to do it while the wanker was signing anything. Half the bracelets are fucked one way or another:

they go off when they warm up, they go off when the sensors throw a wobbler, they go off when the prisoner takes a piss, they go off when it's full moon on a fucking Thursday. Keeps the workshop busy, anyway. Ah—"

The door opened, admitting two guards.

Bevan scowled. "Don't I train you people to fucking knock?"

"I'm sorry, sir, but we have a report of a bracelet fault." The guard's eyes went wide as he realized the identity of the wearer.

"Yeah?" Bevan turned to the screen and queried the system. "Yeah, you're right. Christ All-fucking-mighty. Didn't they check the piece of shit before they fitted it?" He rolled his eyes and sighed. "Never mind."

He stood up. "Come on, Toreth. If you've got to wear the fucking thing, I'll make sure it at least works."

Toreth walked down to the cell levels, biting his tongue the whole way. Bevan obviously had a plan, and was just as obviously getting a tremendous kick out of not explaining it.

In the cell levels, Bevan verbally abused the security technician who'd fitted the bracelet so comprehensively that Toreth half expected the man to burst into tears. The rest of the staff edged away—Bevan had a reputation for a somewhat scattergun approach to discipline. Only the Service guards (of whom there were a number) seemed unimpressed by the performance.

Eventually, Bevan dismissed the quivering tech and removed Toreth's bracelet, putting it in his pocket. Then he selected a new one from the racks and fitted it. He ran through a few screens, then turned to the senior Service guard. "See that? It's working fine. Well, go on. *Look.*"

The woman checked the screen and nodded.

Toreth wasn't confident he could remember which surveillance cameras were active, so he had to keep the questions locked behind his teeth all the way back to Bevan's office. Once they had sat down again, he examined the bracelet. "Looks just the same as the old one."

"No, that's a new one." Bevan pushed his own sleeve back and displayed a bracelet. "This is the old one."

Toreth blinked. "So we're both tagged? That helps how?"

"Because we have two working tags, both registered as fitted to you, but only one listed as active. Yours at the moment." He shook his wrist. "The system thinks you're still wearing this one, too, but it's faulty, so it isn't being tracked. When you want to fuck off, I'll swap the bracelet IDs. As long as the bracelets are within half a meter when I do it, the system won't even squeak."

"Surely the operator'll notice?"

"Not a fucking chance. They see the prisoner ID—you, in this case. The bracelet's hidden. Who wants to look at bracelet IDs with a million fucking digits? A removal or fitting generates a notice, but a matching swap is completely transparent." He shrugged. "Someone might find it if they start poking around, but they'd have to know the system inside out. When it's all over, I'll put them back in the stores together. As long as no one starts comparing surveillance pictures and tagging logs, we're clear."

Toreth frowned, thinking it through. Not a bad plan—a hole in the system, in fact, but it required the cooperation of a senior security officer to make it useful. Not something most prisoners would be able to buy, and in any case, if it was used for a genuine escape… "That means that when I'm out of the building, the system thinks you're me."

Bevan slow-handclapped. "The man's a fucking genius. So you'd better sodding well come back, hadn't you?"

Before he left to keep his next appointment, they discussed a few more things and Bevan offered him a shot of his bloody awful homebrew. He declined. He would need a very clear head indeed if there were to be any chance of pulling this off.

Sara had done him proud—everyone in place in a seminar room, in a quiet part of the building where they wouldn't be interrupted. Toreth was pleased by the readiness with which the others accepted both his information and his suggestion as to what they should do about it. He could get used to the idea of being in charge. Only Chevril held back from the general condemnation, and Toreth added another tick to the list of marks against him. He was almost sure now, and he'd be able to make sure easily enough.

Doral had been given a time ten minutes later than the others. When he arrived, utterly unsuspecting, the five of them closed in a ring around him before he realized what was going on.

"You sold us out to Carnac," Toreth said coldly.

"I—" Doral's jaw dropped. "How did you find out?"

Too damn stupid to lie. "Wrong reply. You should be trying to think of one good reason for me not to kill you right here."

"I'm sorry." Doral looked frantically around the room, clearly looking for sympathy and finding nothing but implacable, professional intent. "Christ, I'm sorry. I thought it was for the best. I thought—"

He listened to Doral's pathetic protestations for half a minute, which was long enough to take Toreth from annoyed to furious. Then he hit him.

After the first few blows he stepped back and let the others carry on. It was too personal, and he was too angry at the betrayal of his plan to keep going—he could feel his temper starting to spiral out of control. Doral dead would be a nuisance. Beaten to a pulp, he would make a useful object lesson in case anyone else thought there was still time to sell out. If they hadn't already done so. Fucking interrogators. Stupid, ungrateful bastards. He should've let Carnac nail the lot of them.

Finally he said, "Enough."

For a couple of minutes the only noise in the room was sobbing and moaning from the curled figure on the floor, then Toreth prodded Doral with his foot. "Stand up."

"I can't—" Two words, then breathless coughing.

"Bollocks can't you." He looked at Doyle and Christofi. "Get him up."

When Doral had been hauled to his feet, Toreth stood in front of him, watching him gasping and struggling to stand up straight. "I'd say I hoped you've learned your lesson, but you're too fucking stupid for that."

"Please—" Doral managed to gasp.

"Shut up." Toreth stepped up close, lowered his voice. "Now, you can fuck off to Carnac's office and explain to his admin that you're going home sick and he won't be hearing from you again. If I see you in the building before I say you can come back, you'll be looking back on the last few minutes here as a fond memory. Understand?"

Doral nodded.

"Not fucking good enough. Do you understand?"

"Yes." He coughed again, and wiped his face on his sleeve, smearing blood and snot. "Carnac's office. Home. I... understand."

Toreth stepped back, and two of the other paras shoved Doral towards the door. He stumbled, caught himself against the wall, and then started up the corridor with more speed than Toreth would've credited.

"Chev, make sure he gets as far as the lifts. Someone will pick him up at the other end if he passes out on the way."

He waited until he heard Chevril's footsteps returning, then said to the others, "Wait for me outside—I won't be a minute."

Chevril passed the others on the way in, turned to follow them back out, then stopped when he saw Toreth still inside.

"Chev, can I have a word? Shut the door."

"Okay. What?"

"Come over here."

Chevril stopped a couple of meters away and waited. "What?" he asked again.

"When did you tell him?"

"When did I tell who what?" Chevril glanced towards the door.

"Yes, they're still outside. I haven't told them yet."

"Told them what?" He pulled himself up to his full, unimpressive height. "If you're suggesting *I* said anything to Carnac, then—"

"It's not a suggestion—I know you did. Give it up, before you really piss me off. And you don't want to do that because I'm having a fucking bad day as it is."

Chevril held on to the innocent indignation for a few more seconds. Then the façade crumbled and he sat down heavily on a desk. "Okay." He looked down at his feet, then up again, trying for defiance. "Yes, I told him."

"Why?"

"I didn't want to die. Is that such a bloody surprise? It's all right for you—you're well out of it either way. Your corporate sweetheart isn't going to let Carnac line *you* up against a wall and have the Service take pot shots. Your stupid bloody plan was never going to do the trick for the rest of us."

"Then why the hell didn't you say so?" Toreth found his anger unexpectedly subsiding to exasperation. It was so bloody like Chev. "You thought of it in the first place!"

"Yes, well, that's how I knew it wouldn't work. Doral came and saw me—it must've been after he'd talked to Carnac. He didn't say anything about that, of course. I told him to fuck off, but then I thought about what he said, and then I went to see Carnac. He—"

"Let me guess. Carnac offered you protection and a job afterwards if you'd fuck the rest of us over for him. Because Doral is too stupid to find his arse with both hands and a map, whereas you're smart enough that there was a chance you could keep it going. But still just about too stupid to see that Carnac's going to kill you along with everyone else, because he isn't going to want to leave any live fucking witnesses. And if you think that doesn't include me, you're even thicker than Doral."

Chevril shrugged, embarrassment laid over fear. "Okay, maybe I was stupid to believe him, but it sounded a hell of a lot better than everyone going down."

"What did you tell him?"

"As little as I could, not that it makes any difference—but I didn't realize then that he'd got it all from Doral anyway. I didn't give him names. And I didn't tell him about you, er... about how you found out in the first place."

No, Chevril wouldn't have. "What did he promise? You get out and everyone else dies?"

"No!" Now Chevril looked genuinely indignant. "He promised that he'd let the seniors go. That includes you, in case you hadn't noticed. It was the best offer around."

Not a bad deal, from a lousy bargaining position, which was only more evidence that Carnac had no intention of sticking to it. "You're a moron."

"Yeah. I suppose that's about it." Chevril squared his shoulders, probably thinking about the sound of boots going in. "Do I get the same as Doral, then? A nice thorough going-over and sent back to Carnac?"

"Tempting. But then I'd have to explain to Elena that I ruined your good looks, and she'd probably serve me my balls on a plate."

"Is there another option?" Cautious optimism brightened Chev's face.

"Yes. Doral's a 'before' picture for plastic surgery. You aren't...yet. So Carnac thinks Doral's blown and you're still useful. Now you stop fucking around, come back onto our side, and then you pass back to Carnac, wherever he's got to, exactly what I tell you to pass back. And you make it sound very, very good."

Chevril frowned, distrustful. "What's to stop me from spilling all this to Carnac as well?"

"I'd say your sense of honor and camaraderie, but actually Bev is going to wire you up and put a feed through to me and him when you're out of sight. If we hear anything we don't like, or the connection cuts out, or if it sounds like Carnac doesn't buy it, I'll kill you. No fucking about, no second chance—you've used that up already."

Chevril stared at him, then nodded. "Okay. I believe you."

"Good. Because I'd hate to have to prove that I meant it."

He laughed, shakily. "I'm not so sure I believe that."

From the sound of it, Toreth had done too good a job with his demonstration with Doral. He went over to sit beside Chevril and put his arm around his shoulders. Chevril flinched slightly, then held himself steady, his hands gripping the edge of the desk. "Chev, I promise you, I don't want to do it. Know why?"

Chevril looked up at him for a moment, then shook his head. "Don't you ever bloody give up? Absolutely no fucking way. No. Never. Not in a million bloody years. Pigs will give formation flying displays first. Clear?"

He sounded annoyed enough, but Toreth felt him relax a little. Good. That was exactly how Toreth wanted him—sufficiently focused on the consequences to do what he was told, but not so scared he'd fuck it up or make Carnac suspect him.

He squeezed Chevril's shoulder, then let him go. "Better behave yourself, then."

Back in the toilets on his floor, he searched the cubicles. Nothing, and nothing, until he found the scrap of paper in the last one of the row. He looked at the message, almost not daring to open it. Finally, he unfolded it. Yes, he was coming. Yes to the time. Yes to the place. Yes, thank you God. Now, it all depended on timing and luck.

He estimated it would take five or six minutes, if he ran it. Then however long it took with Warrick, then another five or six minutes back. If he was more than five minutes late with the next call-in, someone would come looking for him on the strength of his tag signal and find Bevan. More complications, more dangers.

He'd set the meeting time as late as he dared, to make as sure as possible that it would happen. He filled in the remaining time by going around to the seniors, taking Chevril with him. He warned everyone that Carnac had heard about the plan from Doral, and told them to make sure everyone kept quiet if any Service people started nosing around. He didn't have much hope that would help; there was too much information slopping around, and it would inevitably spill. Some people would say the wrong things at some point, but with luck that could be put down to confusion.

Luck. The idea that success depended on luck made him shudder. It was only luck that had kept him in the game so far. Without Payne's forgotten comm, he and Sara would probably be down in the cells right now, waiting for the inspection. Would any of the others have taken the risk of putting the plan into action without him? Bevan, maybe, except that Bevan wasn't a para or an interrogator—he might well have decided a pension was the better part of valor and sat it out.

Everything still depended on him, and that wasn't his favorite feeling.

He contacted Carnac's admin a few minutes early, giving himself as much leeway for the next contact as he could. Then he went downstairs to Bevan's office, and Bevan changed the bracelets and told him which door to use. "I'll be as quick as I can," Toreth said.

Bevan shook his head gloomily. "Just fucking come back. That's all I care about."

He forced himself to walk away from the building until he was confident he was out of easy visible range. Then he ran, wishing he'd managed to put more time in at the gym. When he arrived at the café, out of breath, Warrick was already waiting at a corner table. He'd ordered a coffee and a cake for himself, but nothing for Toreth. Not a good sign.

"What it is?" Warrick asked as Toreth sat opposite him.

He breathed deeply, trying to stop panting. "Warrick, I'm in trouble." Truth, to start with, anyway. "Real, nasty, dead-very-soon, serious fucking trouble."

"Your plans for I&I?"

"Yes."

Warrick stood up. "I already told you that—"

"Don't fucking—" He stopped, realizing that he was raising his voice. Warrick didn't work for him, and shouting wouldn't help. "Don't interrupt, please. Once through, that's all I ask."

"Very well." He sat down again, checked his watch. "I have to get back for a meeting. You have thirty minutes."

If only. He needed to do it in half that to be absolutely safe, but that wasn't going to happen.

"That's fine. First, there's something... okay." He looked around the room—

people eating and drinking, but no one listening, which he'd known already. There was no use delaying it. He took another deep breath, trying to produce the right words without actually thinking them.

"There's something I have to tell you. Don't say anything until I'm done. It's about Kate. She works for Int-Sec—she's a deep cover agent. And..." And he was distracted by studying Warrick's face, trying to work out what he was thinking.

Warrick met his eyes and said, "I know."

He could have spent a week thinking up reactions, and that one would never even have made it onto the bottom of the list of "least likely." "You *know*?"

"Well, that's not strictly true. I strongly suspected."

"How long for?"

"Years. Let me think... she left her office unlocked once. Perhaps something had made me wonder about her; I don't really remember why. But I was about seventeen and excessively curious, and I hunted around in her computer."

"She had classified files on it?"

"Not exactly. But there were other files, enough to make me suspect things weren't as they seemed."

"What?"

Warrick's expression closed. "It doesn't matter, does it? The more pressing question is why you are telling me. Now."

"Carnac knows—not from me. I had no idea myself until he told me. He got it from the Int-Sec systems somehow—he had her security file. I don't think he knows you have a clue about it, because he seemed to get a real kick out of the idea of your finding out. But the real point is that he's threatening to blow her cover to his new friends if I don't stay in line."

Warrick raised an eyebrow. "I'm surprised he would consider that to be a useful inducement."

He didn't know whether to be annoyed that Warrick knew him so well, or relieved that he didn't seem upset. "That's the other part—the part where he m-f's her into implicating me as an Int-Sec agent running an extremely close surveillance on you and SimTech."

There was a brief silence, then Warrick said, "So you thought you'd tell me first?"

Toreth shrugged, trying to keep his voice equally casual. "I've run a few blackmail cases. It only works if people are too frightened of the consequences of owning up to whatever it was to just come clean. Half of the time it would've been better if they'd done it straight away."

"And the other half?"

"Is a total fucking disaster, which is why it works." Which set would this fall into?

"What exactly does Carnac want?"

No mention as to whether he believed him or not. "We're reforming I&I." He waited for Warrick to look properly skeptical, then carried on. "No more high-level interrogations, no more 'torture' at all, in fact—more than enough to satisfy the new Administration and make them leave us alone. Carnac found out about it. He wants me to cancel it, undo everything by nine o'clock tomorrow morning, and let them shut I&I down. His way."

He didn't bother to add the rest of the consequences, because Warrick knew them well enough. It would be interesting to see if Warrick thought his and Kate's lives were an acceptable price to pay to get rid of I&I—only two more on top of the hundreds he'd been happy to see die. Interesting, that was, unless the answer was yes.

"Will you cancel the plan?"

He had the lie prepared, ready for use if the conversation had made it this far. "Yes," he said, without hesitation, and with such conviction that he half believed it himself. "If that's the only way."

If Warrick called his bluff, he was fucked.

Warrick looked at him for a long moment, assessing, and then nodded. "Thank you. However, as I'm sure you're aware, that wouldn't be enough, would it?"

"Probably not. There's nothing to stop Carnac from going through with it anyway. Odds are he will, since I found out about his plan and he won't want me running around knowing all that and hating his fucking guts. And he wants—" And he wants you.

Warrick looked at him inquiringly, and Toreth shook his head. They didn't have time to get into all that right now; Warrick would only think he was being paranoid.

Besides, judging by Warrick's expression, he'd guessed the end of the sentence anyway. All Warrick said, though, was, "So, you're asking me to remove his leverage by getting Kate out of danger and out of his reach?"

"If it was that easy I'd have done it myself. He's already had her arrested."

"Ah." Warrick cocked his head, thinking the problem over with what appeared to be utter calm. "If that's true, then I don't see what I can do except appeal to Carnac's better nature."

God, he hoped that was sarcasm. "Then I'm dead, and so is she."

"Thank you." The calm cracked a little. "I'm perfectly well aware of that."

He thought for a minute or so longer, while Toreth watched him. There had to be something Warrick could do. Because if there wasn't—he *was* dead. He hadn't thought of it so explicitly before, but Carnac would never let him run—he was outside the building now, but the alarm would be raised before long if he didn't return. He wouldn't get far. Carnac would have thought about the possibility and the arrest warrant would be ready to go; the fact that he'd tried to run would only make him look more guilty. Maybe he'd already thought about Toreth turning to Warrick. Maybe it was what Carnac wanted, although he couldn't imagine why. Paranoia again, although after everything that had happened it was becoming hard to distinguish paranoia from common sense.

Finally, Warrick shook his head. "I'll do what I can. I have an idea of something I can try. And if the worst comes to the worst, I can go to Int-Sec and make a fuss in the hope that someone there will hear about it who doesn't like the idea of an agent on trial."

"They won't like you standing there telling them you know who one of their Cit agents is, either."

Warrick smiled dryly. "And that is why it's the last resort. I promise I'll do my best to avoid it. Just to make one more thing clear: I haven't changed my stance on the other question. I won't help you with anything else."

"Just get Kate out and I can manage fine without you."

"I'm sure you can." He stood up, brushing cake crumbs from his jacket. "If that's all, then I should go."

Toreth realized he didn't want him to go yet, however urgent the errand. He hadn't seen Warrick for what felt like weeks, and they hadn't said a word that wasn't connected to I&I. Not that he could think of anything now. "Warrick, what did you find on Kate's computer?"

Warrick glanced up sharply, then schooled his expression into neutrality. "It doesn't matter."

"Yes, it does." Because he so obviously didn't want to say, and because it would keep him here for a little while longer—Toreth only had a few minutes anyway. "Tell me."

Warrick sat down again, slowly, his face still unreadable. "Letters. Letters she'd written to my father. One a week, every week. I've been back in since, a couple of times, and she's still writing them, or she was the New Year before last. There's never anything explicit in them, nothing that says it outright, but if you read enough of them it's obvious what she is. What both of them are."

So he knew about that, too. "Were there any from him?"

"No. But then I doubt she would have kept them there in any case, or even received them in her own name—that would be somewhat suspicious, given that he's supposed to have been dead for over thirty years. There was no obvious evidence of an address to which she sent her letters, if she sent them anywhere. I didn't pry too deeply. However, he may well never have seen them."

"So why do it? It's a stupid risk—you proved that."

Warrick smiled slightly. "People in love do stupid things; as a condition, it's famous for it. Obviously I've never asked why—I've never so much as hinted that I knew—but personally, I think she wanted to give him something of the years they didn't get together. Or rather, the edited version. There's a lot about Dilly and me but nothing about Tar. Not a word. I imagine that all went in the official reports."

"Official reports? Why?"

"You've met him." His voice was cool and distant. "Think about it."

Toreth blinked. "Jesus."

"Yes. Quite. That's something else I've known for a long time. I have to go now if you want my assistance to do any good." He stood again, but didn't leave. "Will you be coming back to the flat tonight?"

"I can't. Not because I don't want to, but Carnac's keeping me at I&I."

His eyes narrowed. "Keeping?"

Toreth turned his sleeve back briefly to show the bracelet. "Until it's all over, which shouldn't be that long. The inspection's got to be sometime tomorrow, or the next couple of days at the latest. Don't worry—he's not going to do anything until after that. He's not even there, for one thing, and he's the type who likes to watch."

Warrick nodded. "I see. Be careful."

"Yes." Had Warrick ever said that to him before? "Of course I will."

He watched Warrick walk away across the café, and started sentences in his mind. Don't go yet. I want five minutes, that's all. One minute. I want you. This could be the last time I see you. This really could be the last time. I want you to—

Toreth looked at his watch and started running.

Chapter Thirteen

❖

Warrick stood, looking at the door, and wondering what to tell Tarin. In a way, he hoped that if Kate had been taken, something would have been said. That it wouldn't be down to him. Now that he was here, he simply couldn't bring himself to do it. What was the point? It would be sheer cruelty to tell Tar now, when it could do no possible good.

For almost your whole life, Kate was running you, stealing your secrets, using you to betray your friends. I have no idea how many of them died because of her. I knew, for years, but I never told you because I was afraid that if everything blew up it would take Jen and Dilly and me with it.

He didn't know Tarin well, but he knew he wouldn't be able to handle that, because who would? And, more pragmatically, he needed Tarin's help now, and there had to be as small a chance as possible of Tarin doing anything to alert Carnac to the fact that knowledge of his plan had escaped I&I. If that happened, Carnac might well have Kate executed straight away. Or worse, processed by the psychoprogrammers, and then Toreth would also die.

So that left silence, both expedient and kinder. He might be able to find a way to tell Tar later, when everything was over one way or another. Kate probably wouldn't be coming back here, whether he managed somehow to get her out, or whether she was executed.

His finger hovering over the button, he realized that he had, finally, stopped even thinking about her as his mother. It was Kate, now, and it always would be.

He activated the comm, wondering whether he'd been worrying needlessly. Carnac might have been lying—Kate might still be here. He didn't really believe that, and any lingering optimism vanished when Tarin opened the door and Warrick saw his face.

"I thought you weren't coming," Tarin said. "Why didn't you reply?"

"Reply to what?"

"I left you a message."

Without thinking, he said, "I didn't get it."

"Didn't—then what are you doing here?"

He picked up the case he'd brought with him. "Are you going to let me in, or do you want to discuss this on the doorstep?"

Tarin moved reluctantly out of the way. Inside the house felt different—sounded different. Vacant. No longer anything like a home. Dismissing the feeling, he set off towards Kate's study, Tarin following him.

"What the hell are you doing here if you didn't get my message? Messages."

"I'll explain later. What happened?"

"They turned up this morning, and they just took her. No explanation, no warrant. They seemed to think the guns were good enough due process. God, I thought... I'd hoped everything like that was over now."

"Who's 'they'?"

"I have no idea. They had Service uniforms on, but I doubt that means anything."

"You're probably right."

They reached the study door. Unlocked. He started to push it open, then hesitated. "Did they go in here?"

"No. Well, not really. She was in there when they came. But they didn't do anything in there, at least that I noticed. They just took her. Keir, what the hell's going on? How did you know?"

"Toreth."

"*Toreth*? They were I&I, then." Tarin paled. "Oh, Jesus. She's there? That place? I hoped they'd closed it down."

"Toreth heard about the arrest, that's all. I don't know how he knew, I don't know who took her, or why, and I don't know where she is." Three lies out of four. Fortunately, Tarin had never been able to read him the way that Dilly could.

Warrick opened the door and went in. He'd hoped that the computer might still be on, but she'd obviously had time to shut it down before they arrived. For a moment he considered trying to power it up and get hold of the information like that, but it was too risky.

Opening the case, he set the system he'd brought on the desk, then started dismantling Kate's system. To his relief, it was as ordinary inside as it appeared to be outside—of course, there was no point having anything in the house which might compromise her cover.

He'd expected Tarin to ask what he was doing, but he simply leaned on the wall and watched for a while. Once Warrick started freeing the memory stores, Tarin shook his head and said, "Tea?"

"What? Oh, thanks."

By the time Tarin returned, with tea and some of Jen's cake, Warrick had the system running. He watched as it scanned through the memory, hunting information. If there was too much encrypted on there, he'd have to take it back to SimTech, with all the dangers that would expose them to. Better to do it here if possible.

"Where's Valeria?" Warrick asked, filling time.

"With her mother. She's going to stay with Philly until everything's sorted out. It seemed like the best idea—the bastards frightened Val badly enough when they took Mother. I thought... well, I thought that if they came back for me, it would be much better for her not to have to see it." He sounded so calm, so matter-of-fact, that Warrick looked up from the system. Tarin shrugged. "I've always known that the things I do, the people I associate with, are dangerous."

"Why are you still here, then?"

"I thought I'd better wait for you. You seemed the most likely person I knew who might be able to do something for her."

He wished he had the same kind of confidence in himself that Tarin and Toreth seemed to have. "Where's Jen?"

"She went to stay with a friend, eventually. Took me a while to persuade her, but she agreed in the end. I told her to go with Philly and Val, but you know how small Philly's flat is and—am I interrupting anything important?"

"No, it's fine." This must be the longest they'd spent together for years without arguing. "I'm waiting for the system to finish the first pass."

"What are you looking for?"

"I need a clue as to where they took her, which means finding out why they took her."

"I thought it was obvious."

He went cold. "What?"

"Me. Or something to do with me. Something I've done, traceable back to this house. Except they took her instead of me."

Warrick didn't know what to say—couldn't think of anything to say that didn't lead towards dangerous explanations.

"It's my fault she's gone," Tarin continued. "I should've asked why they wanted her, I should've said that it was me."

"Tarin, they wouldn't have listened to you. Or they would have taken both of you."

"Maybe. But I didn't try. I didn't do anything except stand there and watch. God. I feel like such a coward."

The only thing he could possibly say to explain that it wasn't true would make things a thousand times worse. So he said, "We'll get her back, Tar. I promise."

Tarin nodded and lowered himself carefully to sit against the wall, mug in his hands. "She doesn't have a lot of furniture in here, does she? I never noticed before. Never been in here much, I suppose."

"Well, it's an office. She's always wanted to keep work and family separate."

He could have kicked himself, except that Tarin had no idea why there was anything noteworthy about the comment.

"She was arrested once before," Tarin said. "Although you were far too young at the time to remember. I waited here, with Aunt Jen, until they brought her back. Only one day. But I thought she was never coming back, like Leo. And you and Dilly asking for her, all the time. Well, you asking. Dilly just crying. Jen cried, too—I found her in the kitchen. Scared the hell out of me, and then she lied and told me she'd been cutting onions or some such rubbish. God, it was awful." He sipped his tea. "I think that's why I couldn't say anything when they took Mother away. I couldn't bear the idea of leaving Val behind, of putting her through that."

It was disconcerting, not to mention discomfiting, to hear Tarin say something like that. "I didn't know you remembered so much about it. You never said anything before."

"Well, it was the big family secret, wasn't it? Mother and Jen used to go on and on about it. 'Don't tell the children, you must never tell the children.' Like I wasn't one of them." He looked up. "You found out, though, didn't you?"

"I did. But then I listened at a lot of doors. I don't think Dilly knows, not about what happened to Leo, anyway."

Tarin shifted against the wall. "That's what I can't understand, Keir. You know how he died, and you're still...*with* that man."

"It's got nothing to do with Toreth. He was hardly born when it happened. I&I didn't even exist."

It wasn't much of an argument. He thought Tarin might pursue it, but in the end he shook his head. "It's your conscience, I suppose, if you can live with it."

"Things are changing, Tar. I&I's still there, but there's going to be reforms." Some kind of comfort, the best he could offer. "Toreth's involved in it. No more interrogations, no more deaths in custody. The kind of thing you've always wanted to happen."

"No. I wanted it destroyed. It's not over until that place, and the rest of Int-Sec, is torn down and everyone who worked there is—" He stopped.

"Dead. Say it, if you mean it."

"No. Yes, I was going to say it, but I don't mean it. You might not believe it, but when I saw the pictures of what happened there...I never wanted it to be like that. More death, more suffering—what's the point? But let's drop it. I don't want to argue."

A surprise and a relief. "Really?"

Tarin smiled tiredly. "First time for everything."

Warrick wondered, for the first time, how much of his hostility towards Tarin stemmed from fear. The fear of putting himself and the people he loved in danger by getting too close to someone whose life span was dictated by his usefulness to Int-Sec. Safer to stay back, as far from danger as was practicable, and to cultivate a dislike based on anything he could find.

"I'm sorry I punched you that New Year," Warrick said.

“What?” Not surprisingly, Tarin looked bemused by the non sequitur.

“You must remember. I was telling everyone about founding SimTech and you said I was still whoring for the Administration, and that the sim would end up as just another tool for oppression.”

“So that’s what it was. Sounds like the kind of bloody stupid thing I say when I’m drunk.” Tarin rubbed his jaw. “All I remember is lying on my back and noticing that you really do see stars.”

“Well, I’m sorry.”

“Forget it. It was a damn good punch.”

“I cracked a knuckle. Hurt like hell.”

“I wondered why you never did it again.”

He laughed. “That wasn’t the reason. I think Jen would’ve strangled me if I’d done it twice.” On an impulse, he said, “You should come and see me.”

“What?”

“Come and stay at the flat for a weekend. When it’s all over and everything’s back to normal, and Dilly’s back from Mars. You can bring Val; we’ll take her to the zoo, that kind of thing. I’m sure we can manage not to talk politics for one weekend. I’ll keep Toreth out of the way—you won’t have to see him.”

Tarin thought it over for a while, then nodded. “Okay. Yes. Thanks. Val would be delighted.” He leaned his head back against the wall. “She loves her uncle Keir.”

“She’s a wonderful girl,” he said, glad to have finally found a topic where he could tell the unreserved truth.

Tarin smiled, looking genuinely pleased. “Yes. She is. I expect every parent thinks the same, but she’s special.”

“Very special. And I’m very fond of her. She’s in my will, you know. Actually, you probably don’t know—I should’ve told you. In fact, I should’ve asked you before I did it. Sorry.”

“It’s your money, you can do whatever you damn well please with it.” Tarin shrugged. “If I haven’t brought her up well enough to use it properly, that’s my fault. But it’s kind of you to think of her.”

“Not at all. And not, I hope, that it’s going to matter for a good long time yet. But I like to know that it’s all settled, just in case it does. She gets a third of more or less everything. And a third goes to Dilly.”

Tarin’s eyes narrowed. “And a third to him?”

“A third to Toreth, yes. He has no idea and I’d be grateful if you didn’t say anything.”

“I can’t imagine I’m ever going to speak to the man.” Tarin stood up and collected the mugs and plates. “I should call Philly and see how Val is.”

“Don’t mention that I’m here.”

Tarin looked at him, frowning, then nodded. “Of course. If you didn’t get my messages…”

“It’s probably nothing. The comm networks are still hiccuping. But it’s best, just in case. Toreth took a risk to tell me about it, a serious personal risk. I wouldn’t want it to backfire on him.”

“All right.” Tarin paused in the doorway. “Val loved him, you know. When you brought him here that New Year, she thought he was wonderful. Mother likes him, too—more than she’s ever liked poor Philly, anyway.” He shook his head. “I love Val, more than anything, and I’d kill anyone who hurt her, but sometimes I think we made a terrible mistake, applying to have her. When a job like his can exist...it’s no sort of a world to bring kids into, is it?”

Before Warrick could think of an answer, he had gone.

It took another twenty minutes until Warrick found something. Not much—a contact number that didn’t crosscheck to anything in the directories, which meant either it had been disconnected, or the name wasn’t real. Since all the other numbers Kate had stored were current, he decided that the latter was at least a possibility. It wasn’t much, but it was all he had so far, and all he was likely to find without more power to apply to the problem. He would have to take the memory back to SimTech after all.

Before he left, he sent a message to the number, from the house comm, saying nothing more than that Kate was in danger and required immediate assistance. Then he warned Tarin to leave, and left himself, back to the city and SimTech.

Toreth had managed to get hold of a gun from the armory, and he had it in his hands, not in the holster. Bevan stood by the door, also armed. It felt like overkill, but however much of an idiot Chevril could be, he was a trained para, and Toreth had made absolutely clear to him the consequences of fucking this up.

Toreth sat watching Chevril, out of line of sight of the comm. He fingered the gun nervously. Things could go wrong in so many ways: if Chevril messed it up, if Carnac didn’t buy it, if Carnac had another insider they didn’t know about, if this was all just part of Carnac’s plan—

“How long, Chev?” He tried not to sound impatient.

“He said about nine, still. That’s all he told me, still.”

“Fuck.” What if Carnac suspected already? “Those Service knuckle-draggers could be back any time. Bevan, find Belkin and—”

“Wait! It’s him.”

Toreth shut up and watched a second screen, set up by Bevan. Carnac’s face appeared on it, and Toreth had a momentary, stupid thrill that he could see Carnac but the socioanalyst couldn’t see him. Things were desperate if that tiny advantage could feel important.

“Do you have progress to report?” Carnac asked.

"Yes. Everything's going fine. Or at least, it's all going how you wanted it." Chevril sounded sour, like someone regretting what they'd done. Well, if that was what he thought would work.

"Good. The systems are restored?"

"Not yet. He had them put in some security blocks, and it's taking the techs a while to undo it all. I can't guarantee it'll be finished tonight."

"When?"

Chevril shrugged. "You know what techs are."

"I neither know nor care. *When?*" Chevril hesitated, and Carnac added, "Will it be ready by lunchtime tomorrow?"

Toreth breathed a silent sigh of relief. That was a risk they'd agreed to take, because they desperately needed at least a hint as to when the inspection would start.

Chevril nodded. "Oh, yeah. First thing tomorrow morning at the absolute latest, they said. Although you know what—"

"Yes, yes. Very well. Everything else has been returned to the status quo? Toreth has given all the other orders?"

Don't look at me, Toreth willed him. Chevril's eyes didn't even flicker from the screen. "Yes."

"Excellent. Thank you for your good work. I shall—"

"Carnac, I want out," Chevril said, interrupting him.

What the fuck? Toreth glanced across at Bevan, who merely shrugged.

Carnac appeared surprised—or possibly like someone trying to seem so. "I beg your pardon?"

"I want out. Please. Let me go. Let me get clear before they suspect something. They will, as soon as it's obvious Doral wasn't the only one. And Toreth isn't going to be that bloody forgiving with me." Unquestionably realistic fear crept into his voice. "I'm dead if he finds out."

Carnac's expression hardened. "Believe me, you are dead if you attempt to run. There is no need to worry about Toreth. Stay where you are, and I promise that everything will work out as predicted. I will require your help for a while longer."

"No. I . . . " Chevril hesitated, doing an excellent impression of a man who has run out of options. "Okay. Yes, okay. But don't forget, we have a deal."

"Of course we do. I will call again in the morning before I arrive—eight a.m. precisely. Don't miss it." Carnac smiled. "And take care."

The link cut out and Chevril slumped forward onto the desk, his head in his arms. "Jesus bloody Christ. Next time do you think you could just shoot me?"

Tempting. "What the fuck was all that about?" Toreth asked, as levelly as he could.

Chevril looked up. "I was trying to act naturally, as per bloody instructions. And naturally, I want to get the hell out of here. But he made it pretty bloody clear what he thought about that."

“I always said you were a prat.” Bevan spoke for the first time. He’d been, or so he claimed, unsurprised at Chevril’s defection. “There was never any fucking chance the bastard would let you go.”

“Yes, I know that now.” Chevril shook his head. “I’ve said I’m sorry, what more do you bloody want?”

“It doesn’t matter. All for the best, as it turned out.” Toreth stood up, putting the gun away. Thinking about what Carnac had said. “He’s going to lock us up. Me at least, probably Sara, too.”

Bevan nodded. “That’s my guess. Me too, do you think?”

“I don’t know—could go either way. You weren’t at the meeting and I deliberately didn’t mention you, so Doral might not’ve known you were involved. Carnac could guess, though.”

“What?” Chevril looked between them. “How do you work all that out?”

Toreth unbelted the holster. “You told him I’d given all the orders—that means my time’s up, whatever he said this morning about giving me until tomorrow. He’d be stupid to leave me loose now, in case I try to change it back. And whatever he is, he certainly isn’t that.”

“So where does that leave me?” Chevril asked.

“In charge of the other paras, until I get out tomorrow.” He handed the gun to Chevril. It made a nice gesture, although Toreth would’ve had to dump it anyway before the guards arrived. “Don’t fuck it up this time, will you?”

Chevril shook his head. “I won’t. I promise.”

“I trust you.”

Bevan, turning away, gave him a frankly disbelieving look. He was right, of course. Toreth didn’t trust Chevril, but then neither did he have much of a choice in the matter.

As he’d expected, they were waiting for them in his office: five troopers and three I&I guards. Flattering headcount, anyway. Sara was still in the office, perched on the edge of his desk and looking pale. When she saw him, she closed her eyes briefly—he couldn’t tell if she was relieved to see him, or if she’d hoped he would’ve heard about it and run.

He surveyed the group—obviously handpicked by Carnac, and not a trace of reluctance on any of their faces for the job in hand. “Can I help you?” he asked.

One of the troopers stepped forwards. “Yes, sir. If you and Ms. Lovelady would accompany us, please. Socioanalyst Carnac’s orders.”

“What orders?”

“Protective custody, sir.” Behind the troopers he saw one of the guards smirk, pulling out handcuffs.

Toreth nodded. "Get on with it, then."

He thought the escort was overkill, until they tried to cuff Sara. As the guard reached for her wrist, she slid off the desk and bolted for the door. Toreth caught her reflexively, stopping a fleeing prisoner, and by the time he let her go the guards had hold of her.

"Toreth!" Her eyes were wide and desperate. "Stop them. Please—Toreth!"

It took three of them to restrain her and get the cuffs on with unnecessary, unprofessional force, and with her screaming his name the whole time. He made himself stand and watch, because there were still the five troopers, waiting for him to try something. He concentrated on the guards, remembering faces. Sara squealed as one of them twisted her wrist viciously, finally locking the cuff closed around it. The bastard was dead, as soon as he found out his name and address. Dead. Dead in an alley. He'd fucking scream by the time Toreth was finished with him.

Then it was done, and they moved on to him. Cuffing his hands in front of him, as they'd done to Sara, which was a small mercy. He submitted without resistance, and followed the troopers out of the room.

All the way down to the cells, he struggled to stay calm and react logically. He'd done everything he could with regards to the inspection. Chevril wasn't the ideal man to keep things going, but with luck there was Bevan to watch him and the head of security would know exactly what had happened as soon as they passed an active camera.

Carnac was doing this to wind him up. It was impossible that he didn't know what effect it would have on Sara—that was why he'd sent so many guards. There was no point making a fuss over it. She'd be fine. She'd have to be fine because they didn't have any choice. She—

They stopped outside a cell and Toreth turned to the trooper who'd spoken in the office. "Put us together, please."

"We have orders to accommodate you separately."

"I don't fucking—" He took a deep breath, wishing suddenly that Payne was there. He looked more closely at the man's uniform. "Does it matter if we're together, uh, Sergeant? Look at her. She's terrified already."

Sara had gone past crying or fighting. She stared blankly down at the handcuffs on her wrists, her lips moving silently from time to time.

"Look at her," Toreth repeated. "Lock her in there all night on her own, she'll be a wreck by morning. Eleven hours in the dark. Doesn't seem very protective to me."

Eventually, the sergeant nodded. "Put them in together."

The cell lights switched on as they entered. They had five minutes until they went off again automatically, and then it would be dark until the morning. He'd hoped they'd remove the cuffs but, naturally, they hadn't. More of Carnac's orders, no doubt.

Single occupancy cell—he looked around, getting a fix on the water, the toilet. Then he sat down on the narrow bed and turned his attention to Sara, standing where the guards had left her. He had to have her coherent and useful tomorrow. Whatever personal kick Carnac might be getting out of tormenting Sara was purely incidental to depriving Toreth of badly needed support.

He beckoned her over, getting the response he expected, which was none. "Sara, come here."

Better if she came on her own, but he'd drag her over if he had to, because he wasn't chasing her around the bloody cell in the dark.

"Sara. Here. Now."

She looked up, staring right through him. She seemed to understand him, however, because after a few seconds she nodded and approached slowly.

"Sit down."

She did, and he took her hands in his, awkward in the cuffs. "Sara, it's less than a day. The—" He caught himself just in time. Someone would be listening, and Carnac mustn't know he knew about Chevril. "I bet the inspection's tomorrow—that's why he came in so heavy-handed. We stay here until then, safe and out of the way, and then he'll let us out. We won't be locked up for long."

"It's not—" She stopped, her breathing accelerating, then caught hold of herself and started again. "It's the handcuffs. Not being locked up. When they did it before. It was..."

At least she was talking now, which was an improvement. "The *cuffs*?" He laughed, startling her into looking at him. "Jesus, I don't know what you're complaining about. You should try it for four days, with your hands behind you."

"It's not...oh, God, I'm sorry I'm being such an idiot."

"It doesn't matter at all." He lay down, pressing his back against the wall, and held his arms out. "Come here. The bed's comfy enough, and I don't know about you, but I could use a lie-in for once. I'm sick of getting up before the fucking sun."

Reluctantly, she joined him, and he lifted his elbow, allowing her to wriggle up and rest her head on his arm. Then he put his arms around her, holding her as best he could.

"You know," he said, keeping his voice conversational, "if Warrick knew about this, he'd be melting all over the place right now. He's got this thing about me in chains."

"Really?"

"Would I lie to you?" And she laughed, almost—he could feel it because she was pressed against him full length. Felt nice, in fact. "Didn't I tell you before?"

"I don't remember."

"Turns him on like mad although, to be fair, that's not difficult." He sighed, only partly for effect. "If I had a comm, I could call him and tell him. Give you something to listen to."

This time she did laugh. "If we had one, I'm sure we could think of something to do with it other than comm sex."

"Probably. But I like comm sex. Better than the real thing, in this case."

"Do you do it, really? Let him chain you up?"

"We tried it a couple of times. That's the weird thing about it—it's only the idea he likes. Except once, at the Shop. I'm sure I told you about that. The party?"

She nodded.

"Right. The rest of the time, the real thing bores me to death and he doesn't get much off it either. But you only have to put something round *his* wrists and he's away. Just goes to show—"

"It's not the handcuffs, it's how you think about them," she finished.

Well, he hadn't planned anything that metaphorical, but it had worked out nicely. "Did that help?"

"Not really." But she sounded steadier.

"Sara, forget about the cuffs. They don't mean anything at all, except that Carnac is a grade-A bastard who gets off on pathetic little power games." He lowered his voice to a whisper, out of the range of the cell microphone. "He should enjoy it while he can, because tomorrow he gets what's coming to him."

She sniffed and swallowed. "Do you really think so?" she asked, also whispering.

"Bevan's keeping an eye on things. Chev'll come through, pillock though he is—he did a great job on the comm. Everyone's been told what to do, so even if Carnac has Service people asking questions, he'll hear the right answers."

"What if it's not enough? What if he still wins?"

Stupid bloody question, to which they both knew the answer. "He doesn't have a chance. Just concentrate on how fucking sick Carnac's going to look at the end of the inspection."

"What about—you know?"

"It'll be okay." Warrick will sort it. Slightly to his surprise, he didn't have to fake confidence in that.

Before she could say anything more, the lights went out and he felt her tense against him. He tightened his hold and kissed her hair, trying to soothe her. It wasn't something at which he'd had a lot of practice. "Shh. Just... shh." Yes. That was how it went. He kissed her again, finding her thick, soft hair and familiar scent to be an unexpected comfort. "Everything's going to be fine."

Warrick was still in his office after ten o'clock, working on the encryption. Since Toreth was at I&I there was little point in going anywhere else—he could sleep when Carnac's time limit expired.

He had an odd sense of déjà vu, which persisted until he tracked down the source. Someone he loved in danger—two people now—and a forced reliance on someone else to save them. Gil Kemp then, and this time whoever at Int-Sec might follow up his message, if anyone did. The uncertainty and the danger were both that much greater this time. The message might never be received, or be ignored. Or it might bring Int-Sec down on all of them.

While the system worked, he passed the time in reading Kate's letters. She wrote them as if Leo had gone away for a month or two—chatty, happy, passing all the news along. "Dilly" and "Keir" filled every page. It was strange, seeing his life set out so completely, full of incidental happenings which he didn't remember. Only Tarin was missing.

Most disconcerting of all was the way that Warrick eventually found himself forgetting the absence, no longer noticing the missing face in the word pictures. Kate had erased her elder son so neatly and absolutely that it was hard to remember whether he had been there with them in any one of the scenes described. The letters held only Kate, Jen, Dilly, and himself, making up, along with the absent Leo, Kate's perfect family. It was worse than he'd remembered it, more disturbing. Or perhaps it was his new sympathy for Tar that had altered his view.

At eleven o'clock, he was in the process of brewing more coffee when the comm chimed. "Doctor Warrick? There's a man in reception who says he has an appointment. He won't give his name, but he says he got your message."

There was only one message that it could be. His first instinctive impulse was to run. Where, he had no idea. "Escort him up," Warrick said, surprised by how calm he sounded.

While he waited he tidied the room, cleared chairs, hardly noticing what he was doing. One man, so it was unlikely he was going to be arrested. Killing him here, in his office, in a building with excellent security and surveillance, would be a ridiculous risk.

Logic could say what it would, but he couldn't pretend he was anything other than frightened. All the years of living with the secret, the knowledge of what Kate was, and finally it had come to this, the thing he had always dreaded. Int-Sec had found out, and the fact that he had virtually told them himself didn't make it any better.

Polite tap on the door, and he went over to open it.

Two security guards and a man he'd never seen before, in a Service officer's uniform, stood outside. Warrick thought of Tarin, of Kate's arrest, and wondered if this man been involved. Tarin hadn't mentioned a senior officer, which he clearly was. He was in his late fifties, at least, with short gray hair that Warrick guessed had once been blond, and he wore the uniform with authority and the confidence of someone accustomed to obedience.

Warrick studied the uniform again, then stepped back from the door. "Come in, Colonel."

"Thank you."

Looking at the guards, Warrick hesitated for a moment before he asked them to wait outside, and then he closed the door behind his visitor.

"What can I do for you, Colonel . . . ?"

The man smiled pleasantly. "Just Colonel will do fine. I'm surprised you recognized the insignia. Not many civilians can."

"We've been exploring a potential contract with the Service, for sim training modules. Would you like to sit down? Coffee?" The inane ritual helped him keep a grip on his fragile calm.

The colonel sat, seeming perfectly at ease. "No coffee, thanks. I try to avoid it late at night or I never sleep." He waited until Warrick had sat opposite him, then said, "You sent a message to me, regarding a mutual acquaintance."

"Yes." After a moment's consideration, he added, "One of your operatives."

"Ah. Thank you for being so honest—it makes things much easier."

"Did you find—" and he almost said the name, before he thought better of it. "Did you find her?"

"Indeed I did. She's in custody, although the circumstances appear to be slightly irregular."

"Can you—"

The colonel held up his hand. "Before we go any further, I have one question."

"Yes?"

"There's a note on her custody file, making a special reference to a para-investigator named Valantin Toreth. He's not to be allowed to see her or speak to her. Is she in danger from him?"

"God, no." Not now, anyway. "He's the one who let me know she was in trouble."

"Ah. And he is . . . ?"

"A friend of mine." He scanned down the mental list of words that didn't fit, and picked one. "He's my lover, if that makes any difference."

"No difference at all."

It occurred to Warrick that the colonel must have known that already, given the reasonable assumption that he'd seen their security files. He'd been assessing the reliability of the information, or rather of the informant. "I also have a question, if I may?"

The colonel nodded.

"How did you know the message was from me?"

"Process of elimination." The colonel linked his fingers and stretched his hands out in front of him, knuckles cracking. "The number was secure and secret, and should have been available only to operatives. However, I knew it wasn't from one, because the message wasn't coded or authorized. That left a small field of people, and probability suggested you. It cost nothing to make sure in person, and a visit is far more secure than a comm link, particularly in these delicate times."

The cool, precise voice strongly reminded Warrick of someone he couldn't place. Had he met the man before? "So, what now?"

"More detail as to the nature of the danger would be useful."

"A socioanalyst called Carnac—" he paused, and the colonel nodded, clearly familiar with the name, "—arranged the arrest. He plans to have her exposed, tried, and executed. And also to implicate Toreth as another Int-Sec agent. He has a psychoprogramming team ready to make it sound convincing."

The colonel's eyes narrowed. "His name wasn't linked to the arrest."

"I didn't think that it would be."

"And he knows for certain that she's an operative?"

"My information is that he had a copy of her security file." That was Carnac's problem now.

"That would be unfortunate." The colonel didn't specify for whom, but the studiously neutral tone chilled him.

Warrick waited for a while, then said, "Can you help her?"

"The operation has been fatally compromised. The operative is no longer a valuable resource and she possesses information that may pose a threat to Int-Sec."

This had always been the danger inherent in this course of action—that Int-Sec would choose the easy solution, the one that he was sure had occurred to Toreth.

The colonel looked almost apologetic. "If I may be honest with you, the current climate is a dangerous one for everyone at Int-Sec, and particularly for the Special Operations divisions. A number of things which occurred under the old regime would make us profoundly unpopular with the new, should they become known. We're endeavoring to maintain as low a profile as possible until the situation stabilizes, and public trials cannot be permitted."

"You're going to kill her." Although if he meant that, why was he here at all?

"That would doubtless be the official course of action, should the matter attract wider attention, yes." Then he smiled, or at least half smiled. "But when confusion reigns, some things may slip through the cracks unnoticed."

"And?"

"An acceptable conclusion, from my point of view, would be if the agent in question was taken from custody and left the jurisdiction of the Administration. Would you find it so?"

"Yes. That would be more than acceptable." He'd work out later how to explain it to Tarin and Dilly.

"How long do I have to arrange her release before the danger becomes acute?"

Warrick checked his watch, vaguely surprised to find it was barely a quarter past eleven. "Sometime tomorrow—that is, Tuesday. I'm not sure at precisely what time, but after nine a.m. the risk increases. You may have a couple of days beyond that, at the outside."

The colonel lifted his head and stared thoughtfully at the far wall, pursing his lips. Eventually, he nodded. "That should be long enough. If all goes well, she'll be free by lunchtime at the latest."

It felt too good to be true, but there was nothing he could do, except be grateful and hope. He wondered briefly if there was any point asking where Kate was being held, but there was no chance that would be disclosed.

"If that's all the information you have," the colonel said, "I think that we're done here. I have work to do. I'm afraid I won't be able to let you know how things go, but the results should speak for themselves."

"I understand."

The colonel stood and looked towards the desk. "Did you remove any materials from her residence?"

Warrick hesitated, thinking of the letters. If Int-Sec didn't know about them, they could be dangerous for Kate. On the other hand, if anyone went to the house it would be obvious that he'd tampered with the computer. "Yes. Data stores. Nothing else."

After pocketing the stores, the colonel offered his hand. "I suggest that if any materials were copied, then the copies are deleted, soon. It's been a pleasure meeting you," he added, with every evidence of sincerity. "Int-Sec would thank you for doing your duty as a loyal citizen, if it knew anything about this. Goodbye, and thank you."

Warrick opened the door for him and watched the security guards escort him to the lift. Two "thank you"s. One from Int-Sec, and one personal? He wondered if the colonel had known Kate, or—strange thought—perhaps even run her. Read her reports on Tarin and his friends. Made the decisions about who to arrest and what then happened to them.

Without noticing, he rubbed his palms together, then wiped them on his trousers. He considered calling Toreth, but decided that a call in the morning would look more natural. If Carnac became suspicious now, when things were so precariously balanced, it would be disastrous.

Chapter Fourteen

It was impossible, Carnac realized for the ten-thousandth time, to leave anything to others. They—any "they"—could make a hash of the simplest instructions. When the cell door opened, and he saw Toreth and Sara sleeping peacefully, if compactly, together, he made a mental note to have the idiots responsible court-martialed, or at least dismissed without references, and turned to the nearest trooper.

"Wake them. Bring him to my office. She stays here." Hopefully that wouldn't tax the trooper's tiny mind too badly.

The morning had been spoiled already, but Carnac's good mood was restored by the sight of Toreth in handcuffs, standing between two troopers and staring sullenly at the floor. Only a small step from that to imagining his execution. A pity the man would never beg for his life—still, there were substitutes that would be almost as satisfying.

"Good morning." He pushed the chess set aside and leaned back in his chair. "I trust you had a restful night?"

"Fuck you," Toreth said without raising his eyes.

Carnac shook his head, tutting gently. "Temper, temper. We shall have guests soon, and I require your presence at the inspection, free and, you will no doubt be pleased to hear, uncuffed. You will be polite, speak when spoken to, and so on and so forth. If you have any other ideas, remember that I have possession of the delightful Sara."

Toreth looked up quickly. "You *bastard.*"

All the reaction he could wish for. He had no intention of hurting Sara (at least not yet—he'd made sure of her inclusion in the first round of executions), but the suggestion provided an excellent restraint for Toreth, should he be considering escape at this point. "The dear woman must learn that there are consequences to her actions. I promise that she is comfortable and unharmed, and will remain so as long as you are a model of cooperation with our visitors."

"I already did everything you fucking wanted. Let her go." His jaw clenched. "Please."

Perfect. "I suggest you freshen up and have something to eat. I'll have a clean uniform sent to your office. You will be brought down at the appropriate time."

He held Toreth's gaze until the man nodded, then he gestured for the troopers to take him away.

Carnac pulled the chessboard back and started to reset the pieces. In truth, the game bored him, although he found the metaphor amusing. It was too easy, and the constriction of the rules made the opposition too predictable. A game such as the elimination of I&I was far more to his tastes—a mildly challenging opponent, and stakes that really mattered.

He would win this one, and Toreth would lose—the game, and shortly afterwards his life. Troopers were already preparing to move in and make arrests. Preparing discreetly, naturally. He didn't want to be seen to anticipate the inevitable decision of his esteemed colleagues.

When everything was done, when all the bodies were burned, he would have made a genuine difference for the better, for perhaps the only time in his life. Without the shadow of I&I lying over it, Europe could begin to change; without the crutch of oppression, perhaps even the Administration would be forced to learn to stand up straight and rule for the good of the people. More realistically, many people would at least now live, and be spared terrible suffering, because of his destruction of the interrogation system. It was true that, in general, they would doubtless be dull and uninteresting people but, innocent, criminal, or resister, they would be far more human than Toreth and his repellent kin.

He rubbed two pawns between his hands, closed his fists around them and opened his right hand. And smiled.

White.

A pity, really, that he didn't believe in good omens.

Barret-Conner stood by the Int-Sec gate, looking at the ID in his hand and wondering whether to swipe it.

Yesterday afternoon he hadn't been able to get access to the complex. When he'd called Sara to tell her, something had been wrong in the office. Her voice hadn't given much away, but he'd known her for a long time. He'd taken the hint and left before the guards took too much interest in a failing ID check.

Staying away today might be smart, too, but if the inspection was in progress then the Para would need all the help he could get.

Today he had no trouble with the ID—not on the way into the complex, nor at the I&I main door, nor on the way through the building. He was beginning to think he might have overreacted, when he reached the General Criminal central office.

The handful of admins were grouped at the far side of the room, talking in low voices. Barret-Connor didn't pay them any attention. One glance told him that he'd been dead right about the trouble—no Sara, and a lot of Service.

He argued for a while but the guards outside Toreth's office wouldn't allow him in. They seemed happy enough to let him go, which was a relief. Around the corner, out of earshot of them, he checked Toreth's comm. No reply. Sara's was dead, too. He changed tactics and went in search of Chevril.

As he headed down the corridor towards the coffee rooms, he saw Chevril's admin, Kel, tapping at the lift call screen. "Kel? Kel! Wait!"

"B-C? Where have you been?"

Barret-Connor jogged down the corridor. When he reached Kel, the lift still hadn't arrived. "What's going on, Kel?"

"The proverbial, my dear, has hit a very fast fan very hard indeed. Sara and Toreth were arrested yesterday."

"The *Para*?"

"Yes. And right now I have to take a message down to Don *and* I'm supposed to wait up here to send a warning when they fetch Toreth out of his office. I'm good, but I'm not superhuman." He tapped the screen impatiently; the lift statuses were all blank. "These damnable things are out of order again."

Swearing from Kel, even a "damnable," meant big trouble. "I'm looking for Chevril, anyway—can I take the message to him for you?"

"Would you? Oh, bless you. I've been up and down those dratted stairs a dozen times already today." The admin did look a little sweaty. "Don's somewhere down on level D, near the interrogation supply stores when I heard from him last. Tell him that Systems say everything is green, and they're waiting for word from him to crash the system for a few hours if Carnac tries to fall back on backups of the old interrogation recordings."

"Got it."

"Thank you. Hurry, now." Kel turned and walked briskly away.

It must be more than the inspection, Barret-Connor decided as he started down the stairs. That had all been planned for and ready to go. Even a surprise start to it didn't account for this, and if Sara and the Para had been arrested yesterday it couldn't be that much of a surprise.

He stopped in midstride, having to keep his balance with a hand on the rail. If the Para *and* Sara were out of the picture, who had taken charge? Taking the stairs two at a time seemed like a better idea.

"Level D" was a vague destination, and Barret-Connor wasn't familiar with the interrogation levels. He saw more security all throughout the building, but especially on the lower levels. Mostly Service and the kind of I&I people whom the Para persisted in calling "resisters" when they weren't around to hear him. Eventually he found Chevril with the head of security and Senior Para Belkin. Before Barret-Connor had taken more than a couple of strides down the corridor, all three snapped to face him, conversation cutting off. Their expressions confirmed his guess—Chevril looked close to panic and Belkin glowered. Even Bevan seemed edgy.

When it registered who he was, Chevril seemed relieved to see him. Belkin merely looked more furious—probably embarrassment.

"I've got a message from Kel," Barret-Connor said quickly as he came up to them. "Systems are ready to go, and they're also set up to make sure Carnac won't be able to use old interrogation recordings."

No one seemed very interested in the news. "Have you seen Toreth?" Chevril asked.

"No. There are Service guards outside his office, though."

Bevan raised his eyes and sighed theatrically, and Barret-Connor braced himself for the invective. All the HoS said, though, was, "I know *that.*" Then he turned back to Chevril and Belkin. "We have to stick to the plan, if we're going to do anything at all."

"He knows," Chevril said.

"There's no reason the bastard should," Bevan said.

"I bumped into him not long after he came in. He's suspicious. It isn't going to work."

They must be talking about Carnac. "The inspection's started?" Barret-Connor asked.

Bevan looked at his watch. "Shit. Soon. Probably very fucking soon."

"And it had better be." Belkin spoke for the first time. "Things won't hold together much longer as it is. Listen, Bev's right—we can't change the plans now. It's too late. People are confused enough about what the hell they're supposed to tell people with all the fucking about yesterday."

Chevril shook his head. "That's the bloody problem. Someone's going to say the wrong bloody thing. They won't know whether they're talking to Carnac or the inspectors or Carnac's Service friends or us. It's hopeless."

"We can't change it," Belkin repeated. "Hopeless or not. Either we see it through, or . . ."

Barret-Connor's heart sank. Were they thinking about bolting? If they were, he could do nothing to stop them. Seniors wouldn't listen to an investigator, and the HoS never listened to anyone. Could he somehow get a warning to the Para?

"The inspectors will have to notice," Chevril continued. "And then they'll ask and some bloody idiot will spill everything."

Bevan looked at him sharply and opened his mouth, then closed it again. Barret-Connor wondered what he'd been about to say. Instead, the head of security turned to him. "Can you find me a half a dozen investigators? Preferably a dozen. Throw in a few admins if you have to, if they know their way around the building and can do what they're fucking told without bollocksing it up."

He ran through a mental list. "Yes, no problem."

"Good lad. My office, ten minutes. Get going."

Carnac met the inspectors in the main entrance. Toreth was there before him, shaved and in a fresh uniform and looking, actually, rather better than he had for some time. The night's rest in the cell had done him good and he had regained control of himself. He had his hands clasped in front of him, though—a reflex position left over from the cuffs.

Chevril was also there, standing as far from Toreth as the reception allowed, hollow-eyed and slightly disheveled. Carnac made a point of going over to speak to him, purely for the pleasure of watching Toreth's composure crack once more as he realized the truth.

"Is everything in order?" Carnac asked.

Chevril nodded, his eyes on Toreth. "Fine. Can I—"

"You will stay."

Now Chevril looked at him, a long, searching inspection. Then he nodded again. "We still have a deal," he said without conviction.

Carnac smiled and returned to his station to wait in silence. Chevril stared at the wall, Toreth glared at his fellow para with murder in his eyes, and Carnac breathed deeply, wondering whether the executions could possibly be more enjoyable than this.

The heavy main doors were, for once, open, letting cold, fresh air into the building, although the light outside was subdued, the sky overcast with threatening clouds. A most metaphorical morning, Carnac thought, as the inspection team's cars drew up outside. He watched them assemble by the reception desk—his own careful choices with a sprinkling of less amenable but necessary men and women with the political clout to make this work.

Less amenable on the surface, perhaps. However, they had ordered the arrests that had provided him with the prisoners downstairs, and done so against his own strongly expressed advice—a nice touch, he thought. Personal responsibility for the horrors on display would overcome any lingering pragmatic feelings they might have about the means being used here to further their selfish ends.

He stepped forward, beckoning Toreth over beside him. He turned to the group, but before he could speak, Toreth whispered, "Let Sara out. Now. She comes round with us or I don't cooperate."

Damn the man—didn't he know when he'd lost? There wasn't time to argue, so Carnac gave the order to a guard, and then addressed the crowd. "Ladies and gentlemen, if I might begin. I would like to introduce you to Valantin Toreth, the Acting Assistant Director of the Investigation and Interrogation Division of the Department of Internal Security..."

Warrick canceled the call for the third time that morning. Toreth's personal comm was dead, Sara wasn't answering, and I&I reception was stoically declaring them both to be "unavailable."

He was waiting in his flat for news once more, this time with only the professionally distant SimTech guard for company. He crossed to the living room window and looked out. A light snow was falling, although it wouldn't settle on the wet pavement. The forecast predicted ice tonight, though.

He'd limited himself to one call an hour, trying to not to attract Carnac's attention. Odd how a man he had once considered, if not a friend, then at least friendly, had become unquestionably the enemy. That despite the harmony of their views about the desirability of the closure of I&I.

He could pretend it was the danger to Kate, or even that he was unwilling to watch so many killed in cold blood when there was an alternative available. Even Tarin had agreed with that, in a way. That wasn't entirely truthful, though. He'd been quite willing to stand aside and do nothing, allowing Toreth's colleagues to die, and I&I staff across Europe to share the same fate. He'd been willing to let Toreth endanger his own life if that was what he insisted on doing.

However, as soon as Toreth was threatened so personally, he had acted without hesitation and without consideration of the risk. No. He *had* considered, and for Toreth he had found it worthwhile. Would he have made the same decision even without the sweetener of reforms at I&I? No way to tell, now. He smiled ruefully at his reflection, wondering what Dilly would say about it all, in the unlikely event that he could ever tell her what had happened.

Three calls were enough. Now he would have to wait for Toreth to call him. He turned away from the window. He might as well go in to SimTech—the odds of getting any useful work done were slim, but there would be some distractions.

Twenty minutes into the tour, Carnac knew that he had lost. The interrogation rooms they saw were empty of anything more offensive than chairs and tables and the staff they spoke to beautifully briefed. In the end, he gave up on his attempts to break the façade. Obviously any potentially problematical employees had been encouraged to take the day off.

At the end of the visit, Toreth stood up in front of the inspection team and gave an impressive presentation about the changes he had implemented. To start with, he made a short but movingly scripted tribute to those I&I staff who had died or been injured in the recent unrest, although without implying that he blamed anyone present for the events, or even connected them in any way. The audience were duly mildly discomforted, and therefore made more receptive.

He explained the new interrogation protocols and restrictions, which would naturally have to be approved by the Administration in collaboration with his esteemed colleagues at Justice before they could become general practice throughout Europe. He spoke briefly about changes to the detention systems, making an oblique reference to how many of the division now had personal experience of the cells. He included a thoughtful section on the use of mood- and perception-altering drugs in interrogations, standards of evidence, and the interrogation of minors, all designed to leave the inspectors with a few mild ethical dilemmas to consider. And, repeatedly, he made sure that all due credit was given to the real architect of the plans, the man sitting in the front row, his highly respected boss, Socioanalyst Carnac.

He spoke fluently and with confidence, and after every section he paused and caught Carnac's eye. At the end he told the audience that Carnac had been a pleasure to work with, and that it had been particularly impressive that an outsider could have such a thorough understanding of the workings and ethos of the division. Then he took questions, and answered them smoothly, charmingly, and without hesitation.

It was a beautiful performance. The only thing Carnac couldn't understand was why Toreth had gone through with it when he knew the price. Obviously he believed that he wouldn't have to pay it—Toreth suddenly developing a self-sacrificing streak was about as probable as his giving up sex.

When the questions were over, the room broke up into small groups, a buzz of voices that made Carnac suddenly claustrophobic. People wanted to talk to him—everyone, it seemed—and he felt himself start to sweat.

As soon as he could manage it, he excused himself and went up to his office. Toreth was waiting for him there, sitting at his desk with his feet up. Carnac studied him for a moment, trying to read his expression. A perfect balance of nerves and anticipation. "You know what I'm going to do," Carnac said.

Toreth smiled at him, tense as a wound spring. "Make the call. Go on. Make the fucking call. I want to watch you do it."

It took only a couple of minutes to discover that Kailynna Avens had been taken out of custody at nine twenty-seven that morning. Knowing it was hopeless, Carnac asked the questions anyway. The warrant had carried Carnac's name, and his authorization, which was why he hadn't been informed. No, no one knew where she was. No one recognized the escort she had left with—three men in Service troopers' uniforms. They had their names, too, of course.

Carnac cut the comm and thought about closing airports and ordering searches. It would be a waste of time. There were too many ways out of New London, particularly for a highly trained operative. Someone might get lucky, but it wasn't worth the risk of publicly tying his name too closely to the fiasco. Bad enough that his name had been used on the release warrant.

Chevril had lied to him, last night and this morning. Comprehensively, and with a skill Carnac wouldn't have credited. The senior must have had a powerful incentive, which Carnac presumed was currently sitting in the chair before him, smirking at his discovery. Payne may well have known, too. For one thing, if Service people were involved there were good odds that Payne was a party to it at some level. Well, Chevril he could take to pieces at his leisure, but he should start with a careful investigation of Payne's recent movements and contacts.

He was still deep in thought when Toreth pushed his chair back from the desk and stood up. The tension had gone, and Carnac realized that he hadn't known for certain that Kate had escaped. "I'm going back downstairs," Toreth said. "Butter up the inspectors a bit more. Lots to do for tomorrow. I'll see you then, shall I? When the preliminary verdict comes in. I think you're going to come out of this looking very good indeed."

"It's not a foregone conclusion yet."

"No?" Toreth headed for the door, only a feint because he stopped behind him, too close. Carnac stayed where he was, waiting for Toreth to go through whatever little charade he felt was necessary to underline his victory.

"What are you going to do about it? Tell them that this was all my idea? That you wanted everything how it was when the bad old Administration ran things? That you wanted to execute the lot of us because you didn't have the guts to handle watching an interrogation?" Toreth put his hands on Carnac's waist and pulled him gently back against him. "Are you going to tell them all that?"

Of course he wasn't—it would be useless and pointless, because no one would want to listen. The idiot inspectors had lapped up every word of Toreth's speech, because it was what they had wanted to hear. They simply refused to understand the danger of letting creatures like Toreth live.

"Do you know, I almost like you like this," Toreth murmured. "Speechless. Suits you. I don't think I've seen you looking better, except maybe when you were flat on your back in bed, telling me all your secrets and begging for more cock." Toreth's mouth moved against his ear now, triggering a memory he didn't know he had. "Do you know what else? You were flying fifteen miles high while you were doing it, but drugs like that don't work on nothing. You wanted it. You wanted me. That came from *you,* not any ampule. Now tell me again how much you hate me and what a lousy fuck I am."

Carnac closed his eyes. Toreth could have been making every word up, because he remembered no details at all about the evening, but Carnac knew he wasn't. Besides, the awful, gaping void of memory was worse than anything Toreth could have done to him physically.

Toreth laughed, then let him go and walked out. Carnac leaned on the desk, trying to pretend that Toreth's voice hadn't any effect on him at all. At that precise moment, he hated himself far more than Toreth, or even the obscenity that he represented. However, he knew that feeling wouldn't last much longer than the erection he was willing away.

The single fact he was most clear about was that Toreth would regret this. All of it, everything he had ever done in his overlong, evil life, but most especially this. Toreth would *pay.*

Kate turned over in the darkness, the narrow bed of the cell hard beneath her. When she had been moved to this place, earlier in the day, she had thought, briefly, that they might be setting her free. Instead, there had been a short journey in a car with blacked-out windows, and then another cell. That was the point at which she had finally given up hope.

How many more Int-Sec agents had been arrested? How many were in places like this? She might have been afraid of what was ahead, if she hadn't been so angry. After years of sacrifice, years of giving her life to the Administration, the thing they had all fought to prevent had happened. It made her furious to think about it. Animals, she would've called them, except that animals rarely behaved like that. Mindless, destructive barbarians.

She'd seen the reports of the damage to Int-Sec, and especially to I&I. The sharpness of her concern for Toreth had surprised her, as had her relief when Keir called to say his lover was safe. She'd been proud of Keir, even as she'd felt cold at the risk he'd taken by going to I&I. He'd laughed, happy and indulgent, when she'd started to fuss. "I was perfectly safe, I promise, Mother. The city's full of troopers now—everything's going to be fine."

If only he knew.

Keir couldn't help her here, wherever here was. They would be coming for her soon. There was no sound, no intrusion from the world outside, nothing but darkness, but she knew the resisters would come soon. She had turned in their families; she had killed their friends and lovers—if not with her own hand, then with her reports. There would be no mercy or reprieve.

Although she would never have said anything of the kind to her handlers, she could understand why they wanted to do it. If anyone hurt Keir, or Dilly, or Valeria, she would move heaven and earth to punish those responsible. The difference, though, was that her children weren't traitors. Resisters played with fire and then whined when they were burned. Tarin's idiotic friends did it with monotonous regularity, and they never learned. They never understood that if they stopped behaving like idealistic fools, they would be accepted and protected by the Administration they professed to loathe. And why? Because they balked at movement registration or comms surveillance, or resented corporate privilege or population control. Pathetic, childish petulance at necessary rules. The selfish desires of the individual overriding the good of the Administration as a whole.

She'd been arrested by Service troopers—*Service*—and she'd known then that she had lived her life in vain. If people who had sworn an oath to the Administration could sit up and beg for new masters, there was no hope for loyalty from the masses. She almost wished now that she'd spat in their faces when they'd come to collect her.

That would have been vulgar, especially in front of poor Valeria. There was no need to stoop to their level. Although it was probably too much to hope for a chance to scorn them publicly at a trial, she would finish her years of service with pride and courage. Whatever they did, whatever they wanted from her before she died, she would give them nothing. There was nothing that—

The door opened, without any warning, spilling blinding light into the cell. Before she could accustom herself to it, a voice ordered her out. She emerged, blinking, only to be hurried away down the corridor.

She almost smiled, thinking how ridiculous they must look—two burly troopers, almost young enough to be her grandchildren, and herself, short and gray-haired between them. Then the conviction of a few moments ago returned. This was the end. She straightened her shoulders and lengthened her stride, trying to keep her dignity. They would get nothing from her.

Then they passed through a security door, into another room lit with harsh artificial light, and she saw him.

He looked terribly tired, and, foolishly, she was surprised by how old he seemed. Nothing at all like the precious photographs, where they were both so young. Still, she recognized him immediately. She had feared, from time to time, that after so many years she wouldn't be able to. That she might pass him in the street one day and not know him. Now that the moment had come she had not a second's doubt or hesitation.

Shock, fortunately, rendered her speechless long enough to register the tiny shake of his head. She stood impassive while the man in Service colonel's uniform completed the transfer paperwork that could only be done with the prisoner present, motioned for the troopers with him to handcuff her, and led the way out of the building.

Two cars waiting for them—one for the troopers, one for the pair of them. She entered the car, sat down, and waited as he sat beside her and the car began to move. She watched through the tinted window as the complex, wherever it was, passed by. Eventually, they passed through a security point and out onto a public road. Leo took her hands, gentle but impersonal, unlocked the cuffs, removed them, and sat back. "It's all right now, " he said. "You can talk freely."

Silence, while she tried to decide what to say. She could tell nothing from his voice. There was one thing, though, that determined whatever else she might say. "Did you get my letters?"

He nodded. "All of them. But... they took a little time to reach me."

"They said they were sending them on, but I was never sure if I could believe them. And when there was nothing back, for so long, I thought—"

He took her hand again. "I asked them to let me see you. I kept asking them for a long time—years—but they said the risk was too great. I'm so sorry, Katy."

"No. No need to be, not now." And there wasn't. She felt as though she had last seen him yesterday, or this morning. However much they had both changed, nothing had changed between them. She looked down at his hand, clasping hers, and thought how beautiful it was, and how she was far too old to think anything so silly.

After a while she asked, "Have there been many Cit agents arrested?" She didn't really care, except that she wanted to hear his voice again.

"No. Int-Sec is keeping it under control, for now. If it starts, it'll be bad, but every day makes it less likely. There have been a few like you—your name slipped out, I don't know how."

"However did you find me?"

"Partly luck. I was one of the senior officers on duty when the message saying that you were in trouble came through. But I recognized the code, so I took charge of it."

Reluctantly, she found herself compelled to ask, "You're working for them? For resisters?"

He shook his head firmly. "I'm working for the Administration."

"But—"

"No. The names at the top might have changed, but not the heart of it." His voice hardened, stripping the years away. "The structure is still in place and that's what matters. That's what is worth fighting for—what we've both fought for."

For so long. She had done her duty to the Administration—endless years of it—and the things that had felt so important in the cell were less compelling now when compared to this miracle. But she hesitated, even so, and he sensed it at once, as he'd always been able to do.

"Katy, do you think I'd still be with Cit if this new council wanted to destroy the Administration?" He squeezed her fingers gently. "You know me better than that."

That she did. The Administration first, over everything else, over herself and Keir and Dilly, and for the first time she realized that she had never once resented him for it, however bitterly she had regretted their separation. Rather, it had been one of the things she had loved about him—his passion, his loyalty and resolve. One of the things that had bound then together. “What now?” she asked.

“Everything’s arranged—it’s not entirely official, but I’m owed a lot of favors. You’ll be met at the other end. There’ll be a safe house, somewhere to stay, and then something permanent can be worked out. For now, the important thing is to get you away.”

“Are you coming with me?” A sudden thought hit her. “Is there—do you have someone to stay for?”

He smiled. “No, no one.”

“Oh.” What was she supposed to say? That she wouldn’t have minded if there were? Of course she would have. “Good.”

“But I’m afraid I can only stay with you for a few weeks.” He put a finger to her lips, silencing the protest. “I’m sorry, but then I have to come back. Just until I can get away permanently, I promise.”

“As long as we’ll be together in the end, I don’t care.” However, she did care, although she knew it was selfish, after he’d done so much. She couldn’t stop herself from adding, “I wish it was for good now.”

“Soon—as soon as I can, I promise. I’m due for retirement, and I’d like to leave as legitimately as possible. We might need friends later.”

We. Everything she had wanted for so long was in that one word. There was one moment, after he held her tight against him but before she kissed him, when Kailynna the professional began to look to the future, and to calculate, and to doubt. Then Kate set her firmly to one side, and never thought about her again.

When the inspectors had gone, Sara attended a brief, tense meeting in Toreth’s office. Herself and Toreth, B-C, Mistry, Bevan, Chevril, Mike Belkin, and the other senior paras in the know. No one had anything untoward to report, and everyone said the same things, over and over again.

It went well. Everything went fine. The interrogation levels looked great. Everyone performed brilliantly. Who came up with the idea of posting investigators ahead of the inspection to warn people it was coming? Brilliant—saved the day. Carnac looked pissed off—that was good, wasn’t it? All level one. The inspectors looked convinced. They *were* convinced, weren’t they? I would’ve been.

Trying to persuade each other.

Eventually, Toreth’s patience wore thin and he threw everyone else out. The two of them sat, him in Tillotson’s stolen chair, herself on the desk. He had his forefingers braced on the edge of the desk, turning the chair a few centimeters left and right. It squeaked softly in the silence. If he didn’t stop it soon, she’d kill him.

“I think it went okay,” she said. She hadn’t been counting, but that must’ve been the dozenth time.

"Yeah. It went fine. We just have to wait for the announcement tomorrow. There's nothing else we can do." He wasn't listening to himself.

"At least it's going to be quick." She hesitated, then asked, "Are you planning to see Warrick? Tell him how it went?"

He shook his head. "Tomorrow. I left him a message to say we were still around. I'll see him when it's all over and done with."

She checked her watch. "I should go. Fee'll be wondering where I am."

"Come to the flat." When she didn't answer, he spun the chair around once, then pushed it back and stood up. "Call her, come to the flat. Some of the takeaways have reopened, and I've already got some things in to drink. I—" He hesitated. "It'll be closer for work in the morning. We should get in early."

Since they'd been arriving early every day for a month, it wasn't much of a reason, but she didn't argue. She knew what he meant. She didn't want to wait alone, either.

Cartons lay scattered across the table, interspersed with bottles. It had taken them longer than they'd expected to find an open takeaway. The meal had been further delayed while Sara tidied up, because the flat was way beyond even her high squalor tolerance threshold. By the time they'd thrown out the last of the broken furniture and generally cleaned everything, even Toreth was willing to admit it was an improvement.

Somehow they had moved onto the topic of birthdays. It made a change from I&I, but in an absolute sense it was still depressing.

"It's just that I feel so bloody *old,*" she said.

"You're twenty-eight."

"And soon I'm going to be twenty-nine. And next year I'm going to be thirty." If we're still here next year.

"Thirty isn't old. I should know, because *I'm* nearly fucking forty and that isn't old, either."

She sighed. She lay on her back on Toreth's battered sofa, her head in his lap, looking up at him. It felt weird, because she hadn't done it for a while, and she was slightly soberer than she usually was when she ended up down here. She was too bloody old to be acting like this, as well.

Toreth didn't seem to mind, though. He'd been remarkably patient while she bitched and moaned over the looming birthdays she couldn't do anything about. Sympathetic, even. Or possibly he just liked the general visual effect of having a woman's head in his lap and he wasn't listening at all. You could never be sure with him. Right now, he was staring thoughtfully into his drink. He'd had more than she had over the evening, which meant that they were about comparably drunk.

She poked his ribs gently, careful to choose the undamaged side. "What're you thinking about?"

"What?" He smiled slightly. "Oh. Nothing."

Meaning Warrick, probably. Not surprising since, apart from one brief meeting, he hadn't seen him for a fortnight. She felt an uncharacteristic sting of jealousy, not so much directed at Warrick in person as at the way he tended to creep into every situation when Toreth wasn't paying attention to anything specific. Toreth had been hers first—her friend first. Now, however desperately he tried to pretend otherwise on occasion, he was Warrick's. Signed, authorized, and submitted, with an unlimited damage waiver.

"What's it like?" she asked.

"What's what like?"

"Having Warrick." Because it was Toreth, she quickly clarified her question. "Having him around as a regular thing."

"Great. It helps if you like chains and you don't mind the noise."

"No, seriously. What's it like?"

"Like?" He shrugged, retreating from the question. "Why should it be 'like' anything? Do you want another drink?"

She knew better than to press him, but she found she really wanted to know. Curiosity and, yes, a touch of envy again. "I mean... always having him there. Knowing he's always going to be there."

"I don't. No reason why he should be."

"Oh, come off it. It's been years now. He's not going to just turn round one day, say 'That's it, I don't want you anymore,' and walk off."

"He could." He wasn't looking at her anymore. "People do. Why the hell would I assume that he won't?"

"Well, because it's *Warrick*. He wouldn't. I mean, he really—"

"Don't say it."

"I wasn't—"

"Don't say *anything*." His voice rose. "Don't—just shut the fuck up."

She stared up at him, appalled by the fear in his voice. "Toreth?" She waited for him to interrupt again, but he didn't. "I'm sorry. I didn't mean to get into a lot of stupid stuff you don't want to hear. Sorry."

"It's... it's no big deal." He ran his hand through his hair. "I don't know why I got so—never mind. What was the question?"

"Forget it."

"No, it's okay. What did you want to know?"

"Well, what it's like, having a regular thing?"

"It's good." He took a deep breath. "It's good—knowing what he likes. It makes it... easy. To... I don't know. To stay in bed on Sunday morning, or whatever, and fuck or not, and not have to think about everything. Anything. It's safe—no, not safe. That's stupid. Just... good."

She could feel him shaking with the effort it took to say that much, and she felt a tiny tug of guilt. It wasn't fair to exploit the fact that he'd do it for her, for no better reason than curiosity. "It sounds lovely."

He nodded, looking even more uncomfortable—at her choice of words or at what he'd said, she wasn't sure. "I don't know why the fuck you're asking me about it. You were the one with the collection of rings."

"They never worked out, though, did they? It was never easy." She snorted, not quite a laugh, and he looked down, suspicious.

"What?"

"I was just thinking—there's you, and I mean this nicely, who'll screw anything you can catch. And you've got Warrick. Then there's me, who's ever so choosy and tries to pick the stayers, and I've got no one. Trying too hard, I expect."

"What about McLean?"

"Total bust." She sighed again. "Wouldn't work. Or at least . . . wrong time, wrong place. Or something."

"Good. He's a tosser." Sympathy, Toreth-style. "You should try my way. Fuck at random until you—" He blinked. "Until you get lucky."

She shook her head. "I don't think it would work. It always ends up messy if I try it."

"You said that before, you know."

"When?"

"Oh, God, years ago. Here. The first time you were here, in fact." He patted the sofa. "When you got so high you tried to fuck me. You said you didn't do casual screwing. Which was funny at the time, because you were lying on top of me trying to unfasten my trousers."

Yes. This was the same sofa where they'd fucked, and she'd pretended in the morning that she didn't remember a thing. She'd been . . . nineteen. Had he really not bought any new furniture in ten years? "Oh, well. Maybe I was wrong."

He smiled. "Maybe."

Pause for thought, a moment of silence while they both wondered if that was it, then he put his drink down on the arm of the sofa and traced his fingertip slowly around her mouth. She managed to resist for the whole length of her bottom lip, and then she opened her mouth and captured the finger.

A second finger worked its way between her lips as his eyes closed. "Mmm. I like that."

I know you do. I remember. She licked figures of eight across his fingertips while she told herself what an incredibly bad idea this was. All the same reasons there had been before, and Warrick. Now there was Warrick.

He need never know. She wouldn't tell him, and Toreth wouldn't either, not about this. Besides, if everything went to hell tomorrow, they might not even have a chance to regret it. His free hand stroked over her forehead, traced her eyebrows. It would be so easy to say nothing and let it happen.

She took his fingers out of her mouth, kissed his palm, and he opened his eyes. "Sara?" he asked, and she shook her head. She had her morals. Not many, and they weren't necessarily very good ones, but Thou Shalt Not Screw Friends' Partners was an absolute.

"I can't," she said. "Not this time."

She thought he might be angry, because his eyes narrowed, but then he laughed. "Fucking hell. I was never sure, you know. Either way."

"Honestly?" She laughed, too, relief that after all this time it was suddenly okay for them to come clean about it. "I thought you were just being polite."

"God, no. I didn't want you to resign, and I knew you would if I said anything and you really didn't remember. Well?"

"Well what?"

"Was it good?"

"Was it—?" So typically bloody Toreth. "God, I can't remember." Then she took pity on him. "Yes, it was. I mean, I haven't spent ten years thinking about it every time I screwed anyone, but it was, oh, I don't know... in the top ten."

He grinned. "Top five?"

Sometimes, like now, she could still fool herself into thinking that she loved him. She sat up, because a little distance was, if not necessary, then at least a good idea. "Shut up and pass me the pineapple fritters."

Chapter Fifteen

❖

In all of Toreth's life, he couldn't remember a day passing so slowly. It wasn't that there was nothing to do—in fact he was as busy as ever. It was simply that he kept looking at the clock, and every time it was five minutes later than the last time he'd checked. Then he'd be angry with himself, and get back to work, forcing himself to concentrate until he knew at least an hour must have passed. Then he would look, and it would be five minutes later again.

Sara brought coffees until he had to ask her to stop. He knew she was only doing it from nerves, but he didn't want to miss the report because he was in the medical unit with caffeine-induced cardiac arrhythmia. They didn't speak much, but there was nothing left to say. B-C was sensibly keeping out of his way, but he caught sight of Mistry wandering aimlessly around in the General Criminal main office.

When Payne arrived in the late afternoon, unannounced, he wondered if he'd come to say the inspectors were ready. That idea was dispelled by the way he slammed the office door behind him. Toreth inspected him with curiosity. He'd never seen him out of uniform, except at the gym, and the effect was mildly disconcerting. His civilian clothes were stained with sweat, and he looked like hell. Now that everything was so nearly over, Toreth had hoped Payne would go quietly. He didn't fancy a protracted, boring scene, although he strongly suspected that was what he was about to get.

"Who did you tell about us?" Payne demanded as he came over to the desk.

"No one." Toreth leaned back in his chair. "Sara guessed, but I'll tell you now she didn't tell anyone else."

"You must have told someone."

"If I had, I wouldn't bother to lie to you about it."

Payne didn't seem to hear him. "Or someone saw us. I suppose someone could've seen us. Fuck."

He'd never heard him seriously swearing before, either. "Yes, easily. Listen, do you think we could get to the point? Because I have a lot of work to do—the inspectors are reporting this afternoon, in case you didn't know."

"I've been suspended, which is why I'm wandering around like this." Payne brushed his hands over his shirt. "Suspended, pending a court-martial." His voice cracked.

"For fucking me? Have they been taking tips from the Americans?"

"The—?" Payne gave him a brief, confused look, then shook his head. "It's for disobeying orders. Carnac's orders. For not telling him what I knew about your plans. For not reporting to headquarters. They've been questioning me all day—he's going to nail me with everything he can think of."

"So what does that have to do with whether anyone saw us or not?"

"Because when they dragged me out of bed this morning and put me in handcuffs and took me in, the bastards who did it made absolutely sure that Mary knew what I'd been doing. With you, that is—they didn't bother telling her about the rest of it. That I'd been . . . oh, Christ."

Payne sat down in a chair abruptly, and covered his face with his hands. "Oh, Christ," he repeated. "That I'd been unfaithful, and that it was with a man. Except they didn't put it quite like that, as you can probably imagine."

For sheer, bloody, beautifully arranged vindictiveness, you couldn't top Carnac. Worrying, though, that he was still sniffing around the wreckage. Didn't the man know when he was beaten? "How did she take it?" Toreth asked, mildly curious.

Payne looked up. "*Take* it? I haven't spoken to her. But when they finally let me go, I went home and found she'd changed the door codes and all my belongings were lying in a pile in the hall, so I'm guessing that she's just a little bit upset."

Toreth shrugged. "She might come round. They do, sometimes. Good luck with it all, anyway."

Payne stared at him. "Didn't you hear me? I'm going to be court-martialed, because I—because I helped you!"

"That's a shame. Nothing I can do about it, though."

"Val—"

"That's not my fucking name. Call me Toreth, if you have to call me anything other than Para."

Payne licked his lips. "What about us?"

"Us?" He always got a kick out of this part, no matter how tedious the rest of it was. "There isn't any 'us.' It was just a fuck, Payne, that's all."

Payne's expression changed slowly from desperation to horrified, unwilling comprehension. Eventually he managed, "Just a . . . ?"

"What else did you think it was? You're the one who said you were happily married." He smiled. "Past tense being the operative one now."

Payne took a few more seconds to pull himself together, but managed it with surprising aplomb. "I see. Yes. Well, thanks a lot, Para."

"My pleasure."

That earned another stare, then Payne said, "Carnac was right."

"He is, sometimes. But most of the time he's lying, manipulative, and ruthless, and I'd keep that very clearly in mind if I were you."

"Whereas you—" He clenched his jaw, stopping the words. "I should tell him the rest, you know. I haven't told them who you asked me to take that message to."

It was always a mistake to let them sit down and start going on. "Payne, I fucked you because I like brunets, and because it's a pleasure to walk down a corridor behind you, but mostly because at the time I badly needed you to keep your mouth shut. At the time." He rested his elbows on the desk and leaned forwards. "And do you know why it worked? Because when Carnac picked you out and gave you to me he knew you were gagging for it and that you'd back me up to the hilt with your bosses so that you could keep getting it. He *knew.*"

Payne looked away. When he finally forced himself to look back, Toreth continued. "You behaved exactly how he predicted. Then you went a bit further than he wanted and now he's spanking you for it, because he's like that. He's a cunt. Don't think that you'll get any favors from him, and don't think he doesn't already know everything you know, and a lot more. Tell him whatever you like—frankly, I don't give a fuck either way."

"And that's it?"

"That's it. If you want some advice, I suggest you keep your mouth shut, and bend over and take it from him like a good little lieutenant. He's like Sara's fucking cat—if you put up a fight you'll only keep him interested." And like Sara's cat, he'll probably finish you off anyway, because he's a bastard. "Now, piss off. Like I said, I'm busy."

Payne stood up, pale but under tight control. Looked good on him. "I hope... I hope Carnac finds some time left over from screwing me into the ground to think up something to do to you, too, because I bet he can come up with something you deserve. And if he doesn't, I just hope you fucking die."

A good exit line, which he made the most of, closing the door quietly this time.

Toreth tried to get back to work, but ten minutes later found himself standing by the window, looking out. They were finally replacing some of the broken windows, and from time to time shards of glass showered silently down into the courtyard.

What were the odds of Carnac simply writing this one off? Given that they were negligible, what was he going to do? Before he had had too long to think about that unpleasant prospect, the door opened again and Sara said, "It's time."

Carnac arrived early for the inspectors' verdict, although there was little point in doing so. There was certainly no chance of inducing a last-minute change of heart in the inspection team. He'd tried that yesterday evening, when he'd spoken to as many of them as he could contact. His attempts to suggest that perhaps a professional body made up in large part of sociopaths was unlikely to experience such a sudden conversion to humanitarian ideals had been received with polite incomprehension. He'd chosen them so carefully, for their previously criminally liberal attitudes, and he now reaped what he had sown.

The tiers of seats filled quickly. At the front he could see Sara, with Chevril beside her. Others sat nearby whom he recognized from Doral's comprehensive betrayal. They all looked nervous. God only knew why, because it should be obvious even to a moron what the result would be.

News of the inspection had spread through the building yesterday, and everyone who could be was here. Soon the large lecture theater was packed to capacity, and he overheard Toreth in consultation with Bevan, deciding which additional rooms would be best for live feeds. Of course. They'd make certain no one would miss out on this.

Once it began, Toreth stood beside him on the platform, listening to the verdict with solemn attentiveness. Only once did the façade crack, when the head of the inspectors began to praise Carnac's personal contribution using the exact same phrases Toreth had used the day before. That drew one cough, which couldn't possibly have been a laugh. When the inspector paused for the audience to show their appreciation, Toreth applauded along with them enthusiastically, leaning in towards him. "Do you think they've got a medal ready for you, you cunt?" he asked through a broad, friendly smile.

For the last ten minutes, Carnac survived only by blocking out every word and staring fixedly at the back rows of the audience, high up and far away, where he couldn't distinguish faces and so didn't have to see the growing delight. Finally, the torture was over—or rather, it moved to a different level.

How quickly he'd picked up the jargon, he thought sourly, as the assembled I&I staff began to clap once more. Applause, and more applause, with the inspection team looking so gratified that he wanted to kill them all.

It took him some time to get away from the crowd, although it wasn't all congratulations and praise. Major Bell was one of the first to reach him. She looked as disgusted as he felt. "Now I see why you froze me out in time for the inspection," she said.

"I'm sorry?"

"These reforms, impressive as they undoubtedly are, weren't quite what the Service had in mind for I&I. Pulling the teeth of Interrogation? In the current climate? Still, I suppose you've made plenty of friends." She gestured to the civilian inspectors, in conversation with Toreth and Bevan.

"Yes, I suppose I have."

To his surprise, she didn't seem to notice the despair in his voice. "I hope for your sake it proves to be a lasting friendship."

"Somehow, I doubt it," he said without thinking, wanting nothing more than to get out of the room while still in control of his emotions.

Now Bell looked at him closely, frowning. "This wasn't your idea?"

With an effort, he pulled himself together, bringing up his professional mask. "I plan for the long term, Major. What happens here this week, or this month, is of less importance than the future of the Administration in the years to come. Whether the council retains its precise current composition or not, I think you will find that it is a civilian future, not a military one."

He smiled thinly, gaining only a little satisfaction from the confusion on Bell's face, quickly followed by a flicker of alarm. That should give her something interesting to report to her superiors. She made her excuses hurriedly and disappeared into the crowd, glancing back over her shoulder once before he lost sight of her.

As he turned to go, one of the inspection team caught his arm and drew him forwards into another conversation he desperately didn't want. It took fifteen minutes before he finally managed to escape, and afterwards he couldn't recall anything they had talked about.

Eventually, he left the stage, stumbling on the steps, horrified to find his vision blurred and his throat tight. Stopping in the corridor, he leaned against the wall, fighting for control, no longer caring what any witnesses might think.

The inspectors and the last of I&I staff who had not been privy to the plan in advance filtered out of the room and down the corridor. A reception of some kind had been laid on in one of the canteens. Carnac couldn't bear to go with them. If one more person patted his back, he was certain that he would vomit. He lingered outside the scene of his victorious humiliation, listening to the medley of excited conversations within. The conspirators, hyped with relief at their reprieve, were reliving the event in gruesome detail.

"Did you see his face?"

"And then when that head wanker from Int-Sec said—"

"What do you think about my stupid bloody plan *now,* then?"

"—the look on his face? Like he was sucking a fucking lemon."

" 'A truly remarkable achievement.' I thought you were going to *die* up there."

"Bunch of bleeding hearts. I can't believe they swallowed it."

"But Toreth, you were standing behind him half the time. You couldn't see his face—"

" 'Continue your highly valued contribution to the unity of Europe.' And Mike said, 'Is he talking about us?' and I nearly—"

"How I didn't laugh, I'll never know, I swear to God."

"Did you see the look on his *face?*" Sara's voice topped the others by sheer delighted volume. "Oh, God, I thought he was going to choke."

"I saw him," Toreth said. Carnac heard an exuberant kiss, and Sara yelped. "I saw him. Best day of my fucking life. I hope Bev got the whole fucking thing recorded."

"Free copies for everyone," Bevan said. He was laughing—they all were. Well, Carnac supposed that they had earned their celebration. It had been excellently planned and executed, he had to admit that.

"Are we going out later, then?" Chevril asked. There was a pause, before he added in significant tones, "I'll get the first round in."

From the chorus of disbelief and abuse that greeted the statement, this would be something of a novelty. There seemed to be general agreement with the idea, though, and the starting venue of "the usual place" was proposed and accepted.

The usual place. I&I vermin drinking their way around the city tonight, and every night for the foreseeable future. In that future, on the levels below him, prisoners—human beings—would scream and plead futilely for their lives, and die in unimaginable pain.

He'd tried his best to destroy I&I, and he hadn't been good enough. Perhaps he had hated too much. Hatred had cleared his vision enough to see past the years of conditioning to the service of the Administration. It had given him the courage to risk his life to change things. However, in the end, hatred had distorted his perceptions and led him to underestimate them. His errors. His failure. Beaten by these psychopathic scum.

They began to leave the room, passing him without a glance, or with expressions of open contempt. Comments and laughter drifted back to him down the corridor as he tried to decide whether the failure or the lack of respect hurt the most.

"What's wrong with you?" Sara asked from inside the room. For a moment he thought she was talking to him, then Toreth answered her.

"I can't make it tonight. I've got to see Warrick."

"Oh, come on. It won't be the same without you. Can't you wait until tomorrow?"

"No. I don't need him any more pissed off with me than he is already."

"God, listen to who's well bloody whipped."

"Fuck off, Chev. As if you'd take a shit without Elena's written fucking permission."

"I've told you before—"

"All right, all right." Sara, placating. "Look, why don't you come out to the bar at least? Then we'll slope off at tennish, when everyone moves on to the club. We can take a bottle of something. I'll say hello, break the ice, and then I'll go back to the party and you can kiss and make up."

"I was planning on fucking and making up, but yeah, sounds okay."

Chevril made a revolted noise. "God, you two."

Toreth laughed, good humor restored. "You still owe me a date, Chev. Your cock, my arse. Don't think I'm going to forget about it."

"I was bloody delirious when I said that, and that doesn't bloody count."

The voices began to move towards the door, so Carnac retreated down the corridor, watching them leave from the concealment of a doorway.

Socioanalysis is both an art and a science, one that is practiced by genuine geniuses, measured on any scale. And a large part of the art is finding the opportunities, and then applying the science of knowing what to do with them.

As Sara well knew, Chevril had offered to buy the first round in the hope that only a few of the conspirators would have arrived at the bar by then. No such luck.

Sara suspected that Toreth had suggested the necessary tactics to a few people on the way over. The group delayed, changed their minds, confused orders, and started again as new people arrived. Other I&I staff already in the bar for celebrations of their own were invited to join in. Eventually, when Chevril was literally sweating at the size of the upcoming bill, Kel called a halt to the persecution and brought out his hand screen.

"You lot need an admin. What's the saying about parties in alcoholic establishments? Names and drinks in order, please, my dears. Rank, brains, or beauty—Assistant Director Toreth still goes first."

Toreth flipped through the cocktail menu, and ordered the most expensive thing on it. When Mike Belkin topped that with a bottle of champagne, Chevril actually whimpered. A dozen more people arrived before the ordering finished, and Toreth insisted they were added to the round. When the bar staff had lined the last of the drinks up on the bar, Chevril handed over his credit card with an expression suggesting he'd rather have parted with a kidney.

"Elena is going to bloody kill me," he muttered, moving out of the way as the crowd descended. "When she sees—"

Toreth leaned down, and Sara didn't hear what he said, but Chevril stopped dead in midcomplaint and looked up at him. She couldn't hear his reply, either, but the mirror behind the bar clearly reflected their faces—Toreth absolutely humorless, with eyes like midwinter, and Chevril suddenly subdued. Chevril said something again, and Toreth shook his head. She didn't catch the first part of the sentence, but as Toreth straightened, she heard him say, "—tell anyone. I mean, I picked you—doesn't make me look very good, does it?"

"Thanks," Chevril said, but Toreth had already turned away. When Chevril saw Sara watching, he managed a sickly smile.

"What's all that about?" someone asked from behind, and Sara turned to find Daedra, still wearing her one black plait.

"Dunno." If Toreth wanted the betrayal kept secret, then she wouldn't spread it. "Have you got a drink? Chevril's buying."

Chevril cleared his throat, and then stepped backwards up onto the rail running around the bar a few inches above the floor, balancing with a hand on the bar. "Listen up, people. Before you're all too bloody wasted on my money to pay any bloody attention."

The crowd offered a few comments that Chevril ignored—mostly suggesting that he stand on something taller—then quieted.

"Right." He coughed again. "Those pillocks this afternoon were right about one thing—this is all down to Toreth. No pissing about—we owe him a lot, some of us more than others. Everyone here, everyone else at I&I. If it wasn't for him, we'd all be back down in those bloody cells right now, and I don't know about you, but once was enough for me. So—Toreth, Senior Para." He raised his glass.

Sara slipped her arm around Toreth's waist as the combination of applause, abuse, and whistles rolled over them. Toreth grinned, actually blushing, and he hugged her shoulders until the noise died down.

"Ah, fuck." Speechless, for about the first time she could remember. "Thanks." He stopped again, running his hand through his hair. "I'll, uh—I'll just say that I didn't do it for any of you bastards personally. I did it to shaft fucking Carnac, and stop him from taking I&I down, and I think I can say that as far as that goes, it was pretty fucking spectacular."

Another pause for more applause. Sara pinched Toreth's waist, and when he looked down, she mouthed, "Bevan."

He nodded, and waved for quiet. "Yeah, and also to say that I'm not the only one you ought to be buying free drinks until they retire..."

As he started the list of names, Sara looked around the room. It struck her that this was probably a new experience for him—he was used to professional respect, and sexual attention, but this was popularity and genuine gratitude. Not a bad achievement, considering who it was from.

Then she looked again, seeing invisible gaps. The people who weren't there. Too bloody depressing a thought for something that should be a celebration, but she couldn't stop herself. Another list of names, this time the dead, unrolled behind her eyes until Toreth squeezed her shoulder again.

"And last but not least, of course, Sara." He leaned down and kissed her on the mouth, firmly and with more tongue than she ought to let him get away with, to the accompaniment of another storm of whistles. He straightened up. "So—to Sara, Bev, and everyone else."

Not sure whether she ought to drink to herself, Sara raised her glass anyway, adding her own silent toast.

Parsons. Starr. Sedanioni. All the rest.

Later that evening, the building security admitted Carnac without difficulty. As he rode up in the lift, he ran through the encounter to come, mapping out probabilities and building contingencies. These were the things he did best and the ritual of planning calmed him.

Outside Keir's flat, the guard checked his ID carefully, and then called in to the flat. Then they waited in silence as the time ticked past. Twenty-three long days since he had been here last. Nineteen since Keir had visited I&I—ostensibly about the curfew passes, but his real motive had been so transparent.

Carnac wished, briefly, that he were the kind of person who could truthfully say, "I don't understand why you're with him." However, he understood both of them better than they did themselves. Therefore, he also knew how slim were the chances that this evening would bring him anything more than a sweet taste of revenge to mitigate the bitterness of defeat.

The door opened. Carnac said nothing. Eventually, Keir nodded, and stepped aside without comment.

They sat down in the kitchen, and he watched Keir as he made coffee. Since Keir had admitted him to the flat, there were two possibilities. Firstly, that Keir knew nothing and therefore had no reason not to admit him, in which case his project would run smoothly. Secondly, that he knew everything, and therefore felt that Carnac posed no threat. In the latter case, things would be more difficult, but not impossible.

Painful as it was, he made small talk, asking about SimTech and Keir's sister. He needed to play for time, and it was safer this way. At the same time, he knew precisely how improbable it was that he would ever have the chance to speak to Keir again, and he found that idea more discomforting than he had expected. He wanted to explain. He had to take the chance, however slim it was, that Keir would understand. Despite his blind infatuation with Toreth, Keir knew the truth about I&I. Yet, for once in his life, Carnac couldn't find the words.

"I hear that you've had some success with the reform of I&I?" Keir said eventually. He tilted his head slightly, waiting for the answer with a half smile that answered any doubts about what he knew.

"Oh, no." Carnac dredged up a cool, professional voice. "Let's not work through all the questions and counterquestions. I would like to think that we know each other better than that."

Keir shook his head. "I don't think I know you at all."

"All I would like is a chance to explain what I did, and why I did it." He didn't hold out much hope that the explanation would be worth anything in terms of altering Keir's attitude towards him, but it would keep Carnac here, where he needed to be.

"I don't think I require an explanation, or that any explanation would suffice. But if you must."

Not much of an opening, but he'd take it. "Reform of that place is hopeless. Impossible. As long as the skills and the will to use them are there, whatever good intentions abound at the moment it's only a matter of time before the interrogation rooms are busy again. It may be years before it's restored to full strength but it will begin to happen in months. It is a habit into which this society has fallen too deeply to extricate itself without help."

Was Keir listening? He was certainly watching with every appearance of interest. "To break the habit the system has to be destroyed, root and branch. All knowledge, all expertise. Everyone who identifies themselves with the organization. I set the situation up to see who would come back, to pick out the ones who believed in the system. I gave Toreth a chance to leave along with the others. You know I did."

Keir shook his head. "You pretended to. And you did so in a way that meant he had to go back. Why?"

"To destroy I&I. And I know that you share that ideal. The Administration doesn't need an abomination like that, and if it does, if it can't survive without I&I, then the Administration should go, too."

"Yes. All true. But I meant, why involve Toreth at all?"

The truth, spoken by himself, would kill the conversation now. "Because I knew that he would be the best tool for the job."

"Was that the only reason?" Keir paused, then continued. "I have a tendency to dismiss Toreth's . . . concerns as unfounded. But in this case, I think I was wrong. Or am I flattering myself unduly?"

"In a sense, you are. The entire purpose of the plan was to destroy I&I. But I won't deny—" Carnac shook his head. Now that it came down to it, he was surprised by how difficult it was, by how few of the carefully prepared words he could remember. "That you are with him is—" Wrong. Terribly wrong. But that wasn't what he wanted to say. He needed to phrase it in terms of himself, not of Toreth. "You are one of the few people I have met in my life who consistently treats me as a person. Not a tool, or some performing freak trained up by the Administration and to be loathed or feared or envied, depending on how much of a threat I pose. You cannot imagine how precious a thing that is. Is it such a surprise that I might hope for more than friendship from you?"

Keir said nothing, his face a mask of polite attention.

"If I might risk the arrogance of expressing a professional opinion on such a personal matter, we are far from incompatible. I know what you get from Toreth; I understand your needs. I'm not as incapable of making compromises as I sometimes appear." The clumsiness of the words appalled him.

"I'm perfectly content with what I have," Keir said. No emotion—he might have been speaking about his flat. "What have I ever said to you that gave any other impression?"

"You have been admirably clear about that in the past. But I hoped that things might change."

"That would take divine intervention, not socioanalysis." Now he smiled coldly. "Of all the people Toreth has been jealous of—and, God knows, there have been enough of them—you are perhaps the least realistic. I wouldn't fuck you again if my life depended on it."

Carnac felt the sting of the anger behind the words, as well as the echo of Toreth in the interrogation room. "Keir, all I wanted—"

"You wanted Toreth out of the way permanently." Keir finished his coffee and placed the cup back onto the saucer, positioning the handle carefully. "And you were willing to sacrifice Kate to do it."

That stopped Carnac dead. He hadn't expected Kate's name and for once he was unsure how to react. Keir's expression gave no clue. At length he said, "That was a threat and nothing more. I never intended to carry it out."

Keir simply looked at him, ice cold and unforgiving, until he was forced to look away. It was hopeless. There was nothing he could say, no way to explain. He could drag the encounter out for a few minutes, no more, and then he would have to go.

"Well, I hope that you suitably expressed your gratitude to Toreth for her swift rescue." He couldn't hide the bitterness in his voice.

"It had little to do with Toreth. I did it. He told me what had happened, and I managed to make contact with someone who could free her."

Carnac waited while the past reordered itself, based on the new information, until he knew what, and when, and how, as clearly as if Keir had already explained it in detail. Payne had held something back from him after all. There were only one or two questions left, things to clarify. "You already knew about her."

"Yes." Then he added, almost apologetically, "I suppose that wasn't terribly likely."

Likely or not, the mistake had been his. It irked him that he consistently underestimated Toreth in this one regard—the strength of his feelings towards Keir. He had believed that Toreth would be too afraid of the consequences to tell Keir of the threat in the first place. The fact that the shock should have been too great for Keir to do anything in time was a secondary consideration.

"You gave them my name?" Carnac asked.

"Yes." No apology in his voice this time. "Now, I think, we've said everything there is to say."

Carnac could only nod. He had hoped for more from him: more vision, more detachment, more…morality. Keir had made the decision to save Kate, and so save Toreth and the rest of I&I. In that way, he had proved a disappointment in the end, like all the others. The other things Carnac had allowed himself to hope for were now forever beyond his reach.

Then, finally, he heard the door to the flat open and Sara call, "Warrick! It's us."

Keir looked towards the door and back, and said, "You knew they were coming."

Carnac contented himself with a smile, pulling his coffee cup towards him. Maximizing the sense that he was at home here.

Sara's voice came down the hall towards the kitchen. "We brought the celebration with us, so unless you're going to be enough of a miserable bastard to throw out a free drink, we—"

She stopped dead in the doorway, champagne bottle in one hand. "What the hell are you doing here?" she breathed.

"Who?" Toreth appeared behind her, and also froze, if only briefly.

Sara put her arm out across the doorway, the bottle hitting the frame, but he pushed her aside without looking at her and came into the kitchen. "Why the fuck is he here?"

Keir stood up. "He came round to talk and I wanted to hear what he had to say, so I let him in."

"I can fucking see that."

"To talk. That's all." Keir turned back to Carnac. "And now we're done, so you can leave."

Sara disappeared from the doorway and he heard her calling for McLean. The watchdogs were clearly still in residence, which was fortunate.

"You can leave, Carnac," Keir repeated, and again Carnac felt the distance between them, a gulf that could never now be bridged. His own fault, to a certain extent, but how much more Toreth's fault.

It angered him to think of Keir wasting his life pandering to the crippled needs of someone so far from being his equal; it made him almost as angry as did the existence of I&I. The scale of the outrage differed, but the core was the same—it was a perversion of the way the world should be. The anger gave him the resolve to do what had to be done. It was dangerous, but a necessary risk, and his last gift to Keir—his freedom from Toreth. Even as he repeated the justification to himself, he felt the sting of anticipation.

Sara and McLean appeared in the doorway, and the cast was complete. Payment time. He stood slowly, savoring the moment. "I had no intention of anything more intimate than tea." He smiled pityingly at Toreth. "Not, of course, that I imagine that makes you feel any less insecure or afraid of the idea of my being alone with Keir."

He heard Sara draw her breath in sharply, and Toreth said, "I'm sick of your fucking games. You don't know a single fucking thing about me." Then he frowned slightly—déjà vu, perhaps, and pathetically predictable.

Carnac took a few steps towards the door, and turned. "Oh, really? Let me see. I know that you like your steak medium rare. I know that you sleep on the left-hand side of the bed. I know that you've come with my name on your lips."

"Carnac—" Keir said warningly. Carnac ignored him, this prepared speech at least unrolling smoothly.

"I know the details of the diagnosis in your psych file. I know that your parents never gave you a second's acknowledgment or approval that didn't remind you of your failure to satisfy their impossible demands. I know how deeply, and understandably, they resented their misfortune that you survived when your brother died. I know that because of them you trust exactly two people in your life, and that the only way you are capable of understanding that feeling is by trying to own them."

He glanced around the room. They stared at him, goldfish expressions, paralyzed by the sudden attack—even Keir. Terrified of the truths they all danced around. Pitiful, all of them. Turning back to Toreth, he lowered his voice. "I know that you want Keir to—"

"No! You *fuck.*" That was Sara, suddenly shocked out of stillness, and he wondered if she had guessed what he was about to say. "Leave him alone!" She started across the room towards him, Toreth moving a split second later.

Carnac didn't have a great deal of personal experience of violence, so he always found it interesting. In fact, except for the pain, he enjoyed it. He particularly liked the way that time seemed to slow, allowing one to appreciate the finer points.

Keir appeared to have been expecting this turn of events, so he intercepted Toreth before he had gone more than a few steps. Because there was simply no way he could hold Toreth back, he had to hit him. If Toreth had had the least expectation of his doing it, he could have stopped him easily. As it was, the blow caught him just below the ribs and he staggered sideways against the wall, eyes wide—not surprising, given his prior injury in the area. It was, thought Carnac, a beautiful sight, although he was under no illusion that it would incapacitate him for long, or that Keir would be able to hold him by force alone.

McLean, caught completely unawares, only managed to get hold of Sara less than a meter before she reached Carnac. He pulled the bottle from her hand and it exploded on the floor, spraying the room. Sara froze, eyes wide, and McLean wrestled her back across the kitchen towards the door, having, in Carnac's judgment, the easier of the two jobs. Winded as he was, Toreth was struggling to get away from Keir and it was a struggle he would win before long.

"Let *go* of me." Toreth was hoarse, barely audible over Sara, who was screaming abuse with impartial fury at McLean and Carnac. "I'm going to break his fucking neck, like I should've done a long time ago."

"No, you're not; he's not worth it."

As Toreth glared at him over Warrick's shoulder, flushed with murderous fury, Carnac caught his gaze, and smiled. He continued speaking, directly to Toreth, ignoring the commotion around them. "I know that you want Keir to love you—"

"McLean, get her out of here."

"—more than you have wanted anything in your adult life—"

"Then if he's still here, call the others in."

"—and that the uncontrollable need makes you sick with terror."

Keir spared him a brief glance over his shoulder. "And you—*you* have one chance to get the fuck out of my home before the rest of the security team arrives and I have you thrown out."

Carnac decided to cut to the end, regrettable as it was to lose any of the effect. It would be enough. He put every ounce of conviction he could summon into his voice, driving the words home like knives. "And, finally, I know that in the end the pathetically little you have to offer Keir will no longer be enough, and he will leave you. And when that day comes, there is nothing you will be able to do to make him stay with you. You're not *that* good a fuck, and really, what else do you have?"

That was it, that was everything. He heard Sara, shrieking elsewhere in the flat, but in the kitchen the only sounds were breathing and the softly fizzing pool of champagne.

Perfect. Absolute perfection, at last. "I'll see you at work tomorrow, Toreth." He turned his back on them and strolled off out of the kitchen, in no hurry at all, glass crunching beneath his feet.

Warrick held Toreth until he heard the outer door close, although Toreth had given up resisting. When he released him and stepped back, Toreth stayed leaning against the wall, his hand to his side, his breathing labored.

After a long silence Toreth said, "Thanks."

"Are you all right?"

"Yeah. Fine." His voice was distant, his eyes fixed on the spot where Carnac had delivered his speech. "Killing him would have been stupid. Although that said, I really wanted to do it and—" He took a deep breath and winced. "Fuck."

"I'm sorry about that—I forgot about your ribs in all the excitement."

"It doesn't matter. I'm fine. Should tell the SimTech security trainers they did a good job with the corporate target self-defense." Silence fell over the room again and Warrick could hear voices faintly outside—Sara and McLean. She seemed to have calmed down, at least.

He should say . . . something, but for once he had no idea what. Acknowledging that he had even heard Carnac's barbs might be the worst thing he could do. The smell of champagne filled the room, overwhelming and slightly nauseating.

"Look, I have to go," Toreth said, sounding almost as though he were asking permission.

Warrick moved away from the path to the door, avoiding the glass. "What I said before still stands—you're free to go, whenever and wherever you wish. You always have been. But I'd very much like you to stay."

Toreth shook his head, but he didn't move away from the wall.

"Carnac was here to talk, that's all." Even as Warrick said it, he knew that it didn't matter this time.

"I know. I know he was. You wouldn't fuck him. I *know* that." Toreth's voice held a hint of anger that came as a relief.

"I realize I never should have let him in." He began an oblique approach to the topic. "It was stupid of me not to guess that he would have some unpleasant parting shot planned. I'm sorry that—"

"No. No need to be sorry. Wasn't your idea, was it? You didn't want anything to do with it. Bloody good plan as well."

"Toreth—"

Toreth pushed himself away from the wall and walked past him out of the room, still not looking at him. "Goodbye."

Warrick stood, debating whether to go after him. On balance, forcing him into a confrontation would do no good. Still, when the flat door opened and closed, it took all his self-discipline not to go after Toreth. It was only as he started to sweep up the expensive mess on the floor that the thought occurred that in all the years they'd been together, he could never recall Toreth saying "goodbye."

They heard the door to the flat close behind Carnac, and after a few seconds Sara said, "You can put me down now."

McLean looked down at her. "Are you sure?"

She wasn't at all, and he didn't look sure, either. He certainly didn't feel sure, arms tight around her, and after the scene in the kitchen it was a welcome feeling. However, he didn't do anything more than hold her—waiting for a cue from her.

"Well... you don't have to put me down." She looked up at him, thinking absently that he must be almost exactly the same height as Toreth. "But I'm not going to go chasing after Carnac with a carving knife."

He kissed her once, then let her go. "I'm still on duty until two."

"Oh. Okay." Well, that sounded promising. "Would you like a drink? I'd like one—a large one."

"I'm still still on duty."

"Well, Warrick's probably making coffee. Or tea. He usually does when something like this happens." Not that something like this happened often. She strained to catch something from the kitchen, but she couldn't hear a sound.

"What are you going to do now?" McLean asked.

"Do?" The question sounded more significant than she could imagine a reason for. "Wait to see what happens here. I was supposed to be going to a party, but I'm not really in the mood now. So I'll probably go home, go to bed, and get some beauty sleep. I've got to go to work tomorrow. Or if you—" His expression stopped her. "What?"

"I thought you worked for Toreth?"

"Well, I'm his admin, but I work for I&I. Why?"

"I thought that . . . well, he won't be going back there, will he?"

So she wouldn't either, and the problem of her job was neatly solved.

"Of course he will. Carnac will be gone in a few days. There's no point in him sticking around any longer. He's lost and he knows it. That was just a goodbye present." And a beauty at that. Still nothing from the kitchen, but as long as Toreth was here, things couldn't be that bad.

McLean nodded. "And you'll be going back with him."

"Yes. He couldn't manage without me—he's hopeless on his own, to tell you the truth." She looked at him consideringly. "So I suppose the conversation is over, right?"

"Sara, it's not that—"

"Don't." She suddenly felt tired. He kissed nicely, but not nicely enough for her to try to get out gently this time, not when there was so much else to worry about. "Let's just stick with 'it never would've worked.' One comfort fuck isn't worth a whole postmortem."

She watched, curious, as his professional blankness covered up the hurt in his eyes. "If that's how you feel, then obviously I *respect* that."

Ouch. She almost said something else, but then she heard footsteps, quick and decisive, and Toreth saying, "Goodbye." By the time she stepped into the hall, the door was closing behind him.

On the way down to the car park, Carnac found himself walking more quickly, suddenly in a hurry to get away. Once in the waiting car, he had barely taken his seat before nausea swept over him. He wrestled the door open again in time to be wrenchingly sick. When he was done, he wiped his mouth and dropped the soiled handkerchief into the gutter. Then he slammed the door shut, desperate to be gone, only to discover that he was shaking so badly he couldn't operate the control panel, and the system wouldn't recognize his voiceprint.

He occupied the ten minutes it took to finally bring himself under control in mentally drafting his letter of resignation from I&I and from the new Administration in general. Now seemed like a strategic moment to distance himself from Int-Sec—he doubted they would take kindly to a threat to expose one of their agents. Besides, he had had his fill of politics. The short-sighted fools wanted to keep the interrogators—very well, then they could rot in the hell of their own making without him. He only hoped that he was still alive when the morons who had congratulated him on his great success at I&I found themselves strapped into a chair down in the interrogation levels, screaming for death. He accepted now that nothing less than that would make them finally see the truth.

At which point, of course, it would be far too late to do the smallest particle of good to anyone.

At least they had canceled his training debt, and he had the paperwork to prove it, signed by everyone who seemed even slightly relevant. He was free of them, finally, of their idiotic demands and breathtaking stupidity. Altruism was a fool's game.

Chapter Sixteen

❖

Being thrown out of a bar wasn't a complete novelty for Toreth, but it happened rarely enough that he felt indignant now. He should've stuck at seven drinks, he decided as he struggled to open the badly repaired door to his flat. Seven since Warrick's flat, that was. Whatever he'd drunk before seemed a long time ago. Seven was always his lucky number, drinkswise, when the alcoholic haze was thick enough to make any problems look better, but the depressant effect hadn't kicked in yet. He should know better than to keep going.

He wasn't even that drunk when they threw him out. But he was obviously planning to be, and the bar staff clearly thought that it would be more responsible to throw him out early rather than to watch him kill himself on their shift. He was sober enough to put up a fight anyway, even if it hadn't lasted long.

He hit the icy pavement on his right-hand side, of course, and the stab of pain from his abused ribs kept him down there for long enough for the cold to really soak through his clothes. After he'd picked himself up, wiped the blood from his lip and finished swearing at the impassive bouncers, he thought about trying somewhere else. He was still barely sober enough for a tiny voice of self-preservation to point out that by the time he was drunk enough to forget what Carnac had said, he *would* be dead. It had taken him five minutes of shivering on the curbside to decide whether that was a bad thing or not, then he'd caught a taxi home.

In the bathroom he pulled out the top drawer by the sink and dumped the contents on the countertop. Looters had stripped his stash out, but he'd filled up in a moderate way since he'd come back. He picked a combination of painkillers and things that might clear his head enough to think, washed them down with water and went to lie on the bed and watch the room spinning.

Carnac's words played over in his mind. It was, he knew, exactly what Carnac wanted, but he couldn't stop it.

The pathetically little you can offer him will no longer be enough. And then he will leave you.

It was true. That and everything else Carnac had said, but in a way the rest didn't matter, because they were the past and present, and this was the future. He knew it was true; he'd known almost from the beginning, the knowledge kept locked deep inside. Now it was out in the light and he found that he couldn't look away.

There is nothing you will be able to do to make him stay.

He'd lied to himself, told himself that the fucking would be enough. He'd even believed it, even if only when they *were* fucking. When he felt Warrick shuddering with desire—when he said "fuck me," and "please," and "I want you"—when the game was so good that he wept in the chains—when he'd wind Warrick up in public, whispering and touching, until he was desperate enough to let Toreth take him in the car on the way home. Even when Warrick had returned the favor and made him screw up Sara's tenth anniversary presentation…

That was what it all meant. He might stay. He will stay. I can make him stay because he needs me. He needs this. He needs it as much as I need him.

It was a lie.

You're not that *good a fuck, and really, what else do you have?*

Nothing. The answer was nothing. That was why the idea of Carnac targeting Warrick had become almost an obsession, because Carnac, bastard though he was, had so much more that Warrick might want. So much more than him.

Forgetting the cut, he bit his lip and winced, tasting blood.

You can fuck me as often as you want. That won't make me love you.

Warrick's voice, except that Warrick had never said anything of the kind to him. He couldn't remember where he'd heard the words, but their truth burned.

He'd proved it himself, over and over, with countless men and women, just like he had with Payne. However much you wanted someone to want you, there was nothing you could do to make it happen. Whatever you did for them, whatever you gave them, whatever you let them take, it could never be enough. Never enough to be sure. Never enough to satisfy them. Never enough to stop them from walking away. Never enough to make them love you.

"How can they expect me to love you, Val?" His mother had asked him that to his face once, exasperated, annoyed with him as usual for fucking up something or other, for still breathing. "You're not a lovable child—you never were."

You want Keir to love you, more than you have wanted anything in your adult life.

For the first time, lying on the bed, sliding slowly from drunkenness to artificial sobriety, he saw it all clearly, everything whole and connected, before the sick fear overwhelmed everything and it was gone, leaving nothing more than fragments.

Carnac had shown him the future. One day, Warrick would be gone. Every day was another day closer to that day, until eventually, unbearable even to think about, there would be the moment he left. "I'm sorry." Warrick's voice in his head again, measured, regretful and, worst of all, kind. "But it was just a fuck, Val. It isn't enough anymore."

That wouldn't be what he'd say, of course, but it would be what he'd mean. How would he do it, really? How would you break up with a possessive fucking maniac who'd been trained how to kill people? He caught himself smiling. Carefully. By comm and from a respectable fucking distance. In a peculiar way, the idea made him feel hopeful. Warrick might stay with him for a good long time simply because he was too afraid to leave. For all he knew, it might even be the reason he hadn't walked away already. The morbid humor evaporated, leaving him cold all over.

Then he saw it. Problem and solution in one, hidden in his own words.

Walk away.

Walk away now. All the pain, all the drawn-out agony of anticipation, that could all be eliminated if he walked away.

He considered the novelty of the idea. He'd never walked away from anything like this before. Not anything that . . . mattered. Technically, he'd done it to dozens of people. Men and women, unimportant fucks he'd enjoyed explaining the situation to if they tried to pursue him. I'm bored. Once was more than enough. You're a lousy fuck, anyway. Whatever made you think I wanted you again? It was just a fuck.

But not Warrick. He'd never thought about it; he'd never even imagined that it was possible. Not that he would say any of those things to Warrick, but that he could leave him and that there was no higher power that could force him back into Warrick's bed unless he wanted—and agreed—to go back. It would be making permanent the feeling he'd had in the flat, the sheer relief of walking away from the inevitable, unbearable conversation.

Goodbye.

It was possible, that was the thing. Warrick couldn't stay with him, but he could leave Warrick. He could do it. The current feeling of resolution might be ninety-five percent chemical, but there was no reason he couldn't stick to it sober. Somewhere inside, beyond the drink and the mask of the drugs, he could hear a voice screaming *no.* He ignored it.

Sara had split up with plenty of boyfriends, and while he couldn't fool himself that it would be that easy after five years, he'd seen how it worked. She was fucking miserable for a day or two, and then she got over it. It wasn't going to be the end of the world.

He pulled the suitcase he'd taken from Warrick's flat out from under the bed and started throwing in the new clothes Warrick had bought for him, and the towels he'd also borrowed when he'd left, and the toilet bag and hairbrush that . . . and he decided to leave the lot. He could buy some more.

Before he left the flat, he realized that he had to tell Warrick now. If he didn't do it straight away, he might not find the resolve to do it later. He sat on the edge of the bed, twirling the comm earpiece between his fingers, until he acknowledged that he couldn't do it like that. He couldn't speak to him. Couldn't even leave a spoken message, which meant sending a note.

Taking out his hand screen, he tried to compose something. In the end he was left with a sparse few lines:

It's over. Don't bother to try to get in touch. I don't want to see you or speak to you again, for any reason. Goodbye.

After further consideration, he changed *over* to *finished* and deleted *goodbye.* Then he sat, staring at the words, until the letters were imprinted on his retinas and he saw them even when he looked away, closed his eyes, and sent the message. It was done. Decided. Irrevocable.

He wouldn't see Warrick again. He would never see him again.

In the morning, Toreth called in sick. To Sara it sounded far more like drunk, even though it was half past ten in the morning. Maybe he'd stayed up all night, rather than having gone to bed and started again when he woke up.

"Where are you?" she asked, and he hesitated. He'd never done that before.

"Not at the flat."

"Toreth, I need to know. In case something urgent comes up."

"I'm at a hotel. The, uh..." and there was a pause. Christ, he didn't even know. "The Bowman," he said eventually. "The one in the Arden complex."

Not too far from work, anyway. "Do you want me to come round tonight?"

"No. And don't tell Warrick where I am."

"Of course not."

"I mean it, Sara." The kind of voice that gave her cold chills even when he used it to someone else. "Not one fucking word to him about me. About anything to do with me."

"Toreth—"

"No."

She decided to leave it. If Warrick came looking for him, she could stall until Toreth was willing to talk some kind of sense. "When do you think you'll be in?"

"Not sure. What's Carnac doing?"

"The rumor is that he's gone already. Handed his resignation to the Administrative Council first thing this morning. They're supposed to be trying to persuade him to stay, but there is a story that he's not even in New London anymore—walked straight out of the building and caught a flight to Strasbourg. I'm not sure I believe that one."

"I wouldn't trust the bastard to stop interfering if he was dead." There was a short silence, then Toreth said, "Sara, how did he know about my parents?"

She froze. Couldn't speak, couldn't think, couldn't breathe.

"You told him, didn't you? When he was writing his bloody report." She wished he didn't sound so calm. "It had to be you, 'cause you're the only one who's met them. You're the only one I've ever told anything much about them. Not even Warrick and, like Carnac said, who the fuck else would I tell? So, really, it has to be you, doesn't it?"

Oh, God, please, Christ, no. "Yes," she managed, wondering if he'd hear the whisper.

"I'm taking the weekend off. I'll be in on Monday." Then the connection went dead.

Sara stared at the blank screen, seriously considering following Carnac's example of resigning and catching the next available flight out of New London, without leaving a forwarding address. But that would mean leaving Toreth in the lurch, and even if he killed her when he came back to the office, she couldn't do it. The least she could do for him was to hold the fort while he took the time to sort himself out.

Toreth wasn't in on Monday. Sara arranged for his hotel bill to go onto expenses, because the division was still paying for accommodation for staff whose homes were uninhabitable. In her opinion, Toreth's flat came close to uninhabitable at the best of times, so she didn't see why he should be out of pocket now.

In Toreth's absence, life at I&I began to return to a strange kind of normality. Every day, the number of Service people in the building diminished, and more staff who had been listed as missing slowly filtered back. Nagra was among the first, B-C having contacted her to say that the coast was clear. The junior para didn't seem at all guilty about her long absence, and Sara didn't have the heart to blame her. For one thing, she was too grateful that she hadn't had to make out a death report for Nagra. It felt weird to appreciate someone simply for surviving.

On Friday, as she sat waiting at her desk, the comm chimed. It was Tillotson, of all people. "Yes?" she asked, surprise making her forget the "sir."

"Is Toreth there?"

"No." Was that relief on his face?

"Then I'd like to see you in my office."

"Okay." She looked at the time on her screen. Two minutes to ten. "I'll be a few minutes."

That really ought to have been politer, too, and she thought he might bring her up on it. In the end he merely nodded.

Sara sat back, wondering what Tillotson was up to. Obviously, he'd decided that I&I was safe again and crept back. Probably wanted to check out the new politics and who he needed to suck up to now. She couldn't find out right away, though, because she was waiting for Warrick to call. He'd called every morning, punctually at ten o'clock, for the whole week. She'd wondered why ten, until she remembered that was when Toreth usually had coffee in his office. By now, their conversation had developed into something of a ritual.

This time, when the call came through, he seemed to be in the corner of a meeting room—behind him, she caught glimpses of Asher Linton and other people around a table, and he kept his voice low. "Good morning, Sara. How are you?"

"Fine. You?"

"Tolerable. Is Toreth back in the office yet?"

"'Fraid not."

"Have you seen him?"

"No, but I've spoken to him, just like every other day." Maybe she could record a message and run it automatically. "He's fine."

"Do you know where he is?"

"Still no." The lie was easier, since Toreth was still adamant that he wouldn't see or speak to Warrick under any circumstances.

He nodded, clearly expecting the answer. "Thanks. Let him know that I called, if it's not too much trouble."

The picture vanished before she could answer.

Tillotson's reception desk was empty, and Sara realized she had no idea what had happened to Jenny. She didn't recall her name on any of the lists. Surely she must be all right? Another name to worry about, another face to dream about. She squashed the morbid thought, and knocked on the door.

When Tillotson offered her a coffee, the surprise temporarily robbed her of speech. She managed a nod, and sat down before she fainted. Luckily, he didn't produce biscuits as well—the shock might've killed her.

Coffees poured, he sat behind his desk. To her disgust, he looked perfectly fit and well: suit neat, face no thinner than usual, not a ginger hair out of place. "Sara," he began with an ingratiating smile. "How are you?"

"Um, fine." This was too weird.

"And your family?"

She nodded dumbly.

"You've got a place to stay, that sort of thing?"

"My old flat was burnt out, so I've been staying with my sister. I thought it would take months to get somewhere, but housing called on Tuesday." He watched her, nodding with apparent interest. "The new place is pretty good, actually—closer than Fee's, even closer than the old flat. I'm moving in at the weekend."

"Well, if you need to take any time off, I'm sure that—" Then the comm chimed. "Excuse me."

Ignoring the low conversation, Sara sipped her coffee and wondered what the hell was going on. Then she almost spilled her cup while resisting the urge to slap her forehead. Of course. It was Toreth.

When the call was over, he went straight to the point. "Where's Toreth?"

"Taking some leave." Mention forms, and I'll slap *you.*

Her face might have conveyed that message more clearly than she'd intended, because he coughed and looked away briefly. "I understand," he continued after a moment, "that he was placed in the position of acting assistant director while... after the recent difficulties. Technically, his operational authority lapsed with the socioanalyst's departure. However, the appointment hasn't been officially rescinded."

He was getting good information from somewhere. "I don't think he'll expect you to salute him when he gets back."

Clearly he wasn't expecting that, because for a moment she saw something that frightened her with its unexpectedness—Tillotson with his mask down. Naked anger and ambition, with a steel behind it she wouldn't have suspected. "Don't try to play games with me," he snapped.

"I wasn't! I—I'm sorry, sir."

He shook his head, perhaps dismissing the apology, perhaps trying to erase his hasty reply. "What I meant is that Toreth's position here is...somewhat ambiguous."

She weighed her answer. The very last thing Toreth needed now was Tillotson with a knife out because he thought Toreth was a threat. "You're telling me. It's a nightmare." She watched him as she spoke, gauging the effect of her words. "People keep calling, wanting him to make decisions. It's only because it's taken so long for the senior people to come back. Everyone really just wants things to go back to how they were. I've been doing my best, but I can only do so much. I have to keep calling Toreth to ask him stuff, and he's really not interested."

That was true, as far as it went, and certainly the part about his lack of interest. She'd called Toreth at the hotel every day, in the late afternoon when he was more likely to be awake and sober, and passed everything along. He'd thanked her, relentlessly polite, made any necessary decisions, and closed the connection as soon as she had run out of things to say to carry the conversation. However, Tillotson, who knew nothing about Warrick and Carnac, was looking more pleased with every word.

"He's trying to have a holiday," she added. "It's not fair, having to keep pestering him with problems."

"Management isn't as easy as people think." Now he looked positively smug.

"Oh, I know that. Really not Toreth's thing at *all.* It's great to see you back." That, she realized as she saw Tillotson frown, was overdoing it rather, so she went for a distraction. "It's all your fault, really."

He stared, taken aback. "Mine?"

"Carnac," the bastard, "only made him take the acting assistant directorship because Toreth did such a good job last time he was here, when you made him Carnac's personal liaison. And considering that when Toreth got back here after the revolt they were threatening to execute the staff, I think he did a pretty good job. Wouldn't have been much for you—for everyone to come back to, without him."

His nose twitched. "Really?"

"You should ask HoS Bevan about it all, if you want to know more, sir. He and Toreth worked pretty closely over the whole thing." Let him know that Toreth wasn't without serious allies, even if Carnac had gone.

Tillotson clearly took the point. "I see that I have a lot of catching up to do. Well, you can tell Toreth that there's no hurry. He can take as long as he likes. And—" He paused significantly, and she wondered what was coming. "Tell him I'll make sure it doesn't come out of his annual leave."

Somehow, Sara managed to get a decent distance down the corridor before she started laughing.

Chapter Seventeen

❖

Why the hell had he come here, Toreth wondered? On a chilly Saturday afternoon the zoo was virtually empty. Even the animals were staying out of the damp, biting wind, curled up under their bedding. Maybe he should have stayed in *his* bed and waited for it to get properly dark. And then what? Go out and find another man he didn't want.

The afternoon was overcast enough that the flamingos were already roosting—standing one-legged in a tight flock in their shallow pool, headless in the gray light. Toreth sat down on the cold stone wall by the pool and jumped back up smartly, swearing loudly enough to cause a few heads to lift from under faded pink wings.

Christ, he was sore. Not surprising, considering how many strangers he'd had—or rather had had him—since . . . since he'd made his decision. Even more of them over the last three days, after Warrick had somehow fought his way through the blocks Toreth had put on his calls.

Toreth, please. I just want to know—

What? Why hadn't Toreth waited until the end of the sentence instead of interrupting? At least he'd been so wasted at the time that telling Warrick to fuck off had been almost painless. He'd thought then that it might be over, that it might start to get better. He'd been almost surprised when he'd woken up the next morning and nothing had changed. Except that he had a slightly sharper memory of Warrick's voice.

Even now, the temptation to go out tonight and find someone tugged at him. He needed something to stop himself from thinking and feeling, if only for a few minutes, and being fucked always did the trick. At least while it was happening. Not afterwards, though.

Enough, he told himself, walking away from the pool. He couldn't face another night of waking up in his hotel room long after his fuck had gone, with the sheets in a sweaty tangle and the pillow inexplicably damp. Lying in the dark, aching and empty, and still tasting Warrick's name. Pathetic, that was what it was. He needed to regain some focus. He needed to stop this morbid obsession, get his life back together and get on with living in the present. God, how many times had he said that over the last week?

Now, though, he had to find a way. He hurt too much to carry on, bruised and torn from saying, "Do it, I'm ready," when he wasn't, to men who didn't care or maybe thought he wanted that. Last night he'd been too high to feel how bad it was, although he'd known, distantly, that it hurt like hell. Was that how it felt for Warrick—there and not there, unimportant?

Afterwards, the man he was with had been worried enough to suggest calling a medic, until finally Toreth had told him that he worked at I&I, and he knew how much blood was too fucking much. The man had left abruptly, and Toreth couldn't remember what he'd looked like—not a single detail. So much for professional observational skills.

This morning, when he'd come down and with a filthy hangover on top of it, the pain had left him sick, and breathless, and angry—with Carnac, with Warrick, but mostly with himself. He'd forced himself to eat a vast and unhealthy fried breakfast, because he couldn't remember eating since . . . well, he must have eaten something, at some point. It wasn't possible to live on bar snacks and amphetamines for a week. The breakfast had been a good idea: it had cured the unpleasant lightheadedness, the tea had made a change from spirits, and for almost ten minutes he'd hardly thought about Warrick at all. Afterwards, he'd had to get out of the hotel, at least for a few hours, and most of the bars he'd passed were shut. Still, why the hell had he come here?

Toreth stopped dead. Walking without noticing where he was going, he'd reached the place he'd been avoiding ever since arriving at the zoo.

The panther lay on the platform in the center of the cage apparently asleep, but when a lion roared nearby, something between a cough and a grunt, the panther lifted its head. It scanned the area slowly. Looking for danger, Toreth wondered, or looking for a way out? It found neither. After a minute it yawned—red tongue curling, ivory teeth revealed as the whiskers lifted, breath steaming—and then sprawled out again, secure in its cage. Now that it no longer paced continuously, grass had grown back over the path it had worn behind the glass.

Visitors were sparse, and Toreth had the viewing area to himself. He rested his forearms on the thick glass, his nose almost touching it, then slapped the glass with both hands. Probably set off an alarm, not that he gave a fuck. The panther didn't react.

Did the animal think it was safe here? Make an allusion, create a metaphor—that's what Warrick had done. He'd looked at the pacing panther and he'd seen Toreth. At the time, Toreth had been pissed off enough to try to scare Warrick properly, but he'd been flattered, too. Sick or not, the panther was fabulous to look at—dangerous, beautiful, rippling with controlled power and self-absorbed strength. That wasn't enough, though. That couldn't be enough.

You're not that *good a fuck, and really, what else do you have?*

Nothing except a psych file with a diagnosis that Toreth had never cared about before.

Cages. You can't get out, and every bastard with a key can get in. He slapped again, harder, stinging his palms. "Hey!"

The panther twitched its ears and opened its eyes halfway. Languorous, that was the word. Like Warrick after a really good fuck. Seconds passed, then the inhuman yellow eyes closed again. Apparently, Toreth didn't even rate a yawn.

He turned away from the cage. No answers here, unsurprisingly, but he knew why he'd come. The zoo was Warrick's place, and there was a tiny, thin chance that Warrick might be here. So unlikely that if it happened Toreth could honestly say he hadn't expected it. He hadn't broken his resolution not to see Warrick again.

The slow walk back to the gate was an effort; he'd spent the whole day walking and he felt shockingly unfit. As he waited for a taxi, Toreth scrubbed his unshaven chin. Jesus, what a wreck. Keep this up much longer and he'd be sleeping on the streets and fucking for money. Much longer than that and he'd end up dead in an alley. He rubbed his chin again, without thinking. Warrick had said that he'd liked the beard.

On Monday, when there had been no word all weekend and Sara had given up hope, Toreth came back. Her first thought was that she should've told Warrick where he was, whatever the consequences to herself. Toreth looked terrible, his face puffy and his eyes black with exhaustion—a week and a half's worth of morning afters, piled one on top of the last. And he walked as if he'd been fucked by all the interested parties in the city. "Morning, Sara," he said flatly and then carried on straight past her into his office.

It took her ten minutes to get up the courage to follow him. She only went at all because of how much worse it would be if she waited until he called her in. He stood by the window, leaning on the frame, and he didn't look around. She managed to persuade her vocal cords to cooperate. "Toreth—"

"You're sorry."

"Yes. God, yes." So pathetically inadequate, for what she'd done to him.

He nodded. "Well, that makes all the difference, doesn't it?"

She went over to him, wanting to say *something*, but no words offered themselves. Besides, it was all she could manage to stay in the room—she trembled with the effort not to run. He frightened her when he was like this. He always had done, because she knew the kinds of things he was capable of.

Finally, he turned and looked at her, and she had the sense of him slowly focusing in from a long distance away. When he was looking directly at her instead of through her, he shook his head. "Christ, you look petrified." He stroked her cheek gently, with the back of his fingers, watching her flinch away. "What do you think I'm going to do to you?" He sounded genuinely curious.

"I don't know."

He pulled her forwards, slowly, until she was right against him, then held her, resting his chin on the top of her head. "Sara, I'm not going to do anything. To start with, it would be incredibly stupid, wouldn't it, here in the office?"

She nodded against him, listening to his heart hammering nineteen to the dozen. He still sounded so calm.

"Besides, it doesn't matter. It's Carnac's job to know things like that. He could have got most of it from my psych file. I mean, I've never seen it. Warrick—" His grip on her tightened. "Warrick probably has. But I expect it's all in there. So forget about it. I have."

I still told him things that couldn't have been in the file, and look what he's done with it. Instead of saying anything she nodded again, because it seemed to be what he wanted. Tentatively, she tried to return the embrace, and at once he released her and stepped back.

"So now that's all sorted, we can get back to work. What's been going on here while I was drowning my sorrows?" He smiled at her, the smile he used for all the other admins when he wanted to charm them into doing something for him. Bright, with a hint of wickedness, and not a drop of genuine warmth.

After she'd given him the news, told him what was on his schedule and offered him a coffee (which he refused), Sara went back to her desk and stared at the screen, and tried not to cry.

Chapter Eighteen

❖

The station was chaos, but Warrick was still glad he'd decided to meet Dilly here. Reports had the Space Center even more heavily mobbed by anxious friends and relatives desperate to meet the first flights back since the unrest.

He waited for an hour before he saw her. For some reason, he'd been imagining her with luggage—everyone else seemed to be laden with the maximum permitted—but she had her usual small bag over her shoulder. She looked as calm, collected, and immaculate as ever, until she caught sight of him.

"Dilly," he said eventually. "Some oxygen would be useful."

She let him go, and he was surprised to see tears on her cheeks. He fished in his jacket pocket. "Here you go. Hankie."

She wiped her eyes and blew her nose. "God, I'm sorry. How stupid."

"Not at all."

"It's being back, that's all. I never realized how much it felt like home. New London, I mean. Until I was out there and you and Mother and Asher and everyone else were back here and I couldn't get hold of anyone and you might all have been dead, for all I knew."

He took her arm gently, and found she was shaking. "Do you want to sit down somewhere?"

"No. I'll be fine in a minute. Can we just go, please?"

As they waited outside the station for the car to make its way through the tangled traffic, she told him about the trouble on Mars base. It seemed to have suffered a restrained version of events on Earth, kept in check by fear of the consequences of serious damage to the sealed environment. She made the journey back on the overcrowded shuttle sound almost the worst part.

When they had taken their seats, before the car had even pulled away, she said, "How's Toreth?"

He looked at her, surprised. "He's... well, as far as I know, he's fine."

"Oh, thank God." She sat back in the seat.

"You could have asked before. When we spoke."

"I couldn't. I thought about it. But I heard about Int-Sec before I managed to get through. About I&I. There were reports, some pictures. I thought he might be dead, and then I thought you'd have told me if he was, but if he was and you hadn't told me then it was because you didn't want to, and so I couldn't ask and anyway the connections were so bad that I didn't want to start anything and then lose you before it was all right." She paused for breath. "If that makes any sense to you. I'm not sure if it does to me, anymore."

He smiled. "I understand. Thanks for being concerned about him."

"I was much more concerned about you." She paused, then added, "I know you know that I don't like him, but I don't want him dead, for God's sake. I'd just, well, rather not have to see him around, that's all."

"Well, that isn't going to be a problem anymore. He's—" And he stopped, realizing that this was the first time he'd said it to anyone. "He says it's finished. We're finished."

"What?" And he saw it briefly in her eyes—her first, automatic reaction. Relief. "When?"

"A couple of weeks ago. Exactly fourteen days, in fact. If you give me a moment to work it out I can humiliate myself for you and do it in hours, minutes, and seconds."

He hadn't meant to sound so bitter, but Dilly ignored his tone. She moved over to the seat beside him. "What happened?"

"There was an extremely unpleasant scene, the details of which I have no wish to go into, and he walked out. Since then I've had one message and a brief but explicit request conveyed over a comm, on the sole occasion that I managed to get through to him."

"What did he say?"

"Over the comm? 'Fuck off,' sincerely meant. I'd like to put that down to the fact that he was drunk, which he undoubtedly was, but in all honesty I can't. After that, I decided not to bother working through his call blocks."

"And the message?"

"'It's finished. Don't bother to try to get in touch. I don't want to see you or speak to you again, for any reason.'" At least the brevity made it easy to remember. "I've left messages for him, but I have no idea if he's reading them."

"And he means it? This isn't one of his attention-seeking 'chase me' things?"

He couldn't help a wry smile. "If it is, he's making it rather harder than usual to catch him."

"And you're... what? Letting it go at that?"

"I don't know. I thought... or rather, I hoped that he would come round on his own. That's the way it normally goes." Her eyebrow went up at "normally."

"Normal for Toreth," he elaborated. "This time is different; I don't think he's coming back. I've looked for him, but he's trying so hard to stay away from me that I don't know if I should keep trying. Besides which, I have no idea what to say to him, even if I did find him." Knowing it probably wasn't a good idea, he added, "What do you think I should do?"

She didn't even pretend to think about it. "*I'm* not going to drive you out onto the streets to hunt him down. I think you're much better off without him, you know that. In fact, you should be grateful you've got a chance to walk away from it—I always worried you wouldn't get that."

One of her fears about Toreth that he'd never even tried to reassure, because it had always been the most valid.

The only way you can understand that feeling is by trying to own them.

Warrick looked down at his hands, seeing ghosts of manacles. She and Carnac were both right. Toreth was inarguably jealous and possessive and, above all, incapable of dealing with those feelings without becoming angry, which only made him more dangerous. He wouldn't take goodbye well, or accept it perhaps at all. Not normally. In a way, then, this *was* an opportunity, one he might never get again, to walk away cleanly—to be free from something that was undeniably hard work at times. Furthermore, from that point of view, rejecting it meant making a serious commitment, even if he were the only one of them who would recognize that. If, in fact, declining the chance of escape was an option. If Carnac's revelations hadn't driven Toreth into a retreat from which he could never be coaxed.

"Keir?"

He looked up. "I was thinking about what you said."

She studied him for a moment, then shrugged. "I'm sorry, but you asked what I thought. If he says it's finished, I say accept it."

Finished. It sounded so final from someone else. The last lingering doubts disappeared. Despite everything, he wanted Toreth—it really was that simple. "I'll think about it."

"Hm. I know what that means. But it's your life, as usual. I just think that—" She shook her head. "No, actually I don't. You've told me often enough that it's none of my business."

Clear enough. Time to change the subject. "What are your plans?"

"I'm not sure. I was hoping I could stay with you until I can get something sorted out. I've got a ton of things to do for work, before I even think about anything else. Although I ought to go and see Mother first. How is she?"

This was the part he'd been dreading most. He'd been using Toreth, in a way, just to keep away from this topic. "She's fine. But she's . . . not at home."

"Where is she?" When he didn't answer, she looked at him more closely. "What's wrong? Is she hurt?"

"No." Truth or lie? Unfortunately, the truth wasn't a realistic option. "She got herself into some trouble. She was arrested, briefly, and now she's gone away. She didn't tell me where, but I've heard from her and she's fine. I can show you the messages from her."

"Arrested?" She looked baffled. "What could *Mother* have done that would get her arrested?"

"I don't know the details—old trouble, I suspect, that all this business turned into new trouble. Something to do with Tarin's father."

Without hesitation she said, "You're lying."

"Yes, I am. Dilly, I can't tell you the truth. It's too risky. It's not that I don't trust you, but the more people who know what happened, the more dangerous it will be for everyone. You, me, Mother, Jen, Tarin. Valeria." And Toreth.

"Keir—"

"No." He held her gaze. "Not on this one. Don't turn it into a fight, please, because I'm not going to tell you. Not now. Eventually, if I can, I promise."

For a moment, he thought she wouldn't believe him, or would believe him and carry on anyway, because Jen always said they were as alike in stubbornness as in everything else. Then she nodded. "All right. If you say so, I trust you."

"Thank you."

She sighed and leaned on his shoulder. "It hasn't changed here, has it?"

"No. No, I'm afraid not. Not that much."

"When I was stuck in the 'port, watching the news, I thought there'd be some point to it all, in the end. That things might be different—better. But it's not going to happen. Everything's going to go on, exactly the same as it was before."

"Not exactly the same."

She shook her head. "Tarin's right. God knows, I never thought I'd say that, but he is. A few things here and there aren't going to make any difference at all. The whole system needs changing. It'll happen again, all this awful mess, until it does change. And before long it's going to be just as dangerous to say that kind of thing as it ever was, isn't it?"

Warrick thought of Toreth's reforms to I&I, and Carnac's conviction that the interrogation rooms would be back in use before long. He put his arm around Dilly and kissed her temple. "I don't know. We'll just have to wait and see."

When Sara saw Warrick striding across the office, loyalty and fear got her out of her chair and in front of Toreth's door before she even had a chance to wonder how Warrick had talked his way past the front desk. Persistent bloody-mindedness, if his expression was any indication.

She'd lied to him at ten o'clock every day, for the whole week, and said she hadn't seen Toreth yet. Hoping that, now Toreth was back at work, she would be able to change his mind. However, he barely spoke to her, and he looked no better when he arrived in the mornings—she had begun to forget that he hadn't always had black rings around his eyes.

Warrick stopped in front of her. "Sara, let me past."

It wasn't a tone of voice she looked forward to arguing with, and for a moment she felt tempted not to try. Once Toreth saw Warrick, once he had to talk to him, then things would either go to hell in ten seconds flat, or everything would turn out wonderfully. She wasn't about to be responsible for the first option, though. He would never, ever forgive her for another betrayal. "I told you," she said. "He's not back."

"Interesting, because the main reception is under the impression that he's been in residence since Monday."

"He's busy," she said, falling back on the automatic admin lie. Warrick merely looked at her until she said, "He doesn't want to see you."

"I am perfectly well aware of that. However, *I* want to see *him.* Don't play games—let me past."

She stared at him, remembering him talking to the captain the day he'd got them out of I&I. Heads had started to come up around the still sparsely populated office. Over his shoulder, she saw Kel mouth, "Security?" She shook her head at him.

"Warrick, if you're going to be like that, I suggest that you go. Before someone calls downstairs and you get thrown out."

"I don't—" Then his voice softened. "Yes. I apologize for being so uncivil. Will you at least tell him that I'm here?"

"He'll know already. Reception will have called it up."

"Tell him anyway. Please."

She hesitated, looking at the door. Warrick walked a couple of meters away and folded his arms. "I give you my word I won't try to go in."

At her desk, she switched the link through to the speaker, leaving no scope for misunderstandings. "Toreth? Warrick's here. He wants to see you."

After barely a second's hesitation, Toreth said, "Tell him to fuck off." Then he cut the connection.

Warrick made a small, aborted movement towards the door, stopping at her squeak of alarm. "Don't worry, I'm not going in."

"Warrick, I'm sorry."

"Can you at least let me know where he's staying? Having no idea where he is is . . . concerning."

She hesitated, before deciding that the lie would have to stand. "No. I still don't know—he didn't tell me. But there's no need to worry about him. He's—" so bloody miserable that I can't bear to look at him. "He's fine, honestly."

"If he were fine, he'd see me."

A hard point to argue with. "Warrick, the bottom line is that he told me not to let you in. I *can't.*"

After a moment he nodded. "I understand." He looked past her, gathering his thoughts, then said, "Do you think he'll come round on his own?"

"I don't know." A reflexive response while she thought about what was best for Toreth. But if anyone deserved to know, it was Warrick. Toreth wasn't drinking and screwing himself into oblivion because he was telling the truth when he said he didn't want to see Warrick again. "No. I don't think he will." She lowered her voice, keeping Toreth's secrets from the rest of the attentive office. "I've never seen him this bad. Not even when you—" She stopped. Did he know she knew? Warrick, however, merely waited for her to continue. "When you screwed the guy at the conference and I called you to warn you he was coming back to the hotel. He's... I can't get through to him, and I have tried—he doesn't even see me properly anymore, never mind listen to me."

"Carnac is very good at what he does. The best." Warrick closed his eyes briefly. "Please, Sara. Tell me where he's staying."

Almost, she did. But Toreth would know it was her. "I can't," she said.

He caught the slip at once. "You do know, then? *Tell* me."

"I can't. He'd kill me, and I'm not just saying that."

The muscles in his jaw clenched, then he nodded slowly. "Very well. You must do what you think is best, of course." She thought that was his exit line, but he continued, his voice cold and every syllable distinct. "But I won't forget this, Sara. Do you understand? If anything happens to him, I won't forget this."

Without waiting for a reply, he turned and strode off, as quickly as he had arrived, the handful of curious spectators scattering out of his path.

Chapter Nineteen

❖

For the last fortnight Toreth had been hunting for women and wanting men. However, he hadn't allowed himself even to look. That was too close to what he really wanted, which was Warrick. Still Warrick. Three weeks yesterday since he'd last seen him, and it was still Warrick.

In his hotel room, in the last minutes of clarity and sobriety for the evening, Toreth counted pluses while he brushed his hair. His arse no longer hurt so much he had to look for soft chairs wherever he went. Daedra was finally supplying again for nonmedical purposes. And…

He dropped the brush, rested his chin on his hands, and stared blindly into the mirror. There must *be* an and. There had to be. Without something else he wasn't sure he could make it out of the room and down to the bar. He didn't really want to, anyway. He didn't want to go downstairs, he couldn't stay here. He didn't want anyone—he didn't want anyone *else*—and he couldn't sleep without it. The thoughts bounced back and forth. The mental equivalent of pacing, because he was too tired to manage the real kind. So fucking tired.

A fortnight ago, when he'd decided to go back to I&I, he'd thought that it might help, but in the end it was only different, not better. The first week there had been the worst, because he'd been waiting. It had taken until last Friday before the thing he'd dreaded most happened, when Warrick showed up.

There, he told his reflection. That's something to be proud about. He'd stuck to his resolution and told Warrick to go. Okay, to split hairs, he'd hidden in his office and let Sara get rid of him. The end result had been the same, though—Warrick had gone. After that, knowing Warrick wouldn't be back, he hadn't minded going to work so much.

At least it had been something to do during the day, and at night he'd fucked women, with skill and concentration. Making it last for as long as possible, so that when he finally came he was too far gone to say anything (or at least to remember saying anything) and he fell asleep immediately afterwards, which was good. For one thing, it meant he had to drink less. There—another plus. Once or twice the women had stayed for the night, so he'd had to think of something to say to them in the morning. "I'm late for work" had done well enough. Anyway, it was all he'd been able to manage after the moment of realization that the warm presence beside him wasn't Warrick.

It felt a little better, though. Was *that* a plus? That it was slightly less fucking awful? At least it was better than the men, and far, far better than the nights when he hadn't been able to find anyone he could pretend he wanted. He looked down at the dressing table, unable to meet his own eyes.

Nights alone in the hotel room, wanking himself stupid over pathetic fantasies that somehow everything could still work out all right. Most of them involved killing Carnac at some point, and at least that part he enjoyed unreservedly. But afterwards he couldn't sleep, his mind too full of images of Warrick that he'd called up when he could no longer stop himself. A few times he'd resorted to sleeping pills, and he loathed those, because whatever it said on the packet they always made him feel like shit the next day. Of course, he felt like shit anyway, but the fuzzy edges they gave the world in the morning left him feeling even more out of control. So he went out, every evening, and took different drugs that blurred things in a different way, and drank and hunted and fucked and tried to forget.

It wasn't working. He knew that it wasn't, but there was nothing else he could do. He was hiding. Treading water, barely, waiting for things to somehow get better. Once or twice he'd weakened and thought about asking Sara to call Warrick for him, and couldn't do it.

You want Keir to love you, more than anything you have wanted in your adult life.

He took a deep breath. Carnac was right. He wanted Warrick, and he couldn't have him, and so that was that. He'd pushed Warrick away, one last time, and he'd gone. Warrick had probably been as horrified by Carnac's analysis as Toreth had. He remembered Warrick's expression in the flat—shocked, stunned into silence. God, how clearly he remembered it.

It had been nearly a week since Warrick had appeared at I&I, and there had been no word from him since. It's too late to go back, Toreth told himself, even if I wanted to.

He desperately, desperately wanted to.

He picked up the new moisturizer that Sara had bought for him—another peace offering like the endless bloody coffees. He probably should've said thanks. He didn't like the silence that had grown up between them, but he couldn't see an easy way around it. Open up a conversation, and she'd want to talk. First of all about whatever stupid bloody guilt trip she was on over the things she'd said to Carnac years ago. He didn't want to hear about it. It was over, he'd forgiven her, and most of all he didn't ever want to hear Carnac's name again. Far worse, though, she'd ask about Warrick.

Still, the moisturizer had been a nice thought. He unscrewed the top and sniffed the open tube carefully. Unscented, just how he liked it. Right. Pretty up, go out, pick someone up, fuck her, don't think about waking up tomorrow.

Unfortunately, the plan forced him to focus more clearly on his face. He looked absolutely fucking awful. Absolutely fucking awful and *old.* This was what it did to you. Getting involved, giving a fuck—this was the result. After a long moment he threw the tube down, hating himself for being so weak. Weak, needy, dependent—all the things he despised in other people. Caught in his own trap. Payne would laugh his bloody head off.

Toreth looked at the assortment of tablets lined up on the dressing table in front of him, took a couple, and then a couple more for luck. Sweeping the rest back into the drawer, he went out to hunt.

The comm woke Sara up, chiming insistently.

"Happy birthday!" Toreth said when she opened the door and, with a rather unsteady flourish, he held out a battered bunch of flowers. Then he looked at his watch and added, "Yesterday. Fuck. I meant to come round earlier but I—oh, shit." He put his hand on the door frame, crushing the flowers further, and shook his head. "Christ, I'm *wrecked,*" he said, sounding astonished by the discovery. "Can I sit down?"

"Of course you can. Come in."

Everything was suddenly and weirdly normal. It was just like all the uncounted times he'd turned up at her old flat, only with the novelty of his spontaneously remembering her birthday. True, it wasn't until next month, but she felt he deserved seven out of ten for getting almost the right day of the month.

He sat on the sofa while she made coffee and put the flowers in water. When she'd finished, the sink was speckled with bruised petals and broken ends of stems—definitely not up to his usual floral standards. Still, some of them might survive. She half expected him to be asleep by the time she'd done it, but when she came through with the tray, he was teasing the cat with a piece of string.

As she entered the room, she heard him say, "Aren't *you* a vile little fucker, then?" in tones of syrupy affection. Bastard, confused by the combination of attention and lack of shouting, kept tapping the string halfheartedly and casting profoundly suspicious glances at him.

When Toreth saw her, he dropped the string hurriedly. "God, that smells good." He took the coffee and sat back. Then he looked at his watch again and frowned. "It's not your birthday, is it?"

"Next month. But thanks for the flowers, anyway."

He grinned up at her, and she noticed how contracted his pupils were. That explained the mood. "Sorry," he said. "I was sure it was today. Should know better than to trust my chronic fucking memory. Woke you up for no reason."

"It doesn't matter." She sat down next to him. "It's Friday tomorrow—I mean, today."

He smiled. "So you can go home early?"

"Yeah." She hadn't dared lately, while he'd been so locked away inside himself. "It's practically the weekend."

He gestured around the room with the mug, somehow managing not to spill it. "I like the flat. Closer to work than the other one. Bigger."

"No, it's almost exactly the same size, except that the hall and the bedroom are smaller, so there's more room in here. How did you find it?" He'd never asked her for the address.

"Called Kel. Twice, I think. Wrote a note and lost it." He chuckled. "The second time, I had to get him to give the address over the comm to the taxi. He sounded pretty pissed off."

"It *is* two in the morning."

"Yeah, well, fuck him." He looked around again, then down at the sofa. "Nice, um, suite. New?"

"Secondhand." She leaned against him, pleased and relieved when he put his arm around her shoulders. "The insurance paid for new but I thought I might as well get this and keep the difference—Bastard will only scratch it all, anyway."

He nodded. "I should get some stuff. Move back into the flat. They'll start kicking up a fuss about the expenses before long. And I hate that fucking hotel." Abruptly, the illusion of normality fractured and she could hear the misery in his voice. "Fucking hate it."

She put her hand on his chest, praying he wouldn't pull away again. "Why don't you stay here until you get the flat sorted out? I'd like you to. No spare room, but this is a sofa bed. Fee stayed over and she says it's really comfy."

"No. Thanks, but I—" He sighed and sat up, dislodging her and slopping his coffee onto the reconditioned upholstery. "I can't sleep here. Nothing personal. I can't sleep anywhere."

"Do you want some tablets? I've got some of Daedra's finest. I was having nightmares about... about I&I."

"Yeah? I used to have nightmares. Still do. About water. I drowned once. Twice. I—" He swallowed heavily. "Old stuff. Doesn't matter. No thanks, anyway—for the pills, I mean. Probably not a good idea. I had something already. Several somethings. I just need to find someone to fuck and then I'll be able to get some sleep."

He said it with such grim practicality that she couldn't think of anything to say except, "You don't have to go somewhere else for that."

Even as she said it, the words horrified her. She didn't know if it was because she'd broken her rule, or because in a way she hadn't—she didn't want him, not in the way she'd wanted him at his flat. She was offering a pity fuck, nothing more. The only kind of comfort he might accept. Not, though, if he recognized what it was, which he clearly did. His eyes narrowed and he looked at her for a long moment before he said, "Do I really look that bad?"

"I didn't mean it like that." Or at least she hadn't meant to mean it like that.

He shook his head, the coldness gone in an eyeblink. "'Course not. It doesn't matter. Look, thanks for the coffee. I have to go." However, he stayed on the edge of the sofa, staring into his nearly full mug.

Maybe a more physical approach would work better. Gently, she pried the mug from his hands and set it on the table. Then she turned his head, kissed him, and held his chin until, finally, his eyes met hers. "Toreth—"

"Fine. If that's what you want. Fine."

Without waiting for a response, he pushed her down onto the sofa, coming down with her, hard and uncoordinated, nearly winding her. She squirmed underneath him, and at least he did shift to the side, letting her breathe.

To begin with, she wondered what he wanted, what he'd like—what would make him feel better. She didn't have to wonder for long, although conversation was clearly out of the question. How the hell had he managed to find anyone over the past few weeks, if he'd had the same fixed, desperate determination he had now? Hands on her, unfastening clothes with automatic skill. Kissing her throat, his body against hers, every fiber of him screaming "Warrick."

A comfort fuck was one thing, but she wasn't sure that her sympathy would stretch to letting him screw her without even seeing who she was. Definitely far beyond the call of duty. But what, honestly, had she thought would happen? She touched his face again, and that did pull him back to the present long enough to kiss her.

When he did, she discovered that he hadn't changed his technique much in ten years. No need to, when he was so good at it. She slipped her hand up under his shirt, finding that he felt as wonderful as she remembered—all smooth skin and hard muscle sliding underneath it. Sara closed her eyes and pressed him closer. It would be all right—or at least it might help. Afterwards, with luck, he'd fall asleep and then in the morning she'd be able to persuade him to call Warrick, and then everything would be really all right.

The last thing she'd expected was that, in the end, he wouldn't be able to go through with it. However, after ten minutes or so, he paused, shifting his hips against her, and said into her hair, "Ironic, huh?"

As subtly as she could, she slid her hand down to the front of his trousers, to confirm the lack of response. Trying too hard, or—more likely—too tired and too high. He caught her wrist, pulling her hand away, but after that, it was only a matter of time. Finally, he stopped moving, stopped touching her, and lay still against her, breathing heavily.

"Toreth?"

No response. She considered options, before deciding that any offer to try to remedy the situation could only lead to disaster. She slipped her arm around him, hoping that if she did it slowly enough, he might not notice. That he at least might stay beside her, might let her hold him—it was no more, after all, than he had done for her in the cell. Almost at once, though, she felt him tense up, and then pull sharply away.

"I don't need your fucking—" He struggled upright. "Ah, fucking *hell.*"

Bastard yowled, a low, warning note. Sara froze on the sofa, waiting for Toreth's anger to pass, which it did, slowly, his hands unclenching.

He rested his elbows on his knees and took a deep breath. "Sorry. Not going to happen, I'm afraid. If I'd known it was my lucky night, I'd have been more careful what I took." He wiped his mouth, then picked up his coffee and drank. Washing the taste of her away, she thought. "Maybe we should make it a fixture—one disastrous fuck every ten years. What do you think?"

"The last one wasn't a disaster."

"But not so good that you wanted to remember it in the morning."

The self-pity, so unlike him, left her unsure what to say. Carefully, she rested her hand on his back. "It doesn't matter."

"No. Right as usual." He smiled, forced and distant, still not looking at her. "Not going to do my reputation any good, though. At least it was only you."

Sara swallowed the hurt, knowing what he meant. She stroked his back, and he didn't move away, which was something. He was staring into his coffee again, so transparently miserable that she felt tears of her own starting. Had she really envied him? She felt suddenly grateful that she'd never loved anyone enough that it could make her this unhappy. "Stay, please," she said. "Forget about the—"

"Sara . . . how long is it going to take?"

Not understanding the question, she couldn't reply. He carried on anyway, his voice soft and desperate. "I want it to stop. That's all. I just want it to stop being like this every fucking minute of every fucking day. Because I don't think I can—"

He stopped and sniffed hard, once, pinching the bridge of his nose.

"Call him," she said.

"No."

"Then let me call him."

"No."

She knew she ought to shut up, but she had to try. "You should've spoken to him at the office. He's worried about you and . . . so am I. He wants—"

"No!" He turned on her, anger flaring up again. "I don't want to see him. I *can't* see him. Don't even fucking think about it. Do you hear me?"

He glared at her until she nodded. Then he put the mug down on the table and stood up. "I'm sorry I woke you up. Thanks for the coffee and—and I'll see you at work tomorrow."

Sitting up on the sofa, she watched him leave, hoping all the way that he would stop and turn around and ask to use her comm. When the flat door closed behind him, Bastard yowled again and jumped up into her lap. She scratched his tattered ears and he purred, wafting eye-watering cat breath up at her, delighted as usual to see an intruder successfully chased off.

She wished she knew where Carnac was so that she could go there and kill him. It was too late to do any good now, but it was the only thing she could think of that would make her feel any better.

Chapter Twenty

❖

Sara had been quiet in the office all day, and Toreth had wondered if he ought to say something. In the end, he couldn't think what, so he let it go. He shouldn't have gone to her flat—bad combination he'd taken last night. Still, despite what he hadn't been able to stop himself from saying to her, it didn't matter. Nothing did, except not thinking about the things he couldn't stop himself from thinking about.

Have another drink.

Different bars, every night. New bars, every night, except tonight. He ended up, by accident, in the bar Payne had dragged him out of once. That meant it was a risk, because he'd been here before, so there was a minute chance Warrick might find him. Still, he hadn't recognized the place until he'd bought a drink, and then he couldn't be bothered to leave—it was safe enough for a while.

He found a woman early on in the evening, who fitted his latest standard: short, blonde, blue eyes, and a light, nondescript voice. Nothing at all like Dillian and so nothing at all like Warrick. He'd almost abandoned her when he found out she wanted to stay in the bar for a while, but he needed someone for tonight because after last night he was sick of pills, and she was a dead cert. In any case, it wasn't as if he seriously expected Warrick still to be looking for him. He'd have to drop that fantasy in the end.

So he sat at the bar with her and talked, or at least made the right kinds of noises while she explained whatever the hell was wrong with her life that meant she'd ended up here with him. Something pretty fucking tragic, presumably. The ring mark on her finger looked reasonably fresh. She'd said her name was Anne, but considering that she wore a silver bracelet with the initials MP in curlicues, he didn't believe her. Could be her mother's initials, of course, or even those of the lover who'd given it to her. Not that he cared either way, but it was something to think about. A few minutes' distraction from—

"I'm sorry?" he said, suddenly noticing an expectant silence.

She shook her head, although she didn't look particularly annoyed. "I said, 'You aren't listening, are you, Marc?'"

He offered her the best apologetic smile he could manage. "Sorry, no. I'm, um—I had a long day at work, that's all."

"What do you do?"

He weighed up a lie, decided that this place was safe enough not to bother. "I work at I&I."

"Oh?" Not much surprise, and he wondered if she'd guessed something like that. "My cousin works—worked there."

He blinked at her, seeing her for what seemed like the first time. "Yeah? What's their name?"

She looked startled by the question. Obviously she didn't want to run the risk of him finding out her own name. "Er, well, you probably wouldn't know her. She said it was a big place."

"Yeah, it's huge. But I'm good with names." Then another possibility occurred to him. "You said 'worked.' Was she killed?"

"No. She wasn't in work that day. She hasn't been back since—she says she isn't going back, if she can find another job." Her eyes clouded. "She lost a lot of friends."

He nodded. "Me too." Or at least a lot of people I knew. Friends sounded better, though, and he couldn't help working on her, even though he knew he already had her.

"I'm sorry." She took his hand, stroking the fingers with her thumb, sympathetic but also sensual. "I won't say any more about it."

He thought about milking it, but decided against it. "It's not a problem, honestly."

"Oh? It's just that—" She flushed slightly. "It's just that you seemed awfully unhappy, earlier, and I wondered if that was the reason."

"No. Nothing to do with that." Or not in any way that made sense without a ridiculously long explanation.

"Would you like to tell me about it?"

To his surprise, he found himself contemplating saying yes. There was no reason why he shouldn't. He'd listened to enough miserable, boring life stories himself in pursuit of a fuck, and presumably they'd all got something out of telling some random stranger everything, beyond a glazed expression and a larger bar bill. "Sure." Trying it once in his life wouldn't hurt. "Would you like another drink first?"

"I'd love one, but it's my turn to buy."

With the fresh drink in front of him, he found had no idea how to start, so he borrowed one of Sara's phrases. "Bad breakup, that's all."

That's all.

"She left you?"

"No. I left them. Him."

He wondered if that had put her off, because she frowned slightly. Some women were funny about it. However, after a moment she said, "So why did you leave?"

"Someone told me some things about him. Which were all true. And... once I'd heard them, I had to go."

She nodded. "I understand. Some things you can't forget. Or forgive." She hesitated, then asked, "Was he being unfaithful?"

"No. God, no. It was... it's a bit complicated. But the upshot was that I realized that it was going to be a disaster in the end. That there was no way in hell it could last." He frowned, wishing he'd paid more attention and was less tired, because he knew there was a formula for this kind of conversation. "Compatible. We weren't compatible. So I decided not to see him again." Put like that, without the desperation he'd felt at the time, it sounded strange.

"So now you're not sure it was the right thing to do?" she asked.

"No. No, I'm sure about that."

She nodded, frowning thoughtfully, staring down at their hands. After a moment, she said, "But don't you think, maybe, it might've been worth it, anyway?"

He thought about it for a moment, then gave up. "What?"

She looked up. "That the time you'd have had with him might've been worth the risk of things not working out?"

"No." He thought about it again. Seeing Warrick—fucking him—swimming with him on Saturday mornings—eating his bloody pancakes—waking up with him and wondering every time whether this would be the day when he'd say, "It's not enough." He knew he wouldn't be able to stand it, but at the same time, could it really be any worse than this? "Maybe. I don't know. I didn't think so when I walked out."

"It must've been bad."

"What?"

"Whatever you heard about him. I mean... I hope you don't mind me saying so, but you obviously miss him. A lot."

Ready to lie, he suddenly couldn't see the point. Who the hell would he be fooling? "Yes. God, yes I do." Every fucking minute of every fucking day.

"But now it's too late?"

"Much too late." If he kept telling himself that, eventually it would be true.

"That's sad. Really sad."

He nodded, letting the conversation fall into silence. He had no idea whether she meant it or not; he didn't much care, as long as she didn't change her mind about leaving with him. She had hold of his hand with both of hers now, massaging the palm. It felt good. Relaxing. He found himself genuinely looking forward to the fuck at the end of the proceedings, for the first time since... since he'd last fucked Warrick.

Then, from behind him, a hand landed on his shoulder and he heard Warrick say, "I apologize for interrupting, but you seem to have hold of something of mine."

Toreth froze, not daring to look around. It was deeply disconcerting to hear Warrick—it was as if admitting out loud that he missed him had, somehow, summoned him. For a wild moment, Toreth wondered if three weeks of drugs and hard drinking had finally brought on an hallucination.

Then Anne looked between them, let go of his hand, and sat back. "Sorry," she said. Then, slightly defensively, she added, "He doesn't have a ring on."

"Nor a collar and tag," Warrick said in a voice that could've snap-frozen a volcano. "But nevertheless, he's taken. At least for the moment. Now, I'd be grateful if you'd excuse us."

She shrugged, standing up. "Sure." Then she smiled at Toreth and raised an eyebrow. Toreth nodded, praying that she wouldn't say anything to Warrick.

She didn't. Instead she clinked her glass gently against his. "Good luck, then. It was nice talking to you."

As she walked away, Warrick took the seat she had vacated, but he kept his hands to himself, folded on the bar. He looked at Toreth's glass and frowned. "What was all that about?"

"What the hell are you doing here?" Toreth asked, ignoring the question. What did "at least for the moment" mean?

"Looking for you. And you've made it hard enough, I must say. You blocked my calls, I&I won't let me in the building, and Sara won't tell me anything. Then I waited outside the Int-Sec grounds for you with no result, so I presume you've been using another exit. The same with the gym. As you can see, I've been reduced to bar-crawling in an attempt to find you."

"So take a fucking hint." He'd been looking for him. He'd been looking for him all this time.

Warrick looked around, dark eyes assessing the room, lips quirking thoughtfully. Toreth wanted to kiss him, right then, as if it would somehow wipe away everything that had happened.

"It's not one of your usual places," Warrick said, "which I assume is deliberate. Or is this one of the usual places that *we* never go to?"

Toreth closed his eyes, shutting away the temptation. It didn't help much, because Warrick was sitting so close that he imagined he could smell him. When he opened them again, he found Warrick looking at him, obviously expecting an answer. He groped back for the question. "I came here with a fuck once, and I was hoping for another one. Thanks for scaring her away. Now will you fuck off?"

"That seems unlikely, don't you think, after all the trouble I've taken to find you? Where are you staying?"

"None of your fucking business."

Warrick carried on as if he hadn't spoken. "I've tried a credit and purchase check, but the systems are still patchy."

"You won't find me. It's going straight onto expenses."

"Ah, of course. I ought to have thought of that. I did get some bars to try, which is why I'm here. Well, the I&I systems will be riskier, but—"

"Warrick..." First time he'd said his name, and Toreth found himself unable to get past it.

Warrick waited for a moment, then said, "I won't stay long, if you really want me to go. I simply wanted to speak to you. And I would like an explanation of why all this rigmarole has been necessary, if that's not too much trouble."

"You won't get one. You don't need one. Now, fuck off." Please. Fuck off, fuck off. Audio loop stuck on the same message.

"No, I don't think so. In an attempt to get this conversation moving, I will assume that the problem is Carnac. Or, more specifically, what Carnac said at my flat."

He willed himself to get up and leave, producing no response. There seemed to be a mutiny in progress from his waist downwards, because Warrick's proximity after such a long absence was having its usual effect. His body didn't care whether Warrick was going to walk out in a month's time, or a year's time, or even in the morning—it simply wanted him, right now.

At least his voice still obeyed orders. "There's nothing to talk about, because he said it all, didn't he?"

"They were only words. Carnac lies as much as—and probably more than—anyone else."

"He wasn't lying, though."

"Lying, talking utter shit, what's the difference?"

Toreth blinked at the uncharacteristic phrasing. "Don't try to—"

"There is absolutely no need for this. For any of this." A hint of pleading broke through, before he sat up straighter and carried on. "What did he actually say?"

"You know. You heard it."

"Some of it. For the rest, I was far too busy stopping you from tearing his head off—something I've regretted frequently since. And of the parts I did hear, I'd still like to know what *you* heard, because I don't think it can have been the same thing."

"He said—no. I won't." Simple denial, no reason, because he couldn't think of one.

Warrick sat and waited, letting the silence do the job of persuasion for him.

Toreth looked down, into his drink, and wished he'd had a few more before Warrick had turned up. "He said that you're going to leave. Me. Because at the end of the day, we fuck, and that's all. And he's right. Why the hell should it last? I might be the world's greatest fuck, but I can't—" He kicked the bar, hard enough to jar his ankle painfully. "But there isn't anything else. None of the shit the rest of you want."

"'Just you. It's enough.'" He looked up and caught the last of a smile fading from Warrick's lips. "A quotation," Warrick said in answer to his expression.

"Yeah? Who? Some clueless fucking idiot."

The smile flickered again. "Very possibly. But nevertheless—"

"No. You can quote whoever the hell you like, it doesn't change what Carnac said, does it? Every fucking word of it was true. About me, about you and Sara. About how much I—" And even though it didn't matter anymore, he still couldn't say it. Because, just maybe, Warrick hadn't heard that part. "What I mean is there's no point dragging it out, so please fuck off and leave me alone."

Warrick shook his head. "Carnac said some things, some of which may have been true to some degree, and then he produced a conclusion as if it followed logically. It's mental sleight of hand, that's all."

"He made a prediction. It's what he does for a living. You're the one who said he was the best you've ever seen." He laughed bitterly. "Not that it's much of a prediction. You can't build a relationship on fucking and nothing else. Or so Elena says."

"Who's she?"

"Don Chevril's wife. You met her at Sara's ten-year thing—you must remember. She's a real stunner: hair down to her waist, legs up to her armpits, absolutely perfect skin. Fuck knows what she's doing with him." Fuck knows what you're—he took a deep breath and went on quickly, talking so that he wouldn't have to say anything. "I fucked her once, at a party, in the dark. She felt like silk, inside and out. She was high as a kite—we both were. She'd never have done it otherwise. We nearly died trying not to laugh, because Chev was there, talking, couple of meters away. He'd kill me if he found out, so don't say anything. Even Sara doesn't know about it. I never told her because she'd only tell someone else and it'd get back to him. He'd go fucking ballistic, even after all this time. He really—"

"I won't leave you."

So calm, so matter-of-fact, that the words gave him one piercing moment of hope, before reason reasserted itself. "Warrick, you don't have to say it to... to make me feel *better* or some stupid—"

"No, I don't. And I'm not saying it for any such reason—I'm saying it because it's true."

Toreth shook his head, resisting the temptation to believe despite himself. "Right. And you just happened to decide to tell me now. Coincidence."

"I've never mentioned it before because I didn't think that you'd want to hear it. Besides, I didn't think it was necessary. I thought it was true enough to be obvious."

"What, you've been taking lessons from fucking Carnac, now? You can't *know* it's true."

"Very well. Here's the version with caveats. While I can't see into the future, neither can I imagine a likely scenario in which I would wish to leave you, taking into account the previous five years. At this moment, I can say that for as long as you wish me to stay and the situation between us remains substantially the same, or changes in ways that are acceptable to both of us, I will stay with you."

It was so perfectly Warrick that he listened, entranced, not hearing the words, just the flow and rhythm of it. Eventually, he said, "I liked the first one better."

"I'm not going to leave you. Or was it 'I won't leave you'? In either case, the intention is the same. I could put it in writing if you'd like me to."

Despite everything, he had to smile at the deadpan seriousness of the offer. "Carnac would love that. He'd want it down and saved so that when everything went to hell he could pull the fucking file out and say that he'd told you so."

"I know. Toreth, if you want me to go, now, I will. And—" He paused, but his eyes didn't waver. "And if you want me to say that I won't look for you again, I'll do that, too. But I would find it extremely annoying to give Carnac the satisfaction of having his prediction come true. Come home—no, I mean, come back to the flat with me. Please. We can talk, or fuck, or sleep, or whatever you prefer." He half smiled. "God knows, you look like you could do with some sleep."

He couldn't argue with the last part of that, at least. And he caught himself thinking, one night. One night and I could leave again tomorrow.

Trying not to think it twice, he thought of something else, an inconsistency in the story that his brain had automatically flagged for attention. "How did you know where to find me?"

The sudden change of subject—or something else—made Warrick hesitate before he answered. "I told you, I did a c&p and found the name of the bar."

"No, you didn't. I've never spent any money here."

"But you said—"

"I said I'd been here with a fuck, and I have. But he bought the drinks, not me. We only had the one round. So you're lying."

Warrick clearly didn't know what to say. There was only one reason why it would be a dilemma whether to tell him the truth. It was the obvious reason, anyway. "It was Sara, wasn't it?"

Warrick hesitated a moment longer, then nodded. "She called me at home first thing this morning and gave me the name of your hotel."

"So why didn't you go there?"

"She sounded so concerned as to the possible consequences that I thought it would be less obvious if I met you somewhere else. I was regrettably unpleasant to her when I came looking for you at I&I, so I owed her a little extra consideration. She... well, to be truthful, she followed you here after work and then let me know where you were."

He thought about the theater, years ago now. "Quite a fucking conspiracy. Again."

"Yes, I'm afraid so. Please don't be angry with her."

"I'm not." He wasn't, which felt strange. He was giving in—had already given in—and what he felt was something like gratitude.

"I'm glad to hear it. Now, will you come back to the flat?"

Toreth knew he shouldn't go with him. He'd promised himself that if Warrick found him, he'd tell him to fuck off again, and keep telling him until he went. He had, at least, tried. Listening to Warrick had been the first big mistake, because he could make the most impossible things sound completely and inarguably logical. Like Carnac.

And there is nothing you will be able to do to make him stay.

So he'd resolved to go first. But he was too exhausted, and too lonely, to remember why it had seemed like a necessary thing to do.

These things can always be mended. Always. Elena had said that, and he didn't know whether to believe her any more or less than Carnac. He liked the sound of it better right now, and she knew more about sleeping with para-investigators than Carnac ever would. And Sara had told him—

Fuck her. Fuck the lot of them. He knew what *he* wanted.

He finished the drink Anne had bought for him and wished him luck with. "Okay. Let's go."

Warrick's shoulders sagged slightly, and he bowed his head. When he looked up again, he said, "Thank you," and leaned forwards and kissed him. It was still a rare enough thing for him to do in public that the knowledge that other people might be watching added another few degrees to the delicious heat that flooded through Toreth.

He's like a drug, Toreth thought, as Warrick broke the kiss and stood up. Except that no drugs were that good. If he could bottle it and sell it, he'd be a billionaire.

On the way out, he noticed the woman whose name wasn't Anne, talking to a dark-haired man who simply had to be Justice, or maybe Service. She obviously had an eye for uniforms, even out of uniform. As they passed, she spotted them and smiled, raising a hand in farewell. He returned the wave, suddenly and ludicrously happy. He was going home with Warrick. They'd fuck, and fall asleep, and in the morning he'd wake up and Warrick would be there. Right now, that was as far ahead as he cared to look.

Outside it was freezing cold—much colder than he'd noticed earlier, when he hadn't been noticing anything much. The world had come back into focus around him, and the effect disoriented him slightly.

He was waiting for Warrick to find a taxi when a female voice said, "I hoped I'd catch you."

When he turned, he found not-Anne, bundled up in a thick coat, scarf, and gloves, which made him feel even chillier. He glanced around, but her recent companion was nowhere in evidence. "Calling it a night?" he asked.

"More than that. I thought I'd copy-and-paste out of your file."

"About what?"

"Forgive and forget. Give things another go." She cocked her head. "Or don't you think I should?"

He hesitated, blowing on his hands, trying and failing to remember anything at all that she'd told him at the start of the evening that might be a suitable subject for a reconciliation. "Sure, why not?" he said, hoping that he sounded as if he knew what she meant and she'd go away before Warrick caught sight of her talking to him. "Good idea. And good luck with it."

"Thanks." She smiled at him, and then unwound her scarf and wrapped it around his neck. "To keep you warm until you get home."

He nodded, mute with surprise, and watched her walk briskly away, her breath leaving a plume in the frosty air. Then he straightened the scarf—soft dark wool that must've cost a packet—and tucked his hands under it.

There was a cough from behind him and he turned back to find Warrick standing by a taxi, door open. "What was that about?" Warrick sounded curious rather than annoyed.

Toreth shrugged. "Christ knows."

Warrick seemed quite willing to drop the conversation. "Well?" he asked. "Are you ready to go?"

"As I'll ever be."

Warrick closed the flat door and dutifully reset the security. He appreciated the necessity, but the delay annoyed him. He'd politely but firmly evicted the guard from the flat before he'd set off to the bar. Optimistic, but he hadn't wanted to have to do it now. No doubt SimTech Personnel Security would call tomorrow to protest—he didn't care in the least.

Now that he had Toreth in the flat, Warrick knew he would stay. Or he was almost sure. He hoped he would. When he turned around, he found Toreth leaning against the wall, staring down the hallway towards the kitchen. "Toreth?"

He looked around and smiled, not entirely convincingly. "Still here."

Warrick crossed over and kissed him, then again, until Toreth started to respond, his hands sliding around Warrick's hips. Then Warrick pulled back and said, "Well?"

"Absolutely fucking fantastic." Toreth shook his head, perhaps dismissing lingering memories of the last time he'd been here. "No, okay—what?"

"What do you want to do? Talk? Sleep? Fuck? It's up to you."

Toreth tightened his grip, pulling him closer. "I'll give you one guess."

It took longer to reach the bedroom than usual, primarily because Toreth refused to let go of him. When they finally made it to the bed, they were only half undressed and the chances of getting far enough apart to complete the operation seemed remote. It crossed Warrick's mind, briefly, that they were far too old to be behaving like this.

However, most of his attention was thoroughly absorbed by the feel of Toreth pressed against him, holding him close, kissing, hips moving against his, hard flesh rubbing together. Even through far too many clothes it was almost unbearably good—much too good to let him frame a request to stop so they could finish stripping. He hadn't realized how much he'd missed this, missed him—or rather, he hadn't let himself think about it. Now that Toreth was here, he wanted more contact, more skin against his; he wanted Toreth on him, inside him. Possessing him. And to hell with what Carnac thought about that.

Toreth shifted against him, rolling them half over so that Warrick lay beneath him, and kissed him again, bruisingly hard. He moaned, feeling Toreth shudder in response, legs locking around his as he thrust against him. Evading another kiss, Warrick leaned forwards, finding Toreth's ear with his mouth. "Fuck me. I want you to—"

Toreth gasped, and Warrick managed to draw his breath in just before Toreth's arms tightened around him. "Warrick—oh, *fuck*." And his whole body strained against him as he came.

When the tremors subsided, Toreth showed no sign of letting go. Warrick shifted his shoulders, trying to gain some breathing space, because suffocation had begun to seem like a real danger. To his relief, Toreth loosened his hold, and moved down the bed to lie against him, panting into his chest. "Christ," he said between breaths, his voice muffled but distinctly embarrassed. "Haven't done *that* for a while. And still nearly fucking dressed. Sorry."

"It doesn't matter in the slightest." Not true, but what else could he say? "If anything, I feel rather flattered."

That was the point at which he expected Toreth to pull away. To his surprise, he moved fractionally closer—fractionally being all that was possible. "So you should. No one else can make me... no. Listen. I'll tell you something." He took a deep breath, his face still hidden. "You're the best fuck in the world—you always have been."

He stroked Toreth's shoulders, feeling the tension in them through his shirt. He didn't know what to say—something was necessary, and in the end too flippant felt safer than too serious. "Well, if there were ever anyone who'd tested a statistically significant sample... "

He didn't laugh. "Warrick, I mean it."

"I know you do."

That was perhaps a touch too sincere, a little too serious, because Toreth let go and rolled away from him, onto his back. He lay with his arms behind his head, still breathing deeply, and looking studiously up at the ceiling. Warrick cast around for a distraction, eventually finding something. "If anyone ought to apologize, then it's me."

That seemed to work, because Toreth looked around and frowned. "What the hell for?"

"I forget the specifics, but I think it was for doubting that you'd be able to thwart Carnac's plans. As you clearly did, I can only say that I'm sorry I underestimated you."

"Fuck, I'd completely forgotten about that. Thanks. But...do you still think he should've closed down I&I?"

The question caught him by surprise. After a moment's thought he said, "Not the way he wanted to do it. If the reforms stick, then I much prefer your solution. If they stick."

Toreth nodded. "That depends on the new Administration letting them stick, doesn't it?"

More or less what Carnac had said, and Warrick strongly suspected that Toreth shared Carnac's opinion of how likely it was. Pursuing the conversation any further would only ruin the night, though, so he didn't reply. Toreth would be happy to let it go, because he always was.

Warrick sat up and stripped off his remaining clothes, then moved across the bed, stealthy approach, until he lay against Toreth, touching full length. He expected a protest, but Toreth instead lifted his head briefly and moved his arm down to hold him, pressing him closer. They lay together, Toreth's fingers tracing patterns on his back, mapping out bone and muscle.

After so long, every square centimeter of his skin ached for attention. Shivers started, up and down his back, running away from the gently exploring fingers. He tried to keep the reaction under control, but it was impossible—he wanted Toreth too much. Flattering as Toreth's loss of control was, that was inadequate recompense for delaying what he desperately needed to make the reunion complete. His cock pressed against Toreth's hip, and eventually he couldn't keep still. He rubbed forwards gently, trying for discretion, opening his mouth to keep the sigh silent.

Toreth lifted his head and looked down at him. "Warrick?"

It was an offer. Warrick shook his head. "I'll wait. I want—" and he stopped to rephrase. "I need you to fuck me."

Toreth's fleeting acquaintance with embarrassment seemed to have passed, because he grinned and settled back into the pillow. "Well...okay. If you insist. Later, then."

"Mm. Not too much later."

Toreth laughed. "Give me a chance. You're fucking insatiable, you know that?"

"You've mentioned it before." It seemed uncharitable to point out that he hadn't been satiated in the first place for quite some time.

He thought Toreth was falling asleep, because the hand on his back slowed and stilled, but after a minute or so, Toreth ran his thumb down his spine and said, "Say it again."

There were two choices, and he took the riskier one. "I'll never leave you."

Whether it was what he'd asked for or not, Toreth smiled. "Never is new."

"That's what you get for asking me in bed. It reminds me why I put up with you."

He cursed himself silently as Toreth's smile froze, then melted away. Warrick knew exactly what he was thinking.

You're not that *good a fuck, and really, what else do you have?*

Warrick didn't plan to add that to the list of topics best not mentioned. "He's right, of course."

Toreth turned towards him again, confusion replacing what might have been fear. "Who?"

"Carnac—and the delectable Elena, for that matter. You can't build a relationship on nothing but fucking, not even when the fucking is this good." He felt Toreth shifting, starting to pull away. "Certainly not one that would last for, say, five years."

Silence.

"I suppose so," Toreth said eventually. "If you want to look at it like that."

Oddly reassured by how uncomfortable he sounded with the idea, Warrick rested his hand on Toreth's chest, feeling his heart beat. "A major flaw in his logic, one might say."

"One just did say." Toreth placed his hand on top of Warrick's, interleaving their fingers. Then he said, "Once more."

"I won't leave you." He hesitated, then added, "And I can tell you why, if you'd like to hear it."

Toreth shook his head quickly. "No. Don't. That's... that was the last time I'll ask, anyway."

"It doesn't have to be. I don't mind telling you, not in the least."

"No. But I mind asking." Toreth turned away again, closing his eyes. "That's enough. It's finished. Let's just forget about it—about everything, and especially about fucking Carnac."

"As you prefer."

Barriers, being rebuilt. In a way, it was almost a relief. Toreth with his guard down, and not even coming at the time, was frankly disconcerting. The openness couldn't last, because the hidden fears that Carnac had dragged into the light were still there and no amount of repetition or reassurance would ever eliminate them.

But they were here, together, now, and that *was* enough.

Chapter Twenty-one

❖

In the third city since they had left Administration territory, Leo watched Kate sleeping in the hotel bed. By the cool dawn light he thought that, despite her gray hair, she looked astonishingly young. And beautiful—no less beautiful than the day he had first seen her in the flesh, at their planned accidental meeting. Then, as now, the picture in her security file didn't do her justice.

He had followed up the message that Kate was in danger from what he'd acknowledged to be a sentimental attachment to the memory of a woman he had not spoken to for a third of a lifetime. The letters handed to him so casually by his son had changed all that. In a way, he was glad that he hadn't seen them before. He had loved her, against all reason and protocol, from the first moment he'd seen her. The years apart had blunted the memory of that and the pain of leaving her; a reminder so sharp, so vivid, delivered every week would have made those years unbearable.

He'd started to read the letters while he organized her release, and then kept reading through the night, right up to the time he had set off to meet her. The opening letter he now knew by heart.

Darling,

Now that you have been taken from me, I know that I should let you go, but it seems so unfair that we had so little time together. If you could have seen me crying every night this week, I'm sure you would have been very cross with me. So now, I promise, no more tears. I will try to accept what cannot be changed, and go on, for the children and for everything our lives together meant. And I hope that, if you can somehow still hear me, you will forgive me this one indulgence to your memory.

Keir and Dilly miss you terribly…

He had loved her, once. He loved her again before he finished the first page, and he loved her more with every letter. They had moved him, amused him, saddened him, and made him deeply grateful for everything she had worked so hard to give him. Thirty-five years of herself and their children, a life in words that now felt more real to him than his own. In return, he had given her a single month, and he bitterly regretted that it was all he had to give.

During that month they had talked about the past, not the future, but it was the future that occupied him now. Tomorrow he was due back at Int-Sec. No excuses or explanations would be accepted for a longer absence. Even now they were being watched. If he failed to return, they faced a life (and probably a short one) of flight and fear. The alternative—defection from the Administration, the bartering of a lifetime of secrets in exchange for safety—would be unthinkable for both of them.

What he had done for her so far had used up many of the favors he had accrued in his long career. It had cost him all the rest to make sure that their son's name would never be connected to any of this—Kate had insisted that the children must be safe, and for this month he had been able to refuse her nothing.

He knew that she missed Europe, missed her home, and that most of all she missed her children, and Valeria, the grandchild he had never met. They must miss her, too, as much he had done, or more. Her letters had given him the sweet illusion of a life lived together, and now her letters to them would have to do the same. He would ensure that they received them regularly.

Stooping over the bed, he kissed her, and told her that he loved her, and she smiled in her sleep. He had made her happy, for this brief time together, and that was some comfort. Not a great deal, but some. From the beginning they had both known the dangers, and the prices that might have to be paid. Once before, for the old Administration, he had given her up. Now, for the new Administration, he did what had to be done.

And, because he loved her, and was grateful, he made quite sure that Kate didn't feel the shot that killed her.

www.ingramcontent.com/pod-product-compliance
Lightning Source LLC
La Vergne TN
LVHW091033080826
845145LV00002B/481

* 9 7 8 1 9 3 4 0 8 1 1 3 6 *